SOMEBODY'S SISTER

Trapped, exploited and left without hope

By

L. P. Holmes

Copyright © L. P. Holmes 2024
This book is sold subject to the condition that it shall not, by way of trade or otherwise, be lent, resold, hired out, or otherwise circulated without the publisher's prior consent in any form of binding or cover other than that in which it is published and without a similar condition including this condition being imposed on the subsequent publisher.
The moral right of L. P. Holmes has been asserted.
ISBN: 9798322399780

This is a work of fiction. Unless otherwise indicated, places, events and incidents in this book are either th imagination or used in a fictitious manner. Any resem living or dead, or actual events is purely coincidental.

To my wife Jenny and my children, Louise, Lisa, Terry, Jack and Calum, for making my life complete.

Thank you, Emily Yau, from Reedsy for your editing advice and support, it is very much appreciated.

CONTENTS

Chapter 1 .... *1*
Chapter 2 .... *9*
Chapter 3 .... *15*
Chapter 4 .... *21*
Chapter 5 .... *36*
Chapter 6 .... *46*
Chapter 7 .... *59*
Chapter 8 .... *71*
Chapter 9 .... *81*
Chapter 10 .... *90*
Chapter 11 .... *102*
Chapter 12 .... *111*
Chapter 13 .... *129*
Chapter 14 .... *134*
Chapter 15 .... *147*
Chapter 16 .... *156*
Chapter 17 .... *161*
Chapter 18 .... *176*
Chapter 19 .... *183*
Chapter 20 .... *195*
Chapter 21 .... *205*
Chapter 22 .... *217*
Chapter 23 .... *224*
Chapter 24 .... *230*
Chapter 25 .... *239*
Chapter 26 .... *250*
Chapter 27 .... *263*
Chapter 28 .... *270*
Chapter 29 .... *275*
Chapter 30 .... *282*
Chapter 31 .... *291*
Chapter 32 .... *295*
Chapter 33 .... *298*
Chapter 34 .... *305*

Chapter 35 .... *310*
Chapter 36 .... *316*
Chapter 37 .... *323*
Chapter 38 .... *330*
Chapter 39 .... *337*
Chapter 40 .... *346*
Chapter 41 .... *351*
ABOUT THE AUTHOR 352

CHAPTER 1

"GET OUT OF MY ROOM!"

Quickly retreating into the hallway – despite having hardly put a toe into his sister's room – Harry was just able to glimpse the raging anger in his sister's face before she lunged forward, slamming the bedroom door in his face.

At 14 years of age, Harry was what you might call 'a little on the geeky side'. In his earlier years he had tried to be a bit 'cooler', but he just couldn't do it. He'd begged his mum for designer shirts and jeans but even when she relented and forked out what she described as a small fortune, the clothes somehow changed nothing. Harry was tall for his age, very slim (his sister called him "Scraggy", like Shaggy from Scooby-Doo but thinner), his hair was very wavy, which made it difficult to control, and unfortunately acne was taking its often-painful toll on his complexion.

His sister, Lilly, on the other hand had similar features but was blessed in that they somehow worked to her advantage. She was tall for her age, slim but not without shape for her 16 years; she, too, had wavy hair. Her good looks made her the envy of the girls and the desire of many hormonal teenage boys. Her skin was unblemished, and she looked good in anything for a girl of her age. She had no worries about flaunting her body and often chose the skimpiest clothes she could, causing huge arguments with her mother to the exasperation of her father. It was clear that with beauty comes confidence and Lilly certainly wasn't short of that. A good brain that could have gone on to achieve great things at school but somewhere along the line the attraction of boys and rebellion had taken her away from her studies. She was still doing okay but as her teachers and parents constantly reminded her, she could do much better.

Harry was brilliant at science and maths and computer studies and anything else the school population thought of as 'not cool'. He lived in constant fear of sports days, seeing them as an opportunity to allow the 'Jocks' to beat the crap out of him, and they would always go unpunished. Even on other school days he would find himself half hiding in the corridors, nooks, and crannies or behind bins in the playground in order to prevent bumping into one of "The Enemy", as he referred to them.

Growing up in middle-class suburban Surrey, his life had generally been pretty good. Sure, his mum and dad divorced when he was only 4, but he got to see his dad and his new family most weekends. It was very rare he would make arrangements mainly because he and his dad had nothing in common. His dad was obsessed with sport, any sport really – football, rugby, golf, cricket, horse racing. Harry had absolutely no interest in sport and usually found himself nodding at the appropriate moment whenever his dad would talk about football, despite the fact he had no idea what it meant to be offside or when there should have been a free kick or something. If he wasn't watching it on the television, he was going out to watch a live game somewhere. And not even games at one of the big clubs, no, he preferred to stand in a cold, wet field watching some rubbish local team play some other rubbish team from a neighbouring town. It wasn't like he couldn't afford a big game either.

Harry knew his dad was rich, at least he was pretty sure he was rich. After all, he was paying for Mum's house – even he knew four-bedroomed detached houses in Oatlands Park, Weybridge, were not cheap – and he also had his own house on the St George's side of the town and those were really expensive. His dad worked up in London somewhere and had something to do with cars but other than that, he didn't have a clue. He quite liked dad's new wife, Amalia. She was Italian and would tell him all about Italy and how beautiful it was. It sounded fantastic.

She would always say to him, "Next time we go to see Mamma and Papa, you come too."

Mind you, she had been saying that since they married eight years ago. Since then, they'd had two children. Sienna and Elena. They were his half-sisters but as much as he had been excited by them when he was younger, they soon became another reason he didn't want to go to Dad's. Amalia was so busy with them, especially Elena who was only nine months old, that he would often be asked to look after or "entertain" Sienna. And how much entertaining can you really do with a three-year-old?

Harry was much closer to his mum. She seemed to understand him. Diane doted on Harry and showered him with affection. He was grateful and yet sometimes a little guilty as Lilly clearly didn't enjoy the same relationship. That said, Lilly didn't enjoy a relationship with anyone in the family.

*

It being a Saturday, Lilly was bored, stuck in her room with nothing to do. Her boyfriend had texted her to say he couldn't see her that day, so she'd have to stay home with her nagging mother and Scraggy, her little shit of a brother. Why he couldn't just disappear like her father, she'd never know. It would make life a lot easier. She was tired of having to look out for him, do everything for him, listen to how great he was. "Oh he's so clever", "Harry's got another A in maths", "Harry is so kind and helpful". *I don't give a fuck*, she thought to herself. *Little shit comes into my room again without asking, he's going to get a slap!*

"Lilly," came the call from downstairs. Lilly turned her music up, hoping she'd go away. *Yeah*, she thought, *Scraggy and Mum can just fuck off and leave me alone. I'm sixteen, for Christ's sake, I don't need this.*

"Lilly," came the call again, louder this time. Lilly didn't respond. Maybe she'd just shut up if she ignored her. "Lilly, I won't ask you again," came the raised, clearly angry voice of her mother.

There was a gentle tap on her door, and it slowly opened. Harry appeared, leaning slightly into the room and – clearly feeling the need to be extra cautious having already been reprimanded once – almost whispered, "Hi, Lilly, erm, Mum said can you come downstairs please?"

"Fuck off out of my room!" she shouted.

Harry quickly withdrew.

Realising the game was likely to be up, Lilly wandered out of her room in time to see Harry running down the stairs. *What's the little shit going to say now?* she thought.

"What do you want?" she shouted to her mother in the kitchen.

"Can you come down, please?"

Her mother had a calm but raised voice, having realised she now had her daughter's attention.

"Why?" Lilly responded in a similarly raised and angry voice.

"Just get down here!"

What now? she thought as she ambled into the kitchen where she saw her mother standing by the kitchen sink, rubber gloves on and a bowl full of dirty plates and soapy water in hand.

"So, what are your plans for the day?" Her mother was trying to sound as encouraging as she could under the circumstances. She knew that the next few moments were likely to result in an argument, but was determined to try and make some sort of connection.

"Nothing," Lilly replied, quite expecting an argument to develop as well.

"Unusual for you, Lilly. Not going out with your friends?" Her mother did her best to keep the conversation going.

"Why?" replied Lilly cautiously.

"Just curious." She paused for a moment. "Not going to see your boyfriend?"

"What?" Lilly snapped at her mother. "What do you know about my boyfriend?"

"Nothing, love, I'm just curious. You've never told me about him."

"Who said I've got a boyfriend?" She had anger in her voice. Lilly glanced over at Harry, scowling at him.

"Not me," said Harry quickly, trying to protect himself.

"It wasn't Harry," their mother quickly interjected, realising Lilly was going to blame Harry despite the truth being that it wasn't him.

"Who then?" Lilly shouted at her mother.

"It doesn't matter who, I've just heard you have a boyfriend so would like to know a bit about him, that's all." Knowing how angry Lilly was getting, she tried to calm things down.

"None of your business!" Lilly shouted and turned to walk from the room.

"Okay," said her mum. "Can you just bring your washing down and tidy your room at some point? That would be great."

"Fine," she responded, and walked out of the room.

"Now would be good," her mother quickly added. "I'm going to put the wash on in a moment."

"Okay, okay, don't go on, I've said yes."

"Jesus Christ," she muttered under her breath as she walked out of the kitchen and headed back up to her room.

Diane doubted this would be the last of the matter. She suspected that Lilly would disappear into a room full of loud music and quickly forget the task she had agreed to. Sometimes Diane could hold her own against Lilly and sometimes she couldn't face it. Today was one of those days.

She had to play the game with Lilly. She knew she was sensitive. Always had been. She cried a lot when she was younger but was also very affectionate. Not so much recently, or for the last few years, actually. She put this down to her being a teenager wanting to rebel against authority and find her place in the world. She was okay with that: she considered her daughter to be normal for her age and guessed she would grow out of it eventually. She did worry about her, though. She often didn't know where she was or who she was with. When she asked Lilly about it, she would usually bombard her with abuse, and she had learned that didn't help the relationship with her daughter at all. On a couple of occasions Lilly had gone missing. Not *missing*-missing, but still missing. She always returned home, just late. She had challenged her about this and tried to make her see that she was only asking because she was worried. Lilly would apologise – with a face that clearly wasn't apologising – and that would be that.

Communication was now at an all-time low. The only things she could find out were from Harry. Harry was her rock. He was also her baby. She had on occasion seen him come home with what looked like bruises, but he would just shrug them off, telling her he had bumped into something, or had done it playing football at school. She worried about him playing sports, he just wasn't built for it. She'd spoken with his father about it but that was a complete waste of time. He just called her stupid and suggested it would help him to "man up". He was such an arrogant pig. He had no idea and never had. How that new wife of his coped, she'd never know. But that was her problem. Diane regularly thought of her as a bimbo.

Harry sat quietly at the kitchen island listening to the exchange, expecting there to have been a huge explosion from Lilly, Mum or both. The fact that there were just a few slightly raised voices surprised yet pleased him. He hated all the shouting and yelling.

He excused himself and went to see if Lilly was okay. She hadn't exploded. Yes, she had stomped off back upstairs but that was good, no shouting, everything was fine. Maybe she'd be pleased if he offered to bring her washing down. He loved Lilly to bits and really missed being close to her. His sister had changed towards him over the years, but he remained forever optimistic.

By chance Lilly's door was open. He walked hesitantly to the threshold and saw that she was sitting on her bed. Clearly, she had not made any attempt to gather her washing together and this gave him the chance he needed to offer help. Still standing in the doorway, he cautiously asked, "Do you want me to take your clo— what's that?"

He stopped mid-sentence, seeing Lilly typing on what appeared to be a brand-new iPhone. Lilly appeared startled; she obviously hadn't heard him coming and instantly regretted leaving her door open. She was about to yell at him to get out but quickly re-thought the situation. If she yelled at him, he'd go speak to Mum. *Damn it,* she thought. *What to do?*

"Get in here," she said. Harry stepped into the room, feeling very unsure of himself. Yes, he wanted to connect with Lilly but the scorn in her voice stopped him from trying. She jumped off the bed and closed the door behind him.

This was worrying. Lilly never let him in her room, let alone with the door closed, but before he could say anything she had grabbed him by the throat with one hand and pushed him up against the back of the door. She pointed a finger in his face and with real anger written all over her expression she whispered threateningly, "Listen, you little shit, one word from you about this and you're fucking dead."

She pushed him tighter against the door, her hand still against his neck. He was struggling to breathe.

"Did you fucking hear me?" she asked.

"Yes," he managed to say before she loosened her grip. "I was only going to ask where you—"

Lilly grabbed him again.

"You never saw it, you never fucking mention it again, got it?" she snarled.

"Okay," he managed to say. At that, Lilly grabbed a pile of her washing and thrust it into his arms. "Now take those down and not one fucking word."

She opened the door and Harry walked slowly from the room. He was quite shaken. He and Lilly were not getting on well at the moment, but he always thought he would have been able to count on her if he really had to. Now she was just another person to fear. He took the clothes downstairs to the utility room where Mum was loading the washing machine.

"You shouldn't have brought her washing down," she said.

"That's okay," said Harry. "I don't mind helping."

"Such a good boy. Shame your sister isn't more like you."

Harry smiled.

CHAPTER 2

Why are they always so cheerful? Zuzanna thought to herself. She had been in Amsterdam for eight years now and yet she still couldn't understand why the Dutch people smiled so much. She had been brought up in Warsaw, watching her mother and father struggling to put food on the table, until she was 14 years old. That was when her father had left them and gone to the Netherlands to work. At the time she didn't really understand what was going on, only that her dad was leaving to try and make a better life for them, but now it made perfect sense looking back.

When her father left, she felt as though he was abandoning her. She was very close to him and being his oldest child, she felt the effects of his going probably more than her brother or sister. Michalina had only been 9 and her brother Szymon 7. They were upset, but they seemed to accept that he was coming back much more readily than she had. Her mother would be cheerful and encouraging with the three of them. She would take them out for day trips, always somewhere cheap but that didn't seem to matter. They just adapted, got on with it. They went to school as always. Did their homework as always. Played out with friends in the park as always. Rode bikes, did cooking, made jigsaws. Everything was normal.

Zuzanna sometimes thought there was something wrong with her. *Why does no one miss him?* she would often think to herself. On occasion, she would hear her mother late at night, crying in her room so she knew her mother, at least, felt the same. Every few days her father would call, and she would get an opportunity to speak with him. "When are you coming home?" she would ask, only to hear him say, "Soon, soon, not long now." She had been told that often.

Two whole years passed and still she had that same conversation with her father. Then one day, completely out of the blue, he walked in the front door. Her mother threw her arms around his neck, and they hugged. They held each other so tightly Zuzanna thought he might hurt her. Her mother was crying with joy. Michalina and Szymon had come running into the room shouting, "Tata, Tata." The room was full of love and joy, but not for Zuzanna. How could he leave her and then just wander back in and expect everything to be the same? It made no sense. Everything was not back to normal; for the last two years things had become a whole new type of normal.

"Come, Zuzanna, come and say hello to your tata," her mother had called over to her. Zuzanna had stood and stared, her feet rooted to the floor. "What is the matter?" her mother continued. "Isn't your tata coming home what you wanted?"

Zuzanna turned and walked out. She went into the small courtyard at the back of the houses where she lived and sat on one of the metal benches. *Why is he home now?* she thought. *What has happened that he needs to come back?* In reality she was pleased, it was just that things were different to when he left. They seemed to have more money than before and Zuzanna was old enough to realise this was because of the money he had been sending home. He had been promising to come home for so long she thought it would never happen. Now he had just walked in and expected it to be back to normal. Zuzanna could feel the anger rising in her.

After a couple of minutes, she caught sight of her father walking through the courtyard towards her. She folded her arms and crossed her legs, turning slightly away from him. He sat next to her, and she moved herself as far from him as the bench would allow.

"Are you not pleased to see your tata?" he said with a gentleness in his voice she had heard many times before. She didn't answer. "I can understand why you are angry with me; I've been away a long time."

He leaned forwards, resting his forearms on his thighs and interlocking his fingers so both hands were together in front of him. He looked out across the courtyard and sighed.

"You know, I thought of you every day," he said. "It was difficult for me too. I know it must have been difficult for you, but you must try and remember how it was before I left."

"That's just it," Zuzanna cried out. "I do remember, you were home, everyone was happy and then you walked out on us."

"No, no, no, you must try and understand, remember how little we had, remember how little work I had. Think, think really hard, I need you to understand."

"Never!" shouted Zuzanna before running back to the house.

The next few days were tense. Zuzanna struggled and yet once again, everyone seemed to be getting on as if nothing had happened. Then after two months came the next bombshell. The five of them sat down to breakfast as they did most days. Zuzanna was still not happy with her father but over time she had at least got used to him being around again. So used to him being around she hadn't even noticed he wasn't working. He would potter around the house doing small upkeep jobs but not work anywhere else. Her mother had always done some part-time work, usually ironing for people or some cleaning when asked, but not full-time. This was the moment she found out why.

"Children," her mother said, "Tata, has some exciting news for you."

Zuzanna frowned. *I knew it couldn't last*, she thought. *He'll be off again soon.*

"Yes, children, exciting news. I have to return to work in the Netherlands."

Just as she thought.

But her father hadn't finished speaking. "...and this time, you're all coming with me."

"What!" cried Zuzanna. "You want to drag us away from our friends, our school, Babcia?"

"Please," said her father. "Just listen."

"Why? You've obviously already decided," she cried.

With that, she stormed out of the room and went to her bedroom.

"Leave her," said her mother. "She'll come around."

"I hope so," he replied.

Of course, that was eight years ago and Zuzanna had grown up. She had finished her schooling in Amsterdam and managed to do quite well. She felt fortunate that many in the Netherlands spoke English. Her command of English was quite good, having been taught it since primary school, and she had also become fluent in Dutch.

She had a great group of friends and a good job working in one of the coffee shops down by the canals. She enjoyed it there: she got to meet people and she was a people person. Being a barista was not exactly a lifetime ambition, but it would do for now, it brought in enough money to help support her parents and her younger siblings.

She craved the opportunity to visit her grandparents more often, but she did get to see her babcia every couple of years and she spoke to her most weeks on the phone. She had thought of teaching her to use Skype but knowing what a technophobe her grandmother was, she decided better of it.

Shortly before her 20th birthday, things had needed to change again for the family. Her father worked in construction earning good money, certainly enough to support the family and get them all the little extras that made their lives comfortable, but the accident changed all that. Zuzanna had been intending to stay on and study at school. She would have loved to get a degree in one of the sciences, she wasn't even concerned about which one. She was good at sciences and loved them all. But then her father was injured at the site: the scaffolding he was under collapsed and his head injuries were so severe that everyone thought he would die. He remained in a coma for weeks and in hospital for 6 more months. Unfortunately, he was never the same. He was angry, sometimes sad, and only occasionally Zuzanna thought she could see signs he was happy.

The impact of this on her mother was devastating. Since they moved to Amsterdam, she had always been cheerful and bright. Forever optimistic. Now she was back to the mother she had been back in Poland when her father was away. She worked and worked. If not out cleaning then at home looking after her father, cooking, caring and looking after Szymon – who Zuzanna thought was old enough to look after himself but didn't.

This all put pay to her ever going on to further education. She had gotten used to it. With her mother's new cleaning jobs and her income from the coffee shop they did okay. They had hoped to get compensation from the building firm for her father's injury but after a lengthy court case it was decided that responsibility fell down to "an act of God", whatever that meant. They would be entitled to some support for his disability but that was it. Her father could no longer work and needed help from Zuzanna and her mother to get by. His condition was reasonably stable, but it couldn't be counted on to remain so. At the moment he was at least still able to dress himself, but he needed help with eating and coordination.

Going to the coffee shop was light relief for Zuzanna and she loved interacting with the customers. The owners realised they had a gem working amongst them, but they also knew that she and her family were struggling, so they tried to give her as many extra shifts as they could.

She was a joy to be around, and the staff and customers loved her. She had been asked out on dates on numerous occasions by all kinds of customers – Dutch, eastern European and other holidaymakers alike. She was flattered but always declined. She longed to socialise with the customers. With many, she had formed a kind of friendship, and they would always ask her to join them. With some of the handsome young men she would flirt, and they would respond knowing she would turn them down. How would she find the time for such things? With the hours she worked and her responsibilities at home it would not be possible. Maybe one day, she would think to herself when she had a moment in her busy day. But not now, was always the answer. She had learned not to even consider the possibility of a relationship.

At 19 years of age, her sister Michalina couldn't have been more different. She was set on enjoying her life to the fullest. She would go out most weekends with her friends and sometimes not return home until the following day. Sometimes there were boys she would talk about and whenever their mother said to be careful, she would always tell her to stop worrying and that she knew what she was doing.

Zuzanna didn't resent this. After all, if she could go out more, she would, but as the older sister she had a responsibility to her siblings as well as her mother and father. Her brother did resent this, though. At 17 he was not working and was reliant on whatever Zuzanna or their mother could spare. *So selfish*, Zuzanna thought whenever he expressed his annoyance.

Life continued with each day bringing new challenges. As Zuzanna looked out at the Dutch people, thinking, *Why are they all so cheerful?* she was also thinking, *One day we'll be like that.*

CHAPTER 3

The office was cold. Not surprising, really. In the Latvian province of Riga, it was only two degrees outside and that was after the sun had been up for several hours. Overnight it had been down to minus eight. When you have a business selling luxury motor vehicles, you would have thought the least the owners could do was replace the small electric fire with something a little more effective.

Anastasjia's job was for all intents and purposes a secretary but in reality, she was far more than that. She had a role, an important role that was not just about filing and taking notes. She was required to get close to clients and establish their weaknesses.

To Anastasjia that wasn't a problem, in fact it was something she found easy to do. So many of these rich idiots fell over themselves to wine and dine her in a desperate attempt to get in her knickers. Sometimes she even allowed it, so long as she got what she needed; information, money, valuables, pleasure and occasionally something the company could use to blackmail the client. With no emotional attachments, this was just business, and she was good at it. These fat greasy slobs thought money would get them anything but most of the time they would be in for a big shock as soon as they signed on the dotted line. Of course, she would play the game when she needed to.

Today was different, though. Today it was her favourite regular and for once, she actually really liked him. Sure, he was another rich fool, but he was good looking, attentive and made her job pleasurable as well as easy. She had been given additional instructions from her employers as to what they needed from him, and it was her job to get it. She would be well paid, of course, and could also have a bit of fun on the way.

Jennings worked for the company as a car importer and exporter from the UK office. Anastasjia knew he would not be aware of other aspects of the company, the parts that were not so obvious, the darker areas that needed to be hidden. Over the next few days, she would make sure that when he was introduced to those parts of the business, he would be prepared to do what the company required. She had met him several times on previous trips and slowly got him to be more trusting of her.

Anastasjia appreciated what her bosses had done for her. Before coming to work for the company in the car showrooms she had worked the streets briefly before moving to the massage parlour where she was forced to work for pitiful pay and squalid accommodation, whilst performing all manner of sexual acts on anyone who was willing to pay. She had been enslaved to the traffickers owning the parlour, with seemingly no way out.

It was actually one of her clients who identified her and introduced her to her new bosses. The company took over the running of the massage parlour. She was told by her bosses, it was "under new management" and was assured the girls left behind were looked after. She had no guarantee of that, but she was sure things couldn't be worse for them. She knew a message had to be sent to the traffickers that they don't mess with the company. She suspected the parlour madam was still not able to walk but that was nothing the bitch didn't deserve. She had been truly evil, thriving on the pain and suffering of the girls.

Anastasjia would often think of the girls; she got on well with most of them. Even though survival was the most important thing, they did manage to comfort each other. She knew she was the lucky one, the one who managed to get away, selected for the role she was now living.

She knew that cooperation was essential, and she would do as she was told, but it was still nice to have some freedom so long as she didn't rock the boat. She was well looked after and had a nice little apartment and even a small group of friends the company approved of. She couldn't jeopardise that.

Her job for the most part consisted of making sure the most valued clients and business owners enjoyed their trip to Riga but signed on the dotted line.

Anastasjia had briefed the showroom staff to make sure the Aston Martin DBS Superleggera was pride of place at the front of the main entrance – the best-lit area of the entire showroom. The other Astons were placed predominantly. It was important that Jennings knew his cars were rated above the Ferraris, Maseratis and McLarens that were also frequently sold to rich Russians.

She understood enough about the working of the company to know that the car sales were a front for another part of the business. They were buying cars from the UK from a company they owned. Not on paper, but she overheard enough to know that was the case. She also knew enough to keep her mouth shut and do her job.

Negotiations would be carried out by one of the sales staff – clearly a senior company member – but that did not mean her role was any less important. If she did her job right, and she usually did, Jennings would be forced to commit to something that would cost him. Something that would make him commit to dealing with the cars that when re-sold would make a lot of money, and make sure he did as he was told. She looked at her role as being insurance, the little extra that guaranteed the deal.

She suspected she wouldn't be home to feed the cat so had asked the neighbour across the hall to call in for her. She knew Jennings was booked into a Grand Suite in the Grand Poet Hotel and if she didn't get to join him, she would consider the day's work a failure. Even better, it was only a short taxi journey to her own apartment so after breakfast she could go home to shower and change before going back to the office.

Jennings was due to arrive in about 10 minutes, time for a quick check of her appearance. She looked in the mirror and checked her makeup and her outfit. The knee-length pencil skirt and high heels accentuated her legs, and the blouse was suitably light that you could see the shape of her figure underneath. *Jacket on or off?* she thought. *Off.* She undid the buttons and pushed her shoulders back, letting it slip down her arms and caught it as it reached her hands. She quickly hung the jacket on the back of her chair and glanced up at the mirror. *Better.*

The door opened and Jennings walked in accompanied by none other than Balodis. She was impressed. They were really going all out to get what they wanted.

Janis Balodis was a thug. This was not just Anastasjia's view but that of the other people at the showrooms. He was highly thought of by the bosses for getting the deals signed but she hated his manner. He was all aggression, over six feet and stocky, muscles in places most people don't have them. He could be charming but was intimidating. You just knew not to mess with him.

"Mr. Jennings," she said, holding her hand out to shake his.

"Oh, I think we're past that, aren't we?" said Jennings. "Please call me Michael."

"Of course, Michael. And you must call me Ana."

She smiled her most alluring smile.

"Ana," he said and smiled back.

Balodis had said nothing, showing a distinct lack of emotion.

"As you can see, we have your cars in pride of place. Demand is fantastic," she said before glancing over at Balodis to make sure she hadn't overstepped the mark.

Still no sign of emotion. She hated him being there but knew if he was involved in the negotiations, it must be important.

"Would it have looked the same had I been here yesterday?" Jennings asked with an even wider smile on his face. Anastasjia hesitated.

"Yes, of course," she replied, smiling back nervously.

Balodis looked at her. She was sure she detected more menace than normal.

"You are our number one supplier, Michael, we couldn't operate without you, you know that," he said out of the blue. A smile appeared on his face; Jennings smiled back knowingly.

From then on, the charm offensive started. That was good, although Anastasjia worried about his comment on how the showroom looked the previous day. She made a short prayer to herself that she wouldn't be made to pay for that later. It wouldn't be today, she had a job to do, but sometime in the next few days she could be punished for it, and it was usually painful. She tried to forget it and do her job. If she didn't give him another reason, with any luck he'd forget.

"Well, I look forward to our negotiations," said Jennings.

"I've booked the three of us a table at Domini Canes this evening and then we can meet back here tomorrow morning for a meeting to discuss our trade arrangements," said Balodis.

"Perfect," replied Jennings.

"I'll get one of the sales team to drop you off at the hotel and I'll arrange for a car to pick you up for the restaurant at seven," said Balodis.

"See you at the restaurant," said Jennings, looking at Anastasjia.

Jennings walked out of the room with Balodis accompanying him. Anastasjia watched them leave through the open door. Balodis called over one of the sales team and she watched as Balodis gave him instructions. Jennings and the salesman walked out and jumped into a waiting DBS before driving off to the hotel.

Balodis returned to the office and closed the door behind him.

"Mind yourself," he said with a menacing stare.

She had hesitated once when speaking with Jennings and Balodis was angry.

"I'm sorry, Janis, I'll be careful."

"Be sure you are, or we may have to play some games and you know I always win those."

He smiled as he walked out. Anastasjia realised she was holding her breath. She breathed out and found she had to steady herself. *No more mistakes,* she thought.

CHAPTER 4

Lilly was at school. Well, for at least half an hour whilst registration was sorted out, then she was off to meet up with Jordan. *Jesus Christ,* she thought to herself. *These sad losers, all waiting to be told stuff that will never be of any use to them.* She waited for the bell so they could all be signed in before shooting off to their first classes of the day. Her friend Julie wandered over.

"What time you are meeting him?" she asked.

"About twenty past," she replied, laughing.

"You're one bad bitch," Julie said, also laughing. "So, where you going?"

"Not sure, maybe just hang out for a while. Depends."

"On what?" asked Julie, with a knowing glint in her eye.

"On whether he wants us to get close." She laughed again.

"You're one bad bitch," Julie repeated.

The bell went and they linked arms as they walked into the school building, still laughing together.

After registration they left together.

"Later," said Julie.

"Later, girl," replied Lilly before heading to the exit at the rear of the school where she could take the short route to the perimeter by the wooded area.

She then made her way unseen to the gap in the fence that for some reason had never been repaired despite it being there when she first joined the school. From there it was a short walk to the end of the alley where Jordan would be waiting in his ST. She was getting excited at the thought of seeing him. He was so cool.

As she approached the end of the alley, she smiled. There was his car but standing by the open passenger door was Levi, his friend. *Shit*, she thought. Firstly, she had been looking forward to spending time with Jordan, alone, and secondly Levi was a complete arsehole. He thought he was really hot, and they weren't. He thought everyone believed his bullshit, but nobody did. *Shit, shit, shit,* she thought.

"Hi, babe," said Levi with a wry smile. "In you get. Don't want to be caught out here in your uniform, do you?" he said.

She could see Jordan in the driver's seat watching her. She walked round to the passenger door where Levi already had the front seat tilted forward so she could climb into the back. She bent forward and leaned into the gap between the seat and the door pillar before climbing in. As she did, she could swear Levi touched her arse. *Dirty bastard.* Levi pulled the seat back, leaving her almost no room. She didn't want to move over to the driver's side as she wanted to be able to see Jordan driving whilst still being able to keep an eye on Levi without him looking round and leching at her.

"Okay?" asked Jordan. "You need to get out of that," he said, referring to her school uniform.

"I know, I know, give me a chance," she replied.

She threw her backpack onto the seat beside her and pulled out her jeans and a tee shirt. She was already wearing a hoodie under her school jacket as it was cold out. The teachers were always moaning about the kids wearing them, but she got the impression they had given up as nobody listened. She undressed, removing the jacket and hoodie so she could get the shirt and tie off. No sooner was the shirt off she saw Jordan glance round to look at her from the driver's seat. She didn't mind, but she did mind Levi turning round and making it obvious he was staring at her.

"Nice tits," he said, laughing.

"Fuck off," she replied.

The car pulled away and Jordan said nothing, which annoyed her even more. She quickly pulled the tee shirt over her head and put the hoodie back on. She managed to pull the jeans up under her skirt so that neither of them could see anything else, then finally removed the skirt and shoved her uniform unceremoniously into the backpack.

"Where we going anyway?" she asked.

They were heading up the A3 into London and she was wondering why.

"We've got some business," replied Levi.

"What business?"

"Nothing for you to be bothered about," said Levi in a tone that told Lilly to shut up and stop asking questions.

Jordan remained silent. She hated that he seemed to do whatever Levi wanted.

He continued to drive on deeper into London, crossing Tower Bridge, then turned off towards Stratford. Lilly had no idea where they were heading. She had been up to London a few times over the years with her mum and brother, but never away from the tourist areas. She was uncomfortable but wanted Jordan to think she was alright.

She had met Jordan at the park while she was with her friends. They were just hanging out when they saw a lowered ST pull into the car park and Jordan got out. He wore a short sleeved open-neck shirt, Levis and Aviators. *So fine.* He wandered over to where they were sitting and asked what they were up to. He explained he had recently moved to the area and was trying to find out where the best places were and what was going on, stuff like that.

He was clearly older than them but not by that much, maybe 18 or 19, she wasn't sure and didn't really care. After a while he asked if anyone fancied going for a drive so they could show him around. Lilly jumped at the chance and she, along with Julie and her boyfriend Will agreed to show him around the Thames hangout spots under Walton Bridge and down by the riverside. They jumped into his car, Julie and Will in the back and Lilly beside Jordan in the front. She could feel the excitement pumping through her body. He was gorgeous and she hoped he liked her. Julie and Will were giggling in the back seat, and all Lilly could think about was hoping they didn't embarrass her. They drove to the river and sat chatting and laughing. They got some vodka, which they drank with Coke – though Jordan just had the Coke as he was driving and then he drove them back to the park.

He stayed seated in the car whilst Lilly got up and let Julie and Will out of the car. She leaned back in the car and said, "Thanks for the drive, great car."

"My pleasure and thanks for showing me round." He paused and looked away and then looked back. "Can I see you again sometime?" he asked.

"I'll be here next Saturday," she nervously said. Did that make it too obvious she was still at school?

That was several weeks ago. Lilly tried to work out where they were. The last sign she had seen was for Stratford but now she was lost. It was definitely East London somewhere. She was okay with it, she was with Jordan, and he would look after her.

She remembered how the week had passed slowly after that first meeting. How she couldn't wait to see Jordan again. Her excitement was fuelled by Julie who was thoroughly supportive and constantly asked her about him. Did she think he would show up, what would they do, what was she going to wear? So many questions.

On Saturday she walked to the park with Julie and Will. Jordan was there already. He picked the three of them up and then suggested they go and visit one of his mates at his flat.

"It could be fun. Bit of music and chilling."

Lilly looked round at Julie and Will.

"Okay with us," said Julie.

"Great," said Jordan and off they drove towards Walton-on-Thames.

Eventually they arrived at the St. John's Estate. Lilly had grown up calling it 'The Bronx' due to its reputation for drugs and fighting. It was known for street muggings due to the network of hidden passageways that joined the parts of the estate. In truth the rumour was worse than reality; she had friends who lived there, and she had been to parties there. Never had she seen any trouble. Jordan parked the car and the four of them went to one of the blocks of flats. The entry pad was broken, and the door was held ajar by an old pushchair that had somehow been wedged into the bottom.

They followed Jordan up to the first-floor landing to a door on the right, which had had most of the paint removed and clearly at some point had a repair done to the lock.

"Yeah," came the voice from inside the flat.

"It's me, Jordan," he called out.

Moments later the door opened, and Lilly saw a girl who looked like she was in her 30s at least, but Jordan later told her she was 20. Her face looked drawn, her skin was translucent, and she was painfully skinny. Lilly couldn't help but notice the track marks on her arms. Although it was now around 2:00pm it looked as though she had just gotten out of bed. She was wearing pyjama shorts and a vest. Jordan put his arms around her and kissed her on the cheek.

"Hi, lovely, you okay?"

"Good, you?" she replied, but Jordan made no attempt to answer or to introduce her and instead walked into the lounge.

Lying on the settee with his bare feet on the large coffee table was the subject of the voice that had called out when they arrived.

"This is Monty," said Jordan.

The girl, still unnamed and unintroduced, climbed onto the settee next to Monty and snuggled into him, closing her eyes.

The lounge was poorly lit with a blanket covering most of the window. There had obviously been wallpaper on the wall sometime in the past but how long ago was difficult to tell. Where the wall was exposed, there were traces of awful paint underneath. Lilly could have sworn it was purple, but it was difficult to tell in the poor light. The floor was bare concrete painted blue and covered by a worn, deep pile rug. In the centre of the floor was a glass-topped coffee table that was far too big for the room and looked like something out of the 1970s with its brass-coloured steel frame. On the table were ashtrays full of roll-up butts and spliff ends. Next to the ashtrays were rolling tobacco and extra-long papers as well as normal papers. There were two or three plastic disposable lighters and a couple of tobacco tins with the lids on. Lilly wasn't a smoker, not really; she had smoked a cigarette from time to time, starting when Julie first offered her one. She didn't like the taste or the smell and couldn't bring herself to inhale. She certainly didn't feel confident using roll-ups and she hoped Jordan wouldn't ask her. She didn't want to let him down.

The air was thick with the sweet odour of smoked cannabis and cigarettes that Lilly knew from being at Julie's house when her mum was smoking weed. In a failed attempt to disguise the smell, an incense burner was alight on a shelf in the corner of the room. There were opened beer cans and Lilly could tell they'd been drinking a while as there were also some empty ones lying on the floor. A television was balanced precariously on a small coffee table in the corner of the room showing some wildlife programme that no one was watching. The sound was turned right down so it couldn't be heard. Instead, Radiohead was playing from a stereo next to the television. The main piece of furniture was a three-seater settee covered with a large throw that although stained, Lilly guessed was better than the settee it covered. There was also an old leather chair that had most of the stuffing knocked out of it.

"Grab a seat, anywhere," said Monty. "Beer in the fridge and some spirits on the side with mixers if you want them."

He indicated towards the kitchen area with one hand. In the other he held what looked like a partially smoked roll-up, the ash of which was about to drop. He suddenly dropped the arm, flicking the ash onto the bare floor by his side.

"Beer for me," said Jordan and walked towards the kitchen.

Lilly, Julie, and Will stood still, not really knowing what to do.

"Help yourselves, guys," said Monty, again pointing towards the kitchen.

The three of them followed him into the kitchen where he was grabbing a can of Stella from the fridge.

"Will?" he asked.

"Oh, yeah, beer for me," said Will.

"Girls?"

"Um, is there any vodka and Coke?" asked Julie cautiously.

"Coming up," replied Jordan, grabbing a half empty half bottle of cheap vodka and a half empty bottle of Coke.

He opened the Coke and the lack of a hissing noise told Lilly it was completely flat.

Lilly was following him with her eyes. She adored him, but she also didn't want to look at the dirt in the room. By remaining focused on him she didn't have to think about it. She was nervous, but somehow found the situation exciting at the same time.

He grabbed a glass from the cupboard above the fridge. The glass was water-stained, but he wiped it clean with the edge of his shirt.

"I'll let you pour it like you like it," said Jordan, passing Julie the glass.

"Thanks," said Julie.

"Lilly?" asked Jordan.

"Same," she replied.

He went through the same process with another glass.

Jordan went into the lounge and sat at the opposite end of the settee to Monty and the girl. Holding the can of beer, he put one arm on the arm rest. He indicated to Will that he could take the chair. Will sat in the chair and Jordan looked at Julie. "You'll have to share the chair, I'm afraid" he said, smiling.

Julie sat on Will's lap and leaned back, partly onto the arm of the chair and partly into Will. Lilly stood, not quite sure what to do.

"Is this enough room for you?" Jordan said, indicating the space between him and the girl. Lilly smiled and sat in between them. Although nervous, this was just where she wanted to be.

"Do you want to sit back?" asked Jordan.

Lilly hadn't even noticed that she was perching on the edge of the seat. She leaned back and settled into Jordan's side. At that moment she realised she would do anything for him, and she hoped he felt the same.

They chatted and laughed and listened to the music. Over the next couple of hours, the girl leaning on Monty never woke up. Lilly was now pushed right into Jordan. He didn't seem to mind, and she certainly didn't. Will and Julie were happily entertaining themselves, drinking, chatting, or kissing. Lilly was desperate for Jordan to kiss her, but he made no move to do so.

"So, are you going to let me try some of your finest?" Jordan asked Monty.

"Help yourself," he replied, "but use it sparingly."

Jordan reached forward to the coffee table, taking his arm from around Lilly. He took one of the large papers from the table and some tobacco, which he spread evenly along the paper. He then reached out to one of the tobacco tins and opened it. Inside were some dried cannabis leaves.

"Only the best," said Monty.

Jordan smiled and took some of the cannabis, spreading it evenly along the tobacco before rolling the paper and securing the ends with a twist. He was careful to replace the lid of the tin before reaching for one of the lighters and lighting the spliff he had put to his lips. As he lit the paper he drew in a deep breath and absorbed the smoke into his lungs.

"Oh yeah, and that's why they call you Monty."

Monty laughed.

"Only the best," he repeated.

"Why Monty? Is that not your real name?" asked Lilly.

Monty laughed again.

"Monty Don, the gardener," said Monty.

Jordan and Monty continued to laugh; the cannabis seemed to be making it funnier to Jordan somehow. Lilly looked nervously between Jordan and Monty, not sure if she should be trying to laugh with them.

Although she had seen Julie's mum smoking cannabis, Lilly still had little knowledge of it. Sure, they had talked about the dangers at school, and yes, she knew people who said they smoked it, but this was the first time she had seen it used so openly. Even Julie's mum would go and sit in the garden where she thought she couldn't be seen.

After a couple of deep draws, Jordan held out the spliff to Lilly, as if to say, 'Draw on it.' She shook her head. Despite the trust she was developing in him, she had been told over and over about the evils of drug use. Will and Julie accepted the spliff and both took deep drags. Julie passed the spliff back to Jordan and then smiled at Lilly and raised her eyebrows as if to say, 'Go on.'

Jordan again offered it to Lilly. Will and Julie were looking at her, willing her to take it. She did her best to hide her fears; after all, she didn't want Jordan to think she was a child. She reached out, taking hold of the spliff. Putting it between her lips she breathed in heavily. Suddenly the smoke hit the back of her throat and she coughed and coughed. They all laughed. Lilly felt embarrassed.

Jordan put his arm back around her and told her, "Don't worry, it takes a bit of getting used to but feels great once you've mastered it, right guys?"

He turned to look at Will and Julie, both of whom were looking really relaxed and with big smiles on their faces.

"Oh yeah," said Julie. "Oh yeah."

Back in the car, Lilly again sat next to Jordan on the way back to Weybridge. They stopped to buy mints to disguise the smell of alcohol and smoking, although Lilly was more concerned about the fact she was feeling really unsteady.

She was not used to drinking and although she had only sampled the cannabis briefly, the combination of smoke and the drug mixed with drink was having an effect that was not pleasant, in fact, she felt quite sick. Jordan dropped her round the corner from her house, so she had less distance to walk. They had already dropped Will and Julie off so the two were alone.

"Can I see you again?" he asked.

"Same time next week?" asked Lilly.

"Okay," he replied. "I'd like to try and see you more though."

Lilly's heart raced.

"Me too, we'll try to arrange something."

"Can I call you?" he asked.

"Best not, my mum gets really funny about people calling," Lilly said and immediately kicked herself mentally. He was going to think she was such a child.

"That's okay, I'll see you next week, same time and we'll sort something out."

As she got out of the car Jordan leaned over and Lilly leaned into him. It was only a short kiss then he said, "See you next week."

When she jumped out of the car her heart was racing.

She had lost track of time completely and it was late, very late, and it was dark. She'd need to get in without Scraggy and Mum seeing her. She carefully made her way through the back door, but her mum heard her.

"Is that you?" she called out.

"Yes, I'm really tired, I'm going to bed."

She quickly ran upstairs and closed her bedroom door behind her. She removed her clothes, which stank of smoke, and put on her night shirt. She made a conscious note to put her clothes in the wash in the morning.

She lay on her back and thought about the day and especially Jordan. She would be seeing him next week. She rolled onto her side and sank into a deep sleep.

The following week she again met up with Jordan. This time she deliberately avoided taking Julie and Will; she wanted to be alone with him. The weather this time was great, sunny, and mild for the time of year, so they went for a drive to the coast. As they walked on the beach, Jordan smoked another spliff. He offered it to her to try again but after the last time she was hesitant.

"Go on," he said, smiling. "It'll help you relax."

She tried again, with a little more success. The secret was not to take in too much. Then they lay on a blanket and looked up at the sky.

Lilly was trembling with excitement and anticipation. Jordan rolled over, putting his face near hers. He moved in for a kiss and they kissed for some time. After a while he gently stroked her breasts with the tip of his fingers whilst continuing to kiss her.

Lilly didn't know how to react, she suddenly stopped kissing him and pulled back from him. It was enough for him to know she wasn't ready to go further. She was a virgin; she didn't want him to know that. She had experienced teenage fumblings with some of the boys at school, but she had never gone further than that.

"It's okay," he said, smiling. "We don't need to—"

Before he could finish, she interrupted.

"No, it's not that, I want to," she blurted out. "I just wasn't ready." She felt foolish.

He smiled again.

"Maybe later," he said, leaning over and kissing her gently again.

"Yes please," she replied, feeling even more foolish. Why on earth did she say 'yes please'? He was going to dump her for sure.

He suggested going back into the car as it was getting cold.

He told her how much he enjoyed the day whilst he drove back to Weybridge. Lilly couldn't help feeling she had blown it with him.

"It was great," she said, hoping he would respond positively.

"Yeah," he replied. "It was, even on the beach."

Lilly's face dropped; he was bothered about her pulling away.

"Sorry," she said without offering any explanation, guessing she didn't need to.

"It's okay, you weren't ready, we'll try next time," he said, smiling.

She smiled back. Had she just agreed to have sex with him? She wasn't sure.

"I'd like to see you more often, if you'd like?" he said to her, like a question.

"That would be great, but like I said my mum is funny about my phone."

She couldn't believe she had said that again. He must have thought she was such a child. Her eyes dropped to the floor.

"Let's see if we can sort that problem out," he said, smiling again.

What could he mean? She was puzzled yet felt she could trust him.

They parked up around the corner from Lilly's again. He opened the glove box and pulled out an iPhone. It was brand new. He handed it to her and said, "My number's already in it."

"I can't take that, it's really expensive."

"That's what I like about you," he said. "You like me for who I am and not what I can give you. Seriously, I get them really cheap. Best not let everyone know or they'll all want one. Keep it between us, keep it hidden. You can call me any evening and I can text you when I want to speak to you, so you don't upset your mum." He smiled at her.

She took hold of the phone.

"Are you sure?" she asked again.

"Yes, of course. I really like you." He leaned over towards her and kissed her again. "Do you trust me?" he asked.

"I don't know what you mean." She was confused.

"Look, I've been let down by girls in the past, but with you I feel I've found someone special. I just need to know that you trust me. Trust is the most important part of a relationship, don't you agree?"

"Yes, of course," she replied, not really knowing the answer to his question.

She had never had a proper relationship and had no idea, but he seemed so grown up and vulnerable.

"Well, can I?" he asked again.

"Can I what?"

She still wasn't sure what she was agreeing to.

"Trust you."

His face appeared to harden towards her momentarily and she noticed it. She felt a shiver run through her body, but she wasn't sure whether it was because of the look, the fear of losing him or because she was beginning to feel out of her depth whilst still desperately wanting to be with him.

"Yes, you can," she replied, speaking very quickly.

"That's good." He kissed her again.

She got out of the car clutching the iPhone. With that, the ST roared up the road.

As the weeks went by she saw more and more of Jordan. He filled her mind. He was so attentive. They spent a lot more time at Monty's. She even got to know the skinny girl who was called Lorraine. She was okay; Lilly never got much out of her as she was usually out of it. She was a smack head. She got the impression that Monty didn't do smack, only cannabis, but a lot of it.

She had started to sleep with Jordan as well. The first time it happened was at Monty's after smoking some cannabis. He told her it would help her relax and it wouldn't hurt, but it did. In fact, it hurt a lot. He was really forcing it and when she said to stop, he continued. She had cried with the pain, but he was gentle afterwards, telling her it would be better the more she did it.

He was right; it no longer hurt, and she was enjoying it, except when she had to do oral sex on him. She hated that but he would hold her in place until she gagged and then he would swear at her and be horrible. She was desperate to be with him so would agree, but she still felt sick, even when he didn't hold her.

She got to know more of his friends as well. Most were okay but she really didn't like Levi.

She hated that Jordan had told Levi about the sex. He had even told him, "She's learned to give good head." Lilly couldn't believe what she was hearing. She told him off after that, it was private. Jordan had apologised and told her he was proud of her because she was so good. She still hated that Levi knew.

She had started to miss school to be with him. She thought the school would be on to her parents, but she was surprised by how easy it was for her absence to go unnoticed. Jordan had told her what to do. "Make sure you go to reception first; the school needs to think you're there." He was right, not once had anyone questioned where she was or who she was with. She didn't like missing school, but Jordan had told her he wanted her with him. Now she was on an adventure with him across London. It was just upsetting he had brought Levi with him.

Eventually they arrived at a terraced house on an estate. Lilly had absolutely no idea where she was, other than London somewhere. They got out of the car and Jordan pressed the button on his keys to lock the doors. They walked up to the front door, which was up a short flight of stairs. She could see there were more stairs down to a basement. She assumed this was another property.

Levi rang the bell, but no one answered. After at least a minute of waiting, Lilly said, "It's freezing out here. What are we doing?"

"Just shut up," said Levi, and eventually the door opened and the three of them went in. First Levi, then Lilly who was almost pushed in by Jordan, who shut the door behind him. They walked through the large entrance hall to a well-decorated lounge on the left-hand side. Standing in the room was a large black guy. He looked at her up and down.

"Not bad. Is she any good?" he asked.

"Any good for what?" said Lilly, feeling alarmed.

"Shut the fuck up, bitch. Who asked you to speak?" he shouted at her.

She looked at Jordan. He looked at her briefly and then looked away.

"Yeah, she'll do nicely," said the guy. "I think me and the guys need to give her some lessons first but yeah, she'll do nicely."

Fear was not something Lilly was used to, but she knew all about it in those few moments.

CHAPTER 5

For Zuzanna, things were not about to get better any time soon. Stepping out the back of the coffee shop at the end of a busy shift, she found Michalina slumped by the side of the dumpster covered in blood. At first sight she thought she was dead.

"Michalina, Michalina." Zuzanna crouched by her sister.

What could have happened to her? She was a free spirit, thought Zuzanna, but not the type of person who would anger anyone. "Michalina," she said again, panic in her voice.

Michalina slowly opened her eyes and looked helplessly at her. Zuzanna couldn't help but notice the bruising on her face and the blood seeping from her nose and the side of her mouth.

"Who did this, who hurt you?" Zuzanna found the words tumbling out of her mouth. "I'll get an ambulance, you wait, I'll call the police."

"NO." Suddenly Michalina came to life, her eyes wide full of fear.

"But I must, you need—"

"NO, please, NO, you mustn't. Please, Zuzanna."

Zuzanna was confused. What had she gotten into?

"But you—"

"NO," Michalina shouted at her. This time she sounded angry.

Zuzanna pulled herself back and looked down at the bruised and bloodied face of her sister. She had clearly been crying, although the tears had long gone and her eyeliner was smudged. The blood around her nostril had also dried and there was a trail of it across her face, as though she had made a half-hearted attempt to wipe it away.

Zuzanna found herself at a loss, confused by the anger of her sister and rejection of her help. Michalina had obviously come here for help but now didn't want it.

"What is it? Why won't you let me help you? I don't understand."

She looked at her sister. Michalina was now trying to sit up, struggling to hold herself and instead leaned back against the dumpster, wincing in pain with every movement.

"I need your help," Michalina said, looking her in the eye, "but no police or hospitals."

"But why—" started Zuzanna.

"I said no police or hospitals, you need to promise."

"But we must—"

"LISTEN TO ME!" Michalina shouted, the fear returning to her face. "Listen, please, no police or hospitals, you must promise me."

Reluctantly Zuzanna agreed. She was sure she could convince her later.

"I need you to loan me some money," she said.

"You mean someone did this to you for money? We must go to the police."

Zuzanna was exasperated. Her sister wouldn't accept her help and she clearly needed medical attention. Now she was telling her she owed money and needed bailing out. *For God's sake*, she thought. *Why am I always the one that has to save the family from catastrophe!*

Zuzanna did have some money; not a lot, but she had managed to put aside a small amount each month. She hadn't checked how much she had for a long time, but thought it was probably about 5,000 euros. Of course, in reality Zuzanna knew she would pay it off. She also suspected she wouldn't get it back, but knew she should still help. After all was said and done, Michalina was her younger sister and she loved her.

"What about your injuries?"

Michalina was still clearly in pain.

"I'm okay," she answered, still wincing as she spoke.

"Well, clearly you're not," replied Zuzanna, finding it hard to hide her annoyance.

"Do you want to help?" said Michalina curtly, bringing the subject back to the money.

"Yes, of course, how much do you need?" Zuzanna asked, wondering how much she'd have left of her hard-earned savings.

"I need fifty thousand euros, and I need it quickly." Michalina looked at her sister pleadingly. Zuzanna looked back at her, frozen and unable to speak.

"Can you help? Please, Zuzanna, can you help?" Michalina asked. She was pleading now, and her eyes began to well up with tears. She must have known she was asking the impossible but having no one else to turn to, there was no other option.

Finally, Zuzanna managed to reply. She spoke softly.

"Fifty thousand euros?" she asked, hoping she'd not heard correctly but knowing she had.

"Yes." Michalina sounded embarrassed.

Zuzanna sat down next to her sister and leaned against the dumpster. The two of them looked straight ahead at the wall opposite.

"What the fuck do you need that for?" It was the first time she had sworn like that in front of her sister.

"Don't be mad."

"Don't be mad?" she echoed back. "What the fuck am I supposed to be?"

She turned to look at her sister who was still staring straight ahead. Michalina looked lost, helpless, as though she didn't know what to say. Zuzanna noticed a tear rolling down her cheek.

"I can't tell you," she suddenly said, almost whispering. "If I tell you, you'll be in danger. Please, just get me the money. I promise I'll pay you back, honest."

The tears on Michalina's face continued to flow, increasing in volume.

"Why would I be in danger? Who do you owe this to? I don't understand, it's so much money, we need to go to the police, they can help you, I'll go with you."

Zuzanna was speaking quickly and trying to get her sister to change her mind.

"No," she snapped. "I can't. If you won't help me, I'll have to try somewhere else. You mustn't tell anyone, understand?"

"But—"

"No one, or you'll never see me again, do you understand?" She said it with conviction so Zuzanna knew her sister was telling the truth. The pair fell into silence.

"Can you help?" Michalina sounded so desperate.

"I can try," she replied.

It was a moment of reflection. It was a moment when the two sisters needed to absorb their troubles together.

But it was a problem Zuzanna had just inherited, and her mind was racing with what she was going to do. She had to help her sister but fifty thousand euros? How on earth did Michalina think she was going to get her hands on that sort of money?

"You know I only work in a coffee shop, right?" she said, breaking the silence.

She didn't want to sound angry; she wanted her sister to know she was trying to be supportive.

"I know, I don't know where else to go."

"Who do you owe this to? It's a lot of money. I just don't understand," she asked again.

"It's not important who to. I'm in so much trouble, I'm so sorry." The tears began to run down her cheeks again as the realisation of the situation returned to her. "They'll hurt me again, they might even kill me, I don't know. I only know if they don't get their money soon…" Her voice trailed off.

Zuzanna stood up and offered her hand, helping her sister to her feet. "I'm not sure how we're going to explain this to Mama and Tata."

"You mustn't say anything," replied Michalina, panic in her voice.

"But they will see, look at you." Zuzanna frowned. How could they keep this secret? It was ridiculous.

"I'll be staying with friends until I heal, I'll be okay, you just need to cover for me."

"But—"

"No, I told you, they mustn't know, it will put them in danger."

"Okay, I'll try." Zuzanna felt she had no choice at this point but fifty thousand euros? How on earth was she to get that? "Look, I think I've got about five thousand euros that I've saved, but fifty thousand, I don't know what I can do to get that."

Michalina began to cry again. Her distress was difficult for Zuzanna to handle. She loved her so much, but she had no idea how she could help her.

"Where are you going to stay?" she asked instead, knowing this was something she could help with.

"I can't say. I'll be safe though." Michalina spoke with conviction. Zuzanna knew there was no point in challenging her so didn't say anything. "Can you borrow the rest from the bank?" asked Michalina. The hope had disappeared from her voice.

"I could try, I just don't hold out much hope. We have no collateral to offer, no property, Tata doesn't work, Mama's only a part-time cleaner and me, I'm a barista on minimum wage. Banks won't want to lend us money."

She could see Michalina trying to stop crying, almost shaking with distress.

"Let me speak with whoever it is you owe the money to. Maybe I can fix something up with them." It was a genuine offer.

"No, it's not safe for you. I've got to go now, please try," Michalina asked, pulling away from her sister. "Please don't follow me," she called out as she walked away.

Zuzanna made no effort to follow her, she could see there was no point.

"Please get the money, I haven't long," she asked one last time as she backed further away. "I'll call you tomorrow." She then turned and began to run away.

After her shift Zuzanna walked to the tram stop and jumped on the first one to her district. She walked the short distance to their apartment and opened the front door. She could hear the television on and guessed it was her father. Szymon was likely playing video games in his room and her mother was probably cooking or cleaning.

"Is that you, Zuzanna?" called her mother from the kitchen.

"Yes Mama," she called back. She desperately wanted to tell her mother about Michalina, but had promised not to.

"I have to go out to work," her mother called back. "Can you finish serving up the dinner and look after Tata until I get back? I shouldn't be late."

Zuzanna could hear the sound of banging cupboard doors and plates as her mother rushed to finish preparing dinner whilst getting ready to go out to work.

"Have you heard from Michalina? I haven't seen her all day."

"Yes Mama, I'll finish up, you go out and I'll see you when you get back." She paused before saying anything further. She knew she had to say something about why her sister wouldn't be coming home that evening. "Michalina called at the coffee shop earlier, she's staying with friends for a few days."

"That girl," her mother said. "She'll get herself into trouble one day." She laughed.

If only you knew, thought Zuzanna. *If only you knew.*

The next day Zuzanna got up for work after managing to sleep for only a couple of hours. She dressed in her uniform and slipped on a light coat. She couldn't stop thinking about the money. What on earth was she going to do? The thought plagued her all the way to work. She thought about Michalina and her injuries and hoped she was okay. Maybe she should have told someone, she thought before quickly remembering what she had promised.

Work was a necessary distraction. It was hard to concentrate and on more than one occasion her boss asked if she was okay. She insisted she was and carried on. A number of her regular customers came in and briefly chatted with her whilst she worked. She even managed to flirt with one of the regulars that had asked her out on a number of occasions, despite her saying that she was not available. She still liked him and if her circumstances were different at home, who knows what might have happened.

It was a busy day and thankfully it passed quickly. Her shift finished at 3:00pm. Her boss asked if she wanted to stay on and earn a bit of overtime. He was clearly worried that her distraction was because of money – if only he knew the truth. She declined, thanking him, and headed off to the bank to ask about a loan.

As she arrived she stood and looked at the doors, which looked unusually large to her. She hadn't noticed their size before, maybe it was because she knew she was about to ask the impossible. She pulled herself together and still wearing her uniform she gathered her nerves and as confidently as she could she strolled inside.

The bank was not busy, that was good. At least there was some chance of her seeing someone. She noticed a pedestal at which a young female member of staff stood, looking very smart in her banking uniform. There were customers at the machines either withdrawing or paying in money. She came here periodically to use those machines. She was only just getting familiar with using them for paying in the small amounts her mother earned and those went straight out to pay the rent.

Speak to the young girl, she urged herself. It was strange to her that she thought of her as young, after all, she was very likely older than she was. Maybe it was because she didn't have the problems in her life that Zuzanna had. She approached the girl, whom she could now see from her name badge was called 'Saar.'

She explained that it would be a personal loan, and after a conversation where Zuzanna disclosed that she couldn't apply online, Saar told her she would see if a loans agent was free. She returned after less than five minutes to explain that Zuzanna would need to make an appointment, the loans staff were all busy.

She asked what sort of amount Zuzanna was looking to borrow, and when she told her it was fifty thousand euros, the look on Saar's face told her everything she needed to know: she had little or no chance of borrowing that amount.

Zuzanna decided to make an appointment anyway and Saar turned to the computer screen next to her and brought up a calendar. The first space was next Wednesday – a full eight days away. Saar gave her a leaflet about personal loans, which explained the paperwork she would need.

Zuzanna walked out of the bank and went to sit on a nearby bench. She knew the answer, but she sat and read the leaflet anyway. Sure enough, it confirmed she had no chance of borrowing that sort of money. In fact, she would be lucky to borrow five thousand on her wages. She sat back on the bench and looked over at the busy streets, full of tourists enjoying Amsterdam, many for the first time. The locals were smiling and happy and bikes were everywhere.

After a while she became aware of someone sitting down on the bench next to her.

"You okay?" came the question.

She looked up and saw the young man from the coffee shop. She smiled; it was good to see a friendly face. Alright, she had turned down his offer of a date on a number of occasions, but they still got on well and she was happy for the company.

"Yes, I'm fine, thank you."

"Fine?" he repeated. "When a girl says 'fine' it usually means she's anything but." He smiled as he said it.

"Nothing for you to worry about," she said, and tried to change the conversation. "I've only ever seen you in the shop."

"I hope it's not something I have to worry about," he said, ignoring her attempts at idle chat, a sudden more serious look on his face. "Did you manage to get the loan from the bank?" he asked.

"What?" she replied, not quite understanding what he was saying.

"I hope for Michalina's sake you have managed to get the money. I wouldn't want her to suffer more than she already has."

"What? I don't understand." This was no longer the friendly face she had frequently seen in the coffee shop, the one who had flirted with her and asked her on a date. Was this some kind of joke? What was going on? "What do you know about Michalina?" she asked, still confused.

"Are you stupid?" he responded, now sounding angry. "Michalina told me you were the clever member of the family." He laughed. "She owes us a lot of money and interest is increasing each day, so it needs paying back one way or another."

Zuzanna looked at him in horror.

"I'll go to the police," she managed to splutter out.

"No, you won't," he replied. "You saw her face. You know what we can do to her, and we can be much worse than that."

Zuzanna was horrified. She stared at him with fear for her sister and anger for him. Had he only been nice to get to her?

"And of course, there's that waste of space brother of yours on his PlayStation. He's another possibility. Of course, we could target that disabled father of yours or your overworked mother. She's easy enough to get while she's on one of her cleaning jobs…"

She could feel the fear for her family. It was so real she was shaking; she was struggling to make sense of what she was being told. How could he know so much?

"What, what do you want?" she asked.

"I told you; we want the money your sister owes, and we don't care how we get it."

Tears began to roll down her face; she didn't know what to do. She knew her sister had gotten into trouble – how could she not have if she owed that much money? – but this young man was something else, this man who had tricked her. She had really liked him, but it appeared that it was all a lie. Now he was showing his true self, threatening her and her whole family.

"I don't know what to do, I can't borrow the money, they won't let me." She found herself pleading with him.

"Don't worry, Zuzanna, we have other ways you can pay it back. Come with me."

He stood up and offered his hand. She ignored him but stood up anyway. "Come with me," he said. It was not a request.

"Where are we going?" she asked, desperately wanting to know what was happening.

"You'll find out," he said.

It was clear that her role was to follow and do as she was told. She could only think about the injuries to Michalina and how she didn't want that to happen again.

CHAPTER 6

Jennings had been around the business long enough to know when he was being played. He had not had the pleasure of negotiations with Balodis before, but he knew his reputation that he was good at his job. But being good was not enough, you needed to be exceptional. And despite the fact that sex with Ana would be a nice little bonus, he was not about to let that sway him.

Normally he would deal with one of the company's minions. Whenever he had been over before he'd have some wannabe salesperson who clearly thought he knew it all. At least this Balodis knew how to dress himself. Normally they would be wearing some cheap ill-fitting suit, clearly imported from some fake market somewhere with a designer name woven into the pinstripes of the fabric. What was it with these amateurs? If the designers had really made that shit, they would be out of business within months. And what was it with them all wearing cheap deck shoes, no socks and open-neck shirts? There was a way to do business and they didn't understand it. At least Balodis's suit seemed to fit, and he was wearing a shirt and tie.

From his haircut and stern face, Jennings suspected he was ex-military although it was hard to tell, they all had military haircuts. The difference being the others normally had this solemn facial expression as if constantly worried, whereas Balodis was straight faced and hard to read. He certainly didn't look worried. Clearly, he thought he could intimidate him.

Well, think again. Let's see how our business dinner goes later, thought Jennings. *Then we'll see how arrogant you are before I break you down to get what I want.*

Jennings looked in the mirror in the bathroom of his hotel suite. He admired his physique. *Not bad for a guy in his fifties,* he thought to himself, smiling. He reached up and felt his cheeks with his hands. *Have another shave,* he thought as he stroked one side and then the other before brushing under his chin with the back of his hand. And with that, he ran the hot tap until steam rose from the boiling water entering the sink. He lathered up his face and set about making sure he was cleanly shaved the best he could. He knew Ana would sleep with him tonight as she'd want to butter him up for a sweet deal tomorrow. He knew it was a buyers' market and having an eastern European garage selling on his company's cars is a luxury most executive dealers don't have, but he wasn't about to make it easy for these amateurs.

He was going to enjoy fucking Ana; she was stunning and had a body to die for. Then tomorrow he would make it clear they didn't throw all the punches. He had a few up his sleeve as well. *Fucking stupid eastern Europeans,* he thought.

He stepped out of the bathroom to where he had laid his trousers and shirt on the bed. Simple quality trousers and a clean white open-necked shirt. *Don't let her get lipstick on the shirt,* he thought to himself and laughed. Explaining it to the wife was something he didn't want to have to do. She was difficult enough without that. She knew he was a 'player' and she did well out of him. He was like this when they met, he was like this when they got engaged, he'd been like this since they married; he was not about to change now and you know what? If she didn't like it, she could fuck off. Again, he smiled to himself. She was never going to do that.

Jennings dressed and wandered down to the reception at the Grand Poet ready for his collection, just giving him time to check at reception to see if there were any messages left. He didn't know why he did that in this modern time, he never had a message. Everything was instant email on his phone, text message or social media, but there was still something about asking at reception and he couldn't stop himself from doing it the 'old fashioned' way.

He turned around to see the car had arrived. Of course, from reception he couldn't actually see the car but there was that salesman. He knew straight away – shiny fabric suit, much too small, huge belly hanging over his belt forcing the buttons of his shirt to strain the cheap cotton material and trousers that looked uncomfortably tight – just what he expected. He smiled to himself.

"Hello, Mr. Jennings. I'm Joseph, to take you to the restaurant," the salesman said in English that was surprisingly good.

"Great," he replied and stepped towards the doors, putting a hand out for Joseph to lead the way.

The car was parked, or abandoned as Jennings would describe it, on the grey block footpath outside the hotel. As he suspected it was one of their Astons. The door was open, and he climbed into the passenger seat.

"Have you been to Domini Canes before, Mr. Jennings?" asked Joseph excitedly.

Before responding, Jennings thought to himself, *Obviously you haven't. Doubt you could afford to buy water there,* then said, "Yes, one or twice, very nice. Have you?"

There was a short pause before Joseph responded, "Erm, no," and that was the end of that conversation.

Jennings made no attempt to engage him again, opting instead to look out of the side window at the night-time Riga before him.

Joseph drove smoothly, which was a surprise to Jennings. He was expecting some idiot trying to show off the car, but this was a nice enough journey and for that he was grateful. He enjoyed the short drive along the Daugava River, which was very beautiful. Joseph pulled up by the side of the road near the restaurant then just sat there. He was obviously not getting out, so Jennings stepped out of the car and closed the door behind him. No sooner had the door

SOMEBODY'S SISTER

closed, Joseph drove away, leaving him standing on his own. He stopped for a moment, shaking his head. *Fucking eastern Europeans,* he again thought to himself.

He walked to the restaurant door and entered. Glancing to his left, he immediately saw Ana and Balodis sat at a table. A waiter approached and was about to speak, Jennings assumed to ask him about a table, and he indicated where Ana and Balodis were sitting. The waiter nodded knowingly and backed off towards the bar area.

As he approached the table Ana and Balodis stood to greet him. Balodis offered a hand, which he shook, and Ana leaned forward, allowing him to kiss her on both cheeks.

"Please, sit," she said, indicating to the chair next to her and opposite Balodis.

He slid his jacket from his shoulders and immediately the waiter reappeared asking if he could take it. He handed him the jacket with a mumbled, "Thank you," and then looked at Balodis.

Jennings had been right when he assessed Balodis earlier. Once again, he was dressed in appropriate clothing: a white long-sleeved shirt, and beautifully tailored and smart, well-cut chino trousers. He was going to have to be on his guard with this one. He looked at Ana. She really was stunning and now wore an off-the-shoulder, figure-hugging long red dress with slit on the side from the ground to her hip, revealing a beautifully shaped leg. Red stilettos completed the look. *Keep your wits about you,* he thought to himself. *This is going to be difficult.* But at least he'd get to fuck her before the main meeting. He hoped the meal wouldn't drag on for too long.

"Are you ready to eat, Michael?" asked Anastasjia.

"Starving," he replied.

Dinner passed uneventfully. Jennings was pleasantly surprised by the easy-going chat of Balodis. He didn't look like someone who could do small talk, but he was clearly very good at it. Ana was easy company but to be honest she didn't really need to say anything. He did wonder if she had been instructed to keep quiet but to be honest, he didn't give a shit. At the conclusion of the meal, Balodis offered him a glass of Latvia apple brandy.

"No, thank you. I think I need to get some sleep before tomorrow," he replied, hoping the next move would be Ana offering a lift to the hotel. Balodis stood and reached into his trouser pocket before handing the keys to the Aston over to Ana.

"Here, could you run Michael back to the hotel?" he said. "I need a walk. I'll see you both tomorrow. 10:00am, is that okay?"

Anastasjia took that key and thanked Balodis.

"Of course, I'll make sure Michael gets to the hotel safely and I can make sure he gets to the meeting on time tomorrow. If that's okay with you?" she asked, looking at Jennings.

"It's fine to me," he said, and then looked back to Balodis.

"Excellent, I'll see you both tomorrow." Balodis smiled. Jennings wondered how he could look threatening even when he seemed to be happy.

Balodis walked towards the door followed by Anastasjia and Jennings, where they were handed their coats by the already waiting waiter. Outside Jennings and Balodis again shook hands.

"See you tomorrow," said Jennings.

"Tomorrow," replied Balodis before leaning in to kiss Anastasjia on both cheeks, making sure to look her in the eye long enough for her to know what was expected of her.

In the car Anastasjia slipped off her shoes to drive the short way back to the hotel. After parking Jennings walked around the back of the car to where Anastasjia stood. He leaned forward and gently kissed her on one cheek before saying softly, "Would you like coffee?"

"I'd prefer brandy," she replied, smiling.

He grinned as he took her hand.

"Just a moment."

She leaned into the footwell of the car and grabbed her stilettos, dropped them to the floor and put them on. She took Jennings' arm and locked the car before walking with him to his room via reception to the lifts.

When they reached his suite, he opened the door and stepped back to allow Anastasjia to step in.

"Very nice," she said as if this was the first time she had ever been in one.

"Room service?" he asked.

He didn't need to comment on the room, he knew he had been put up in the best room in Riga, it was all part of the plan to soften him up. He smiled and told her to ring down and order whatever she wanted and to order him a scotch.

"Make yourself at home, I'm going to have a quick shower," he called to her as he walked to the bathroom.

He knew she wasn't going to object, and she knew he knew it.

"Oh, and keep your dress and stilettos on for the time being."

It wasn't a request.

*

Anastasjia rang room service and ordered a bottle of 12-year-old malt for Jennings and a glass of cognac for herself. She ordered a bucket of ice and then set about carrying out her job. She secreted the tiny cameras around the suite, ensuring she worked out where they would be best positioned to catch her and Jennings in the best possible light.

*

Jennings finished showering and wrapped a towel around his waist. It had been a long day and although he had showered earlier before going out he thought to do it again in fairness to Ana. *If she's going to do me the honour of sucking my dick I might as well make it as clean as possible.* He smiled at the thought and then walked into the room, pausing to look at her. She looked even more desirable than she had earlier. He started to walk towards her when there was a knock at the door. *Room service.* He turned to the door and opened it. The house staff carried in a large tray on which was the bottle of scotch and a glass, a small ice bucket and the glass of cognac.

"Thank you. Put it on the dresser, please," he said to the young man and handed him ten US dollars.

The young boy thanked Jennings as he left.

When the door was closed, he turned to see Anastasjia pouring a generous glass of whisky for him and adding ice from the bucket. She handed it to him. He took a small sip and then put the glass down on the dresser, brushing up against Anastasjia as he did so. He then took the glass from her and did the same.

*

Jennings pulled her close and pressed his lips against hers, parting them gently with his tongue. She responded to the kiss passionately. *I always liked him,* she thought. *Might as well enjoy the room and make the most of the situation.* She reached up with her left hand to unzip the dress.

"No!" he almost shouted at her. She was startled. "Please," he said calmly. "Let me."

She dropped her arms to her sides, and he reached around her and took hold of the zipper pull, carefully sliding it down to below her waist. He then moved his hands lightly up her arms, so lightly he only just touched them, and gently took hold of each sleeve, pulling them forward, freeing them from her upper arms and allowing the silky dress to drop to the floor, revealing her panties. She'd chosen the smallest ones possible that matched the colour of the dress and shoes. Jennings took her hands and stepped backwards, allowing her to step forward out of the dress. When she went to kick the shoes off, he shouted again.

"No! Leave them on."

She smiled at him. "Of course," she replied, and he smiled back.

He pulled her close and kissed her again, this time more passionately than before. She reached down, released the towel from his waist and let it drop to the floor.

She could feel his erection pressing against her, throbbing and ready. He stepped back and applied gentle pressure to her waist with it. She knew what he wanted, and she lowered herself to her knees, taking him in her mouth. Jennings put his head back and groaned in pleasure. He held the back of Anastasjia's head, allowing her to do her job, stroking her neck and face in appreciation. Anastasjia was good and she knew it. She moved her head back and forth, knowing exactly what she needed to do.

Not long now, she thought to herself, and sure enough he was finished moments later.

She stood up and reached for the cognac, taking a mouthful, and swilling it slightly around. She handed Jennings the glass of whiskey and he took a sip.

Then she moved in and kissed him.

"Thank you," he said.

"Please don't thank me, it was my pleasure," she responded. "Would you like me to take off my shoes now?" she asked.

"No, please let me…"

He slid off her panties until they had passed her thighs and dropped to her ankles. Now she was naked apart from the shoes. He pulled her close again and began kissing her. Whilst they kissed, she could feel him up against her so knew he was ready again.

This time she led him, taking him to the bed and turning him around so his back was to it. She gently pushed him down, so he was lying on the bed, feet still on the floor, and climbed on top of him. She knew this could take a while. *Might as well enjoy it,* she thought and set about making sure Jennings was enjoying himself.

Afterwards they lay next to each other and within minutes

Anastasjia heard him snoring. Like all men it was all about them. She guessed he knew she was there to try and get him on side, but it was beneficial for both of them. At least he wasn't violent or mean. When she was sure he was asleep, she gently got out of the bed and gathered up the cameras she had set earlier. She sent a short text message to Balodis that simply said, 'Ready.' Moments later there was a gentle knock at the door. She took a look at Jennings, still asleep, and walked to the door. She positioned herself behind it as she wasn't wearing anything and opened it enough to see Joseph waiting on the other side, still in his suit despite it now being 3:00am. As she handed over the cameras, Joseph tried to push the door open a little further to get a glimpse of her. "Do I need to report you to Janis?" she snapped at him.

Joseph retreated, holding the cameras. She closed the door very gently and looked back at Jennings. Still sleeping. *Good.* She crept over to the bed and climbed back in. *Mission accomplished.* She smiled and then closed her eyes, needing to get some sleep before morning.

She managed to fall asleep faster than she thought she would. Jennings awoke at 7:30 and woke her as he got up for another shower. When he came back out, he leaned over and kissed her on the forehead.

"What time is it?" she asked.

"7:45, why?" She quickly sat up.

"I need to get back to my apartment to get ready for work. Then I'll come back to pick you up for the meeting." She quickly jumped out of the bed and reached for her panties.

"Don't worry about it. If we're a bit late, so what?" He seemed so casual about it, he obviously didn't know Balodis like she did.

"I'll be back soon," she said as she pulled up her dress and tried to fasten the back.

Jennings stepped forward and helped her with the zip.

"I was hoping we could make love again," he said in a slightly pleading voice she actually found quite endearing.

"Later, lover, I promise," she said.

She picked up her shoes and, barefoot, walked out of the room.

Anastasjia drove quickly to her apartment and showered. She then changed into her business clothes, a sharp pencil skirt suit. One last glimpse in the mirror and she was out again, driving back to the hotel to pick up Jennings.

When she arrived at the hotel, Jennings was waiting outside. He jumped in the car and leaned over to kiss her. She kissed him back. She really felt for him. *I really think he likes me,* she thought. She was pleased; she liked him. She knew her feelings towards him were more about pity than desire. She knew it was impossible for it to come to anything, he lived in the UK with his wife. One he was unlikely to leave, and definitely not for her. She also knew she was indebted to the company and Balodis would ensure she remembered she was doing what she was paid to do, and until the company decided she owed them no more, she couldn't leave.

They arrived at the offices at 9:55am and went up to the boardroom. Balodis was already waiting. Immaculately turned out in a very expensive well-tailored suit with a white shirt and dark tie. For a moment Anastasjia felt panic. Had she got the time wrong? Was she in trouble?

"Good morning, Ana, Michael. I hope you both had a pleasant evening." Balodis smiled knowingly.

"Great, thank you," replied Jennings.

"It was very nice, thank you Janis." Anastasjia was relieved Balodis appeared happy with her.

*

Balodis offered coffee and then they sat down to talk business.

"Michael, before we start, I have a proposition for you," he began.

"Oh yes," replied Jennings, thinking he was to be taken for a fool.

"Go on, give it to me, what's your pitch?"

"Michael, we know you make a lot of money from the cars you arrange to be shipped to us," Balodis started, but Jennings interrupted.

"Yeah, obviously, I'm not a charity."

Balodis smiled menacingly.

"No, you don't understand, I know you make a lot of money, but I also know you make a lot of money that is rightfully ours," he continued.

"You don't know what you're on about," Jennings said as he sat back in his chair. *This idiot can't prove anything,* he thought to himself.

"Let me see if I get this right," began Balodis. "You tell us how much the cars will cost, we agree on a fee, and delivery charges, you ask that the money is transferred to a holding account so that it will sit and wait until we are happy the cars have been cleared through customs. Am I close?" Balodis asked.

"Well obviously, we wouldn't expect final payment until the cars are delivered and you're not going to pay for a car you don't have. I thought we were here to negotiate a new deal. If you're not interested, I'm going." He began to stand.

"Sit down," Balodis said firmly. Jennings sat again.

"So, what is it you're saying?"

"You purchase the cars at a rate you have arranged, and this is below the value that you have arranged with us. You take the money from the holding account and transfer it to cash, where you then split the money between two new holding accounts, one that pays for the cars and one that goes to you." Balodis smiled again, knowingly. "Am I right?"

Jennings felt he had a choice to make, front it out or admit. The safest option would be to admit it.

"So, what are you going to do? You can't prove a thing," he said sarcastically, confident he had covered his tracks.

"Actually, we don't need to. You are going to help us with another of our commodities and when you do, you will be paid well."

"Fuck you, Balodis, you can't prove fuck all. Do you want to do business or not? I'm sure we can find some other fuck we can work with." His anger was getting the better of him. And fear of Balodis had gone.

"We need you to move cash to one of our clients in London. How you do that will be up to you, but I would suggest the easiest way would be by train across Europe to France and then jump on the Eurotunnel in a hire car," said Balodis, sounding very confident.

"Are you fucking mad?" said Jennings. "Firstly, you can't prove fuck all and secondly you can go fuck yourself." Jennings went to stand up to leave again.

"Sit down, you fuck, before I do something you'll regret." The message was clear and again Jennings sat down.

"Now, we have fifty thousand euros in the suitcase in the corner of the room." Balodis indicated the case that Jennings hadn't noticed. "I would like you to take this to London, and then it needs to go to an address I shall give you when you get there. When you deliver the case, you will be rewarded with ten thousand euros. Obviously if you are stopped the money will be taken from you and you'll probably go to prison. If you mention us, you will be killed."

"What?" Jennings couldn't believe what he was hearing. His emotions were all over the place, anger had been replaced by fear.

"I take it by your response you heard me, you will be killed." Balodis continued, still sounding as menacing as he could. "To help you decide, I have a little movie for you to watch." He picked up a remote and turned on the screen on the wall. On it, as clear as day were Anastasjia and Jennings engaged in sexual intercourse.

"What do you hope to achieve by that?" asked Jennings as he looked over towards Anastasjia, seething with anger. "Not even a good fuck but passed the time, fucking whore," he said.

He could tell Anastasjia was upset. Even if she knew the film would be used as leverage, he could tell she really did like him.

"So, do we have a deal?"

"You bunch of eastern European cunts, who the fuck do you think you are?" He was enraged and despite his initial fear was not going to let go. "You don't fucking frighten me, you can't prove fuck all, that fucking whore can fuck off and you can fuck off with her."

He had worked in the car export business for years and was not going to be pushed around. He knew the garage in Riga relied heavily on the value of the cars he exported to them so they could make heavy profits when sold on to Russians and other former eastern bloc countries. "You need our business more than I need yours so why don't you take the whore, fuck her yourself. But before you do, call me a taxi because I'm out of here. You fuckers have lost a contract."

He stood to leave and walked purposefully towards the door.

*

The sound was deafening. Anastasjia instinctively put her hands to her ears to stop the pain. Balodis had moved smartly and professionally. Like a trained assassin he had reached into his jacket, pulled out the gun and fired it into the back of Jennings' head in a single movement. The blood sprayed across the door in front of him as he collapsed to the floor dead. Anastasjia realised she was sprayed with his blood as well.

She looked at Balodis, wide eyed and in fear. She tried to scream but no sound came out. Balodis calmly returned the gun to the inside of his jacket.

"Well Ana," he said in a quiet voice, "it appears you have a trip to London, and don't forget the suitcase." He laughed.

Anastasjia cried and shook with fear, but she knew she had no choice.

CHAPTER 7

Harry woke at 6:30am to the sound of the front door closing. His room was immediately above the door so he couldn't miss it. He guessed it was Lilly as she didn't come home last night. He could hear her stomping up the stairs and slamming the door to her room behind her.

*

Lilly lay on the bed and closed her eyes, opening them quickly as images of everything she had experienced filled her thoughts, placing her in a world of turmoil and pain.

"Lilly."

Shit, she thought as her mum called.

"Lilly."

Please just go away, she thought, followed by a knock on her bedroom door.

"Lilly, open the door."

"Go away, I'm tired." Lilly wasn't angry – which was unusual for her – she was tired. She wanted to sleep and try to forget what had happened to her.

"Lilly, I called the police last night, they've been looking for you."

"What did you want to do that for?" She should have known her mum was going to call them; it wasn't the first time she had come home late to find they had been called and this was the next morning.

"I didn't know where you were. You could have been dead for all I know, I've been worried." Her mum sounded angry and upset.

"Please, just leave me alone, I need to sleep."

"Just let me see you're okay, please Lilly, just open the door." Lilly knew her mum was not going to go until she spoke to her. Now she was getting angry.

"See, I'm okay. Now please just let me sleep."

"Where were you? I've been worried sick." Her mum was sounding more and more angry.

"Oh, for Christ's sake, just leave me alone, will you?" she shouted. The anger had fully caught up with her and she just wanted to be left alone.

An argument between Lilly and her mum was on the way and she decided the best thing would be to ignore her mother until it all died down later. She slammed her door shut in her mum's face.

"You've not heard the last of this, my girl," said her mother indignantly.

*

Then Harry heard his mum on the mobile to the police, saying Lilly was okay and by her responses he guessed they were going to come to the house and see she was okay. Mum was asking if it could be later, saying that Lilly was sleeping, but it sounded like they were insisting. They needed to check on her welfare. Mum gave up in the end and hung up the phone.

It was nearly 7:00am and Harry decided he may as well get up. It was Saturday so no school, which was good in that he wouldn't have to hide from the 'enemy' but bad in that the only friends he had were the ones he saw at school. He hadn't heard from Dad or Amalia, so he guessed they didn't want him over this week.

He would stay at home and work on his computer. He was learning about coding and programming, and it was something he enjoyed. The only issue was that he knew Mum would insist he go out to play and get some fresh air. He so hoped that wouldn't be the case. Every time she forced him out, he'd go to the park and then have to hide every time he saw a group of teenagers in case any were the 'enemy.'

After dressing he went down to breakfast and got himself some cereal. He and his mum went through the normal morning pleasantries around how he was, and what he was going to do today. Not a mention of Lilly. Harry guessed his mum knew he had heard the argument. After he finished breakfast, the doorbell rang. His mum went to the door, and he heard her talking to the police officers.

"She's in bed, I'm afraid. I did tell them, you'll have to come back later."

"I'm sorry," said one of the officers in a female voice that was quite forceful, "we have to see her to check that she is okay. We're not looking to stay long but we need to see her to satisfy ourselves she hasn't come to any harm."

Harry recognised the voice. She was a female detective that had visited when Lilly had gone missing before.

"Okay, I'll get her but she's very tired so please don't be too long."

Harry heard his mum go upstairs and call for Lilly. He couldn't hear Lilly's response, but he guessed she was arguing because he could hear mum shouting.

"Just get up and get downstairs. If you're not down here in two minutes, I'll send them up and you can see them in your room!"

"Fine," he heard Lilly shout at her mother.

Harry heard her stomp down the stairs and head into the lounge where the police officers were waiting. He heard the officers ask Mum if it was okay to speak with Lilly on her own so she would be free to speak. He guessed his mum had agreed because he heard the door to the lounge close and moments later she walked into the kitchen and put the kettle on.

*

In the lounge the officers – one male in uniform and a female detective she had met when she was late home before – tried to engage Lilly in conversation but she was having none of it. "Just go away and leave me alone." But she knew they wouldn't just leave.

"Lilly," said the female officer, who Lilly guessed was the more experienced of the two; she didn't look much older than her but was obviously the more qualified. "We need to know if you're okay and where you have been."

"I'm not saying," she said defiantly. "Just go away," she repeated.

"Listen, Lilly," said the male officer this time. "Would it be easier for you to speak with me or my colleague on our own?" He glanced at his female colleague before looking back at Lilly.

"No, just go," she said again.

"Are you hurt?" he asked.

"No," answered Lilly, making it clear she didn't want to hold any sort of conversation with either of them.

"Okay, Lilly," said the female officer, "we'll let you get some sleep but what we'd like to do is call back later so we can have a chat with you. Is that okay?"

"Do what you like," said Lilly before walking herself out of the room and heading back up to her bedroom.

*

The following morning was one of those bright and yet cold mornings when the sun was out and there were few if any clouds in the sky. The sun streamed into Harry's room, waking him at around 8:30am. Sundays were the only day that Harry allowed himself to sleep in. He sat up and turned on his TV. After he had been watching for a couple of minutes there was a soft knock on his door. He knew it wasn't his mum as she would knock quite loudly and call his name at the same time.

The door opened slowly, and Lilly put her head through the gap.

"Can I come in?" she asked.

This was a first. Lilly had never asked to come into his room before. Normally she just stormed in and made various demands of him or complained about him.

"Okay," he said cautiously.

Lilly stepped in and closed the door. She sat down on the side of his bed uninvited and asked him what he was doing the rest of the day.

"Nothing, why?" he asked, still unsure why she suddenly felt the need to talk to him. After all, she hadn't spoken to him for ages except to shout at him or order him about.

"Will you come out with me today?" she asked, her voice surprisingly cheerful.

"Where?" Harry responded. He wasn't sure what was going on.

"Please, Harry, I need you to help me." She never called him Harry. What was going on?

"Why?" he asked, still curious.

"Look, if you won't help, just say so," she snapped. That was more like the Lilly he knew. "Please," said Lilly.

There was something different. He could tell she was pleading, and she seemed desperate.

"Okay, where?" he asked.

"Get dressed, we'll go after that."

"Yep, I'll just let Mum know."

"No," snapped Lilly. "Just tell her you're going to the park, and I'll meet you there."

"But…" started Harry.

"No, Harry, you promised to help." He didn't actually promise, thought Harry, but okay.

"I'll see you there then," he replied.

After telling his mum where he was going, Harry left the house and took the short walk to the park where he sat on a bench and waited for Lilly. He was confused and a little apprehensive. She had been so horrible to him recently and although he loved her and looked up to her, she quite frightened him, especially after he saw the iPhone. Maybe he should have told someone. *No, she would have been really mad.* Moments later he saw Lilly walking across the park towards him. She seemed even more agitated than earlier.

"Come on," she said as soon as she reached him and began walking towards the exit of the park on the far side from their home.

"Where are we going?" Harry just wanted to be told something.

"Not far," which wasn't much of a reply.

When they reached the car park, he saw some guy sitting in his ST Focus. As they approached, the guy climbed out and extended his hand to shake Harry's. Automatically Harry responded. Jordan immediately tightened his grip so that Harry couldn't let go.

"So, you're Harry?"

"Yes."

"I'm Jordan, Lilly's boyfriend. I hear you're going to help us out?" Without waiting for a response, Jordan turned to Lilly.

"You've not told him anything?"

"No," replied Lilly. "I thought it best for you to do it." She sounded really nervous.

"What do you want me to do?"

"We'll discuss it on the way, jump in." He opened the passenger door and tilted the seat forward so Harry could climb in. When he was in, he put his seatbelt on.

"Got enough room?" Jordan asked.

"Erm, yes, thanks."

"Seatbelt." Lilly reached back for it and pulled it around her body. "That's better," he said as it clicked in place.

Then he started the car, revving it before pulling away with a wheel spin.

They headed towards London. Once on the A3 Jordan started to explain to Harry why he was there.

"The thing is, Harry; I've got some friends and unfortunately, I owe them some money that they want back really quickly. Lilly has tried to help but she doesn't have a lot of money, so she helped me out in other ways, but my friends are saying it's not enough."

"I don't get it, what's that got to do with me?" asked Harry.

"Well Lilly has said she doesn't want to have to entertain my friends again, so we are looking for other ways of paying off the debt. I've suggested to my friends that you might like to do some delivery work for them, and that way they can be paid out of your wages."

Harry could only see the back of Lilly's head as she was slumped further down in the seat. Her head hung forwards. She had said nothing.

"What deliveries?" He didn't understand. Why was he being asked to pay off this guy's debts? It didn't make sense. What had Lilly gotten into?

"We'll talk about it when we meet up, shouldn't be long provided this traffic clears."

Slowly they crept through the traffic, making their way towards Stratford, eventually arriving at a terraced house. It was obvious that something wasn't right. He had never seen his sister like this before. She remained stationary in her seat looking towards the footwell, deliberately avoiding looking at the house as though it was going to harm her in some way. Harry continued to be cautious. He didn't know what Lilly had gotten herself into but knew he needed to help if he could.

Jordan climbed out of the car and walked around to open the door for Lilly. She still never moved, which again, Harry thought odd. What was she so afraid of?

"Come on, it will be okay," said Jordan, holding his hand out to her. She took it and he helped her from the car. He leaned towards her and kissed her on the cheek.

"You okay?" he asked. Lilly nodded. "Good girl." And with that he tipped the passenger seat forward allowing Harry to get out.

Lilly didn't look at Harry as Jordan led them towards the house. The door opened as they approached, and Jordan and Lilly walked straight in. Harry stopped for a moment.

"Come on," said Jordan, beckoning him to follow.

Harry looked up and saw the door was being held open by a very large black man. He was the biggest man he had ever seen. Whatever Lilly wanted him to do was not on his mind at that moment, only the fear this guy instilled in him.

"Get in, man, we don't have all day," the man said to him in a loud voice. Harry quickly stepped through the open door and the man closed it behind him. Lilly and Jordan had disappeared into the room off of the hallway.

"In there," the guy said, pointing at the room.

As Harry walked in, he followed uncomfortably close behind. On the far side of the room, Lilly was standing so close to Jordan that most of her body was against his. She appeared to be using him as a shield and was very slightly behind him. Also in the room was a young black woman. She was very beautiful. She was chewing gum and smoking a cigarette at the same time. She looked Harry up and down but said nothing. Harry was frozen, not knowing where to stand or if he should speak. Moments later the other door in the room opened and two other men walked in. Lilly moved further behind Jordan. Still, no one said anything.

"This the main man?" asked the first guy, pointing at Harry.

What does that mean? he thought, looking nervously from person to person. Jordan nodded. Lilly continued to look down.

"Okay then," said the first man. "You know what this is?" he said to Harry, holding up the small yellow closed container.

"It's the inside of a Kinder Egg where the toys are," replied Harry.

"Yeah, it is. Well done," he said. The other two men laughed. The young woman just continued to look at Harry whilst chewing her gum.

"You like Kinder Eggs?" he asked, still holding the yellow container up.

"They're okay," he replied.

"Okay, well in the trade we call this a 'G' pack, you know what a 'G' pack is?" Harry shook his head. "A 'G' pack is the way you and your sister are going to help pay off Jordan's debt to us, you understand?"

Harry shook his head; he still didn't know what the man was on about or how he was going to pay off a debt with a Kinder Egg. Despite feeling very afraid he was beginning to wonder why he should anyway. It wasn't him who owed the money. He didn't understand why Lilly didn't just stop seeing him and go out with someone else.

"Let me explain this in very simple, easy to follow steps so you get it," he said in a very patronising tone. The other men continued to snigger as he spoke. "This is a 'G' pack, we fill it with gravel and 'H'. You know what that is, yeah?" Again Harry shook his head. "You sure he's bright enough?" he said, looking towards Jordan.

"He'll be good, man," said Jordan, nodding.

"Okay, gravel is rocks, crack, yeah, and 'H' is heroin, you get it now?" Harry was horrified as he realised what he was being asked to do. He was unable to open his mouth and respond.

"We fill it, and you deliver it, you get it?"

"What… No, I'm not delivering drugs, what if I get caught?" He finally managed to get the words out.

"You said he would be okay," the guy said to Jordan.

"He will, he'll be fine," replied Jordan, "won't he?" Jordan turned and looked at Lilly.

Lilly didn't look up but in a muffled, quiet voice she said softly,

"Please." The message was for Jordan and the man, that was clear. It certainly wasn't for Harry who was getting very scared about the whole thing.

"Okay, bitch, this will be down to you," the man said, looking at Lilly. "And with interest. I think you'll be enjoying the Fam's company for some time to come." The other two men moved towards her, grabbing hold of Jordan's arm so they could get behind him.

"No, no, please, please no, please." Lilly sounded absolutely terrified. Harry was shaking with fear. He looked at the scared face of his sister.

"Harry please, please," she screamed, tears streaming down her face. They grabbed hold of her and pulled her away from Jordan.

"Let her go!" Harry shouted, not knowing where they were taking her but guessing it wasn't good. They ignored him. He noticed that Jordan did nothing to stop them. And they began to drag her towards the open door. He stepped forward to follow her, but the man grabbed him. He knew not to resist.

"No, no, Harry, no, no!" Lilly was screaming and pleading. She had tears streaming down her face, which was contorted in fear.

"Shut the fuck up, bitch," said the large guy, who was still holding Harry. "Can't hear myself fucking think, stupid fucking bitch."

"Please let her go," cried Harry, feeling tears of fear for his sister welling up in his eyes.

As she was dragged to the entrance of the other room, Lilly was sobbing.

"Okay, okay. Don't hurt her, please." Harry managed to get the words out as quickly as he could. He was still unsure exactly what he was agreeing to, and he was terrified, but he could see Lilly was even more frightened and he would do what he could to protect her.

The two men holding Lilly let go and she ran towards Harry. She wrapped her arms around him and held him tight. From where she had buried her head in his shoulder, she was still sobbing and unable to speak.

The large man pointed towards her and nodded to Jordan. At this Jordan stepped forward and without saying anything pulled her away. She again stood behind him holding his arm. "Okay," said the man. "Now we all know our responsibilities, let's get started." The man handed the 'G' pack to one of the others. "Take young Harry and show him how to plug the pack, then we'll arrange for his trip to deliver the food. You go with him," he said, indicating that Harry should follow the man into the other room.

Harry looked at Lilly who looked back pleadingly. A tear rolled down her cheek and Harry could feel his eyes begin to well up again. Knowing he had no choice but to help, he turned and followed the man into the other room. The door was closed behind him.

*

Lilly didn't want to cry but she was worried about her brother.

"Where's he going?" she asked, not to anyone in particular, the words just came out.

"So long as he does as instructed, he'll be fine," said the man before turning to the other guy that had remained in the room.

"She can go upstairs with you; I've been told she was pretty good." He laughed.

Lilly started to shake, realising what he was talking about.

"Please, no, please, you promised," she pleaded, tears flowing down her face. The other man grabbed her arm and went to pull her away. Jordan twisted his body sideways, forcing her to lose her grip on his arm, allowing the man to pull her away.

"Sorry," he said softly.

"No, please, no, no, you promised, please!" she cried out as she was pulled from the room into the hallway. The man slapped her hard across the face.

"Shut the fuck up, bitch!" he yelled and pulled her towards the stairs.

"Good move, my man," she could hear the other guy say to Jordan.

"No problem, Fam," replied Jordan.

CHAPTER 8

"Get upstairs," the man with the gruff voice barked at Michalina.

She had done as she was told and had begged her sister for help to pay off her debt. She was not dependent, but the craving was growing. She was going to need a fix soon and Zuzanna was her only hope.

"Second room on the right," he said after her.

She could smell sweat, urine and dirt. There were flies on the walls, which were stained with nicotine, and she stuck to the carpet as she walked. In the open doors to her left she saw the rooms were full of men, drawn, dirty, wide eyed. She guessed some of them were addicts like her. In the first room she passed filthy mattresses littering the floor on which lay other young girls. Like her she guessed they were addicts who had gotten themselves into a similar situation. She wondered if they had someone like Zuzanna who would borrow the money for them and help them out. She hoped Zuzanna wouldn't take too long. She had no idea how much time it would take for a bank to loan her the money, she just hoped it would be soon.

"Get a move on." The voice behind her was getting agitated. She didn't want to upset them, not after they beat her up before. She quickly hurried into the next room. It was every bit as bad as the first. The girls didn't even look at her. They just stared at the ground.

"Take a seat, you could be a while," the man said as though he was asking her to wait for a bus instead of for her sister, waiting to be rescued from this hell she had gotten herself into.

She sat on the edge of one of the mattresses next to a girl who she guessed was even younger than her, maybe fifteen or sixteen. Surely, she couldn't be an addict at that age, she thought, before seeing the track marks on her forearms. At least Michalina hadn't gotten that bad. She had only smoked her 'H.'

Michalina looked around the room. As well as the young girl next to her, there were five other girls. None of them engaged her in conversation, in fact they seemed to be deliberately avoiding eye contact. One of the girls who appeared almost skeletal was curled up in the corner of the room shivering. She was wearing a pair of dirty denim shorts and a red vest top. Her long, dark, unkempt hair hung over her face as she leant against the wall. Michalina could see sores on her legs from injecting. Some of them were now infected. She wore no shoes, and her feet were black. It was difficult to see how old she was as she was covered, but Michalina guessed she was a similar age to her, maybe a year or two older.

The man who had led her to the apartment building was called Thomas. He was okay, better than some of the others. She didn't know the names of the ones that beat her up, she only knew that Sebastian – her dealer – had called them in to make sure she did what she was told. It was her own fault. Smoking a bit of puff with the guys from college was no big deal but going on to smack was a big mistake. She had known it at the time, but it was such a hit she didn't care. Nothing came close to that feeling. The only problem she had was funding her problem and that was how she had got into the situation she found herself in now. Initially she thought she could handle it. Just small amounts of money involved. But as her habit increased, she found herself struggling to pay. That was when Sebastian made her an offer to help her out. All she had to do was a bit of dealing around town and she would be rewarded with her own supply. No problem for a few weeks but then she was robbed of the profits when a couple of guys jumped her. In the bag was over a thousand euros for Sebastian.

Sebastian was really good about it and didn't seem to be angry with her, in fact he even let her have her fix before he explained that she would need to do a bit more work to pay off the money she had lost. Over the months her debt had increased and with interest, as did her need for 'H', and she reached a point where she couldn't pay. That was when Thomas, a big lump of a man but very docile, had come and found her. He told her that Sebastian wanted to see her and that she had to come immediately. She was at a canal-side bar with friends, but Michalina guessed she needed to go with him; Sebastian was not someone you messed with.

When she arrived, Sebastian was initially businesslike, explaining that she owed very nearly fifty thousand euros and she needed to pay it back fast. She told him it was impossible: it would take years for her to earn that type of money, which was when he told her that she would have to either borrow it from family or steal it if necessary. It didn't matter, but he wanted it back and she had a week. But after a week, she still didn't have the money and was texting Sebastian begging for another fix. She offered to pay back the money another way, all he had to do was say how.

"So," said Sebastian, "all I have to do is say how." He paused, and Michalina nodded. "I have various contacts that can put you to work. You can pay off the debt that way. How does that sound?" He wasn't cold and he sounded like he was trying to help.

Michalina was beginning to go into withdrawal; she could feel the craving rising and she could feel herself sweating.

"Yes, anything," she said. "Please, just help me and I'll do whatever."

She was worried that she would be asked to have sex with him. She was okay with it if it meant she got the 'H' she needed but she knew it could end up taking her down a path she didn't really want to go down. She began to undo her shirt. It was important to let him know she was available if that's what it took.

"Stop," he suddenly said, causing her to pause, fingers holding one of the buttons. She looked at him unsure of what to do next.

"You misjudge me," he said, smiling. He raised his hand as if to speak but then put it down again, holding the tension. "I understand you have an older sister? Zuzanna?"

"Yes." Michalina was curious. "Why?"

Sebastian reached in his trouser pocket and pulled out the small wrap of paper, holding it up so she could see it. Her eyes lit up; she needed the wrap so bad.

"I think you have an opportunity to pay back the money before the interest increases too much." Michalina said nothing, she didn't know what he was talking about. "I suggest you tell her about the difficulties you are having. What you tell her about your habit is up to you, but she needs to know you owe us this money and she needs to help you to pay it off."

"She won't do that." Michalina's head was racing. How could she explain it to her sister? And how could Zuzanna get that sort of money? "I don't understand, how can she—"

Michalina never finished the sentence as she was cut off by Sebastian.

"Let me explain. Zuzanna works and has for some time. Your parents are struggling, and your brother is due to go to college."

"How do you—" Again she was unable to finish the sentence.

"How do we know this?" he asked.

Michalina nodded.

"You owe us a lot of money and we will get it back; do you think we are stupid?" Michalina shook her head, still not saying anything. "No, that's right, we make sure when we lend money that we can get it back. So, Zuzanna can go to the bank and borrow the fifty thousand euros." Michalina was sure she saw him trying to prevent himself from laughing. He seemed to realise he was going to and quickly became serious again. "If she can get it in one payment, we'll ignore the additional interest that is currently building. If not, we'll make sure we get it paid another way." His eyes narrowed. He looked terrifying.

Michalina was shaken but knew she had no choice. Sebastian passed her the small fold of paper, and she opened it, revealing the gold she craved so much. He reached into a drawer behind him and pulled out a lighter and a burnt piece of foil. He also passed these to Michalina. She took them, poured the powder into the foil and began heating the bottom with the lighter. Sebastian rolled a piece of paper into a tube and handed it to her. She put it to her mouth and as the fumes began to rise, she inhaled them through the tube, drawing them deep into her lungs. Instantly she felt the calm wash over her.

The following afternoon, when she was at college, she was approached by two men she had not seen before.

"Have you spoken to Zuzanna?" one of them asked in a strong eastern European accent.

"Not yet, no." She had guessed they were something to do with Sebastian and this confirmed it.

"You seem to think we are not being serious?" he said.

"No, I just haven't had time, it was only yesterday." The other man just stared at her.

"You need to come with us so we can explain things to you. We'll also provide you with a message for Zuzanna that might help when you ask her."

"What message?" she asked.

"Later." Again, the first man spoke, the other still remaining silent.

"Where is Zuzanna now?" he asked.

"She's at work. I promise I'll ask later." Michalina was getting worried.

"Yes, you will," he said coldly. At that moment she was grabbed by the other and the two forced her down a nearby alleyway.

"Please, you're hurting," she cried.

Neither of them spoke. The first punch hit her in the stomach, winding her and making her double over. More blows followed. Both of the men appeared to be enjoying the assault. Slapping her across the face, one side and then the other, whilst continuing to punch her midriff and ribs.

The assault went on and on. When they stopped Michalina slumped to the floor. They picked her up under the arms and dragged her to the end of the alley where they put her into the back of a waiting car. Closing the door behind her, the car set off. The driver, another man she didn't recognise, said, "Where to?"

"The coffee shop," the first man answered. He looked at her and smiled. "Do you think Zuzanna will get the message?" he asked. Michalina was shaken and felt dizzy. She couldn't bring herself to say anything.

"Yes," he said, "I think when she sees, it will help you get the message over." He paused, looking at her again. "You need to ask her for the money and ask nicely, make sure she understands. One look at you should convince her of the urgency. Make sure she says yes. We wouldn't want her to suffer the same fate." Michalina looked up at the back of the driver's head and then at his eyes in the mirror.

"No, please, please don't. I'll convince her." She felt the tears flowing down her face. She didn't care, the pain of knowing what might happen to her sister was too great, she had almost forgotten her physical pain from the beating.

"No police, and make sure she understands what could happen if you don't get the money," he said, making sure he caught her eye.

After a short drive, the car stopped. The man spoke again. "Once you have told her, you need to go see Sebastian. I would suggest you have your passport and documents so you can prove your age when we arrange a job for you. Understand?" He looked at her again, she nodded in response.

"Good," he replied. "Now get out."

Michalina had climbed out of the car, and it immediately drove off. She had looked around and realised she was at the back of Zuzanna's coffee shop. Her legs were shaking, and she collapsed against a nearby dumpster. Moments later Zuzanna had come out of the back door.

That was a couple of days ago. Hopefully by now Zuzanna would have arranged the money. Getting her passport from home had not been easy. She had to sneak into the house when everyone was asleep and retrieve it from the sideboard in the lounge. She managed to get in and out of the house making as little noise as possible, but she still was unsure as to whether she had woken anyone. When she got to Sebastian's apartment building, Thomas had been waiting. He took her documents, "For safe keeping."

Michalina leaned back on the mattress. She was beginning to feel cold. The room wasn't heated. She had already been supplied with a dose of 'medication' as she preferred to call it and was feeling okay. She looked around at the other girls but none of them looked back. On the mattress between her and the young girl was a blanket, although it was so dirty that Michalina wasn't sure she wanted to touch it. She turned to the girl, leaning slightly towards her, and asked, "How long have you been here?"

The girl turned towards her and without answering turned away again. The skeletal girl in the corner glanced at her through her greasy hair and then also looked away. The others in the room didn't look at all.

She turned back to the young girl on the mattress.

"Do we get food, or do we have to go out?" Again, the girl briefly looked at her and then looked back down. A voice came from behind her.

"Shut the fuck up, will you?" She looked round to see a girl who, at a guess, was in her early twenties. She was lying on a mattress, propped up on one elbow.

"They don't like us talking," she said in a raised whisper. The look on her face was one of anger rather than fear. "Just be quiet and wait."

"Why not?" Michalina asked just as a man she didn't recognise stepped into the doorway.

"No talking," he said before looking at the girls one at a time, making sure they had gotten the message.

He stepped back and turned away, walking out of view.

Michalina decided silence was the best option. *Shouldn't be long now,* she thought to herself. As soon as the money was arranged, she could get back to the family and help Zuzanna pay the money off. Maybe with her sister's help she could even get off her habit. She had convinced herself that she could do it despite the feeling of the heroin still coursing through her body.

Time passed. Michalina had no idea how long she had been there. She was hungry and cold. She could tell it was getting dark outside, so guessed it was early evening. She hoped this meant they would be given food soon. The other girls had still not said anything. Occasionally one of them was taken and would be gone for a short time before returning. Michalina guessed this was to give them their fix, so they'd be ready for work if required.

She then heard heavy footsteps coming up the stairs and down the hallway, finally coming to a stop outside the door. She looked to see Thomas's frame filling the doorway. He stepped to one side revealing Sebastian behind him. Michalina held her breath. She wondered whether Zuzanna had got the money, hoping beyond hope. She looked into his eyes desperately.

"Milou," he said, looking at the young girl next to her. "Good news, we have work for you so you can begin to pay back your debt." He smiled at her. The young girl looked at him, saying nothing.

She climbed to her feet and stood head bowed. To Michalina she looked fragile; her clothes were dishevelled and dirty, and her face smeared with dried tears. Sebastian looked her up and down, shaking his head.

"Oh dear, Milou, you'll need to clean yourself up before you meet your date, looking like that you're enough to frighten anyone." Sebastian laughed. Thomas did also, although Michalina got the impression he was only joining in the laughter because it was expected of him, rather than because he found what Sebastian had said funny.

"Michalina," said Sebastian, looking at her. "Bad news, I'm afraid. It appears the bank was reluctant to loan your sister any money so you're going to have to work off the debt. Don't worry, though, we'll provide you with the work."

Michalina didn't know what to say. She just stared at him, still looking for signs of hope. "But," he said, "Zuzanna is going to help you pay off the debt."

"How?" asked Michalina, wondering how her sister could help.

She hadn't even considered that the bank would reject her loan application, although she guessed that was more through hope than logic. Why should the bank loan money to someone who works in a coffee shop, who has a mother who is a cleaner, two siblings at college and a disabled father, all living in a rented apartment? It was obvious really.

"You don't need to worry about Zuzanna, you need to worry about yourself. We will be back later and hopefully we will have fixed you up with some work," he said before leaving.

"Thomas," Michalina asked before he had a chance to follow, "please could we get some food?"

Thomas looked down the corridor as if looking at Sebastian and then turned towards her.

"I'll get some sent in," he said before walking out.

Ten minutes later a man she didn't recognise stepped in the room and put a large shopping bag on the floor.

"Sandwiches," he said, and then left. The girls looked up, but none moved. Michalina grabbed the bag and looked inside. The food was clearly from a local supermarket. She pulled out a cheese sandwich and then passed the bag to one of the other girls. No one said anything but the bag was passed around until empty.

Michalina ate with such pleasure it was obvious she hadn't eaten for days.

CHAPTER 9

"This is Sebastian," the man from the coffee shop said.

Zuzanna looked at the man and then towards Sebastian with disgust. She was in a portacabin on the outskirts of Amsterdam, which stood adjacent to a building site for new office space. The portacabin was sparsely decorated with images of sports cars in cheap frames on the walls, the pale grey interior giving it a light yet industrial appearance. Sebastian was standing in front of a very elaborate, old wooden desk that didn't go with the interior and Zuzanna guessed it had been reclaimed from somewhere. Behind the desk was a black leather swivel chair, which again didn't fit with the sparse decoration of the room. In front of Sebastian and the desk was a padded office chair and a couple of cheap wood and metal chairs against the side walls, the sort you would see in a canteen.

"Zuzanna, the pleasure is all mine," said Sebastian as he extended a hand towards her.

She stood unmoving and making it clear she was not about to partake in niceties with him or anyone else who was threatening her family.

"As you wish," he said, withdrawing the offer of his hand. "As you know, your sister owes us a considerable amount of money—"

"Who's us?" asked Zuzanna, interrupting him, making it clear that she was furious with the situation.

"Please, Zuzanna, be nice," Sebastian said, smiling at her.

"Be nice? How can I be nice? You've beaten up my sister for God knows what. This person – who I assume works for you – makes threats against my family. Apparently, we owe you large amounts of money for something Michalina has done, and you expect me to be nice?" She spoke quickly, wanting to make sure she got out everything before he interrupted her.

Again, Sebastian smiled at her.

"Please have a seat, let me explain." He indicated to the padded chair.

She sat down. She quickly glanced back at the young man from the coffee shop who had taken a seat by the door then back at Sebastian, who had perched on the edge of the desk, directly in front of her, one foot on the floor and the other bent at the knee swinging back and forth.

"Michalina owes us a considerable amount of money," said Sebastian as he leaned towards her.

"Yes, you've said. I don't know how. She doesn't own anything and has only ever done a bit of part-time work so if you've lent her money, you are bigger fools than I thought," Zuzanna said, still spitting venom towards him.

"Your sister is an addict and cannot pay back the money quick enough, so she needs your help. We will get the money back." He looked into Zuzanna's eyes to make sure she was paying attention.

"No, she's not an addict," Zuzanna barked at him. "I expect her, and her friends may smoke a bit of weed, but she's no addict." She paused. She had said her piece and now wanted to hear what Sebastian had to say. She continued to stare at him, not trying to hide the anger she felt.

"Michalina is an addict. Heroin, to be exact."

Zuzanna couldn't believe what she was hearing. "No," she managed to say.

"Yes, and she has borrowed and borrowed and now her debt is due. As you have seen, we do what is needed to ensure we are paid and believe me when I say, you have seen nothing yet." His eyes narrowed. "Do I have your attention?"

Zuzanna sat and stared back, not knowing what to say.

"I said, do I have your attention?"

This time he said it in a raised, commanding voice that demanded a reply.

"Yes," she replied in a softer voice.

"Michalina will be staying with us for a while and will be working off the debt in a factory or a kitchen or somewhere, we haven't decided." He spoke in a calm voice, much like when she had arrived.

"Where?" asked Zuzanna.

"It doesn't matter where, what matters from your point of view is that she will be okay and provided you do as we require, you and the rest of your family will be okay." He smiled again. "We own some properties that we would like you to work in," he began, clearly avoiding getting to the main issue. "Do you know the De Wallen district?" he asked in a casual manner.

"Of course," she replied.

She knew it was the red-light district in the heart of Amsterdam, nowadays a tourist attraction as well as an area of shame, both for the city and the girls who worked there so far as she was concerned.

"What of it?"

"We have some shop fronts in which the girls work. They can earn large amounts of money, the sort of money that could help to pay off a large debt in a relatively short space of time."

"You can't be serious." Zuzanna looked at him. "She's too young anyway. If the police did checks you'd be found out and then what? You'd get nothing."

Zuzanna couldn't believe they would even think such a thing. Yes, Michalina was beautiful and looked older than her 18 years, but she was still too young to work in the De Wallen district. Then the thought crossed her mind: how well did she really know her sister?

She hadn't realised she was a drug addict and didn't think she would ever get herself into fifty thousand euros of debt.

"Please, you can't expect her to do that," she said, hearing herself pleading more than she wanted to.

"You are right, of course," said Sebastian. "She is too young, and it would be wrong to set her to work there."

Zuzanna breathed a sigh of relief.

"As I've said, she can work for us in a factory or something. You, on the other hand, will work the shop. You can pay us eighty percent of your takings." He smiled again.

"No way, you can't be serious, I can't..." The words burst from her lips in a frenzy. How could they even think she would do that? Her fear of Sebastian was overridden by her shock at what she was being told.

"You will," he responded. "You will rent the space and you will entertain any patrons and when we are happy the debt is paid you can go and carry on with your sad coffee shop life."

This was said with menace. Zuzanna felt herself shaking and she stood and turned towards the door. The man from the coffee shop stood up, blocking her path.

"Out of my way," she shouted at him.

He didn't move.

"Sit down, Zuzanna." Sebastian's voice resonated around the portacabin walls. Zuzanna didn't move, just stared at the man in front of the door. "I said, sit down now!" It was an order. She slowly turned back and sat in the chair.

"Better," said Sebastian. "I understand you have a disabled father?" he asked in a gentle voice.

If she didn't know better, she would have thought he cared. She nodded her head.

"And your mother works long hours for small amounts of money.

Cleaning?" Again Zuzanna nodded her head. "You have a younger brother," he laughed. "Going to college, I understand. It's important to get an education."

Zuzanna wondered if he was now mocking her. "Yes," she replied, gritting her teeth.

"Okay, this is how it is going to work," he said as he began to explain, sounding like a teacher giving a lesson. "You will be able to continue working at the coffee shop, best to keep up appearances for the customers and I understand you're very popular?" He looked towards the man by the door who nodded. "Yes, very popular, so you can keep that up. I expect you also help to pay the bills at home, yes?"

"Yes," she replied, much of the life knocked out of her by his deep knowledge of her. *What has Michalina told them?* she thought.

"This will mean you need to work an evening shift for us, shall we say seven pm until three am? That way you should be able to grab a few hours to sleep."

Zuzanna's head was spinning. "I can't. Don't you see? I can't. Please?" She was pleading now. Surely, they couldn't be serious.

"You don't seem to have grasped the situation, Zuzanna. Your choice is do as we say, or you never see Michalina again. And you and the rest of your family will still owe us the money."

"Why? What would you…" Zuzanna was struggling to get the words out. It made no sense to her. She wasn't a sex worker, she had only had a boyfriend once and even then, sex wasn't particularly good. How could she have sex with strangers? It was impossible.

"I can see you're struggling," said Sebastian.

He sounded caring, which confused her even more. How could he be like this? So casual, as if he were offering her an office job or asking her to do some cleaning. But no, he wanted her to have sex with strangers.

"I'll tell you what, how about you try now with young Lucas here and get some practice. I'll wait outside. Just think, the quicker you do it, the quicker it's over and then you can get dressed. Simple logic." Zuzanna looked at him in disbelief. He walked past her to the man and whispered to him. Then the male, who Zuzanna now knew as Lucas, walked towards her. She looked at Sebastian and called out as he left.

"You can't be serious."

"Be quick," he called back, then closed the door behind him.

By the time she turned back, Lucas was leaning against the desk smiling.

"No way," she told him, full of anger.

"Zuzanna, you have to. If you don't, you saw what Sebastian and his friends are capable of. It's best to just get it done." From the tone of his voice, she got the impression that he was also being asked to do something he wasn't happy with.

"I can't, please," Zuzanna almost whispered, tears welling in her eyes.

"First time's the hardest," said Lucas, as he stood in front of her and undid his belt buckle before pulling down his jeans.

He reached down and took hold of Zuzanna's hands, pulling her gently towards him. She stood, realising that there was not much hope of getting out of it. Lucas eased her coat off and undid her jeans for her before easing them down over her buttocks and letting them slide to her knees.

"You need to take them off," Lucas said in a matter-of-fact way. She eased them to the floor before stepping out of them and leaving them crumpled on the linoleum.

"I don't have protection," she suddenly said, realising.

"Here," he replied, thrusting a condom that he must have pulled from his jeans into her hand.

She looked down at the unopened condom and then at Lucas. She was still in shock and wasn't sure what to do.

"Give it here," he said, holding out his hand. She handed him the packet, which he unceremoniously tore open. "Have you put one on a man before?" he asked. She shook her head. "Here." He handed back the condom and pulled down his boxer shorts, revealing a partially erect penis.

She looked at it. She was right, he clearly wasn't keen. This is something they both had to do. He took her other hand and put it around his penis. She pulled away. More from surprise than anything.

"Zuzanna, you must," he said gently.

She put her hand back and as she did, she felt a tear roll down her cheek. He grasped her wrist and moved it gently back and forwards until it was clear what she was expected to do. She continued until he was ready.

He took the condom from her other hand and spoke, and still trying to be as gentle as he could, guided her as to how to put it on. She did as she was told. He turned her back to the desk and suggested she climb onto it as the alternative would be to lie on the floor. Tears continued to stream down her cheeks.

"Wait," he suddenly said. "Panties, it will be easier if you remove them now."

She stood up again and putting her thumbs into the waist elastic, pulled them off. She was now naked from the waist down and felt exposed. She could feel a chill in the room; it seemed even more sparse than before. "Oh, wait," he said again.

He really didn't know what he was doing. He quickly went around the desk and opened a drawer. Despite the awful situation she found herself in, she almost laughed at this ridiculous young man wearing a tee shirt and nothing else running around a desk. He pulled out a jar of what looked like Vaseline. "I think you'll find it more comfortable with this," he said, handing her the jar.

She undid the jar and took a handful. She felt rather than saw Lucas climb onto her and she lay still whilst he moved himself, very quickly as if he wanted it to be over as much as she did.

"Was that, okay?" he asked when he'd finished.

She realised he'd never done this before. Sure, he may have had a girlfriend at some point, but she didn't think he'd ever been told to have sex with someone. Maybe they were both victims.

"It was fine," she replied.

"That's good." He seemed genuinely pleased. "You'd best get dressed," he said to her as he began dressing himself, dropping the condom into the wastepaper basket.

Zuzanna grabbed her clothes from the floor. She was stunned. What had she just done? She couldn't believe it. Thinking back to what Sebastian wanted her to do, she recoiled. She certainly didn't think she could do something like this with complete strangers.

"Are you sure you're okay?" he asked again. He seemed genuinely concerned. Amazing, considering he had just raped her. She guessed he didn't see it like that.

The door opened and Sebastian walked in.

"You can leave now, Lucas, well done." He looked at him without answering, glanced once more at Zuzanna and then left. "It's a start, but you need to be more enthusiastic. Remember, the quicker you are with them the quicker you can get through them." He smiled and pointed at the CCTV dome in the corner of the room. He'd watched the whole thing.

"You bastard," she exclaimed.

"Now be nice, Zuzanna. You've a lot of work to do and that means a lot of customers."

She stared at him. At that moment she thought it would be impossible to hate anyone more than she hated him.

"Let's say the first two customers of the night cover the rent of the shop and anything you earn after that can go towards the debt."

Zuzanna said nothing. What could she say?

"Remember, the more customers the quicker you pay off the debt, and the less interest you incur." He laughed. "You best go home and get changed for your first shift. Be back here for eight. After all, we don't want you overworking on your first night, do we?" He grinned again. "I'll introduce you to one of the girls who can get you dressed appropriately. Dowdy coffee shop barista is not a look most clients are looking for."

"I can't work there, please, what if my friends see me?" She wasn't really pleading, that time had come and gone. She was just concerned now.

"Oh, I wouldn't worry too much," he said jovially, still smiling. "Believe me, once we've dressed you and done your makeup your mother wouldn't even recognise you. Now, off you go." He pointed towards the door. She walked away from him and left, not looking back and still feeling numb. "Don't forget this," he called. She turned as he threw the jar of Vaseline towards her. Instinctively she caught it. "You're going to need plenty of that." Again, he laughed as he said it.

CHAPTER 10

Please not Balodis, please not Balodis, Anastasjia thought to herself. The idea of a thirty-five-hour train journey with him filled her with fear and dread. Not only had she seen him murder Jennings without a second thought, she also knew of his unusual and painful sexual preferences.

When she first joined the company one of her responsibilities was to entertain him. Thankfully, she had been lucky to come away with nothing more than a few minor bruises, but other girls had not been so fortunate. At least two girls were so badly scarred they had to be put to work in establishments where the clients wouldn't be too fussy. She was fairly confident she was important enough to the bosses not to be harmed seriously but in the world she lived in, this was never a certainty. After all, they were prepared to risk her going to prison for smuggling vast amounts of money across Europe.

Anastasjia also knew she was definitely going to be travelling with someone. She may be trusted but not with two hundred and fifty thousand euros.

She arrived at Riga Central railway station at 7:30pm. She knew better than to be late. The train was due to depart at 8:15, heading towards Molodechno in Belarus on the first stage of the journey. She wanted a good seat but also knew she should leave plenty of time to receive her final instructions and the suitcase with the money. She had packed herself a leather holdall with enough clothes for up to four days; she guessed it wouldn't be much longer and if she needed anything she could buy it when she got to London.

She hated being away from home. Saying goodbye to the cat was the hardest thing. To Anastasjia, Minka was the only living thing she could trust and even then, she knew being a cat, it was only after what it could get. She had always wanted a dog. She had always thought they would be better company but with the long hours she worked, it was impossible.

It was getting near to 8:00pm, 15 minutes before the train left and still no sign of anyone. Maybe the company had altered the plans and she wouldn't have to go. She was about to leave when she saw Balodis walk in. *Shit,* she thought. *All I fucking need.*

"Hi, Janis," she said, trying to sound cheerful.

"You're fooling no one," Balodis replied. "I know you'd rather be travelling with someone else." He smiled and then gestured to a man behind him. Anastasjia had been so focused on Balodis she hadn't seen the slim, athletic-looking man. "You're in luck. This is Uldis. He'll be travelling with you."

Anastasjia guessed he was about 25 – he must be new to the company and at least he wasn't wearing some cheap suit. Instead, he was wearing jeans and a tee shirt with a leather bomber jacket.

"Anastasjia, a pleasure," he said, looking her up and down, checking her out.

"Say hello, Ana. You know how to be polite, don't you?" said Balodis, the grin on his face getting even wider.

"Hello," was all she said. She was not minded to say anything more.

"Uldis will be accompanying you on the journey. He will be within sight of you at all times, especially at the stations where you change trains and on your overnight stops."

"Overnight stops?" she asked. "I thought we were just changing trains and carrying on until London."

"There is a thirty-five-hour train journey to Brussels followed by a three-hour trip to London." Balodis sounded almost exasperated at having to explain. "The plan is to break up the journey with a couple of stops where you can get some sleep and something to eat. We're just thinking of your wellbeing." He laughed.

Uldis, clearly trying to impress Balodis, laughed along with him.

"Here are your tickets and the details of the hotels you will be staying at." He handed her a plain white A5 envelope. "I'm sure I don't need to tell you what will happen to you and of course that cat of yours should you do anything you know we would not be happy with, yes?"

"Yes, of course," replied Anastasjia, knowing exactly what was expected.

She had no intention of crossing Balodis or the company and never had. She also decided that she would not be doing anything with Uldis either. She could see by the way he looked at her he was expecting something from her.

"Hurry now," said Balodis. "The train is leaving at any moment, you don't want to be late."

Anastasjia put the envelope into the side pocket of her holdall and lifted the strap, pulling it over her shoulder. Uldis made no effort to help and just lifted the small suitcase he had brought with him. As she walked towards the platform, she caught sight of Balodis whispering to Uldis. *Final instructions,* she thought.

She looked at the ticket for the first train. She noted you couldn't sit with large cases and so she would have to put the case in the luggage rack near the door. She noted her reserved seat was very near the case. *Okay,* she thought. *That will be okay.* Uldis, she was pleased to see, was not seated next to her, though from his seat could clearly see every move she made. He was also in a reasonable position to stop anyone stealing the case. She found that reassuring; the last thing she could afford to do was lose the case.

She glanced out of the window onto the platform. Balodis was standing looking straight at her. He intimidated her even through the train window. Minutes later the train slowly pulled out of the station. An overnight journey, arriving in Belarus at 6:05am, she would have to try and get some sleep. Shame the train wasn't a sleeper. She walked towards Uldis, and he looked up at her.

"I need to sleep. You watch the case, wake me in about four hours and you can get sleep then." He nodded and she returned to her seat. She leaned back and closed her eyes. She knew she wouldn't sleep well but if she could just doze a little, she would at least function when she needed to.

Anastasjia woke with a start. She looked around, panicking, unsure of where she was. A man was leaning over her.

"Time to wake," he said. She realised it was Uldis. She had clearly slept much better than she thought. She looked over to where she had put the suitcase with the money. Still there. She calmed down.

"What time is it?" she asked.

"3:30."

She'd slept much longer than she had anticipated.

"You won't have time for much sleep," she said apologetically.

She wasn't worried about him but was grateful he had allowed her the extra time to sleep. The stress of the last few days had clearly taken their toll on her.

"I don't sleep much," he said, smiling before returning to his seat.

She watched him for a few moments as he sat back and closed his eyes. He didn't move. She wondered if he had already fallen asleep. She stood to go to the bathroom and immediately he opened his eyes, looking directly at her. How on earth had he heard her? She pointed towards the toilet sign, and he nodded, closing his eyes again. She thought for a moment about the case and then smiled to herself. No one was going to take it from a moving train.

When she returned to her seat his eyes were still closed. She reached into her holdall pocket and pulled out the envelope with the remaining train tickets and the detail of her hotel stops. Change trains at Molodechno, time for coffee and breakfast before travelling to

Grodno and then Warsaw. Arriving at 8:25pm. She looked at the details for the hotel. Premiere Classe Varsovie Hotel, not a top hotel but at least she could get a good night's sleep and a shower before the journey to Brussels and then the Eurostar.

The train pulled into Molodechno on time, and she got up to depart. She moved towards the case, but Uldis got to it first.

"Let me," he said, lifting it from the rack and carrying it to the doors.

She followed him out, carrying her leather holdall over her shoulder. He put the case on the platform and pulled up the handle.

"No, let me," she said, reaching for it. She didn't trust him enough to let him wander off with the money. He stepped back.

"Breakfast?" he asked.

For a moment she was taken aback. He had been polite but businesslike.

"I thought we were meant to be travelling separately?" she replied.

"I won't tell, if you don't," he said, smiling.

It took her by surprise. He was actually being unprofessional. She couldn't help but find it quite endearing. Setting off towards the exit of the station, she pulled the case behind her, and Uldis followed. They found a nearby café that was open and ordered breakfast. They sat down at a table, an awkward silence between them.

The food came and they ate, and still, they did not speak. Anastasjia didn't feel like engaging in conversation. She could see he appeared awkward, shuffling from side to side. Obviously, he had been brought up to be polite, but with nothing to say. She had a guess that Uldis didn't know how to do small talk. That suited her; she just wanted the journey over with.

After breakfast they made their way back to the station for the next part of the journey, towards Grodno. When the train pulled in, they made their way to their seats. Anastasjia smiled to herself.

Similar seats, similar view of the case in the rack, Uldis still watching her. The journey to Grodno was much shorter and they arrived in time for lunch. In the same way as their arrival at Molodechno, Uldis offered to take the case off the train and in the same way, once on the platform Anastasjia took it and the two of them travelled to a nearby restaurant for some lunch. This time they did speak. A difficult conversation about the trains and the weather. *He really can't do small talk*, Anastasjia thought. She smiled. *Never mind*.

The journey to Warsaw was a similar affair. When they arrived, it was dark. Fortunately, the hotel was nearby so it was no more than a very short walk. When they arrived Anastasjia went up to the front desk and spoke to the young male receptionist.

"A room for Anastasjia Grigorjeva?"

"Oh yes," the young man replied, "Mrs. Grigorjeva, I have that booked and paid for you and your husband." Anastasjia couldn't help rolling her eyes. *Husband*, she thought. *Whose idea was that?* She looked at the receptionist and smiled at him.

He handed her the card for the room door. Once in the lift Anastasjia turned to Uldis.

"Really, Mr. and Mrs. Grigorjeva, you never thought to tell me?"

"Ana, I do as I'm told. They could have booked it in my name. I was told you would take charge and so best to book in your name." He looked at her. He could see she was annoyed, but he didn't really care.

"It's the Mr. and Mrs. I'm annoyed with," she said.

"There was no way they were going to leave you alone with the money." She knew that, she just didn't want to hear it.

The room contained a king-size bed and a small desk, as well as a small but clean bathroom. Not bad; she had certainly slept in worse places.

"And where are you sleeping?" she asked, with a voice that implicitly implied 'not in the bed'.

"In the bed. Where are you sleeping?"

She scowled at him slightly. She knew the room was not his idea and there was nothing he could do about it, but she wanted him to know she wasn't happy. There was no way she was going to give up the bed, that was for sure.

"So long as you know the room isn't the only thing around here that costs money and you can't afford what I can offer, got it?" She looked him in the eye.

"Fine by me," he answered. "We can put a line of pillows down the centre of the bed if it makes you feel more comfortable." She wasn't expecting that as a response but was pleased he was being so reasonable.

"Yes, thank you," she said, smiling.

He smiled back. "No problem."

The following morning after sleeping remarkably well Anastasjia woke to find the bed next to her was empty. She then heard the sound of the bathroom light switch and Uldis appeared. He had his trousers on but was barefoot and topless. Although slim he was incredibly muscular. He was drying his hair with a towel.

"Morning," he said in a cheery voice. "After you shower, we could get breakfast."

She nodded and got out of the bed. Heading to the bathroom, she grabbed her clothes on the way.

Breakfast was a surprisingly pleasant experience. Uldis appeared to have gotten over his awkwardness and was suddenly very talkative, asking her if she had ever been to London before and telling her what she should try to see while there. She returned the conversation by asking him the same questions, as well as a few personal ones such as where he was from and how long he had worked for the company. She discovered he came from a small village just outside of Riga. Once he left school he quickly discovered that if he was to find a job, he would have to leave the village. He told her the story of how he met Balodis. He had been working in a bar when a fight broke out. He quickly stopped the fight and threw out those involved, and a while later, Balodis, who had been sitting in one of the booths, handed him a card telling him to call and that he could give him a job that earned far more than his current one did.

"The rest is history," he said, smiling. "They ask me to make sure people do as they are told. They hold me on a retainer, so I get plenty of opportunity to do what I like to do."

"And what is that?" asked Anastasjia.

"Go to the gym mostly, sometimes play football with friends," he replied.

She guessed that was the case, looking at his physique.

The next part of the journey took them to Wuppertal in Germany via Berlin. A different train but the same as before. She was seated on her own with Uldis able to see her and the case in clear view to both of them. They didn't arrive at Wuppertal until just after 10:30pm so Anastasjia was pleased the hotel was close by. They had eaten at the stop in Berlin and purchased sandwiches on the train so all she wanted to do was go to the room. They checked in and made their way up to the room, Uldis carrying the case.

"If you want a shower before bed, you can go first and I'll have one when you're out," said Uldis.

Uldis was always the consummate professional, thinking of her needs. She thanked him and went into the bathroom. While she showered, she thought about him. She found it quite exciting that he didn't seem interested, almost erotic. As the water cascaded over her body and the lather was gently rubbed over her, she found herself changing her plans. She had previously told herself she wouldn't engage with this young muscular man, a company man, a man who followed Balodis's orders. She was wise to the world where sex was concerned and knew he may just use her, but having sex with him may also be something she could enjoy. She found herself getting turned on at the thought of it. She finished showering and climbed out of the bath, drying herself with a large towel.

Returning to the room, Uldis was still dressed. He went into the bathroom and closed the door. Moments later, Anastasjia heard the shower start. She stood for a moment looking at the bed. She then glanced at the bathroom door. The sound of the water stopped and there was a pause before Uldis walked out wearing a clean pair of boxer shorts he had clearly taken in with him.

Anastasjia stood with her hair still wet, and a towel wrapped tightly around her. She could feel the excitement of anticipation coursing through her as she slowly walked towards him, catching his gaze. He smiled at her. Without saying anything she put one hand behind his head, standing on tiptoe, and leaning towards him, she kissed him gently on the lips. He pulled away slightly, enough for Anastasjia to know she was being rejected.

"What is it?" she asked. "Don't you find me attractive?"

He looked her in the eye. "Of course, but like you said last night, the room isn't the only thing that costs money so—" He didn't finish what he was saying.

"This one's on the house," she said, smiling.

She leaned towards him again and this time he met her kiss. Anastasjia let the towel fall and pushed her body against his.

They made love on the bed. It had been her choice, the first time in a long time that Anastasjia felt like it was. She had instigated it and she had called the shots. At no point had he tried to make her do anything she didn't want to, which was something she was not used to, and she had loved every minute of it.

The next morning there was no awkwardness and they continued to converse easily. She found herself hoping she would get to spend more time with him in London.

The trip to Brussels would only take three hours but it unfortunately meant a short coach trip followed by two trains. But at least there were no long stops. They managed to get to Brussels station just after 1:00pm.

A line of taxis waited for passengers outside the station but suddenly a large BMW saloon car pulled up in front of them, causing the taxi at the front to sound his horn, the driver gesticulating towards the BMW. The man then opened the door of his cab but when he saw the driver of the BMW glare at him, he quickly got back in and closed the door. Balodis always had that effect on people.

"Ana, good journey I hope," he said, looking towards her and Uldis. "Quickly now, you're holding up these gentlemen." He held open the rear passenger door for her to get in, and indicated to Uldis he should get into the front, taking the case with the money and throwing it into the trunk as if it weighed nothing.

When he climbed back into the car, he looked at Uldis, who sat with his holdall on his lap.

"Uldis, you can't travel like that," he said. "Put your bag next to Ana's on the back seat."

Looking a little nervous, Uldis complied.

"I wasn't expecting to see you here," said Anastasjia, trying to sound like she wasn't concerned.

"No, you weren't, were you? Neither of you were," he responded. "Let's get you booked into the hotel and then we can discuss what you are to do next," he said, looking in the rear-view mirror and catching sight of Anastasjia looking back.

"We're booked on the Eurostar for later this afternoon," Anastasjia said, confused. They weren't due to stay in a hotel.

"Yes, that was the original plan and I hate wasting money on a train ticket we won't use, but it is a must and the job we need you to do is very important."

"What job?" she asked.

"All in good time," replied Balodis.

Uldis said nothing.

Balodis parked in the car park of a hotel and remained in his seat. "You can go book in and take the bags to your rooms. Shall we say twenty minutes?" He looked at Uldis.

"Twenty minutes. No problem, Janis," Uldis replied with an enthusiastic tone that showed he was desperate to please.

"Excellent. Hurry along and be back here in twenty minutes." He said the latter part in the most intimidating way, which really meant 'don't be late or I'll be angry'.

They went to reception and Anastasjia introduced herself.

"Yes, of course," the receptionist said, confirming with the two of them they had reservations in separate rooms on separate floors.

Separate rooms, thought Anastasjia. It made sense. After all, Balodis now had the case with the money so there was no requirement for anyone to be watching her.

They walked to the lift and Uldis pushed the 'Up' button. The doors opened immediately, and they went inside, the doors closing behind them. Uldis pressed the buttons for floor one and floor two and the lift whirred into life.

"No need for us to stay the night in separate rooms," said Uldis.

Anastasjia stepped into the corridor. "Absolutely not," she replied, smiling as the doors closed and Uldis disappeared from view. She walked to her room and opened the door, all the time thinking of why she was so attracted to this man she had only recently met. The feelings were overwhelming, something she had not experienced for years.

*

Back in the car park Balodis drummed his fingers on the steering wheel. *Eighteen minutes*, he thought. *They had better be on time*. He could feel himself getting more and more wound up despite the twenty minutes not being up. At that moment he saw the two of them walking out of the hotel and over to him. *Nineteen minutes*, he thought. *Just in time.*

Uldis and Anastasjia climbed into the car in the same seats they had left.

"Nice rooms?"

They both nodded.

"Good," replied Balodis. "Let's go and get a drink and I can tell you what I want you to do."

Uldis and Anastasjia said nothing as the car pulled away.

CHAPTER 11

"Stop your crying, man," the man said. Harry could feel a tear rolling slowly down his cheek. He wiped it on his sleeve and looked at the man. "Better," he said firmly.

Harry had no idea what was expected of him other than to take drugs somewhere. He was confused and worried about Lilly. He would have to do it, so she was safe.

The man produced the yellow plastic Kinder Egg container from the pocket of his jogging bottoms. He wrapped it tightly in some cling-film.

"You watchin'?" he asked. He looked directly at Harry who nodded. He then handed it to Harry as well as a jar of Vaseline from the mantelpiece. "Now plug it." The man looked at him. Harry looked back, not knowing what he was talking about. "Plug it, man," he said again, only this time he sounded like he was getting annoyed. "Up your arse, man, plug it up your arse."

Harry was shocked.

"What?" What on earth was he on about? How could he do that? The yellow package looked huge. "I can't, I can't." In a sudden movement the man grabbed Harry around the neck and pushed him back against the wall. Harry was choking.

"I can't breathe," he managed to say. The man had him pinned to the wall. Harry dropped the Vaseline and the Kinder Egg container on the floor as he tried to grasp the hand around his neck.

"Don't fucking drop it, you fucking idiot." Harry started to cry again. He had never been so frightened. "You wanna help your sister, you need to start doing as I tell you, understand?"

He pushed harder.

"Yes, yes," he managed to say. The man released him and stepped back. "Now fucking pick that shit up, you fuck, and plug it."

"I don't know how." Harry was crying and shaking as he reached for the packet and the Vaseline. He really didn't know what to do.

The man snatched them from him, opened the Vaseline and smeared a handful of it all over the Kinder Egg. "Now drop your trousers and pants." It was an order. Harry continued to cry but did as he was told. "Now turn around and bend over."

"Please," replied Harry.

"I won't ask again, you little fuck. Turn around and bend over the back of the chair."

Harry did as he was told. He felt vulnerable and terrified. He then felt the man pushing the packet against his anus. "Don't tighten, man." The man was clearly angry. Harry tried not to resist and eventually felt the package go into him. "Now stand up."

It was so uncomfortable but surprisingly not as painful as he thought it would be.

"Good," said the man. "That's how you travel, that way it's not found on you. Got it?" Harry nodded. "Get dressed then, for fuck's sake, man. Do we have to tell you everything?"

As he pulled up his pants and trousers, he could still feel the package. It was more uncomfortable than painful, and he found himself shifting from side to side trying to find a better position.

"Stand still, man." The man looked at him, clearly still angry. "You don't want to draw attention to yourself. You got a phone?" he asked. Harry nodded. "Turn it off and give it to me." Harry did so and was handed a cheap basic phone as a replacement. "In there are the numbers of the people you are going to see, so you need to call them when you get near. There's also a number to get hold of us in an emergency. You fuck this up, you never see your sister again, understand?"

Harry was already terrified and now he knew that he had to do everything he could to help her. Once again, he nodded in acknowledgement.

The man handed Harry a piece of paper with an address written on it, as well as a train ticket. "That will get you to Eastbourne where you need to deliver the package. Got it?"

"What if I get caught?" he asked nervously.

"Don't," the man shouted back at him. "Remember, you come back here without the money, and you don't see your sister again, understand?" Harry nodded again. "Dry your face, man. Like I told you, don't be drawing attention to yourself, okay?"

They walked out of the back door and took a short walk to Stratford rail station.

"Okay, man, you go from here to Victoria and then from there you go to Eastbourne, got it?" The man looked closely at him.

"How do I know where the address is?" Harry asked.

"Ask someone, man." He sounded annoyed again.

Harry was worried about how long this trip would take. "I think my mum will be expecting me back before dark," he said, genuinely concerned about getting home on time. He wasn't one to stay out late and knew his mother would worry.

"Better hurry then. You go to the address; you deliver the package to the girl. You hear me?"

"Yes," was all Harry could manage.

"You make sure you give it to the girl. She'll give you the cash, you plug it and bring it here. When you get back here you call the number on the phone and we'll come and pick you up, then you go home, okay?"

"How do I put the money there?" Harry couldn't think how he would put money in his bottom, and he guessed he wouldn't get the

Kinder Egg back.

"I don't care how you do it, just do it. You get found with it and it gets taken from you, you owe us, and your sister pays, now get on the fucking train."

Harry was so busy thinking about what he had to do he hadn't even noticed the train pull into the station. The doors were already open, and people had started boarding. He jumped on and turned to look at where the man had been talking to him on the platform, but he had already gone. He still wasn't confident about sitting down so stood all the way to London Victoria.

*

Back at the house in Stratford, Lilly lay numb as the third of the gang members climbed off her. The other two in the room, both of whom had already raped her, clapped as the man stood. Her jeans and underwear were somewhere on the floor where the gang members had thrown them. She was in shock and couldn't feel the pain she guessed was coming.

"Really quick, man, we thought you'd last a bit longer than that," said one of them.

"Fuck you," the man replied. The other two laughed.

"Get dressed, bitch, you're going on a journey." As he spoke, he pulled his own jeans back up.

When she was dressed one of them walked out of the room. He suddenly stopped and turned back to look at her. "Come on then, don't make me wait." Lilly followed him out, as did the other two. They went downstairs and into the main room again where the large man was waiting.

"Good time?" he asked, grinning.

It wasn't directed at her. One of the men, Lilly thought he was the second one to have sex with her, although she had no idea by this point, replied, "Yeah, she'll do."

"For what?" asked Lilly, panicking.

"Never mind for the minute, you'll find out soon enough."

"Where's my brother?" she asked, worried for him. Despite her own problems, her concern for him was growing. It had been at least an hour since she last saw him.

"He's running an errand. Don't worry, he'll be fine."

She didn't believe him.

"Please don't hurt him," she said.

"He does as he's told he'll be home this evening." Lilly was told to sit down, which she did. They put on the television and handed her the remote.

"Watch what you want," the large man said in an almost friendly tone.

She could feel the tears drying on her face and was just beginning to get the feeling back in her body, but that only made it worse. She could now feel the pain. She was sore like she couldn't imagine, and she had stomach pains, like a really bad period.

"Where's Jordan?" she asked.

No one replied. Two of the men glanced at her but didn't say anything. The large man left the room, going through the door that she had seen Harry go through earlier, leaving her with the three men. She started shaking. Surely, they weren't going to force her again. When the large man walked back in, he was accompanied by a woman in her mid-forties and a man in a leather jacket and jeans. The woman was very smart but looked weathered. Lilly noticed the length of her skirt was a little too short and her blouse was unbuttoned to the point where her bra could just about be seen. In Lilly's eyes she was dressed far too young for her age.

"Have you tried her?" the woman asked.

"Yeah, we all gave her a go," said one. He laughed whilst the others joined in.

"Stop that," the woman scolded them, and they immediately stopped laughing. "This poor girl has been through an ordeal." She turned to Lilly and asked, "Yes?" Lilly nodded. "Yes, I thought so, and what is your name, child?" She spoke with compassion.

Lilly wanted to trust her; she needed to trust someone after all she had been through.

"Lilly." She looked up at her face and had a feeling the woman was not there to help her. She was certainly not about to trust her just yet.

"Lilly," she replied. "A beautiful name." She smiled, and Lilly tried to smile back. "Come, come with us," she said, putting out her hand for her to hold. Lilly didn't move.

"Where are we going?" she asked.

"Away from here."

Lilly was getting more and more suspicious of her. "But where?" she asked again.

The woman didn't respond but looked to the man she had come in with and indicated towards Lilly with a nod of the head. Without saying anything the man grabbed her by the arm, dragged her to her feet and marched her out of the room.

"Where are we going?" Lilly was getting frantic. "Please, let me go, where are we going?" she cried out.

"Shut up, bitch, just go with them," the large man called after her.

The woman handed him a roll of banknotes. "Thank you, we'll be in touch."

She followed Lilly and the man out into the back yard and into the alley where a new-looking Ford Transit van was parked, one of the larger ones with a raised roof. Standing by the door was another eastern European man, also wearing a leather jacket. As they approached, he opened the back doors. In the back was a mattress on which were four other girls. Lilly guessed they were all around her age. They all looked terrified.

"Get in," said the man. "We haven't got all day."

"Where are we going?" Lilly asked again, though by now she knew not to expect an answer.

The man holding her slapped her hard across the face. "Just get in," he said.

She climbed into the back of the van. Two of the girls moved to give her a little more space. And with that, the doors closed, plunging the inside of the van into darkness.

Lilly could hear the men and the woman talking outside. She didn't know what the language was, but she did know it wasn't English. She couldn't see a thing; her eyes wouldn't adjust, and it was pitch black. She knocked on the side.

"Please, let me go!" she cried out.

Knock, knock, knock.

"Please!"

The doors burst open.

The man who had slapped her grabbed her arm and slapped her hard again.

"Quiet. No more noise." He pushed her hard, so she fell backwards, partially landing on one of the other girls. The doors slammed shut again. Lilly sat up. Her face throbbed and she was still sore and in pain.

Moments later she heard the doors at the front of the van slam shut. The engine fired up and the van pulled away.

Lilly couldn't see well but could just about make out the other girls. They looked at her and she tried to smile back. After what seemed like an eternity the van stopped again. With the side of her face still throbbing she was not about to make any noise. A few minutes passed and the back doors flew open again.

"In you get."

It was another girl. This girl looked eastern European. She climbed in the back and sat next to Lilly. Again, the doors closed and moments later they moved off.

The van drove on. Lilly had lost all track of time, but she knew that if she didn't use the toilet soon, she was going to have an accident. Finally, the van stopped, and the back opened. "Everyone out."

The six of them shuffled out and stood at the roadside.

"This way," the man spoke.

Lilly knew not to question anything. They followed him to a very run-down-looking property on a housing estate that had clearly seen better days. Lilly had no idea where they were, but she was sure she could smell the sea.

The other man and the woman from the house followed them in. The house smelt of sweat and cigarettes. To the left of the hallway was a lounge area, the floor of which was covered in stained mattresses with a few blankets strewn around. In the room were a couple of men. They looked frightened.

"Upstairs," The man said, now behind them. The girls walked up the stairs, where Lilly could see a filthy-looking bathroom through the open door. The door was supposed to have frosted glass in the top half, but it was broken with only part of it still in place, meaning anyone could see in.

There were three other rooms, all of which had mattresses on the floor.

"Find yourself a space," the woman said.

"Where should we—" One of the girls from the van started to speak but before she could finish the woman interrupted.

"Anywhere, we really don't care. If anyone needs the toilet it's there." She indicated the bathroom with the broken window. "Make yourselves at home. I don't expect you to be here for too long. Oh, and keep the noise down, there's a number of men sleeping downstairs who I'm sure would like to keep you quiet." She smiled before she and the men headed downstairs.

Lilly and the girls stood in the corridor looking around. Finally, one of them walked into one of the rooms and sat on one of the mattresses. Lilly and the others followed her. They still didn't know each other, yet being in the van had somehow formed a bond between them and they stuck together. How funny humans were.

CHAPTER 12

It was 6:15 and Zuzanna knew she was going to have to leave for De Wallen. She was in jeans, a tee shirt and an old sweatshirt and was sitting on the bed counting down the minutes. Her mother had offered to make her something to eat but she couldn't face it. Michalina was nowhere to be seen. God knows where she was. Zuzanna didn't know whether to feel anger or fear of what might be happening to her. She guessed whatever was happening it wouldn't be good, so she had to do what she could to help. But this, she couldn't, could she? Have sex with anyone who was willing to pay? How did she get here? She shook her head and looked up at the walls of her room. It was just the same as always. Somehow, she expected everything to look different; it certainly felt different.

She grabbed her shoulder bag, which still held the Vaseline, and walked slowly downstairs. She looked into the lounge where her father, always loving but with some real problems that affected his moods, was watching television, which now seemed to be his life. He looked up and smiled before looking back.

"Zuzanna, you going out?" her mother asked, clearly surprised. Going out was something she never did. Michalina, yes, all the time, but not her.

"Yes, Mama, don't wait up."

"Where are you going?" asked her mother.

"Just out, I'm meeting some friends from the coffee shop."

"That's good," her mother replied. "I worry about you never going out. You need to go and spend time with people your own age."

If only she knew, thought Zuzanna. *If only she knew.*

As she opened the front door Szymon appeared in the hall. "Where are you going?"

"Nothing to do with you," she replied scornfully. She was not in the mood for questions.

"I was going out. Who's going to help Mama with Tata tonight?"

Zuzanna was the one who always helped her mother with preparing food for her father and dressed him for bed before tidying up ready for the next day. She turned back towards Szymon suddenly and unexpectedly, resenting that she was the one to do all the helping.

"Listen, you spoiled little child, you are going to help Mama, understand?" She could feel the anger rising in her.

"That's not fair. I was going to go out with friends—"

Before he could finish Zuzanna slapped him around the face.

"You think the world revolves around you? Well it doesn't." Zuzanna was fuming. *How dare he?* she thought. "You need to start taking some responsibility and start helping around here. We're all busy and we've all got problems, now get in there and help Mama."

She indicated towards the lounge where their mother and father were seated.

"Yes, Zuzanna, sorry." Szymon was shocked. His eyes welled up, but he fought the urge to cry. He held his hand up to his face where she had slapped him and walked slowly into the room. Zuzanna walked out the front door into the cold night air. It couldn't have been much above four or five degrees. She pulled her coat collar up, so it partially covered her face, but it was more to hide from anyone watching than the cold.

As she walked, she thought about Michalina. She couldn't understand how she had become dependent on drugs. She had kind of guessed that she had smoked a bit of pot. This was Amsterdam, everyone did – well, everyone except her. At that moment she wished she did, anything that would make what she was going to have to do easier.

She remembered the look on Szymon's face when she slapped him and regretted it. It wasn't his fault, he was a young boy, still at college. What did she expect? He was probably wondering what was going on. She had never been violent towards him before, or anyone for that matter.

When she arrived at the portacabin the lights were off. The building site had clearly locked up hours ago and no one appeared to be present. She walked up to the door and tried the handle. Locked. What did she do now? Maybe they had changed their minds? They used her this afternoon, so maybe that was enough to satisfy them?

"Are you Zuzanna?" The voice came from behind her.

Her hope that the nightmare was over vanished in an instant. She turned around and saw a very made-up woman who Zuzanna thought must be about 25, although she had on so much makeup it was difficult to tell.

She was wearing a leopard-print faux fur coat that went down to just above her ankles, and red stiletto shoes. Zuzanna guessed she hadn't walked far in them.

"I've been told tonight is your first night?" She wasn't smiling. It was clear to her that this woman didn't want to engage in conversation, and she didn't want to talk to her either.

"Yes," Zuzanna replied, saying as little as she could.

"Come on, let's get you back to mine and we'll get you set up," she said and then started walking off without looking back.

Zuzanna took a few quick steps and caught her up. Just a couple of streets away they arrived at a small apartment building. The building was old looking and run down. She unlocked the external door and stepped in, leaving Zuzanna to catch the door, then follow. Entering the ground-floor apartment Zuzanna was surprised by how clean and tidy it was. Certainly not like the outside of the building.

Zuzanna followed the girl through the lounge area and into the bedroom. Again, she was surprised by how nice it was. It went against everything she had been expecting.

"Strip to your underwear and take a seat." Zuzanna didn't answer and saw that the only seat in the room was in front of a mirror on a dressing table. She slowly removed her coat and went to lay it on the bed.

"Please," the woman said, "hang it up, there's hooks on the back of the door."

The woman had already hung her coat up and put her shoes neatly together by the door. Without her coat on, Zuzanna could see she was already dressed for work. She wore stockings and suspenders, which hung from a revealing leather Basque, held at the front with leather laces. Her breasts, which were very large, sat on the top with her nipples on display. She wore a leather choker around her neck and leather bracelets on each wrist, which were all lined with metal studs that matched those on the Basque.

As requested, Zuzanna stripped down to her underwear. She felt very conscious of her appearance. Wearing little makeup, her hair straight with a simple style and very pale skin, she looked nothing like what she was expected to, and her underwear was simple and plain, the bra not even matching her panties. She folded her clothes and put them on the floor, not sure where she should put her things. The woman said nothing, just waited. Zuzanna took a seat in front of the mirror.

"Try not to worry, I know how nervous you are. We've all been there, believe me." For the first time since they met the woman came across as kind.

"What should I call you?" asked Zuzanna in response.

"Call me Charlotte," she replied. "Or Lotte, whichever you prefer."

"Is that your real name?" she asked.

"Yes, what did you think?" She sounded cross with her.

"Sorry," said Zuzanna, "I just—"

"Don't worry about it, just relax and we'll get you looking right. We're running out of time."

Her words reminded her why she was there and the sinking feeling in her stomach returned.

Charlotte's efforts to make her over were good. Zuzanna wondered if she had ever been a professional beautician or something similar; maybe she still was. When she finished, she had completely transformed Zuzanna's face and hair. Zuzanna actually thought she looked quite good, certainly she was very different without her plain makeup and hair. She would never have thought about doing anything like this normally but perhaps for a night out or similar, it could be something she might try.

"Now clothing," Charlotte said.

Zuzanna looked away from the mirror, to where Charlotte had opened a wardrobe door revealing a number of items hanging up, all of which looked as if they were fresh out of a sex shop. She had every type of material from leather to latex, to plastic, to rubber.

Zuzanna got up from the chair and went over to look in the wardrobe. There were more conventional items, pretty bras and knickers, lacy or flowered, some plain, some with revealing cut-out areas.

"How recognisable do you want to be?" she asked.

"Not at all," Zuzanna quickly replied.

"What are you prepared to do?"

"What do you mean?" she asked. She wasn't expecting Charlotte to ask but had guessed what she meant.

"Well, if you wear leather or rubber you wouldn't be very recognisable, but it would indicate you might be up for a bit of BDSM. If you wear plain cotton or lace it would mean you probably only do straightforward sex, but you'd be more easily recognised. Latex maybe both, maybe not. I can even give you a cut out, if you fancy anal?"

Zuzanna winced.

"Not anal then." Charlotte laughed.

"Just cover me as much as you can." Zuzanna felt deflated. All hope had been lost.

"Leave it to me, I'll hide you but not make you too kinky."

Charlotte selected her clothes and helped her dress. The red latex top had cap sleeves and a high neck but was cut out around her breasts, leaving her nipples exposed. The material clung to her body and emphasised her physique. It stopped just below her midriff, leaving a gap before her matching knickers.

"I don't think I can stand with my breasts out," said Zuzanna, looking at herself in the full-length mirror.

"It's like this," said Charlotte. "You need to see customers, the quicker you get to see the customers the quicker you pay off the debt. It's not nice but that's what it is."

"I know, I know, I just don't think I can look like this." She could feel tears beginning to well up in her eyes.

"Hey, don't cry, please don't cry, you'll ruin your makeup." Charlotte smiled, trying to cheer her up and it did for a moment. But then Zuzanna looked at herself again. "I know it's hard and this is your first night so it's going to be really difficult. Honestly it gets better, I promise. You look really sexy so boys will want you. You can let in the ones you want only, just make sure you're not too choosy, you do need to see some of them." Zuzanna nodded. "So, we're staying with the top?" Zuzanna smiled nervously. Charlotte opened a drawer and pulled out a pair of red lace hold-up stockings. "Here, put these on."

Zuzanna did as she was told, taking them off her. She was pleased to see that they were brand new, still in their packaging.

"Good, right, let's talk you through things. First, make it clear what you're prepared to do, okay?" She looked at Zuzanna, who nodded back. "They will knock on the glass and ask how much. Make sure you get them to agree to the money and what they are paying for. You only need to do what you agree to do, but remember you can make more for oral or anal but only do what you want. Any trouble, you hit the panic button and shout out, understand?" Again, Zuzanna nodded. "Do you use contraception?"

"What? No, no I don't," Zuzanna replied. She surprised herself that she hadn't even thought of it with so much going on in her head.

"Hey, come on," said Charlotte. "You need to think, keep your wits about you. Look, the room will have condoms available, make sure they use them. No condom, no sex. Some will want without. For them, definitely no sex but it's up to you with other things. You can get more for no condom, especially for oral."

Charlotte made it sound so easy, but Zuzanna felt herself gagging already.

"How much do I charge?" she asked, not sure she wanted to hear the answer.

"Right," Charlotte said, and began to explain. "Sebastian will see us at the window, and he will set the price. Generally starting prices are about fifty euros for twenty minutes: that's why it's important to finish them off as quickly as you can, then they can get out and you can rest before the next. The first hundred euros pays for the window, so you don't start earning straight away. Look for the sober young boys and play up to them. They're always horny but only last a couple of minutes. I tend to avoid middle-aged drunks; they go on forever and are the ones more likely to get violent. Okay?" Zuzanna nodded. "Okay, let's get you some heels and we need to get going."

Charlotte opened the wardrobe again and selected a pair of red stilettos. They were not as high as Charlotte's – only four inches or so – and she was grateful for that.

"These shouldn't be too difficult to walk in," she said, handing them over.

"Could I wear my trainers until we get there and put them on later?" she asked.

Charlotte smiled.

"Yes, of course," she said. "Here, let me." She took the shoes back and put them in her shoulder bag. Charlotte put her coat back on and Zuzanna followed her lead. Charlotte looked at her appraisingly.

"No, that's not going to work." Zuzanna looked down and realised her coat was nowhere near long enough. Charlotte grabbed another from the back of the door and handed it to her. "This will be better." This one was full length and warm, with a fur collar.

"Come on," said Charlotte. "Let's get it over with."

They made the journey to the De Wallen district in silence. Not because it was awkward but because there was nothing more to say. Thirty minutes later they arrived. The narrow alleyways were all lit – mostly by the shop fronts, which produced a red glow. There were already groups of young people wandering around, many drunk despite it not yet being 8:00pm. Zuzanna made a mental note of the advice from Charlotte about drunk men. There was a group of girls who appeared to be on a hen night. They all wore sashes saying things like 'Mother of the Bride', 'Bride's Best Friend' and 'Maid of Honour'. They also looked slightly worse for wear. Some of them appeared to be more scantily dressed than she was. At least she was wearing a coat, they must be freezing. In a strange way it made her situation more manageable.

The girls in the windows watched them as they walked past. Many of them had a vacant look. A few of them smiled. Zuzanna had the impression they knew Charlotte and therefore knew the situation she was in. They were all various levels of scantily clad and between them every type of sexual fetish was covered.

Zuzanna saw Sebastian standing outside one of the buildings.

"Zuzanna, you look fantastic," he said, grinning at her. "Ready to earn some money." He laughed. Zuzanna glanced at Charlotte who

SOMEBODY'S SISTER

was scowling at him. "You can get to work, Charlotte." He indicated towards the empty doorway on one side of the alley.

Charlotte didn't answer but walked to the door and let herself in. It wasn't locked but as soon as she got in, Zuzanna heard the click that meant it was now. Charlotte pulled the curtain across and disappeared from view.

"So, this is your room," Sebastian said as he indicated the door next to Charlotte's. "You will find everything you need in there; I will be waiting to see you. Don't be long!" he said with menace in his voice. "We'll keep an eye on you tonight to make sure you're okay." He laughed again.

The hatred she felt was almost overwhelming. He obviously noticed.

"Remember to smile, you need customers."

She went in, closed the door and pulled the curtain across.

Inside, the room was sparse. There was a bed covered in a red sheet. It looked clean but knowing what happened in the room it was probably dirty. The floor was tiled with a black and white chequered pattern and the walls were decorated in flock wallpaper that somehow didn't go with the rest of the room. On the opposite side to the bed was an old sideboard. It was quite elaborate with carvings on the corners. It had two small drawers and two larger doors below what looked like a marble top. She looked in the drawers. One was filled with condoms and another with Vaseline. She realised she'd left the pot Sebastian threw at her back at Charlotte's apartment. There were also tissues and surface wipes. She then looked in the cupboard underneath, where she found clean sheets and all manner of sex instruments – cuffs, whips, paddles, feathers, ties. She quickly closed the doors. *I won't be needing any of that*, she thought. At the back of the room was a door. She looked in to see a toilet and basin. There was soap and towels and behind the door was a coat hook. She took off the coat Charlotte had lent her and hung it up. She looked in the mirror. How could she do this?

She went back into the main room and looked around again. She saw that there were two light switches. She turned off the main light and switched on the other. The room was immediately illuminated with a red glow. She quickly turned it off again then sat on the edge of the bed. Suddenly there was a knock on the door.

"Problems?" It was Sebastian.

"No, just a moment," she replied.

She couldn't do it. Her emotions were all over the place: anger, fear, distress. Her breathing was becoming erratic, and her heart was racing, she was beginning to hyperventilate.

"Hurry, the room needs paying for and waiting around you're making the debt larger, not smaller." Zuzanna took a deep breath as she tried to control her breathing and stood up, flicking on the red light. She then pulled back the curtain and stood in the doorway. Sebastian looked at her and then turned away, disappearing from her view. But she knew he was still outside, watching.

Groups of men and women wandered past. She knew that photography in the De Wallen was forbidden so thought she was reasonably safe, but she could see that some had cameras, which made her uneasy. She glanced up and down the alleyway and could see the girls in the other rooms standing in the doorways. Some were moving seductively from side to side, gently stroking their own bodies whilst others stood completely still. Some of them were pouting at groups nearby. She saw a man reach for the camera around his neck and the girl in the room opposite grabbed the curtain, pulling it across herself, hiding her body. She stuck her fingers up towards the man. "Fuck off," she mouthed. He put his camera down and she lowered the curtain.

In the corner of her eye, she saw a group of men who looked quite young. They were speaking English and were egging one on.

"Go on mate, you can do it."

She watched as one walked towards the room next to hers where Charlotte had entered earlier. From inside her room she could no longer see Charlotte's door, but guessed he had gone inside.

"Yeah, go on," one of them shouted. "Give her one for us."

They all cheered. They hung around for a couple of minutes before walking off. A few minutes later, she saw the boy half running after them. He was pulling on his coat. She guessed Charlotte had dealt with his needs.

As she stood in the doorway, she saw groups of men and men on their own come and go. She also saw couples and groups of girls. These would stop and look but there was a definite distinction about the way the men took an interest. She watched the men entering and leaving Charlotte's room as well as the girls opposite.

Zuzanna had stood there for over an hour, and no one had shown her any interest, not that she wanted it, but she knew she had to do something. Then Sebastian appeared. He stood in front of her and called, "Open up."

She unlocked the door, and he pushed her back in the room and closed the curtain.

"What is your fucking problem?" he said to her, his voice full of venom. She thought he was going to hit her, so she stepped back. "Listen to me, we're not fucking around, either you start making some money or your sister has the shit kicked out of her and we show your parents the video of you and Lucas, not to mention the beating you'll get as well. Now fucking start performing and start fucking them before we fuck you. Got it?"

Zuzanna was shaking. He didn't wait for a response and turned to walk out. He pulled the curtain back and opened the door.

"You've got twenty minutes to fuck your first client, or I'll be back to fuck you up and then you'll owe me for the room." He stepped out and slammed the door behind him.

Zuzanna watched the girls, trying to figure out what they were doing that she wasn't. She watched as the girl opposite, a beautiful black girl with a shaved head, smiled at the small group of men in front of her, seductively moving her body from side to side. To Zuzanna it looked like she was doing a kind of erotic dance. The men moved off but one of them stayed and continued to look. She put her hands on her hips and looking directly at him, she pouted. Leaning forward slightly, she slid her hands up her body towards her breasts before stopping slightly short and bringing them back down. The man stepped forward and they exchanged words that Zuzanna couldn't hear. She opened her door, and he stepped inside. The curtains closed behind him.

Okay, she thought to herself, *I can do this*. Moments later a group of very drunk men staggered in front of her. They stood making rude gestures and in Dutch asked her how much. She sneered at them, remembering what Charlotte had said about being too drunk. As they moved off, a balding, grey-haired, older man, aged at least seventy, stepped forward and knocked on the door. Zuzanna closed her eyes briefly, hoping he would be gone when she opened them. But he was still there looking hopeful. That was when she saw Sebastian standing on the other side of the alleyway staring at him. Realising she had no choice she opened the door. The old man asked for a price. The minimum to accept was fifty euros for twenty minutes but there was no way she was going to do anything with this man for as little as that.

"One hundred for twenty minutes," she said, still with the door open, half expecting him to walk off. She smiled at him, remembering what she had seen the other girl do. She put her hands on her waist and pushed her breasts out towards him. *At least it will look like I'm trying*, she thought.

The old man stared at her breasts for a moment and then looking her in the eye he reached into his pocket and pulled out his wallet. He handed her two new-looking fifty-euro notes. She stepped back and let the old man come inside. As she closed the curtain, she caught a glimpse of Sebastian grinning at her.

Turning back into the room, she saw the old man was already removing his trousers. She got the impression he was not new to this. She went to the drawer, pulled out a condom and handed it to the man.

"Please, could you do it?" he asked.

He sounded so polite, so she nodded and undid the packet. She looked down to his penis which was only half erect. She paused, looking at it and then at the condom in her hand.

"Please?" he asked again. It was almost as if he was pleading. She felt sick; it took all her concentration not to heave. Taking another deep breath, she reached between his legs and rubbed him gently to a full erection. Then she placed the condom on him.

"Would you like to get on the bed?" she asked, not really knowing what to do next.

"Can I lie with you on top of me?" he asked. "It's easier for me than having to support myself on top," he added.

She nodded and he lay down on the bed. He was face up and was looking directly at her. She looked at him and thought about what she was about to do. The feeling of nausea returned. Closing her eyes for a moment, she then went to climb on him.

She suddenly stopped and stood back up.

"What's the matter?" he asked.

"Nothing, nothing. I shan't be a moment." She opened the other drawer and grabbed the pot of Vaseline, disappearing into the toilet. She put a large handful of the lubricant into herself and went back out. The man was seated on the side of the bed; his erection was almost gone.

"Sorry," she said. "Shall we start again?"

She took his hands and got him to stand again so she could more easily pull his penis back to an erection. She then let him lay down, climbed on top of him and, pushing the crotch of her knickers to one side, she guided him into her. As she did, she felt a tear roll down her cheek. She reached up and wiped it away. The man had fortunately closed his eyes so didn't see.

Within a couple of minutes, she felt him tense and sensed he had finished. She was relieved it was ending. She stopped moving and he let go of where his hands were on her breasts. He opened his eyes and looked at her and then looked away. He began to cry.

"Are you okay?" she asked.

He sat up and pulled off the condom. She noticed a bin in the corner of the room and held it out for him to drop the condom into it. He was gently sobbing, tears rolling down his cheeks.

"Here," she said, handing him some tissues. She was confused. Why was he crying? She should be crying. Instead, she found herself acting like his carer.

He took them gratefully. "Thank you," he said. "Please, can I see you again?" he asked.

"What do you mean?" She was confused. Did he think this was some sort of date they just had? He had paid one hundred euros for a couple of minutes of paid sex.

"You're the first person I've had sex with since my wife died of cancer two years ago," he said.

Shit, she thought. *What am I supposed to say to that?* Her head was spinning. She was disgusted by what she had done and yet she felt an overwhelming pity for this sad, lonely old man.

"Okay, I guess so. If you see me here." Although he was an old man, at least he was quick, and he was polite.

"Thank you."

He dressed and as he was about to go, he pulled out his wallet again and handed her another fifty-euro note.

"But you've already paid," she said.

"I know, but this is for you." He obviously knew how it worked with Sebastian taking her money. As she pulled the curtain back and unlocked the door, he said, "Thank you," once more.

She smiled back at him and closed the door, locking it again before closing the curtain. Then she sat on the bed and cried.

After a few minutes, she pulled herself together. She stepped into the bathroom and washed her face. Her makeup was smudged. She looked in the pockets of Charlotte's coat and found lipstick. It was nearly the same colour so she grabbed a tissue and wiped away as much of the old lipstick as she could, and then reapplied the new one. Using one finger she tried to spread the remaining eyeshadow on her eyelids so it looked as acceptable as she could make it. *That will have to do*, she thought.

She went back into the main room and pulled back the curtain. She looked out onto the alley. It was now full of people, who were all looking at the girls and more importantly, looking at her. Within seconds of her opening the curtain, a young man, who she guessed was in his early twenties, knocked on the door.

"How much?" he called out.

Zuzanna wasn't expecting that. A number of those in the alley stopped and looked. She glanced up and down. In some ways having everyone look made it worse.

She mouthed, "One hundred for twenty minutes."

She knew that was a lot, but the old man had paid it, so why not him?

"I've got seventy," he called back. Some of the people in the alley had begun to laugh, waiting to see what she was going to do. She opened the door.

"Okay, quickly." She almost pulled him into the room and closed the door and the curtain. She held out her hand and he put the notes into it. "Take your trousers off and get on the bed," she commanded.

She didn't know why but she found herself being quite dominant towards him. Maybe it was disgust because this young man was paying for sex. She went to the drawer again and handed him a condom.

"Put this on."

The boy did as he was told and as opposed to the old man, getting erect was clearly not an issue for him. She went to the bathroom and reapplied Vaseline before returning to the room and climbing on top of him. He came almost immediately.

Charlotte was right. The sober ones were fast. She got off him. He seemed embarrassed.

"Can I just stay a moment, please?" he asked.

She guessed he had friends who would laugh if he came out too quickly.

"If you wish," she said, remaining as stern as she could.

He sat without talking until his twenty minutes were up and then eventually said, "Thank you," as he got up to leave. As he walked out onto the alley, she heard a cheer go up. She guessed it was his friends.

That was two, and it wasn't even 10:00pm. How many more was she expected to have sex with? She shook her head as she thought of the hours to come.

She continued until it was about 2:00am, when the last man left. Over the course of the evening, she had had sex with no less than eleven men. All different ages and types. Old and young. Fortunately, only one or two came across as quite aggressive but even they were okay. A couple had offered more money for oral sex, but she was not prepared to do that, and they seemed to accept it. She sat carefully on the bed, tears in her eyes. She was exhausted, embarrassed, disgusted with herself and angry. She knew this was going to happen again and again and she didn't know if she could do it, but then she knew she had to.

At 3:00am Charlotte appeared at her door. She had her coat on. "Come on, Zuzanna, time to go."

Zuzanna went and got her coat and put it over herself.

"You've done well," said Charlotte. "It will get easier, I promise," she said.

Zuzanna hoped so, because it didn't feel easy at the moment. In fact, it felt like the worst possible nightmare anyone could be in.

As they went to step out of the room an elderly lady was waiting to go in.

"Cleaner," said Charlotte.

Suddenly there was another overwhelming feeling of disgust and embarrassment that came over her. Zuzanna could only think of the dirty tissues and full condoms that the cleaning lady would find. Evidence of what she had done. The woman went in, closed the curtain and switched on the main light.

Zuzanna and Charlotte started to make their way back to Charlotte's, where Zuzanna had left her belongings.

"Wait," came a call from behind them. Zuzanna immediately tensed. Sebastian. "Zuzanna, you had a good evening. Now you need to pay." He grinned at her.

"Come on, Sebastian, you could wait until later, we're both tired," said Charlotte.

"No time like the present." His grin seemed to grow.

Zuzanna reached into her pocket and pulled out the money. She hadn't even counted it; she hadn't had time, and she had no idea how much was there. She knew that the minimum she had asked was fifty but that was less than most. She went to count it, but Sebastian snatched it from her hand.

"I'm sure this will go some way towards things." He smiled.

"You bastard." Zuzanna was fuming. She guessed that he knew she would have been given extra cash from some of the men and now he had taken that as well. She had no idea how much money she had raised.

"Now be nice or I might forget to count all this, and you'll have to do some overtime."

"Come on," said Charlotte, trying to pull Zuzanna away.

"Yes, hurry along, Zuzanna, go with Charlotte, you've got an early start tomorrow. See you back here at seven," he sneered.

CHAPTER 13

Michalina had been in the apartment for two days. She was restless but at least she wasn't having to find money for drugs – that was something that came in a regular steady supply. The young girl 'Milou', who had been taken out the day she arrived, had since returned. When she got back, she was black and blue. It was obvious that someone had assaulted her. Michalina couldn't understand it. They said she was going on a date, but she had come back in a dreadful state. It looked as though every step was painful. Her jaw was so badly swollen she couldn't speak, and she struggled to eat.

When they came to give Michalina some 'H' to smoke, they would periodically come and inject Milou, which seemed to calm her and take her mind off the pain. The other girls kept themselves to themselves, as instructed, but Michalina had taken it on herself to try and help her. The only time they had been allowed to leave the room was to use the toilet and wash, although the facilities were hardly what you would call inviting. There was often a queue, and she would find herself standing in line with a group of men. They were a combination of drug users, alcoholics and the homeless, who all seemed to be looking for something. Whatever this was seemed to be provided. Michalina guessed there would be payback for them at some point, but she didn't care. Zuzanna was going to pay her debt as soon as she got the bank to loan her the money and she had what she needed – a roof, food and most importantly 'H.' she knew it was the devil, but it also felt so good. She guessed others were in a similar position to her.

Michalina had just covered Milou with a blanket and was watching her fall asleep when Thomas entered the room.

"Ladies, good news," he announced. "We have gainful employment for you." He was smiling. "Please follow me." Michalina went to wake Milou, but he stopped her. "No, not Milou, she's too young, and Tess, you can stay as well." He indicated to another young girl who was sitting at the back of the room. Michalina had not really noticed her before. She looked young, maybe 16 or 17. Tess looked over but said nothing. Milou was still sleeping. Michalina got up so as not to wake her and followed Thomas out of the room with the other girls. The skeletal girl struggled to walk. She looked really unwell.

They followed Thomas down the fire escape at the rear of the property where there were two waiting minibuses at the bottom. One was already full of men and the other contained at least six girls aged between 18 and 30.

"In you get," Thomas said.

Michalina and the others climbed in and found seats. No one said anything but they all looked at each other.

Thomas closed the door and the minibus pulled away in a convoy with the other.

"Where are we going?" one of the girls asked.

The driver said nothing, ignoring the question.

The minibus drove for over two hours. Some of the girls started to get restless and were saying they needed to find a toilet. Eventually they pulled into a service station and parked alongside the bus with the men. One at a time the girls were allowed out to use the facilities. A large man from the front of the men's bus stood by the door to the toilet. Michalina was sure he was there to make sure they didn't run off.

They all got back in the bus and before driving off the large man who had previously been standing outside the toilet, came to their bus with sandwiches and crisps for them. He handed the bag to a girl near the door and returned to the men's bus. Again, they drove off.

Michalina watched out of the window, trying to guess where they were headed, when she saw them cross the open border into Belgium. They continued on until they reached a small house in a village just outside of Brussels. They pulled up alongside the other bus in the driveway. The driver said nothing. Michalina watched as the men got out of their bus and were led into the house. After a few moments the large man opened the door to theirs. "This way, follow me," he ordered.

They filed out and followed him into the house. The men were standing, cramped, in the lounge area. She guessed there were at least twelve of them, maybe more. The man led the girls to a rear room that she guessed had been a sitting room or dining room at some point, but like the apartment building they had left was now just a room with mattresses on the floor.

"Take a seat," he said. They all filed in and sat down.

Some of the girls had started to speak to each other. They were whispering and some were speaking Dutch, but others, Michalina could not understand. She could just about make out that a couple were speaking English, but she didn't recognise the language of some of the others.

After an hour or so the large man returned to the room.

"Whose passports do we have?" he asked. Several of the girls put their hands up. "Excellent, and who has their passports with them?" Michalina and a couple of the other girls put their hands up. She had been told to bring the passport with her so she could be identified as eligible to work, not for travel. "Okay, I'll take those now," he said. It was not a request.

Michalina reached into her pocket and pulled out hers and handed it to the man.

"Polish," he said. "Thought you were Dutch."

"I've lived in Amsterdam since I was ten," she replied.

He put the passports into a brown envelope with what Michalina guessed were the men's.

"Who does that leave?" he asked. Two of the girls put their hands up. One of them was very young, maybe 14 years old, petite and blonde. The other was about 18 and had long, flowing but unkempt dark hair. She had a dark Mediterranean complexion.

"You two come with me," he said and then addressed the petite blonde girl. "We have some special clients who would love to see you." He smiled.

She didn't respond; she just followed him out of the room with the older girl.

Michalina lost track of time. She had been given a small amount of 'H' to smoke, which she knew was enough to keep her quiet and so far as she was concerned, that was all she needed at that time.

It was beginning to get dark. Two men appeared at the door. Michalina could tell they were eastern European. She was sure she had seen them getting off the other bus. They pointed to two of them. Both girls had been noticeably quiet and had stuck together closely. Michalina suspected they were related to each other; they were so similar in appearance.

"You and you, come with us." Michalina looked at the girls they had pointed to.

"What do you want?" one of them asked.

"Don't fucking argue, you fucking whores," the other man said.

Before the girl could say anything more, the two men came in, grabbed the girls, dragging them from the room.

"Let go, let us go!" she cried.

The men ignored her and then they were gone.

As they dragged them up the stairs, Michalina could still hear the same girl crying out, "Let go, please, let go, you're hurting me."

The sound softened as they moved further away until a door was slammed, and it went quiet.

Michalina looked around. The girls were all looking frightened; she guessed she looked the same. She was terrified. She had thought she was going to be taken to work in a factory or something, but now was beginning to doubt that.

CHAPTER 14

The car headed into the centre of Brussels, away from where their hotel was on the outskirts, and finally pulled into the car park of the Hotel Amigo. Anastasjia had heard of this place, having spoken with customers and business bosses from various top-end car dealerships who had stayed there. They usually couldn't wait to tell her how splendid it was.

Balodis led the two of them into the reception area and told them to take a seat. They sat opposite each other, no need to advertise they were getting on so well. She smiled at Uldis who smiled back. Balodis spoke briefly with the receptionist and then returned and sat next to her. She felt herself squirming.

"Mr. Daniels will be with us shortly," he said.

"Who is Mr. Daniels?" she asked.

"All in good time," he responded.

Balodis sat staring ahead in silence. Anastasjia thought he looked quite nervous. She wondered why he was there. If he was going to be where she was, why not accompany her on the entire journey instead of just turning up here? He was not looking at Uldis despite being almost immediately opposite him. Anastasjia caught Uldis's eye. Neither of them smiled. What was this all about? They had no idea.

After waiting in silence for what seemed like an eternity to Anastasjia, an immaculately dressed grey-haired man arrived. Balodis got up and turned towards him as he approached, putting his hand out to greet him.

"Balodis," he said.

"Mr. Daniels, a pleasure to see you again," he responded.

"Yes, we'll see," the man replied, clearly not impressed by Balodis. He then turned to Anastasjia. "You must be Anastasjia." He held his hand out and she met it with hers. He leant forward and brought the back of her hand to his lips, brushing them gently. "An honour," he said.

Weighing up the situation as quickly as she could, she noticed that Balodis was fearful of this man. She had never met him before but knew to play the game.

"Please," said Anastasjia, "call me Ana."

"Yes, Ana, of course, and you she must call me Oliver," he said, smiling.

"Oliver," said Anastasjia. "This is Uldis."

"A pleasure," said Daniels as he shook his hand. "You must be starving?" he said to them. "All that travelling."

Anastasjia smiled in response.

"Good, I've booked us a table in the rooftop restaurant. I tend to find that in the cold weather it is not used as much as at other times and yet with the heaters it is very pleasant, is everyone okay with that?"

Anastasjia got the impression he was used to getting his own way and that the question was more rhetorical than it sounded. As they made their way to the restaurant, Anastasjia had an opportunity to get a better look at Oliver Daniels.

He was classically handsome, his grey hair making him particularly good looking, and with a great physique for a man who was probably in his fifties. His English was impeccable with not a hint of an accent.

At the table, Daniels held the chair for Anastasjia and once she had taken her seat he sat on her left. Balodis sat opposite her, and Uldis took the seat to Anastasjia's right.

"It's my intention to have a steak, medium rare, which from experience is cooked to perfection. With that in mind I intend to order a bottle of red wine, probably from southern Italy, certainly very dark. You are welcome to try it but, please, have whatever you want, it's all going on my account," said Daniels.

Anastasjia, Uldis and Balodis looked at the menu and placed their orders.

"Ana, a well-done steak is a cremation," joked Daniels.

Anastasjia laughed. "I know, I've been told that many times. I can't help it, it's just the way I like it," she responded.

"Then how you like it is how you should have it," he said. "Balodis tells me you've been with the company for some time," he said. Anastasjia still didn't know who this man was, but she guessed he was important, and she should answer his questions.

"Yes, a number of years. Are you with the company?" she asked.

"In a way. I'm part of the car group that supplies your garage with Aston Martins. I believe you know Jennings?" he asked. It was a knowing question.

"Yes," she said nervously.

The waiters arrived with their food. Nothing was said while it was served up. The bottle of red wine was opened, and a small measure poured for Daniels to try. He held the stem and swirled the glass, looking at the clarity, and then took a deep breath, sampling the bouquet. He then sipped the wine.

"Yes, excellent," he said confidently.

"Sir," replied the waiter, topping up his glass. "For the lady?"

"Please," replied Anastasjia. The waiter continued around the table, arriving last at Balodis. "Sir," he said.

Balodis didn't say anything; he just put his hand over the wine glass indicating he didn't wish to have any. Anastasjia was sure she caught a glimpse of annoyance from Daniels at this.

Daniels was right about the steak; it was cooked to perfection.

"Ana, what is it you think we do?" Daniels asked, continuing the conversation after the waiters had left them.

"Sell cars," she answered, knowing that she shouldn't let on how much she actually knew.

"Yes," he laughed, "we do, and I know enough to know you know more than that. I've heard good things about you."

"In that case, you know I know when the best time to keep my mouth shut is," she said, smiling at him.

"Yes, of course." He smiled back. "And what do you think Jennings' role in the business was?" he asked, looking her in the eye, presumably looking for a reaction. The honest answer was that she didn't know. What she did know, was that he was dead. The question unnerved her.

"He was a senior salesperson; he could arrange transactions and negotiate the best deal for you whilst ensuring we were able to sell cars at a profit." Anastasjia wondered where the conversation was going, whether he knew what had happened to Jennings and the fact that his killer was sitting to his left.

"Yes, that's exactly what he did, and can I ask if you know why you've been asked to bring that case to Brussels?" he asked.

Anastasjia paused before responding. She guessed it was something to do with money laundering; you don't deal in that amount of cash if you have something to hide. She decided that keeping her response simple was the best way to answer.

"Because Mr. Jennings refused," she replied. She glanced at Balodis, whose eyes had narrowed.

"Yes," Daniels laughed. "He did, didn't he?" He laughed again.

He looked at Balodis, who looked back. Balodis put his knife down and reached for his water. Almost in a single movement, Daniels reached for Balodis's steak knife, and spun so the blade pointed down. Then, to Anastasjia's horror, he rammed it full force into the back of Balodis's hand. It was so sharp the blade cut into the tablecloth, and she could hear the chink as it hit the reinforced glass tabletop. Balodis didn't scream, but visibly tensed in pain as blood began to flow from the wound. She glanced at Uldis, whose stare was transfixed on Daniels. Uldis said nothing but stared, open mouthed, not quite believing what he had seen. Anastasjia could feel her heart racing. She tried to stay as calm as possible but her legs were shaking under the table. She put her hands down to try and steady them. Who was this man who was so in control of Balodis?

Then, Daniels pulled out the knife and wiped the blade on his napkin. He raised his hand for the waiter who appeared almost instantly.

"Mr. Balodis has had an accident," he said calmly. "Please get him cleaned up and bring him back when ready."

"Yes of course, sir," the waiter said as he placed a hand on Balodis's shoulder. With his other hand he grabbed Balodis's napkin and handed it to him to wrap around his hand. Balodis glanced at Anastasjia; he looked furious. She guessed it was made worse for him to be subservient to Daniels in front of her. Balodis stood and walked away with the waiter.

"Balodis thinks he's important," Daniels said after he was out of sight. "The fact is, he is monumentally fucking stupid and has caused us too many problems over the years. I'm sure I don't need to tell you about his sexual history." He looked at Anastasjia knowingly. "That has caused us many issues and a lot of money, not to mention his heavy-handed incompetence."

He returned to his steak, cutting another piece using the knife he had just stabbed Balodis with, and put it in his mouth. He paused to finish chewing before continuing.

"We will of course compensate Jennings' wife; I know he was a weasel, but he did a job for us. Not wanting to transport the money was not an issue to kill someone for. Jennings honestly thought he was just a car salesman. He would have known it was only a small part of what we do, but he knew better than to tell anyone about the business workings of the organisation." Daniels cut himself another piece of steak. "Hurry up, you two, don't let it get cold," he said.

Anastasjia and Uldis continued to eat.

"Why do you think we needed you to bring a case of cash to Brussels?" he said.

Anastasjia looked at Daniels. "I'm only guessing, but I would think to pay for things that you can't get away without using bank accounts for." She didn't want to say too much as she was unsure of his intentions.

"Balodis was right about one thing," he remarked. "You are very clever as well as beautiful."

"Thank you," she replied.

"Indeed, we use the money to pay for rentals, housing, goods and services where we can, and to provide drugs to those workers who need it. Purely medicinal, of course." He smiled.

"Of course," she replied.

"Next question," he said, as he took another sip of wine. "Where do you think the cash comes from?" It was another knowing question.

"I'm sure I don't know," she replied.

"Good answer, but I think we both know that's not true." He put down his knife and fork and rested his elbows on the table, putting his hands together under his chin. He paused for a moment and then separated his hands. "I like you, Ana, and I'm usually a pretty good judge of character." She looked at him and at Uldis and then back to Daniels. She was hoping for a glint of support from Uldis, however he sat motionless and expressionless.

"Okay, thank you," she said.

"How about, we all meet up in my suite tomorrow?" he said. "It's a beautiful room with views of the Grand Palace, and we can have a business discussion. I would love your input, Uldis. How about it?"

Anastasjia looked at Uldis, who nodded towards her. "That would be wonderful, we'll look forward to it," she said.

"Okay, now finish up your steak and wine and when you're ready I'll get you a cab back to your hotel. Please don't rush, but I've got to go." He stood up to leave. Uldis and Anastasjia both went to stand but he waved a hand to say they shouldn't. "No, please, stay and finish. I'll see you tomorrow, have a good evening." He smiled and took Anastasjia's hand again, gently kissing the back of it before letting go and waving towards Uldis. "Tomorrow," he said as he walked away.

They sat in stunned silence whilst they finished their meals and drank the last of the wine.

Anastasjia looked at Uldis. He was staring at his empty plate, not looking up or saying anything. She wondered what he was thinking. She was sure he wasn't expecting to be involved in such activities as outlined by Daniels. She found herself feeling sorry for him.

She put her knife and fork together on her plate and as she did, the waiter who had taken Balodis approached them.

"Your taxi, sir, madam." Neither she nor Uldis had asked for a taxi, so she guessed it was Daniels.

"Thank you," she replied as the waiter took the back of her chair to help her up.

He showed them the way out of the restaurant, and they headed down to reception. Walking out into street level, they saw the executive limo waiting to take them back to the hotel. The driver opened the back doors for them and Anastasjia climbed in, shuffling over to let Uldis in beside her. Within moments they were driving back.

The limousine pulled up outside the hotel doors and the driver jumped out, opening the rear door to let them out. They thanked him and he offered to pick them up at 1:00pm the next day and drive them to Mr. Daniels' hotel. They gratefully thanked him and said they would be in reception for 1:00pm. Not having to rush due to Balodis and his threats felt great. He was clearly scared of Daniels and Anastasjia guessed he wouldn't trouble them again.

They made their way to the lift and called it in the same way they had on arriving earlier, but this time with less pressure. The lift arrived and an elderly couple walked out of the opening doors, leaving it empty. Uldis pressed the buttons for floor one and two and stepped back as the door closed. They both looked at the back of the door.

"We need to talk," Anastasjia said, breaking the silence as the doors opened on the first floor.

"Half an hour?"

"Half an hour," replied Anastasjia as she stepped into the corridor.

The door began to close. Before it closed completely, Uldis stepped in the way. "Your room?" he asked. She smiled at him.

"Of course," she replied. He stepped back, allowing the door to close and again he disappeared from view.

Anastasjia went into her room. Her bag was still on the bed from earlier, no time to unpack or get sorted. She looked around the room and noticed a dresser on which was note paper and a pen with the hotel insignia. Moving the pen and paper to one end, she then removed the suitcase from the bed and placed it on top of the dresser in the space she had created. She thought about Uldis. She really liked him. If she was honest with herself, she expected he would let her down, men always did, but with him it felt different; she was hopeful he wouldn't be like the other men. She wasn't counting on it, but she was prepared to find out.

She went to have a shower and within minutes the hot water was washing over her. It felt great to just relax after the travelling and the meeting. She wondered about Balodis, and how Daniels had such a hold over him. Most people were terrified of him, but Daniels couldn't be less concerned. And to stab him in the hand like that, ruthless!

She stepped out of the shower and dried her hair. She looked at herself in the mirror. Even though it might feel big headed, she knew she was beautiful. Even with no makeup she knew she was stunning. She wrapped the towel around her body and stepped into the room. She decided the best bet was to wait in the towel for Uldis.

Moments later there was a knock at the door. She turned the lock to open the door, smiling at the fact that Uldis had spared no time in coming to see her, but it burst open and instead Balodis stormed in, rage on his face. He grabbed her throat with his bandaged hand and squeezed. It hurt and she was choking.

"Fucking whore," he shouted at her. "Who the fuck do you think you are?" he asked.

"I don't, I don't—" She was struggling to speak.

She reached up to grab his arm with both hands. With the hand not on her throat he grabbed the front of the towel, twisting it, so it tightened around her body. She still couldn't breathe. She was becoming more panicked. She stumbled backwards onto the bed.

Before she knew what was happening Balodis reached for his fly and undid the zipper.

"I'll fucking teach you," he said, his face raging.

Anastasjia pushed herself back on the bed, but he grabbed her by the ankles and in a swift single action dragged her back towards him. She tried to fight but he slapped her across the face. The towel she was wearing was still somehow clinging on to her top half but her body from the waist down was exposed. Balodis was clearly getting aroused by the violence. She had heard the stories. Most girls were only bruised; it was the cut ones who suffered the most. Many were disfigured for life. He undid his belt and pulled his trousers and underwear down to just below his balls, revealing his erection. He leaned over her and forced her legs apart, leaving her terrified and frozen. She knew what was about to happen and also knew there was nothing she could do to stop it. But for some reason, he flew off her suddenly, rolling off the bed and landing on the floor. He was gasping in pain. Then, as if out of nowhere, Uldis leapt onto the bed and over to where Balodis was lying on the floor.

He immediately tried to get up, but Uldis landed on his chest, winding him.

"You fuck," Balodis managed to gasp as Uldis knelt and punched him hard in the face, causing his head to hit the ground with a thud.

"Get dressed," Uldis shouted to Anastasjia. She was holding the rapidly appearing bruise on the side of her face. She grabbed her pile of clothes from the chair and began to dress.

Uldis stood over Balodis, making it clear that he was no longer in charge.

"I helped you," Balodis said to him as he wiped blood from his mouth.

"And, I'll be forever grateful," Uldis replied. "But you ever touch her again and I'll kill you, understand?"

Balodis pulled himself to his feet. He looked at Uldis and then at Anastasjia.

"You might want to put that away," said Uldis, pointing at the now flaccid penis that was still exposed. Balodis pulled up his trousers and buckled his belt.

"You think you can tell me what to do?" he asked, looking at Uldis.

"Not at all, but you touch her—"

"I get it," interrupted Balodis, clearly still raging at the situation.

"You need to leave," said Uldis and he pointed towards the door.

Balodis began to walk slowly past Uldis, glancing at where Anastasjia stood. But suddenly he grabbed the pen that was on the dresser and rammed it forcefully into Uldis's cheek. The first two inches of the pen disappeared into his flesh and blood began to spurt out. Balodis let go of the pen and punched Uldis in the face full force, sending him sprawling across the floor.

Balodis turned to Anastasjia and grabbed her by the hair, pulling her face down, level with his hip. Before she could react, he was bringing a knee up and smashed it into her face. Her nose exploded in pain, the sensation shooting right up into her skull. She was dazed and staggered back.

"You fucking whore," he repeated.

She was struggling to focus; her head was throbbing. Blood was streaming from her nose, slowly covering her tee shirt. She stood against the wall waiting for the inevitable blow, but it never came.

Suddenly he collapsed to the floor on his knees before falling face down. She had to jump out of the way as his head smashed against the wall beside her. She looked up to see Uldis standing where Balodis had been. Blood still poured from the wound in his face, and it was now over his hands. Especially the right hand, which she could now see he had used to pull the pen from his cheek, before ramming it into Balodis's ear.

"Is he dead?" she asked, her voice trembling as Balodis's body twitched slightly before falling still.

Uldis crouched down and felt Balodis's neck.

"Dead," he said, looking up at Anastasjia who was still shaken and dazed. She managed to pull herself together just enough.

"What do we do now?" she asked.

"Police?" It was a question.

"I don't think we can draw attention to ourselves," she replied as she held the bottom of her tee shirt up to her nose, which was still pouring with blood. "What about Mr. Daniels? He didn't seem to have a lot of time for Balodis," she said.

"Do you have his number?" he asked.

"No, I was hoping you would," she replied, trying to work out how they could contact him. She didn't know if Daniels could help but she guessed he wouldn't want attention being brought to the business. Uldis searched Balodis and found his iPhone.

"Screen is locked," he said.

"Let me," she said, taking it from him.

Yes, the screen was locked but only by fingerprint. Using a tissue, she picked up Balodis's hand and began to press his fingers to the reader, starting with his index finger. When she swiped the middle finger over the reader the phone fired to life. She scrolled through the contacts, but no Mr. Daniels.

"Shit," she said, looking at Uldis. "Not in there."

"What time did we leave here to go see Daniels?" Uldis asked.

"What?" She looked at him, confused.

"What time did we leave here to go see Daniels?" he asked again.

"I don't know," she replied. "Maybe two, I can't be sure."

"Look at outgoing calls around 2:00pm. I'm guessing he must have called to let Daniels know we were on our way."

She scrolled through the few outgoing calls on the phone and saw that at 1:58pm there was a forty-second call to a mobile number that had no name attached to it. She pressed the green dial button and heard the phone dial and then ring. It rang four times. *Pick up, pick up*, she thought to herself.

"What is it, Balodis?" they heard when the call was finally picked up. "You better not be wasting my time." It was Daniels.

"Mr. Daniels, it's Ana."

"What is it, Ana? You sound alarmed." He sounded worried. "And why are you using Balodis's phone?"

"He's dead, I'm sorry," she replied, not really knowing what to say.

"Dead? What do you mean, dead?" he asked, not sounding particularly angry, more concerned.

Anastasjia took the towel she still had held to her face and looked at it. It was red with blood. She felt it dripping down her face. She quickly put it back to her nose.

"He attacked me and Uldis. He stabbed Uldis and then Uldis killed him." Her words made it sound like he had murdered him, but she knew he had to: he had saved their lives.

"How is Uldis? Where was he stabbed?" asked Daniels, sounding rather 'matter of fact'.

"He's okay, Balodis stabbed him in the face, there's a lot of blood but I think he'll be okay." She looked at Uldis again, who nodded towards her, acknowledging that she was right: he would be fine. He, too, was holding a towel against his cheek. It was slowly turning red.

"Who have you told?" asked Daniels.

"No one, just you."

"Okay, Ana, what is your room number?"

She told him.

"Okay, you stay where you are, make sure you and Uldis have all your belongings ready and I'll send a car for you both."

"What about Balodis?" she asked, looking at his limp body.

"Leave it to me," he replied. "I shall see you both shortly, try not to worry." With that, he hung up.

Anastasjia looked at Uldis. "He said to get all our belongings and wait here."

He looked her in the eye. "Will you be okay whilst I grab my stuff?" he asked. She nodded. "Okay, I'll be back in a couple of minutes." He leaned forward and kissed her on the cheek before hurrying out of the room, stepping over Balodis's body as he left, closing the door behind him.

How had she ended up here? First, she saw Balodis murder someone and now she was looking at his lifeless body on the floor. She turned and went into the bathroom again, removing the blood-stained tee shirt and rolling it up. She put it into a sanitary bag and using wet tissues she wiped the drying blood from her face and neck before flushing them away.

She looked in the mirror at her swollen nose and face. It looked as bad as it felt. A small drip of blood began to appear in one of her nostrils. She thought it had stopped enough to not use the towel anymore. Slowly she gathered up her cosmetics and toiletries, putting them into her wash bag before returning to the room.

She finished packing her bag and left, taking one last look at the lifeless body of Balodis before closing the door behind her.

CHAPTER 15

As he climbed off the train Harry looked around at the other passengers. He guessed some were shoppers and some may even be going on a day trip to the seaside. He made his way to the exit, passed his ticket through the machine and put it back in his pocket, saving it for later so he could get home.

By now it was early afternoon, and he knew he would have to make up an excuse to his mother as to why he was back so late. He wondered if Lilly would get back before him and if she would say anything. He assumed she wouldn't. After all, why would she draw attention to him being out if it led back to her?

He was still upset at her for getting him involved in this. He knew she was frightened and that wasn't something you often saw from Lilly, so whatever was going on must be bad. He, too, was terrified about what might happen to him. He wasn't brave at all, certainly not as brave as Lilly. He remembered the look on her face when they were in the room together in London. All he had to do was deliver the drugs and it would all be over later today, he told himself.

He'd removed the 'G' pack when the train had pulled out of London, wrapped it in a tissue and put it in his pocket. He guessed this was a risk, but it was so uncomfortable inside him he didn't fancy sitting on it all the way to Eastbourne. When the guard announced the train was approaching the station, he quickly went into the toilet and put it back in. Surprisingly, putting it back was not as uncomfortable as he thought it would be, especially with some lubricant: it was nowhere near as bad as when the man had pushed it in.

Harry looked at the piece of paper with the address. As he left the station, he looked for anything that might give him a clue what to do next. He felt as though everyone was looking at him. He began to wonder whether they might know something. He'd seen police programmes on television where the drug dealers had been followed by undercover detectives. Maybe they had followed him from the house in London? He found himself looking at his feet, trying not to be seen. The people who had left the station with him had gone away, and new people were arriving in taxis. He looked back towards the station and saw an information board on the wall.

The board was faded in places but not enough that he couldn't see the names of the roads. He again looked at the piece of paper from his pocket. The index of road names by the side of the map was so faded he couldn't read it. He would have to search the map without the index. Harry's logical brain kicked in and he started scanning the street names, going from the top of the left-hand square first before moving to the second square along and so on. It felt like it was taking ages, but it was the only way. Eventually, he came across the street he wanted on the fourth row. He guessed he was about ten minutes away on foot. After memorising the map, he set off hoping that no one was watching him.

When he arrived at the road Harry's heart sank further. It was a really long road, full of Victorian or Edwardian houses that seemed to go on forever. Worse still, the numbers of the houses were not all clear and some of them didn't even appear to have numbers.

He began to walk up the road. He decided to walk up one side and then back down the other, that way he would end up walking towards the station again. He found himself laughing at the misplaced logic in his plan; the house would be in the same place, so it doesn't really matter which way he went.

It was after he had walked for about 30 minutes that he saw the dirty-looking house; it had rotting window frames and blankets up in the windows. The black door was covered in scratches and marks as though something had attacked it with a hammer and the paint was peeling. No number anywhere but Harry knew it was the address, it had to be. He looked back to the last numbered house and counted down to the run-down property to check. *Yep. That's it.*

Once again Harry found himself looking left and right in case he was being followed. But the street was clear, no one around, just the occasional car racing past far too fast for the speed limit.

He went to the door and pressed the bell. Nothing, not a sound. He stood for a moment and then pushed the button again. Still nothing. He wondered if it even worked, he guessed not. He could see the knocker plate in the middle of the door but the knocker itself had been broken off. Clenching his fist, he banged on the door. Again, nothing. *Maybe they're out.* What was he supposed to do if they weren't in?

He reached for the phone he had been given and pressed one of the buttons, bringing the screen to life. As he did, there was the sound of a bolt going back on the door and it opened just enough that he saw a woman looking at him.

She looked him up and down before opening the door enough to grab him by the upper arm and pull him into the house. When he was inside, she let go of him, closed the door and pushed the heavy bolt back into place. Harry looked at her; she was skeletal in appearance with rotting teeth that just about held onto a rolled-up cigarette that hung from her mouth. Her clothes hung on her body and looked far too big. He guessed they probably fitted at one time, but not now. Her arms were covered in tattoos that joined together across her chest and crept up her neck. She pulled the cigarette from her mouth and smiled a slightly toothless smile. Harry thought she was maybe forty years old, although the condition of her made it hard to tell.

"You bring supplies?" she asked. Harry nodded. "Speak up, lovey," she said. "No need to be afraid."

"Yes," replied Harry, still cautious of this woman.

"Good," she replied. "Give it here and we'll get you something to eat."

"Do you have a bathroom?" he asked politely.

"Listen to you," she said, laughing. "Just get it out now." Her tone had changed to something more aggressive. Harry looked at her face. The smile had disappeared, and a scowl had taken its place.

"Please," he managed to say. His eyes were beginning to well up again. He was sick of crying; he must have cried more today than he could remember.

Taking pity on him, she said, "Go on, in there," and pointed at a closed door near the entrance. Harry opened it and the smell of faeces and urine hit his nostrils. Thick brown smudges stained the toilet pan and the urine-stained floor.

"Hurry up," the woman shouted from behind him. He stepped into the room, feeling his trainers sticking to the floor. He closed the door behind him and undid his trousers, before pulling down his underwear enough to be able to get the end of the cling film and put the 'G' pack out. He could see the pack was stained with faeces and even a little blood, and it was still smothered in the Vaseline too. He washed his hands and shook them as dry as he could. There was a towel, but he had no intention of touching it.

There was a loud knock on the door.

"Come on," she shouted.

"Coming," Harry shouted back. When he stepped out, he saw she was standing with her hand out. He handed over the 'G' pack, and she smiled again.

"I need to go now," he said, hoping she would just give him the money he was expected to collect and that he wouldn't have to ask for it. She turned away and walked down the hall into a kitchen area. The kitchen was not any cleaner than the toilet and didn't smell much better either. "Please," said Harry, "I need to get going."

"Not yet." This time a male voice coming from behind him replied. "You go when the food is sold," he said. Harry thought he must have come from a room at the front of the house, but he hadn't heard him coming.

The man was not big but was lean. He also was covered in tattoos, although they weren't enough to cover the track marks over his exposed arms.

"How long is that? Only my mum will be expecting me," he said, getting more and more concerned.

"We've got buyers coming and once it's sold you get the money," he said.

"I don't understand," said Harry. "I've got to get home, my sister—"

"Stop fucking whining." The man was clearly becoming annoyed with him. "Look, if you help with some of the deliveries, we could get the money quicker, else you can wait here until it's all gone. Up to you," he said, staring at him with cold eyes.

Harry was thinking. He wanted to get away, but he didn't want to be selling drugs. It was bad enough he had to bring them here in the first place. He looked at the woman who was sitting at the kitchen table and was now separating the tiny, compressed plastic wrappers she had found within the 'G' pack. She had made a small pile of brown ones and a small pile of white ones.

"That's Sally, and I'm Peter," said the man. "This is her place, but she helps us out," he said.

Sally looked up and gave another toothless smile before looking back to her increasing piles of drugs. Harry was amazed how many there were and how they all fit in the Kinder Egg box.

Peter opened the fridge and pulled out a beer bottle before hammering the top on the edge of the table where Sally was sitting. The top flew off and Harry watched it fall to the floor and spin around before falling flat.

"Help yourself to food," Peter said as he took a swig from the bottle, pointing towards the cupboards.

"No thank you," he replied, not quite knowing what he was supposed to do next. Harry was still standing, not moving, just watching. Eventually Sally stopped what she was doing. Peter had taken a seat at the table opposite her and was drinking his beer. He sat back in his chair and put the bottle on the table, holding it with both hands.

"So, what's your story?" he asked.

"I don't know." Harry looked down at his feet. He really didn't want a conversation. "Please can I have the money? I've got to get home." He tried to remain as polite as he could, as he guessed asking for money might anger Peter. But Peter didn't seem angry. He just leaned further back in the chair, so the front legs raised from the floor. He then grabbed the seat between his legs and spun the chair, so he was now facing Harry.

"What exactly have you been told your job is here?" he asked.

"I was told to bring the drugs here and you would give me the money for them that I have to take back to the man," Harry blurted out in one breath.

Peter nodded. "Yes, that's about right. Like I've told you, you can help us sell them. We have some customers already. As soon as they are gone, we take our cut, and you take the rest back to London. If you don't want to help us that's fine but it will take longer, do you understand?" He looked Harry squarely in the eye as he spoke.

"How long will that take?" he asked, hoping not to annoy Peter again.

"I don't know, a couple of days."

"What?" replied Harry, completely shocked. "I can't wait a couple of days, my mum will be looking for me. What about my sister?"

"Who the fuck is your sister?" replied Peter.

"Lilly, I was told that she could come home when I brought you the drugs." He could feel tears welling up in his eyes again.

"Don't cry, deary," said Sally, giving him another toothless smile.

"Look," started Peter, "I've got to get rid of this stuff. Quite a bit will be going today, and the rest should be gone by midday Tuesday if you give us a hand."

"Tuesday!" exclaimed Harry. "I've got school tomorrow," he blurted out.

"Not anymore," said Peter, laughing. "Look, get used to it," he added.

"Can I call Mum please?" Harry asked, surprising himself at how polite he was managing to remain.

"Don't be so fucking stupid," replied Peter.

Harry heard a phone buzzing. Peter pulled it out of his pocket and answered it.

"Yeah… Yeah… Five minutes." He hung up and placed it back in his pocket. "You're in luck, first delivery." He smiled. "Ten rocks and ten brown," he said to Sally, who proceeded to count out ten wraps from each pile. "Sit down, kid, you're making me nervous," he said.

Harry walked to the only other chair in the room, which was between Peter and Sally on the far side of the table, and took a seat.

Moments later the doorbell rang, shortly followed by another buzz coming from Peter's pocket.

"With you in a moment, my man," he said, answering it.

He gathered up the wraps that Sally had counted and slipped them into a zipped plastic bag he took from a kitchen drawer. Harry watched as he disappeared from the room and headed towards the front door. Out of view, he heard the heavy bolt pulled back and the door open. There were muffled voices, and then the door closed, and the bolt was pushed back again.

Peter walked back into the kitchen with a beaming smile on his face.

"First bit of business completed," he said, waving a roll of twenty-pound notes in his hand. As he did, the phone in his pocket buzzed yet again. "Yeah… Yeah… No problem… Yeah, see you then." He grinned towards Harry. "You might be out of here tomorrow at this rate."

For the rest of the afternoon and into the evening there was a steady flow of callers to the address. Harry never saw any of them but the two piles of drugs on the table were getting gradually smaller. None of the 'deliveries' were as big as the first one; some were all white packages, and some were all brown packages, but down they went.

At one point Sally got up from the table and pulled out a saucepan and a tin of baked beans, which she proceeded to cook on the hob. After putting bread in the toaster, she presented Harry with a plate of beans on toast, though no butter on the toast.

"There you go, lovey," she said.

"Thank you," replied Harry, taking the knife and fork she handed him. He wasn't hungry, he just wanted to go home.

"Come on, lovey, eat up." Sally looked at him with some concern.

Harry eventually ate the food, clearing the whole plate. He was obviously hungrier than he thought. He noticed Peter never ate; he was checking his phone at the table and appeared jumpy. His legs shook, which made the table shake.

"TV?" said Sally suddenly, looking at Harry.

"Sorry?" he replied, not sure what she meant.

"Do you want to watch TV?" she asked.

"I don't know." He was still nervous, not sure what to do.

"Come on," she said, getting up and walking out of the kitchen.

Harry followed and Peter watched them leave. Harry got the impression Peter was drunk. He had definitely consumed a lot of beer; there must have been at least ten bottle caps on the floor and the open-topped bin in the kitchen was full of empties.

They went into the front room. Sally turned on the TV and handed the remote control to Harry. "Watch what you want, deary," she said, smiling. "Do you want a blanket?" she asked. He hadn't noticed but the room was freezing.

"Yes please," he replied, and Sally pulled out a folded, slightly musty-smelling grey blanket. "There you go."

"Thank you," he replied, taking a seat and pulling it over himself.

Sally turned to go and then stopped, turning back.

"Look, I know it's all been a bit much but hopefully you'll be on your way tomorrow and your sister will be home. In the meantime, make yourself at home and try to get some sleep, busy day." She smiled again. Harry did his best to smile back.

CHAPTER 16

After waking from a fitful sleep Lilly sat up. Her hair was unkempt and stuck to her face and with a hand she brushed it away and over her shoulder. She could see the other girls lying on mattresses. Most of them were covered with dirty-looking blankets but it was so cold Lilly didn't think they cared about how grimy they were; she certainly didn't. All she wanted was to go home but it didn't look like that was going to happen any time soon. She didn't understand what was happening. Jordan had told her that if she got Harry to help out everything would be okay, and she wouldn't be harmed again. She thought back to the previous day and immediately her stomach began to hurt again. She just prayed she wasn't pregnant. Some of the other girls were coming round and sitting up. None spoke or even looked like they wanted to.

She could hear voices downstairs and guessed that at least one of them was the man who had hit her in the face. She gently touched her cheek, feeling the swollen flesh she suspected was now turning blue. Another voice downstairs was the woman she had met at the house in Stratford, but there were others. They were chatting and laughing but Lilly couldn't hear well enough to know what they were saying.

She hadn't really taken the time to get a good look at the other girls, having only really seen them in the dark of the van and for a few minutes when they arrived at the house. Her initial thoughts about their ages were probably right; she guessed at least three were 16 or 17 but one of the others must be younger, maybe even 14, it was hard to tell. The eastern European girl was a little older, she could have even been 20. But she looked more terrified than all of them and spent her time shaking and looking at the floor.

Lilly needed a shower; she could smell the stale, bitter smell of sweat from her clothing and couldn't help but notice that the other girls smelt equally bad. Suddenly the young-looking girl broke the silence.

"Do you think we'll be here long?" she whispered.

She wasn't speaking to anyone in particular but to the group as a whole. A couple of the girls shrugged but the eastern European girl never looked up.

"I don't know," replied Lilly softly. "I hope they'll let us go soon." That's when the eastern European girl finally looked up and made contact.

"You fucking silly little girl. Don't you get it?" She spoke softly but with anger in her voice. "You belong to them until they say otherwise, just pray you get a factory job or a farm job." She turned away and looked again at the floor.

"I don't want to work in a factory or on a farm," said Lilly indignantly.

"Yes, you do," the girl responded. "The alternative is you fuck."

"What?" Lilly looked at the girl open mouthed.

"You fuck," she said again. "You can't work for them; you fuck for them."

Once again, Lilly felt the fear and a tear ran slowly down her cheek. The young girl openly wept, her body trembling with each sob.

Another hour or so passed, it was difficult to tell, to Lilly it felt like a lifetime in this continuing nightmare that seemed to get worse and worse. The girls had remained silent after that exchange, the only sound in the room was the occasional sobbing from the young girl and even that had dropped off.

The talking downstairs stopped, and Lilly heard doors opening and closing.

"Come on, move it." The man's accent was not English, and she didn't recognise it. It was coming from downstairs and was quite muffled. She heard people walking on the wooden hallway floor and going out of the front door. She felt tempted to get up and look out of the window but thought better of it.

More footsteps and talk; this time they were making their way up the stairs. Moments later, the woman she had met in Stratford was standing in the doorway. She glanced to her side to someone that was out of view and then back into the room.

"Some of you will begin your new employment," she announced. "We have jobs for four of you," she continued. "Who wants to help out at a factory packing chicken?" She was so positive, speaking as though they had just been successful in an interview. Lilly looked around and saw that the eastern European girl already had her hand in the air. She looked at Lilly, nodding ever so slightly and raising her eyebrows. Lilly didn't need a second cue. She quickly raised her hand as did the others.

Only one of the girls didn't raise her hand, in fact she didn't even look up. Lilly hadn't really taken much notice of her, she was sitting on her own at the back of the room, hunched over and not looking at anyone. Lilly willed her to look up so she could give her a cue, as the eastern European girl had done for her. But she never moved or looked up.

"All very keen to work, that is good," the woman said, nodding. "Unfortunately, I only need four of you and I'm afraid Lilly can't come along with that nasty bruise, it would cause too many questions."

Lilly instantly felt panic. Did that mean she was going to be used for sex?

"Please," replied Lilly. "I'll work hard." The thought of the alternative struck fear into every muscle in her body. She could feel herself beginning to shake.

"Don't worry, Lilly, we have other plans for you. If you behave and do as you're told you won't come to any harm." She again smiled and Lilly slowly put her hand down, fearing the worst.

"So, Lilly and Ella, you stay here for the moment, the rest follow me."

The young girl started waving frantically. "No, no, me, I want to come, please," she cried. Lilly guessed she was Ella.

"I'm sorry, Ella, but you're too young for the factory. And anyway, we have a very special customer who is waiting to see you." The woman smiled again. This time it was not a pleasant smile but very sinister. Instantly Ella began to sob again.

"Don't worry, Ella, you'll be fine," said the woman. It wasn't convincing.

The three girls who had their hands raised stood up to leave but the quiet girl still hadn't moved.

"Come on, Milena, now!" the woman shouted, but the girl still didn't move.

The woman stepped back into the hallway and glanced to where the person out of sight was still waiting. She nodded towards the mysterious figure and then towards the girl. A man walked quickly into the room. Lilly recognised him as the one who had slapped her. He grabbed the girl by the upper arm, lifting her effortlessly to her feet and dragged her towards the door. Still, she said nothing as she was pushed out of sight and down the hallway.

The woman looked at Lilly and Ella one more time. "Won't be long now, I'll be back shortly."

With just her and Ella in the room, Lilly couldn't help noticing how loudly the young girl was sobbing. Despite her own fears she couldn't help but feel sorry for her and she shuffled alongside her to offer some sort of comfort. She put an arm gently around her shoulder. Instantly Ella put her face into Lilly's neck and wept. She could feel the moisture of the girl's tears on her top. She put her other arm around her and just held her. *How on earth did this girl get to be here?* she thought to herself. She knew she was here to help Jordan, but this girl was Harry's age. Nothing made sense anymore.

It was difficult to tell how long had passed when another man came to the doorway. He threw a plastic bag into the room and said, "Eat," before turning and walking away. Again, an accent that Lilly didn't recognise, but he only said one word. Lilly still sat with an arm around Ella, who had finally stopped sobbing. Letting go of her, Lilly reached for the bag and brought it back to where they were sitting. Sandwiches from Tesco wrapped neatly in their containers with bags of crisps and bottles of Coke. The sandwiches were cheese and the crisps cheese and onion. For the first time in ages Lilly smiled. It was the absurdity of it. They even got 'meal deals' to save money.

Lilly shared them out with Ella and the two of them ate for the first time in what seemed like ages.

CHAPTER 17

Zuzanna was exhausted. Six straight nights she had worked at Sebastian's demand but finally he had promised her a night off after tonight. She lay on her bed in her and Michalina's bedroom looking at the ceiling. *How am I surviving?* she thought to herself. She knew the answer, it was the only way she could help Michalina and stop her family coming to harm. Not that they knew. Michalina hadn't been home since she last saw her. Sebastian had assured her that so long as she continued to make money it wouldn't be too long before she saw her again. But still, she had no idea if she was okay.

Her mother was getting frantic; she knew Michalina was rebellious but to not see her for a week, had never happened before. Zuzanna had tried to placate her.

"You know what she's like, Mama," she had said. "She will come home when she's ready, I'm sure she is fine."

Her mother had at one point tried to call the police, but Zuzanna had stopped her, knowing that was not a good idea. Although having previously told Zuzanna she was pleased she was getting out, her mother was getting annoyed with her.

"It's no good, Zuzanna, every night, it's bad for you," she scolded her.

If only she knew the truth, Zuzanna thought.

"Your brother is helping every night so I can work. Why can't you do your share, cleaning up after your father, cooking, washing? It's not fair on him, he has schoolwork."

"Not fair? Not fair? What's not fair is you working your fingers to the bone and me out each day working at the coffee shop while

Szymon sleeps all day, that's not fair!"

She hadn't meant to shout, but she was so angry with the world. Seeing the shock in her mother's face, she instantly regretted it. She knew it was wrong to take it out on Szymon.

"Sorry, Mama, I'm tired," she had said, her head hung in shame.

"I'm not surprised, out every night. You need to stay in and look after your father and then get a good night's sleep."

Zuzanna had nodded in agreement but knew there was no choice in the matter, she would have to go out again.

Time was ticking by, and she would need to go to Charlotte's soon. She closed her eyes again and prayed to herself that this nightmare would soon be over. With each night her body was getting increasingly sore and although Charlotte was right – that each night would be a little easier – her body needed a rest. Just as she was about to get up there was a gentle knock at her bedroom door.

"Come in," she called, and the door slowly opened.

"Hi, Zuzanna." It was Szymon. She wondered what he wanted: he never came to her room, even when Michalina was home and the two of them were really close.

"You know it's my birthday tomorrow," he said.

"Yes, of course," she lied. With everything going on she had forgotten all about it. She made a mental note to get him something on the way to Charlotte's.

"My friends have offered to take me out for my birthday so I hoped you would stay in and look after Tata."

Knowing she had tomorrow off, it was the least she could do.

"Okay, no problem, you enjoy yourself." She smiled at him.

"Thanks, Zuzanna, I'll make sure Tata is comfortable before I go, it probably won't be until about seven."

"What, seven?" said Zuzanna, sitting quickly up. "Do you mean tonight?" She couldn't do tonight, she had to work. She had no idea what Sebastian would do if she didn't turn up, but it wouldn't be good. Szymon looked at her with a concerned face.

"Yes, I promise not to be out too late, but it is my eighteenth."

"It's tomorrow, you're only seventeen." It was ridiculous. She knew a day wouldn't make any difference, but she had to say something to put him off. Szymon looked confused.

"I know but it's not the first time I've been out for a drink, Zuzanna."

"I know." She wanted to help him but knew she couldn't. "I can do it tomorrow, but I have to go out tonight."

"Why?" he said, clearly distressed.

"Look, I promise I will stay in tomorrow, but you have to stay in tonight."

"This isn't fair." The look on his face reminded her of when he was a small child and couldn't get his own way, only this time, he was right; it was his eighteenth but what could she do? Szymon left the room, slamming the door behind him. She heard him stomp down the stairs and guessed he was talking to their mother.

As she stood up, she caught a glimpse of herself in the mirror. She did look tired and even she could see the sadness in her face. Grabbing a sweatshirt and her bag, she headed downstairs, pulling the sweatshirt over her head as she went. She decided to just leave. Even though she knew she would be early she couldn't face the argument with her mother that she knew was coming.

Zuzanna slipped into her trainers and grabbed her coat from the end of the banister.

"Where are you going?" It was her mother.

"Not now, Mama, please. I'm in a hurry."

"You're always in a hurry. Where are you going?"

Zuzanna shook her head and just said, "Out," not wanting to get into a discussion.

"What is it with you, Zuzanna? You were always the good one, the helpful one, the one I could rely on."

"You have no idea." She found herself raising her voice more than she had wanted. After everything she was doing to make the family safe, she couldn't hold in her temper.

"So, tell me!" her mother snapped back. "Tell me what is so important you can't stay in for one night to let your brother enjoy his eighteenth birthday. Tell me that."

Of course, she couldn't say why. She knew her brother was upset, and she hated upsetting him and her parents but there was nothing she could do.

"I've already said I just can't, now I have to go." She quickly stepped outside and slammed the door behind her. As she stepped away, the door opened again.

"I don't know what it is with you, Zuzanna, but this isn't right, you know it isn't right," her mother called after her. Zuzanna never looked back, she carried on walking, tears in her eyes.

When she arrived at Charlotte's, she pushed the button to her apartment.

"You're early," Charlotte said as she buzzed her in. As she walked into the lounge area, she saw that Charlotte was wandering around in a pair of brightly coloured knickers and a tee shirt. "You okay?" she asked cheerily before she caught sight of Zuzanna's face. "What's up? Is it getting too much for you again?" She paused, waiting for a response. When none came, she continued, "It gets difficult sometimes. You have to battle through it, it's the only way."

Zuzanna looked at her as the tears rolled down her cheeks again. She had cried more in the last week than she had in the rest of her life. Charlotte went over to her and put an arm around her shoulder. Although she had only known Charlotte for a week and knew what she did, she couldn't help but like her.

"It's my brother's eighteenth tomorrow," Zuzanna said. She

wasn't sure Charlotte wanted to hear her problems, but she had to tell someone.

"Well, that's great, you're not working tomorrow. You can try and enjoy it." She sounded so cheerful.

Zuzanna smiled and shook her head. "He wanted to go out tonight, but our mother was working. One of us has to be home as our father isn't well. I told him I had to go out. It's not fair on him."

Charlotte squeezed her arm gently, in a reassuring manner. But Zuzanna still felt bad. She had managed to get a card on the way to Charlotte's, but they had nothing else worth buying for a present for him. She'd just have to put fifty euros in the card.

Charlotte made them coffee and got out the biscuits. They sat and chatted for a while until Charlotte announced it was time to get ready for work. She provided Zuzanna with clothes again. She was getting used to the revealing nature of the underwear despite hating what she was being made to do. She had learned to convince herself this scantily clothed person in the mirror wasn't actually her.

"How are you holding up after a week?" Charlotte asked, with genuine concern.

"Okay, I guess," replied Zuzanna. "I am getting sore; I do use the Vaseline, but it still hurts so much."

Charlotte smiled. "Try not to tense. I know it's difficult but relaxing helps."

"I know," replied Zuzanna. "I try."

Charlotte stopped what she was doing and looked directly at her. "You could just do oral instead. Do you do oral?"

"What? No, no I don't." Zuzanna looked disgusted. She had never considered the idea of putting a penis into her mouth. The thought made her feel sick.

"Zuzanna, it's about making them cum and then getting rid of them," she said and looked sternly at her. Not angry but serious.

"You have to do whatever you need to get them finished quickly. Have you done oral before?" Zuzanna screwed up her face. "I'll take that as a no."

She left the room and returned with a large dildo and a condom.

"Sit down and take hold of this."

Zuzanna sat in an upright chair and Charlotte handed her the dildo. She took hold of it and rested it in her lap.

"No, not like that, hold it up."

Zuzanna realised what was required and held it up as if it were an erection. Charlotte then passed the condom and told her to put it on the dildo. She then took the dildo and standing in front of her, Charlotte held it in front of her as if it were her erection.

"Go on then, put it in your mouth." She smiled.

Zuzanna looked at her and then at the dildo. She started to laugh at the absurdity of it.

"Come on, Zuzanna, be serious for a moment, just put it in your mouth."

Zuzanna did as she was told and held each side with her hands.

"Slide your hands up and down each side as if you're tossing it off." Zuzanna did as she was told. "After a few minutes, lower your mouth over the end, maybe run your tongue around the end before taking it further in."

Zuzanna leaned forward and opening her mouth took the end just beyond her teeth. She could taste the latex. *What did she say?* thought Zuzanna. *Oh yes, tongue.* She slowly ran her tongue around the end of the dildo. Charlotte put one of her hands on the back of Zuzanna's head and gently pushed her down onto the dildo.

Suddenly Zuzanna gagged and pulled her head away. She coughed.

"Basic mistake," said Charlotte. "Never let them take charge." Zuzanna was still getting herself together from the effects of choking. "Try again, but if they put a hand on your head, you bat it away or pull your head back. Take it from me, they'll stop."

She held the dildo up again and nodded that she should try once more. Zuzanna leant forward and opened her mouth, letting the end go in beyond her teeth.

"That's good," said Charlotte. "Move your head back and forward, and remember, you control it, this is just about making them cum as quickly as possible."

Zuzanna did as she was told. Suddenly Charlotte grabbed the back of Zuzanna's head and instinctively Zuzanna pulled her head back, stopping what she was doing.

"Good, well done," said Charlotte, grinning. "You do that, and they'll let go."

Zuzanna nodded, trying not to cringe.

Despite the nightmare she was living, she couldn't help but worry about her sister and what she was going through. *I pray to God Michalina is safe after all this.* She at least knew there would be a day when this was over.

Instinctively she put her arms around Charlotte and hugged her. Charlotte responded, hugging back. The physical touch brought tears to Zuzanna's eyes, and she felt them roll down her cheeks. She said nothing but just stood, feeling soothed by the comforting warmth of Charlotte's body against her.

"Come on." Eventually Charlotte released her grip and moved away from Zuzanna until she was standing opposite. "Time to get ready," she said, leading her toward the dresser. Zuzanna complied. She knew the routine now and sat in the chair whilst Charlotte helped with her makeup before helping her choose an outfit to wear.

"Good evening, ladies, ready to make some money?" Sebastian sneered towards them when they arrived at De Wallen. Zuzanna just stared back, the anger rising inside her. "Into your offices," he laughed. "Try not to take too long, time is money." He was grinning from ear to ear.

"Fuck off." Zuzanna surprised herself. She never would have spoken to anyone like that a week ago. Now it was easy.

"Now, Zuzanna, be nice." He smiled again.

She turned her back and stepped into her room, closing the door behind her and pulling the curtain shut.

She sat on the bed looking around the tiny room. *That fucking bastard*, she thought. *If I ever get the chance, I'll fucking kill him.* She had never hated anyone like she hated Sebastian. It wasn't so much what he was making her do; it was that he was changing her, and she was becoming a person she didn't like. She had known her brother was the spoiled one in the family, but she had spoiled him herself. She hadn't shouted at him, she had helped her mother but no longer had time. She resented not having time to help her father. She was becoming aggressive, rude, not the person she knew she should be.

She looked towards the cupboard that held all the sex toys and towels. Although she needed the money to pay off Sebastian and to help Michalina, she hoped for a quiet night. She would have tomorrow off, so she just needed to get through one more night. She never imagined that the opportunity to stay home and look after her father could be so inviting. *I must be sure to give Szymon some money to take with him when he goes out to celebrate,* she thought. Although she considered him to be spoiled, she also recognised it was hard for him having to help out every night and he had no idea where Zuzanna had been going. In his eyes she was out enjoying herself. If only he knew. She shook her head, stood up and got ready to open the curtain.

No such luck on the quiet front, the De Wallen was heaving with groups of people. Many wandered around and looked at the girls out of curiosity. She knew it was a tourist attraction, but she couldn't understand why these sightseers never tried to understand the true story behind the girls and why they were here. Did they even consider they were being forced or coerced into the work? Did they think they all wanted to do it and loved to make money? She would never understand.

At that moment, her first customer knocked on the door. It was the old man, her very first client. The man who had lost his wife. She opened the door and let him in.

"Hello," he said with a slightly shy look on his face.

"Hello," she replied. "Are you okay?" She remembered his tears the first time and how he had told her about his wife dying.

"Yes, I'm sorry I'm back, I hope you don't mind?"

She smiled at him. Sex with an old man wasn't something she really wanted, but he was being nice.

"Of course not." She smiled again. "Would you like me to help you undress?"

"Please," he replied, looking directly at her face for the first time.

She helped him remove his clothes and coaxed him to erection before putting on the condom and guiding him onto the bed. When he finished, he thanked her and as before gave her an extra fifty-euro note. Then he quickly put his arms around her.

"Thank you and bless you," he said before letting himself out without looking back. Zuzanna stood still. She couldn't help but feel concerned for him, despite him using her.

Her second customer was a young English boy. Very confident with his mates and equally confident when in the room with her. His first question was, "How much for a blow job, darling?" said with a big grin on his face.

Not this one, she thought. She could smell the alcohol on his breath. Although she had already taken him for a hundred euros and knew he was willing to pay more, she couldn't quite bring herself to it just yet.

"Not with me," she replied. "You want sex or not?" she snapped.

"Okay, luv, easy does it."

He dropped his trousers and left his tee shirt on and pulled down his underwear. *This should be quick,* she thought, and sure enough it was.

"Cheers, darling." He laughed towards her. "Still no chance of a blow job?" She opened the door, and he stepped out of the room to a loud cheer from his friends.

She pulled the curtain closed and thought for a moment. *I can do this. I can do this,*. Why had she turned down the opportunity to make more money? *The next one who asks, I'm going for it*, she told herself.

At that moment she heard the sound of a group of young men walking down the alley. They were speaking Dutch so she knew they would not be as easy to please as the English, but she knew she needed to get back to work. As she pulled the curtain back, she could hear the group getting closer.

"Come on, lads, let's get you laid," one of them called out.

She could hear them laughing. Then she recognised one of the voices – Lucas. She had initially felt sorry for him, believing he may have been a victim himself, but now he and his friends were trawling the alleyways of De Wallen looking at the girls, undoubtedly looking for sex. Well, not with her. She closed her eyes and shook her head.

"What about this one?" she heard him say and knew that he was encouraging one of his group to come up to her window. She was seething.

As she opened her eyes, her eyes landed on another familiar face. He was standing right in front of her with the group of young men. Szymon. His mouth dropped open. Zuzanna stared back and felt herself beginning to shake. She caught a glance of Sebastian who was leaning against the wall opposite. At that moment she knew he had arranged for Lucas to befriend Szymon, intending on this moment. He was smiling in the knowledge that he had managed to go further in ruining her life. She quickly pulled the curtain closed and sat on the bed.

"Best find another, more accommodating," she heard Lucas say.

"Come on," he said. She guessed that Szymon was hesitating to move on. The sound of the group moved away, and it went quieter with only the usual sounds of people walking by.

After sitting for a couple of minutes there was a knock on the door. She pulled the curtain back far enough to see Sebastian, an angry look on his face.

"Come on," he said through the closed door. "Time is money."

She shook her head and closed the curtain. *Fucking bastard*, she thought. He's fucking ruined my life, well fuck him.

She opened the curtain and said, "Fuck you, you fucking cunt," then pulled it shut. What had he turned her into? She was shocked by her language. Only two weeks ago those words would have never come from her, but more important to her was the look of horror on Szymon's face. She was mortified. What must he be thinking? He was certain to tell their parents, and what then?

There was more loud banging on the door.

"Open up, Zuzanna, NOW." It was an order. She ignored it. More banging. "Open the door now, you fucking whore, or your life won't be worth living." Again she ignored it.

He had ruined her life, ruined her sister's life and she had had enough. She grabbed her coat and pulled it over her shoulders. She just wanted to leave. She pulled back the curtain and unlocked the door.

"Where do you think you're going?" asked Sebastian.

"Fuck off," she shouted, and she started to step out of the room.

He blocked her way. Some people had stopped to look but Sebastian didn't appear to be concerned. Instead he pushed her back, so she stumbled. She caught her heel on the step into the room and fell hard onto the floor. Sebastian followed her in and turned to close the door and the curtain.

Zuzanna pulled herself to her feet. Her bum hurt from hitting the hard floor.

"Get that fucking coat off and get back to work." Sebastian was raging but Zuzanna was equally mad.

"Fuck off, Sebastian. I've had enough and I'm going."

She felt the blow to her stomach almost before she saw it happening. Winded, she doubled over in pain. Sebastian grabbed her coat by the collar and pulled it back, causing her to spin and fall to the floor. He pulled the coat off of her.

"Get up!" He was standing right over her. She looked up at him.

"What else can you do that you haven't already done to me?" she asked with spite in her voice. Sebastian grabbed her hair and lifted her to her feet. "Let go! Please let go," she cried in pain.

Now on her feet and with Sebastian holding her hair behind her head, she looked at him.

"Please, Sebastian. Please let me go home. I need to speak with my brother." She looked at him imploringly.

But instead of letting her go, he grabbed her below the chin with his free hand.

"You'll do as I fucking tell you and you'll do it when I tell you." She could feel the menace from him. "Let me show you what I can do." With that, he released her chin and spun her around, still holding tightly onto her hair. He pushed her onto the bed, so she was face down and kneeling on the floor. He continued to pull her hair tightly as he knelt between her legs. She was frozen with fear knowing what was about to happen.

"Please don't, please, I'll do what you ask," she pleaded with every ounce of energy she had.

"You will do as I ask, you're right about that." She felt his hands in the waistband of the tiny panties she had been given by Charlotte and in a single moment felt them ripped from her body. The cord dug into her skin and caused more pain before the material snapped.

"Please, no, please, argh..." She felt the searing pain as he forced himself inside her.

Suddenly he thrust his hips hard into the flesh of her backside, forcing himself into her even further. She had never experienced pain like it. "Argh! No, please, argh! Stop, please," she cried.

Tears streamed down her face. Sebastian continued to thrust into her. Gripping her hair tightly with one hand whilst the other pinning her to the bed. She screamed in pain as he stopped. She guessed he had cum.

He pulled himself free and stood over her. She continued to look ahead. She was in pain and yet was strangely numb. Her legs had gone, and she felt like she couldn't move. She was still exposed to him, and she wanted to cover up. She felt like her world had ended. She sobbed into the bed.

Sebastian pulled up his trousers and was about to leave the room.

"Like we've agreed," he said calmly. "You'll do what I say, when I say, okay?" Zuzanna didn't answer. "I said, OKAY?" He raised his voice, as if say 'answer me'.

She nodded. "Yes," she said softly.

"What was that?"

"Yes," she said again, this time loud enough to be sure he heard.

"Good, I'll be back at 3:00a.m. I'll expect at least five hundred euros, shall we say?" He smiled as he left the room.

Zuzanna got up and quickly locked the door. She went to sit down on the bed, but the pain stopped her. She could feel the blood trickling down her leg from where he had torn her.

She remembered what Sebastian had said and realised she needed to clean up and get back to work. She knew he would be back and was terrified of what he might do. She went to the bathroom and pulled some tissue from the roll, wetting it in the sink. She proceeded to dab at the bleeding until it stopped. The pain was excruciating.

She looked in the mirror at her puffy, swollen face and the tear-streaked makeup. She was never going to make five hundred euros looking like this. She washed off the streaks and tried to re-do the makeup. She was nowhere near as good at it as Charlotte, but she did the best she could. Her panties were in shreds on the floor, so she dropped them in the bin. Manoeuvring her skirt as best she could, she pulled it down sufficiently to cover herself.

She returned to the window and, taking a deep breath, pulled open the curtain. Sebastian was back leaning against the wall opposite. He acknowledged her as she froze in fear. Then he wandered out of sight. At that moment a young man knocked on her glass.

"How much?" he asked in a posh English voice.

"One hundred for twenty minutes," she replied, looking him in the eye.

"How much for a blow job?" he asked.

"One twenty."

"Okay," he said, pulling out his wallet.

She was still repulsed by the idea of taking someone in her mouth but after what had just happened to her, she knew she needed the money fast. *Got to start somewhere*, she thought.

At 3:00am Charlotte knocked on her door. "Ready to go?"

Zuzanna had actually been ready to go for ages. She had stopped as soon as she made the minimum five hundred euros. As she stepped out Sebastian was waiting.

"A productive evening, I hope," he said, sneering towards them. They both handed over the cash. He looked at the money. "Only five hundred? Not much for you, Zuzanna, any problems?" She was terrified of him. All her anger and hate had turned to fear. She shook her head. "Well, a day off today, let's hope for a more productive day tomorrow," he said.

The girls walked back to the apartment, where Charlotte gave her a long hug. It was very comforting.

"Don't worry, sweetheart. I know it's hard, but we can help each other get through it. If you ever need a chat, you know where I am."

Zuzanna started to cry.

"Come on, don't let him win. Are you going to be okay?"

Zuzanna nodded and wiped her tears on her coat sleeve before setting off for home.

As she walked the dark streets, she wondered what she was going to say to Szymon. What must he think of her? As she approached her own apartment and saw what was outside, she knew the answer. Piled to one side of the door were several bin bags full of her possessions.

She tried her key in the door, but it had been locked from the inside. She rang the bell hoping above hope that she could explain herself. Perhaps tell them about Michalina, though it might also get her harmed so maybe not. She rang the bell again and moments later the hall light came on.

"Who's there?" her mother asked.

"Mama, it's Zuzanna," she called out.

"Go away, I have no daughter called Zuzanna."

"Please, Mama, let me explain," she continued to plead. She couldn't bear to lose her family.

"Go away. You are a whore, a worthless whore and no daughter of ours, you are not welcome, and we want you to go."

Zuzanna couldn't believe it. "Please, Mama, please." There was no response. Moments later the hall light went off and Zuzanna guessed her mother had gone back to bed.

She was alone.

CHAPTER 18

Another week had passed, and Michalina was still spending her time in the room with the other girls. Most nights the same two men would come and take the same two girls out. From the fear in their eyes when the men appeared Michalina could guess what was happening to them but in a selfish way, she was just glad it wasn't her. She remained hopeful. Maybe it was because they were still waiting for Zuzanna to pay them and so they didn't want her to come to any harm. She was also given a daily supply of 'H', which kept her satisfied.

The young petite blonde girl was away for a day and then came back. She spent most of her time sobbing. A couple of the girls had tried to speak with her, but she didn't reply. She was beginning to look quite ill too: she hardly ate anything.

Evening approached and the two men came to the door but this time they turned to Michalina and told her to follow them. She was terrified. She had seen the state the other girls were in and feared what happened to them was likely to happen to her.

"Where are we going?" she asked cautiously.

"What is it with you bitches?" the first man said. "Don't ask fucking questions, just do as we tell you." He paused, staring at Michalina. "Come on, don't keep me waiting, we have work for you." Hesitantly, Michalina stood up and prepared to go with them. "Come on," the man said again, walking out of the room. She followed and the other man waited for her to pass before leaving with them. They got to the kitchen where there were two other men and a woman she hadn't seen before.

"Michalina, we have work for you." The woman spoke with a

Dutch accent she guessed was from the Amsterdam area. Michalina said nothing. "I am, however, concerned about your drug habit," she said. Her tone was surprising, as she sounded as if she was genuinely concerned. "I think you will find it difficult to work off the money for drugs as well as your accommodation and food."

"Accommodation and food?" Michalina responded, confused. She thought she owed for the drugs; she never considered being charged for anything else.

"Yes, silly girl. You didn't think it was all free, did you?"

"But—" began Michalina.

"Nothing is free," the woman said. "Let's begin with a bit of fun."

Michalina looked at her and at the men. "What fun?" she asked, the fear rising.

"These men are my associates, and they help me with running this section of the business. They are away from their wives and in need of stimulation to keep them happy." She smiled at Michalina. "In a moment they will drop their trousers and you will suck them off one at a time."

"No way," Michalina shouted. "Are you fucking mad?" She looked at her and the woman calmly looked back.

"Michalina, you owe us money, you need heroin, you need food, and you need somewhere to stay. You will do whatever we say."

"No way," said Michalina again. "Zuzanna is paying you."

"Who is Zuzanna?" asked the woman.

"My sister," said Michalina, confused. "She was getting a loan to pay off my debt."

"What debt is that?" asked the woman. A knowing smile crept across her face.

"I don't understand. I owe Sebastian money and Zuzanna was getting it." She looked at the men who were leaning against the kitchen units. The woman folded her arms.

"I think you've been misled," she said.

"What—" began Michalina before being cut off.

"We have already paid off your debt to Sebastian for you," she said, still smiling.

"Who are you?" Michalina was desperate. "Why have you done that?"

This time the woman's smile was no longer friendly. "You go to a drug dealer for drugs, we go to Sebastian for people like you who cannot pay their way. We have paid off your debt by buying you for our use, in any way we chose."

None of this made sense. What was going on? Who was this woman who seemed to think she could make her do anything she wanted?

"I think you are due another fix," she said. "Unfortunately, nothing more will be arriving, and neither will any food until you have tasted these men." Her face suddenly hardened. "Unpleasant as that may seem, it will help us decide what line of work you will go into once you arrive in England."

"England?" said Michalina.

"Yes, Michalina, you shall be going to England and so will some of your associates. There you will be given work. What work will depend on how cooperative you are now."

"No fucking way am I going to England and I'm definitely not sucking off anyone," Michalina shouted at her.

"Okay," the woman replied calmly and then turned to the two men who had fetched her. "Take her back to the room and remember, no food and no drugs." The two men nodded. One of them grabbed her arm and pulled her towards the door.

"Let go, you fucking ape," Michalina said. He ignored her and she was marched unceremoniously back to the room where she was pushed onto the mattresses.

The two girls who were normally taken out looked at her as she sat on the mattress, angry. They seemed unsure as to why she did not look broken in the way they had. After all, they had been systematically raped every day for over a week, treated like sex toys for four grown men in the house. How could this girl just be angry? Maybe that was how she dealt with it.

"Are you okay?" one of them asked, concerned for her.

"No, I'm not fucking okay, I'm pissed."

"What did you have to do?" she asked.

"Nothing," replied Michalina. "I refused so they threw me back in here." The two girls looked at each other and then back at Michalina without saying anything, as if they had never realised that was an option before now.

Later that evening the two men came for the girls. By now they seemed almost resigned to their fate and walked out with them. It had been almost 24 hours since she had last eaten and Michalina was starving, but that was nothing compared to the craving she was beginning to develop for a fix of heroin. She had already started sweating and was getting agitated, wondering when they would relent and give her what she so desperately needed.

Time went on. Eventually the girls were returned, and they curled up together under a blanket. Michalina was rocking on the mattress. She was sure she could last out. After all, she didn't inject, she wasn't a serious addict.

Time ticked by and as darkness fell, all the girls in the room went to sleep. Only Michalina remained awake, her heart racing so fast she thought she would explode. With the sweating and the hunger came a feeling of nausea. Eventually unable to stand the pain developing in her stomach she got up and left the room to look for the woman. She knew she had been defeated. She just needed to stop the pain and at that moment, she would do whatever was asked of her.

Hearing the noise, one of the men stopped her in the hallway.

"What are you doing up?" he asked in his strong eastern European accent.

"I'll do it," she said, feeling dizzy and unsteady. "I'll do it, just please let me have something, please." The man looked at her, eyebrows raised. "Where is she?" she asked. "I'll tell her."

Smiling at her, he replied, "She won't be back until morning but if you show me what you are prepared to do, I can help you out." She looked at his face. He was smirking, but she didn't care. She just needed the pain to go away.

"I'll get your fix now and then you can continue with my friends in the morning."

She agreed and he led her to the kitchen where he produced a bag of powder from his pocket. He waved it in front of her. She went to grab it.

"Not so fast," he said, quickly putting the bag back in his pocket. "First you get on your knees and work, then you get rewarded."

Knowing she was defeated she sank to her knees and waited whilst he freed himself from his trousers. As she got nearer, she could smell him. It was a sour mix of body odour and semen, and she immediately thought of the girls. He had just been with them and now it would be her. She slowly opened her mouth and took him in, hoping it wouldn't take too long.

Wiping her face on her sleeve, she felt sick but was rewarded with the bag of heroin. The man never spoke as he zipped up his trousers. He just took her by the arm and led her back to the room.

The following morning, she woke up in the room with the other girls. She didn't know if they knew what she had done, but she didn't care. As promised, the man had given her the heroin she needed, and it acted almost like a miracle drug to cure her. She felt calm but knew there was more to come. Her debt to the woman still needed to be paid.

As she sat on the mattress waiting for the men to come back, she thought of her sister. Why had she not gotten the money? It had been days ago she had asked, and she must have had time to go to the bank by now. According to that woman, she'd been sold by Sebastian. It made no sense. And now she was going to have to do this, and God knows what work they had in mind in England. *What a bitch*, she thought to herself. Zuzanna had a nice easy life, she worked and had savings. *Why won't she help me? I know I always left her to help Mama but surely, she doesn't hate me so much as to not try and help me.* The anger she felt for her sister was something she never thought would happen.

Some of the girls were talking to each other. None of them spoke to Michalina, probably because she had snapped at the two girls the night before. She felt bad about that, especially after guessing what they had been through. The man from the previous night appeared at the door with a tray of food. Michalina saw the two girls who went out each evening visibly shrink where they sat.

"Breakfast," he said cheerfully.

The man looked at Michalina and grinned without saying anything. He then left the room leaving the tray on the floor.

Michalina was starving. The 'H' had fixed her needs but not her hunger. She grabbed one of the bags of food from the tray. Sandwiches again. She didn't care and ate like it was her last meal.

Waiting for the men to collect her felt like an age. She had no desire to do what was asked but knew that without doing it, she would be forced to endure another night without her fix. Yesterday had shown her the withdrawal effects were unbearable. It suddenly occurred to her what the woman had said – "Paid off your debt." In her anger and revulsion at what she was being asked to do, she hadn't taken in the full conversation, but now the words were coming back to her. She suddenly realised that she had been sold to this woman, whoever she was. Who buys and sells people? She wasn't keen on Sebastian, but he dealt drugs, he didn't sell people.

Moments later the two men appeared. Again, the two girls cowered on their mattresses. Michalina knew what was going to happen and she had no choice. She stood up and followed the first man while the other man followed behind her.

The kitchen smelt of fresh coffee. But even the wonderful smell couldn't stop her from dreading what she was going to have to do.

"Morning, Michalina," the woman said. "I understand you needed some support in the night." She smiled. Michalina nodded. "Good, now let's see what else you can do. On your knees." Without a word Michalina sank slowly to her knees. The woman pointed towards one of the men. "You first."

The man smiled and unzipped his jeans, pulling them down to the top of his thighs.

"Don't be shy," said the woman in a matter-of-fact tone. Michalina slowly shuffled her way over to him.

By the time she had finished with the third man she was feeling sick. Only the man from the night before remained.

"Only one more, Michalina, I'm very impressed." She smiled.

With this man it took longer than with the others. Michalina guessed it was because he'd already been with the other girls, and it wasn't long ago she had sucked him off.

When he finished, Michalina sank backwards so she was resting on her heels.

"Very good, Michalina, up you get. We have a big day today. You will be off to England later." She smiled and indicated to the men to take her back to the room.

Returning to the room, Michalina felt disgusting but also knew it was never going to feel as bad as the withdrawal effects she had gone through.

CHAPTER 19

"Please sit." Daniels indicated towards the small sofa in his suite. Anastasjia and Uldis both sat down, saying nothing.

"Coffee, or something stronger?" he asked, smiling.

"Coffee, please," replied Uldis.

Anastasia shook her head. Daniels turned to the coffee and poured a cup.

"Milk?"

"No, thank you," replied Uldis politely. Grabbing a saucer to go with the cup, Daniels turned and walked to where they sat, passing the drink to Uldis.

"Ana, are you sure there is nothing I can get for you?" Again, she shook her head. She was struggling to concentrate, refreshments were the last thing on her mind.

"Thank you," she managed.

Her nose and face continued to throb in pain. She watched as Uldis picked up the cup of hot coffee, but then remembering the deep wound to his cheek, replaced it back in the saucer and put it down on the table.

"I should have thought of that," Daniels said, also realising that hot coffee was not practical. "We'll get you stitched up in no time, and we'll sort some kind of pain relief for you." Uldis nodded in thanks. "You've been through the wars." Daniels looked at the two of them. "Are you concerned about Balodis?" It was not a question Anastasjia was expecting. She looked at him, furling her eyebrows and showing her confusion. "Yes, of course you are." Daniels answered his own question. "Try not to be. The police will of course carry out an investigation, but you'll be happy to know they won't find anything connected to you." He paused. "Either of you."

"But—" began Anastasjia, but she was interrupted by Daniels.

"Please," he said. "The CCTV system in the hotel is faulty and has not recorded anything. The night staff did not see Balodis arrive and the fire escape at the rear of the hotel has been left open, which will suggest that that is how he got in."

Anastasjia tried to process the information. "But we were booked into the rooms and my blood is all over the place, on the towels, in the sink… I suspect our DNA and fingerprints are everywhere." She felt frightened, concerned and in pain.

"Not in the room he will be found in. His body is in another room's bath, soaking under the running shower. Your room is at this time being thoroughly cleaned, so there will be no obvious reason for you to be involved." Anastasjia looked from Daniels to Uldis and back to Daniels, still concerned. "You need not worry," he continued. "We are professionals. I have booked out a room here in Amigo for you to both get some rest. I assume one would be suitable?" he asked knowingly.

"Yes, thank you," replied Anastasjia before looking at Uldis who nodded in agreement.

"Yes, thank you," he said, finally speaking.

"I'll have a doctor come and see you about your injuries and then the two of you can get some sleep before we meet up. Is one still okay?" They both nodded. "Good, here's the key card, you're on the floor below. I'll have the doctor with you in about thirty minutes." He handed her the card and indicated to the door. It was clearly time to leave.

They both thanked him and made their way to the lift. Neither spoke or looked at each other. On the floor below Anastasjia struggled with the card for the door. She was angry and frustrated. The stress of all that had happened suddenly overwhelmed her and she began to cry.

"Here," said Uldis softly, and reaching out he took the card from Anastasjia, opening the door. She sat on the bed and Uldis joined her.

"We need to wait for the doctor," he said as he looked at her swollen face. She nodded. "It looks painful," he added.

"It's okay, how are you?" she asked, knowing he must be shaken by the events of the night. It's not every day you kill someone.

"Okay," he replied, though she could tell that was something of a lie, so as not to upset her further.

When the doctor arrived his English was bad. Not as bad as their Flemish but still it was difficult to understand.

"No broken," he said, pointing at Anastasjia's nose, and then said, "Big," moving his hands apart as if indicating she had a huge nose. She guessed he meant it was just swollen. He handed her some loose tablets.

"What are they?" she asked.

"Take," he said, and motioned putting them in his mouth, clearly not understanding her question.

"What?" she asked again, holding one up. "What?" she said again.

"Codeine," he replied. "Two." He held up two fingers and then began to repeat the number 'two' at her and tapping his watch meaningfully. She translated this to mean she should take two tablets every four hours.

The doctor turned to Uldis and held his face with one hand, turning it to get a good look at the gaping wound on his cheek. It had not stopped bleeding but at least it was no longer pouring out. The doctor reached into his bag and pulled out a small packet marked with the words 'MITSU sterilised surgical needled suture'. Pointing towards the hole in Uldis's face, he said the word 'stitch', and made a stitching movement with his hand.

Uldis nodded and the doctor got to work. He went back into the bag and pulled out a syringe and needle. He pointed at the injury again and managed to say, "No pain."

Anastasjia guessed he meant he'd numb the pain with the injection. She nodded and felt herself reaching out to hold Uldis's hand like a protective mother. Uldis looked at her before looking back at the doctor and nodding in appreciation for what he was going to do.

After stitching Uldis's face, the doctor covered it with lint and tape. He then handed him a pack of tablets the same as the ones given to Anastasjia and then he left the room.

Anastasjia and Uldis undressed down to their underwear and climbed into the bed. Uldis had to lie on his right side to keep the injury away from the pillow, which meant he was looking into Anastasjia's face. They had turned off the main lights but kept on the small lights by the skirting boards. Somehow, she needed some light in the room; it was also comforting to be able to see Uldis. Of course, he had agreed, it was clear he would do anything for her.

She smiled at him.

"Would you be okay to put your arm around me?" she asked, knowing the answer.

"Of course," he said, wincing slightly as he spoke.

She turned over and shuffled back into him and then felt his arm around her. It was reassuring and made her feel as though despite the trauma of the day and the violence she had been involved with and witnessed, things were going to work out for them.

They woke up late. Anastasjia opened her eyes and looked at the clock by the bed – 11:45. She could feel Uldis's arm around her still, heavy; she guessed he was still asleep. She edged away from him and crawled out, letting his arm fall gently to the bed. The room was light enough to see despite the curtains still being closed. She looked down at where Uldis slept, peaceful despite the lint covering his injury clearly on show. As she wandered into the bathroom, she caught sight of her face. Some of the swelling had begun to reduce but had been replaced by the ever-increasing array of colours from bruising. She put her hands up to her nose and touched it, wincing at the contact. Still very painful. *More codeine*, she thought to herself.

She would have loved to soak in the bath, but knew Daniels was expecting them at one, so she opted for the shower instead. Keeping him waiting was probably not a great idea. After the shower she dried herself and walked back into the main room, holding the towel in her hand. Uldis was awake.

"Morning," he said, looking at her body. She smiled.

"How are you feeling?" she asked.

"Okay," he replied. "You?"

"Okay," she said.

She wondered what he was really thinking. He was clearly still in pain and continued to wince as he spoke. She hoped he was really 'okay.'

"You need to get showered; Daniels will be expecting us at one."

"No problem," he said, pulling himself up. As he moved, he seemed to struggle, as though every muscle in his body was stiff and painful. She guessed it wasn't only his face that hurt from the fight with Balodis.

He walked around the bed to the bathroom and deliberately brushed his hands across her lower back as he passed. As he did, she felt the thrill of anticipation and excitement rush through her body.

"No time," she said to him. "Later."

When he was in the bathroom, Anastasjia looked around the room. She realised she had not seen their bags since they left the other room, where Balodis was lying dead. Here, they only had the blood-splattered clothes, which, of course, they couldn't put back on. She instinctively opened the wardrobe and was relieved to see that their clothes were neatly hanging up and folded on the shelves. The shirts and other items had even been ironed.

1:00pm and they were at Daniels' door.

"Welcome," he said, inviting them in. "I hope you managed to get some sleep. I'm afraid your injuries still look very painful."

"Thank you. Yes, they are, but we'll be okay."

Uldis just smiled.

"Okay," said Daniels. "If you need the doctor again, just let me know. Please come in. I've ordered us some lunch." They walked into the suite and could see the dining table set for three. "Do you think you'll be okay to eat?" He was looking at Uldis's face and injury.

"I'll try, thank you," he replied, though Anastasjia was not really sure whether it would be possible or not.

"Please help yourself." Daniels indicated the food before sipping from his drink.

The three of them finished off most of the food, even Uldis despite struggling a little with the discomfort.

"Ana, I asked you yesterday what we did as a company." She didn't reply, knowing he had more to say. "We do, as you say, 'sell cars'. We also move cash about in order to pay for things that we would rather the authorities knew nothing about."

Anastasjia nodded.

"Tell me, Ana, how did you come to work for the company?"

Anastasjia found herself cringing. She was unsure how much Uldis knew of her past, but she really didn't want to say in front of him how the company had saved her from her job in a brothel.

She looked at Uldis and he looked back at her. She then looked equally nervously towards Daniels. Reading her concerns, Daniels continued. "I understand the company rescued you from somewhere that was trying to force you into sex work?" he asked.

"Yes, yes, that's right," she managed to say, looking to see whether Uldis's expression had changed. He continued to stare blankly. She was unsure if that was a good or bad thing.

"And how do you think the company knew about the premises you were living in?"

It was a simple question, but one she hadn't really considered. All she knew is that they had stopped her from having to work there, and had punished the owner of the establishment.

"I don't know, I've never thought about it. I am grateful to the company for giving me the opportunity to work in the sales department though," she said, not quite convinced that that was the right answer.

"We have a number of very legitimate businesses." Daniels looked at Anastasjia, eyes unblinking. "We also have a number of not so legitimate businesses that we feel we can help to improve, and at the same time make profitable on a reasonably large scale." Daniels paused. "Can I get either of you another drink? Perhaps something stronger?"

"No thank you," they both answered together.

"Probably a good idea with the medication you're both taking." Daniels smiled. "We do need to launder money, you have identified that yourself, Ana, but the purpose of the money laundering is to help fund our other activities."

"Drugs?" said Anastasjia without thinking. It was an automatic response.

"No, no, not drugs. We do need on occasions to supply drugs to our users but not as a profit enterprise. No, the activities I speak of are personnel. We provide personnel for various businesses across Europe mostly, but also Africa when required and Asia on occasion."

Anastasjia looked back at Daniels.

"Sort of a recruitment agency," he said, laughing to himself.

"What businesses?" Anastasjia asked, but she had already guessed the answer.

"Mostly the sex trade, but also building sites, farming. On

occasion we get a request for domestic staff. They tend to be rarer, and the employees have very specific requirements, so we tend to get those from various African states. We find them more..." He paused and then finished his sentence. "Compliant." He smiled again, not taking his eyes off Anastasjia. She noticed Uldis's expression had not changed. "So, Ana, have you any thoughts?"

She looked at Daniels, not quite sure what he expected of her. Anastasjia had been caught unawares. She knew the car company was only part of the business and knew they were not all legitimate, but trafficking of humans? Wow, that was something else.

"I don't know. I'm not really sure what to say," she managed to splutter out.

Daniels laughed. "Ana, we... and by we, I mean those of us in the company who know you, think a lot of you. We would like to think you could move up in the organisation and perhaps become more involved in management decisions. Balodis, although an oaf and an idiot, had managed to put himself into that position, mostly through violence, but we feel you could replace him. What do you think?"

"What about Jennings? I don't understand. Are you saying he worked for you?" Anastasjia was now asking the questions. "Why was he being blackmailed into moving money?"

"Good observation, Ana. Indeed, the death of Jennings was totally unnecessary. Not everyone working for the company knows the set-up or the other aspects of the business. Although Jennings was a weasel, he was actually a very good car salesman. That was his job. He had no idea at all about the other parts of the business. We did know he was syphoning off some of the profits on the luxury car business and we allowed this to some extent. But we then decided that with a bit of persuasion he could be useful in other ways."

"Like moving money," said Anastasjia.

"Exactly," said Daniels. "The plan was to bring to his attention what we knew and perhaps set him up with some sort of evidence we could use against him."

Anastasjia shivered as she realised that she was the evidence, that night in the hotel with him. She kept quiet, hoping Daniels wouldn't bring it up in front of Uldis.

"But as we know, that fucking clown Balodis shot him. I still cannot get over how monumentally fucking stupid he was." He paused again. "But of course, you were there, so you know all about that, and for that, I'm sorry. Anyway, you stepped in and with help from Uldis fulfilled what Jennings would have undoubtedly done. But you did it without the level of persuasion Jennings required and with far more skill." Daniels smiled. "Obviously there is still part of the journey to go for the money but thank you for bringing it this far. For that, we would like to reward you."

Anastasjia was not sure she was ready to be rewarded or come to think of it, what Daniels even meant by that!

"Tomorrow, we have two minibuses leaving Brussels for the UK. On board are a number of workers, mostly women but also some men. The first will be travelling from Dieppe in France to Eastbourne on the south coast of England and the second from Zeebrugge, here in Belgium, to Hull in the northeast of England. We would like the two of you to accompany them." He looked from Uldis to Anastasjia, but neither said anything. "Ana, I would like you to make the journey to northern France in order to catch the ferry to England from Dieppe. I took the liberty of booking your ferry ticket in anticipation of your acceptance."

"But how would I get—" She began to respond only for Daniels to interrupt.

"You will be pleased to know that everything has been taken care of. Your journey has been programmed into the sat nav to make it nice and simple."

"Sat nav—" Again, she was interrupted.

"Yes, after working so hard to sell our Aston Martins I thought you might like to drive one to England. If you are stopped you are simply an employee of the company driving a company car, although we tend to find well dressed and finely turned-out people driving Aston Martins are rarely stopped." Anastasjia suddenly thought about her swollen nose and black eyes. Daniels must have guessed what she was thinking. "Don't worry, you still look very beautiful and with the application of a little makeup, and some dark glasses, you'll look as good as new."

He turned to Uldis.

"We have a similar plan for you. You have the more difficult of the tasks as you will need to drive from Hull in the north of England down to the south coast, accompanying the minibus."

"Why not catch the ferry to the south coast somewhere?" He didn't understand. Why did he need to go to Hull before travelling to the south? Why not go straight to the south coast? That was what Anastasjia was going to do. Despite his confusion, he tried to sound as reasonable as possible. He had witnessed how violent Daniels could be and was not sure he could afford to anger him.

"A good question, Uldis. I knew I could rely on you to think of the logistics. You seem a thoughtful person and that is why I am trusting you. Yes, of course it would be easier." He nodded towards him and paused before continuing. "We need to use different ports. Using the same one each time would soon attract unnecessary attention. This way, you have no obvious connection to Ana, and she has no obvious connection to you. We will provide you with a cover story similar to that of Ana's for if you are stopped. As a young man in a nice car, you are the most likely to be challenged so we will make sure you have all the documentation you need your story ready in full before you leave. After attending one of our other businesses in the north of England you will drive down to the south coast to meet up with Ana."

"What's the catch?" Uldis found himself saying. Anastasjia looked at him, concerned.

"No catch," replied Daniels. "I'm afraid there will be no Aston Martin for you, only a Volkswagen Golf, but still a nice car. Some of those you are travelling with have no idea what the future holds and are looking for a better life. Most of them know they have to work. Perhaps not the work they are expecting but nevertheless, they have something we need them to do. This is the one thing they all have in common; they need to work for us." Daniels smiled again. "Uldis, you will meet up with the minibus at the port. The driver and my associate travelling with them will be looking out for you, understand?" Uldis nodded. "Ana, you will be doing the same."

Anastasjia looked to Uldis and then back to Daniels. "What about Uldis's face? His injury is not going to be covered up by makeup."

"True," replied Daniels. "But we are aware of a report at a police station here in Brussels of a fight in a bar where unfortunately a man was stabbed in the face with a broken bottle. The police officer even has a statement, but unfortunately the offenders ran off before they could be found."

Daniels waited for either of them to speak. Both had worked out that he had their stories covered.

"Ana, I would like you to take the money you brought to me to England. We will ensure it is hidden in the car and we will remove it after you have arrived. The money will be used to pay for replacement workers who will require bringing across to France. I'll give you instructions before you return. Do either of you have any questions?"

Anastasjia had a lot of questions, too many, but she thought better of asking them. "When do we leave?" It was the only thing she felt safe to ask.

"Excellent. Tomorrow morning you can pick up the Aston from the car park and drive to France. It shouldn't take you longer than four hours to get to Dieppe but to play it safe I'd give yourself an extra couple of hours. You can always grab a coffee and maybe something to eat before the ferry. I'll get you the ferry times so you can judge for yourself. Obviously Zeebrugge is only a couple of hours away, Uldis, so you can leave later."

The two of them said nothing. Anastasjia wondered if Uldis was as stunned by everything as she was. He was a hard-working guy who had been dragged into this world of crime. In a short space of time, he had been seriously injured, killed a man and was now getting involved in people trafficking. She wondered what he was thinking. She had some understanding about the company. She knew the car business was not what it purported to be and had witnessed Jennings being murdered by Balodis. She had been a sex worker in another life and the company had taken advantage of this by getting her to sleep with clients and where necessary blackmail business associates and customers. What did he know? She had no idea.

"Very good, now the two of you can enjoy Brussels this evening or take advantage of room service. I leave it up to you. Don't worry about the cost, it's our pleasure."

With that, Daniels stood up. It was time to leave.

CHAPTER 20

Alice took the latest missing person report from her sergeant. No matter how hard she tried, she struggled to show enthusiasm. Six years in the police including a year's training as a detective and here she was dealing with stroppy teenagers who didn't want to be helped.

"When you qualify, where would you like to be posted?" She remembered the conversation with the DI who had pushed her down the detective route. Before him, she was more than happy running around in uniform, dealing with public order and driving fast on a blue light run. She enjoyed the thrill. She didn't like everything about it, like when she nicked offenders and found them back on the street a couple of hours later. That really pissed her off. Why did no one know what they were doing?

As a police officer, she was used to frustration. Arresting someone for a domestic only for the partner to be banging on the counter pleading for their return, sometimes before they even got them booked into custody. People needed help because they were having a breakdown and having to drag them off the street for their own good, only for some psychiatrist to let them straight out of the hospital where they were vulnerable again. Drunken idiots on a Friday and Saturday night thinking they're funny when for the twentieth time in a night they shout out, "Oh, look, the strip-a-gram arrived." Wankers, the lot of them.

The DI – Jameson – was the one who suggested she had an aptitude for investigation, but she could guess that his attention was for a different reason: getting in her knickers. She was used to it; she had been fending off unwanted advances since she was a teenager, so this was nothing new.

She passed her detective's exams with the highest mark in the class, and had been shown to be the best student. So even if the only reason she got on the course was because of a DI lusting after her, then she would go with that. She also suspected that having told him where to get off and threatening to tell his wife was the reason she ended up dealing with missing persons. "Anywhere but public protection," in other words she wasn't interested in dealing with domestic disputes, child protection cases that should be dealt with by social workers, vulnerable adults who should be in hospital or missing persons, usually stroppy kids. "Major Crime would be great," she had told the DI, who assured her he would be her sponsor. But then she refused his advances.

It was no surprise when her posting came through. Sitting at the breakfast bar at home she tore open the envelope and then pulled out the A4 sheet of paper.

"Fuck," she found herself saying out loud.

"What, what's the matter?" her girlfriend – Nyakim – had asked, clearly concerned.

"Missing fucking persons," she said. "Fucking bastard." She knew that Jameson was the one who'd done this. He'd pretty much promised her Major Crime, her performance on the course had shown him she was worth the place. *Well fuck him.* She was so mad.

That was over a year ago and she had been stuck here ever since. The others in the office seemed to love it; she couldn't see it. To her this just didn't feel like real police work. As the months had passed, she had grown to understand the importance of the work, it just wasn't for her. She wanted to be out dealing with the big villains. She had put in for a move, but it was refused on the grounds that she was needed here.

To make matters worse the wanker Jameson was now the divisional DCI.

"I wonder who he shagged to get that job," she told Nyakim when she heard.

Today, as she got into the car to drive to Weybridge there was something troubling her. Someone like Harry going missing did not follow the pattern she usually saw. She kind of guessed that his sister was the one leading him astray, she was a complete waste of time. Nothing but trouble, skipping school day in and day out. And every time Alice tried to speak with her, she either got a tirade of abuse or the cold shoulder.

She had first come across Lilly about a year ago. Over the months she had gone missing with increasing frequency but had always turned up. To start with she would just be a bit late home. This then developed to coming in late at night and eventually coming back the next day. Since she turned 16, she'd been a complete nightmare. Harry, on the other hand, up until recently had been the model child, but not anymore. Alice mused, not now his sister had obviously got him into something, but what? Three times over the last couple of weeks he'd gone missing only to turn up a day or two later.

Shame, really, Alice quite liked him. When she did home visits on returning missing persons, Harry was normally reasonable. Her biggest concern was his deteriorating attitude and the fact that his sister had decided to stay out longer and longer. She was last seen a couple of weeks ago. Her mother was frantic, and Harry clearly knew something but was saying nothing.

She got on okay with the mother – Diane – but thought the father and his show wife were stuck-up arseholes. The dad especially was so far up himself, he spoke to everyone like they were his inferiors. Well, not with her.

If she could get to Harry, she may – and it was a big may – just be able to stop him going down the same route as his sister. She decided she would do her best with him. She might hate this job, but if she could stop Harry turning out like Lilly, she'd be happy.

*

Harry was in his room. He'd been back for a couple of hours. Three times now he had gone down to the house in Eastbourne and each time he had been told Lilly would be back when he got home. She wasn't and Harry was desperate to get help. The only problem with that was they had warned him Lilly would be harmed if he said anything, and now he was a 'drug dealer' he'd be locked away. Harry felt like his head would explode, there was so much going on. He was missing school; he was not seeing his friends – not that he had many – and he was worried about Lilly.

Jordan had forced him to take some money, over two hundred pounds. He'd been told to hide the phone and the money as it could lead the police to them. If that happened, then Lilly was dead. He was terrified.

He knew his mother was falling apart, she wouldn't stop crying.

"Where the hell have you been?" she had shouted at him. "How can you do this to me? First your sister and now you. I don't get it. What have I done that is so awful?"

How desperately he wanted to tell her everything, to have her put her arms around him and reassure him everything was going to be okay, he just knew he couldn't. The risk was too high.

Hearing the car pull onto the driveway he looked out of the window. His head dropped as he saw the brand-new Aston Martin pull in and grind to a halt. He let his head drop so his chin nearly hit the top of his chest. *Dad, that's all I need.* He looked up and watched as his dad climbed out of the driver's side of the car and slammed it shut, with far greater force than it needed. Harry could see his dad was not in a good mood. His mother must have called him. He sat on the bed and tried to think of what to say. It wasn't going to be easy, but he had to protect Lilly.

The doorbell never rang so his mum must have seen him arrive too. He did hear the door close, though, the slamming suggested his dad had used the same force he had used with the car.

He could hear his dad's raised voice. "what the hell...", "your fault...", "better off without..." and occasionally replies from his mum: "why can't you...", "for fuck sake...", don't blame..." and so it went on. He could hear his mother crying. Harry sunk onto the bed; he felt awful.

More tyres on the gravel drive. Harry turned and looked out to see the unmarked police car.

He had seen this police officer before. She came round both times after he got back from Eastbourne. She was okay, she never shouted. If anything, Harry thought she was a bit disinterested. Each time she would ask about Lilly, but he just said he didn't know where she was, and she left it at that. Hopefully it would be the same today. And he hoped his dad wouldn't make it worse by shouting and yelling. That's how he normally dealt with not getting everything he wanted.

This time he did hear the doorbell. He couldn't hear what was being said, so he guessed they had gone through to the kitchen, either that or they were whispering. Harry moved over to the door and opened it quietly. Still, he couldn't hear anything. He crept onto the landing and over to the banister, surprised by how noisy the floorboards were.

Suddenly he heard the kitchen door open.

"Just let me have a word—" The police officer was interrupted.

"Why should I let you speak to my son without me? I have rights," dad shouted.

Just what Harry expected.

"Please don't—" His mum tried to intervene.

"I'm coming with you; he'll talk to me." His dad was being firm. That was his 'I expect to get my own way' voice.

Harry darted back into his room and shut the door, not before hearing the police officer say, "Please, Mr. Voclain, it will be best if you let me speak to him without you."

With the door closed it was difficult to hear but his father's voice was like before. "He's my son… This wouldn't happen if…"

He sat on the bed.

Suddenly the shouting stopped, followed by quiet footsteps on the stairs. It only sounded like one set of feet. There was a knock on his door.

"Harry, can I come in please?" It was the police officer.

"Come in."

The door opened.

*

Alice walked in and saw Harry sitting on the bed. Unlike most missing teenagers she came across Harry looked terrified, but terrified of what?

"Hi, Harry, how are you today?" she asked in the most pleasant voice she could muster.

"Fine." He didn't look fine though.

"Can I sit down?" she asked, indicating the office chair by his desk. She noticed he didn't have a computer set up, only a television and a PlayStation. She knew he could probably access the internet on that, but something told her he didn't.

This whole thing with Harry going missing was odd. He was a good kid who did well at school, he was the perfect child at home and well thought of by his parents and teachers, so why this sudden change? It had to be Lilly; Lilly was nothing but trouble.

"You look upset, Harry, you certainly don't look fine. If something's troubling you, you can tell me."

Harry looked away and said, "I told you, I'm fine, okay!"

She could tell he was trying to sound annoyed, but his voice was trembling.

"Is it Lilly?" As she spoke, Alice leaned to one side so as to catch

Harry's eye.

"No," Harry shouted.

"It obviously is, Harry. Where is she?"

"I don't know, how should I know?" It was totally unconvincing. Alice couldn't help wondering what that bitch had gotten her brother into.

"Look, Harry, I really like you. You're a nice guy and I know you're sensible, that's why I think Lilly is getting you involved in something, and I don't think it's something you want to be involved in. Am I right?" she asked more out of hope than any expectation of an answer.

"No, no she's not, I don't know where she is, leave me alone, I don't want to see you, please go." Tears had started to roll down his cheeks. He quickly wiped them with his sleeve.

Alice looked at him sympathetically. She could see whatever it was, caused him a lot of distress.

"Okay, Harry, I won't ask about Lilly again today, but I've got to ask, where have you been for the last couple of days?"

Harry looked at her then looked away again. "Please go," was all he could say.

"Okay, Harry, I might be back to see you later. Please don't go missing again." It was a throwaway comment, she knew there was every chance he would go missing again, especially if Lilly had her claws in him. She stood up to leave and reached into her jacket pocket for her business cards. She handed one to Harry who took it without looking at it.

"If you want to talk to me, any time at all, just give me a call on the mobile number. If I don't pick up, leave me a message and I promise I'll get back to you, okay?" Harry nodded. "See you later," she said as she walked from the room.

"Bye," came the polite reply.

Nice kid, she thought again as she closed the door behind her. As she reached the bottom of the stairs, Harry's dad was waiting.

"Well?"

"Something's troubling him and he's not talking just yet—"

"I'll go speak to him; he'll talk to me."

She looked him in the eye. He was still angry. She knew his type, rich people used to getting their own way and looking down on everyone else, never listening to anyone.

"Please, just give it a while, he's upset about something. I suspect it's to do with Lilly but he's not saying."

"Bloody girl, this is your fault." Alice instantly regretted mentioning Lilly. He turned to his ex-wife. "Too bloody soft with her." Diane looked fearful of him, that was obvious. She had enough training in coercive and controlling behaviour in domestic abuse, to guess what the relationship was like between them and how affected Lilly probably was by his overpowering behaviour.

"Please just leave it with us. I'm going to speak with Lilly's best friend this afternoon and that might help us work out where she is." She knew he wouldn't leave it.

"So, you're saying that Harry's going missing because of Lilly, and that Julie Porter girl knows about it?" He snapped it back at her.

"No, I'm not saying that. I'm saying I'm going to find out if she can help us find Lilly," she said as firmly as she could. "Now I've got to go but I'll let you know how I get on." She turned to go.

"If you can't find her, I will!" He shouted at her.

"Thank you for your time," she said as she walked out. There was no reply.

*

Harry watched her leave from his window. He worried that she might ruin things by looking for Lilly and the men finding out. He really wanted to tell her what he knew. She seemed really nice, he just couldn't take the risk.

*

After getting back to the office Alice got on with her paperwork. It had been a productive afternoon and she had forwarded several files to her sergeant for review and hopefully filing. Alice grabbed her bag and her car keys. She didn't normally do visits in her own car but after speaking with Julie's parents, she couldn't see her until 4:00pm. Apparently Julie had missed so much school that they didn't want her missing out when she did go. The only good thing was that Julie Porter lived on Alice's way home. Using her own car was a small price to pay as after a quick visit to her she could head home.

As she walked to the car her mobile rang. She recognised the number. It was Julie Porter's mother. *Please don't put it off*, she thought before swiping right to answer the call.

"Hello?" Through the sobs on the phone Alice could make out Julie's mum's voice.

"Hi, I'm really sorry but we're going to have to cancel, Julie's in hospital."

Alice was surprised. "Sorry, what? What happened?"

"We don't know yet, she's in surgery. Her jaw's been broken and she has a heavily bruised eye socket." Alice could hear she was struggling to speak.

"Sorry, how did it happen? Do you know who?" The questions raced through her mind. Poor kid.

"We don't know, she can't speak at the moment. I'll call you when I know more."

"What hospital is she in?" asked Alice, half wondering whether she should go to there or if she could get away with sneaking off home early.

"We're going to St. Peter's; we're going to wait there to see her."

"Okay," replied Alice. "Call me when you know how she is, I'll leave my mobile on."

"Okay, we will." With that, Julie's mum hung up.

Alice wondered who had hurt her and couldn't help feeling a little jealous for whoever at the station would be dealing with it. Now a good GBH, that's a proper crime for a detective. That's what she should be investigating.

*

"Tea's ready," Harry's mum shouted up the stairs.

"Thanks," he shouted back.

After the police lady left, his dad had come up and had a go at him, saying things like, "How could you do this?" and, "Don't we give you enough?" Then he'd gone and shouted at his mum, upsetting her again. Much as he loved his dad, he really didn't make speaking with him easy. He left after that and roared off the gravel drive in his car. Harry could hear the sound of the stones on the driveway hitting the body of the Aston Martin. Harry guessed there would be a few new stone chips on the paintwork after that.

Harry wandered into the kitchen and sat at the breakfast bar where his mum had laid him a place.

"Okay?" she asked, clearly trying to keep things together.

"Yeah, sure," he replied. "Sorry I upset you," he said, even though he knew Jordan would call in the next few days and he'd have to disappear off to Eastbourne again.

"That's okay," she replied. "Let's watch a film together tonight."

Harry didn't hear her. His eye had been caught by the television in the kitchen. It had the local news on. The large recovery vehicle was lifting the bright orange Ford Escort ST from the Thames. The reporter was saying a crash had happened earlier this afternoon and the body of a young man had been recovered from the vehicle. It continued to say police had not yet released the identity of the man.

Harry didn't need to be told who it was. He knew it was Jordan.

CHAPTER 21

Bzz… Bzz… Bzz…

The mobile on the side table continued to vibrate, desperate for an answer.

Alice opened one eye and glanced over to where the light from the screen illuminated the room.

Bzz… Bzz… Bzz…

She could feel one of Nyakim's arms around her, which made it difficult to reach and the last thing she wanted to do was wake her. Leaning over as far as she could without moving Nyakim's arm, she picked up the phone and glanced at the screen.

A number she didn't recognise.

Bzz… Bzz… The phone continued.

Alice pulled herself away and rolled up into a sitting position. Unplugging the charging cable, she gently stood up and walked out of the room. *Bzz… Bzz… Bzz…* The phone continued to demand her attention.

She swiped the answer button as she closed the bedroom door behind her.

"Hello?" she half whispered. Nothing, no sound came back. "Hello, who is this?" Alice spoke again. She reached the stairs and began to make her way down. "Who is this?" she asked again, sounding a little more annoyed than she intended.

"Hello," came a whispered reply. "Is that the police lady?"

"Harry?" asked Alice. She wasn't expecting that. "Harry?" she repeated. "Is that you? What time is it?" She didn't mean to infer he was calling at the wrong time, but it was a natural question. She knew it was still very dark outside.

"Erm, I'm not sure, I think it's about four thirty." He sounded as though it was perfectly natural to call at this time although clearly, he must be distressed to be calling her in the middle of the night.

"What is it? Why are you calling at this time?"

"You said to call you any time." It was true, she had said that, she just didn't expect him to take it so literally.

"Okay, Harry, you've got me now. What can I do for you?" She waited for a response, but Harry stayed quiet. "Harry…" She waited; nothing came. "Listen, Harry, I know it must be difficult to call, but you have so the hard part is over. What is it? Is it about Lilly?" There was another pause. "Okay, Harry, it's the middle of the night and I'm—"

"I don't know where she is," Harry finally said. He sounded frantic.

"Okay, so why are you telling me now? You told me that earlier." She was trying not to sound exasperated.

"Because Jordan's dead," blurted out Harry.

"Jordan? Who's Jordan?" Alice had not heard of anyone by that name related to the case.

"He's the one who was going to tell me when Lilly could come home," Harry said. "If he can't pick me up, I don't know how Lilly gets to come home."

Harry was speaking so fast it was making little sense to Alice.

"Where are you now?" she asked, suddenly concerned he may have run off again.

"I'm at home." He sounded surprised.

"Okay, how about I come to yours at 8:00am before you go to school?" Alice needed time to think about what Harry was saying.

"No, no you can't do that." He still sounded agitated.

"What then?" Alice replied. She didn't understand but she could tell it might be a good way of finding Lilly.

"Can you meet me at the end of my road at 8:15?" he asked.

"End of the road? Which end of the road, where?" she asked, knowing Oatlands Park was quite a big area.

"Oatlands Chase, where it meets Oatlands Drive?"

Alice thought for a moment. She could meet up with Harry, get the information about Lilly, run him to school and be at work for about 9:30. Having driven off early in her own car the night before, she knew work would disapprove of her using her own car for another visit.

"Okay, 8:15 and you can tell me about Lilly."

"Okay," he replied. "Don't tell anyone." He was still panicking.

"Why's that?" Alice wanted to know what he was so afraid of.

"Please," he pleaded.

"Okay, no problem, I won't tell anyone." She made a mental note to let someone know where she was, knowing she was going to break her promise. And why she was going to be late.

"If you tell anyone, I won't tell you anything." Harry was still pleading.

"Okay, Harry, I've promised, don't worry." Alice tried to sound as reassuring as possible despite it not coming to her naturally.

Harry hung up, leaving Alice holding the phone against her ear. She glanced at the clock on the cooker and saw the time was now quarter to five. She could go back to bed; the thought of snuggling into Nyakim was certainly inviting but the risk was that she would wake her, and Alice knew she needed the sleep.

Today she needed to leave a little earlier in order to make her way over to Weybridge to see Harry. *It better be worth it*, she thought to herself as she switched on the coffee machine.

After showering and dressing Alice went back down to the kitchen and laid the breakfast bar for her and Nyakim. She knew it was still a little while before she would be up, so she grabbed the remote control for the small TV on the wall and turned on Breakfast News. *Same old stories*, she thought as she scanned the screen for the headlines. They were so depressing and yet each day she was drawn to the news as though it was the most important thing she did. She found herself watching it whenever she could, on TV, on her mobile and her computer at work.

Nyakim would tell her to turn it off, especially when she was looking at it on her mobile in the evening. "You prefer that damn news to me," she would say.

"Of course, I don't," she would reply, whilst craving the opportunity to look again. Seeing the news reminded her of what she wanted most from her job, to work in Major Crime.

The national news switched to the local news. The irony being that as they lived near to London, most of the news was the same. They covered a couple of the local stories, like the car going in the Thames near the Chertsey Meads. She already knew about that as it had been on the evening news yesterday.

"The driver has been named this morning as Jordan Winter from East London," said the reporter, standing in front of the severely damaged car on the recovery lorry.

Alice was still tired, the details of the car and the driver not registering in her mind. The camera then switched to a local complaining about cars racing on the Meads and how it was all related to drugs. "We always knew something like this would happen," said the elderly lady.

Job for the traffic department, thought Alice to herself, dismissing it as a young driver going too fast and crashing. She poured another cup of coffee.

She heard Nyakim coming down the stairs and glanced at the clock again – 6:55, right on time. Nyakim kissed her gently on the lips. "Morning. You were up early," she said.

"Yes, I took a phone call from a kid I've been dealing with, he seemed in quite a state."

Nyakim smiled. "That's a funny time to be calling."

"Four thirty, would you believe?" She smiled back. "I didn't want to wake you, you looked so peaceful lying there." She was beautiful, absolutely stunning. She felt so lucky to be with her.

"What did he want that couldn't wait?" Nyakim asked, interested, but Alice did wonder whether she was really annoyed about it.

"I'm not sure, he sounded really distressed. He's only young but has started going missing. I've a feeling it's to do with his sister."

"Do you ever switch off?" asked Nyakim. She smiled, knowing how hard Alice had needed to work to become a detective and that she was in a part of the business she didn't enjoy. She did her best to be supportive, but Alice knew she worried about the amount of work she did and the constant need to prove herself to her colleagues.

"You can talk," replied Alice. Nyakim was always working late, putting in long hours.

Nyakim left for work and Alice left shortly after, grabbing her coat, bag and keys before stepping out and locking up. As she got into the car, she saw her elderly neighbour was putting out the bins and cursed to herself. She'd forgotten about them.

"Morning," she called to him, smiling. He was a nice old boy, she and Nyakim got on really well with him. He was one of the few people who knew Nyakim lived with her, although she doubted he knew they were partners. In fact, no one knew they were partners. She wasn't ready to come out as gay. She had suspected her not going to Major Crime was because she had rejected Jameson. She had no idea what he would do if he knew she was gay.

Nyakim had different reasons for not wanting to come out. Her family were devout Muslims and although they had allowed her to continue with her education, they were not about to accept that she was gay. To them, her living with another woman, and a police officer at that, suited their perception.

"Morning, Alice, early start?" He smiled back.

"Yeah, you wouldn't be a lamb and do my bins, would you? I'm running a bit late."

She hated to ask but it was a friendly neighbourhood and they helped each other out.

"No problem." He waved. "Have a good day."

"Thanks," she called back before climbing in the driver's seat and reversing off the drive.

The journey to Weybridge was awful, as she suspected. *I could bloody walk there quicker*, she thought as she stop/started all the way through the town. The traffic began to move a little quicker heading to Walton-on-Thames. As she approached the junction with Oatlands Chase, she saw that Harry was already there. He hadn't seen her. She turned into Oatlands Chase and pulled up on the grass verge. Finally seeing her, Harry climbed in.

She had forgotten to tell work where she was going. It was a foolish oversight; telling people where you were going was basic safety. *Oh well,* she thought. *A woman of my word*. After all, she had promised not to tell anyone.

"Alright?" she asked. "Do you want to talk to me?" Harry nodded but didn't offer any further information. It was going to be like pulling teeth if this carried on. "Okay, Harry, you called me in the middle of the night and got me out here this morning. I've done that so you need to speak to me. What is it that you wanted to tell me?" Harry looked at her again and then looked down.

"They've got Lilly and I don't know what to do." He had started to cry. Big fat tears rolled down his cheeks.

"Who? What? Harry, who has got Lilly?"

"I don't know." He was shaking.

"Okay, Harry, I need you to explain to me, who has Lilly?" She tried to keep her voice as friendly as possible.

"It was her boyfriend but now he's dead, so I don't know who it is now."

"Who's dead?" she asked.

"Jordan," he replied.

"Who's Jordan?" It was not making any sense.

"Lilly's boyfriend."

Alice tried again by going back to the beginning. "Okay, Harry, listen to me. I want to help but I need you to go over what you know as slowly as possible and explain to me where Lilly is."

There was a pause before he answered.

"I don't know where she is. Jordan knew, but he's dead now." He sounded exasperated but Alice couldn't work out what he meant. She tried a different tack.

"How do you know Jordan is dead?"

"I saw his car on TV. They were pulling it out of the river."

She remembered the news that morning. "Was the boy driving the car Lilly's boyfriend?" she asked even though she already suspected the answer.

"Yes, that's what I've been saying." Harry looked relieved.

"Okay, Harry, how do you know all this?" Her curiosity was growing.

"I was with Lilly just before they took her, but they promised they would let her go if I did as I was told. They've still got her but now Jordan's dead I don't know who else to speak to and I don't know where she is!" The words repeated in her mind: 'they took her.'

"Okay, how about you come with me, and we can have a proper chat. What I'd like to do is go to a special room where we can record what we're saying, and you can tell me everything."

It was part of a rehearsed speech she used whenever she needed to video interview children.

"No, we can't." Harry sounded suddenly frantic.

"Hey, hey, don't worry," she replied, trying to calm him. "We can get your mum to be present to make sure you're okay. Don't worry, you haven't done anything wrong, you'll be fine."

"No!" he shouted at her.

"What then, Harry? What would you like to do? You asked me to come here, I can't do anything if you won't talk to me." She looked at his face, which was wet from his tears.

There was a pause.

"Can I show you?" He almost whispered the question.

"Show me what?"

"Where they took her."

"Harry, you're going to have to be more specific. What do you mean, where they took her?"

"We were both there and they said they would let her go but they didn't."

"Right, so you can take me to where they took Lilly? Yes?" He nodded. "Where is it?" she asked, hoping for a specific location.

"Near the Olympics."

"Near to where the Olympics were in Stratford?"

"Yes, that's it, Stratford. I know the house, it's near the station." Alice thought it through as quickly as she could. If Lilly had been taken, she needed to get back-up and put an operation in place.

"Right, Harry, you'll have to come with me. We need to go to the police station, and you need to tell me everything. We'll then try and find Lilly."

"No," Harry shouted. "You're not listening. No, I can't."

"But—"

"No, I said no. I'll show you but I'm not talking to anyone, and you can't make me. I'll deny everything."

Alice was at a loss. "So, you want me to go with you to Stratford to point out the house?"

"Yes, but you can't tell anyone it was me."

Alice knew she couldn't do what he was asking, the risks were too great. "Look, I know you're scared but—" Harry interrupted her.

"If you don't want me to show you I won't." He was angry.

"It's not that, it's just that you'll be missing from school, and I can't go over to Stratford without telling someone. I'll be missed. I'm going to end up late for work as it is."

She was trying to think how best to keep Harry onside, knowing this was an opportunity to be involved in solving a serious crime. A young girl taken away, it was what she craved.

Harry reached out to open the door.

"Just forget it," he said as he wiped the tears from his face with his free arm.

"Wait," Alice called, loud enough to stop him in his tracks. She couldn't believe she was even considering the idea of going to London with him, but this was possibly the only chance of getting the information she needed. It could also get her recognition, if it led to solving what she suspected was something serious. She weighed up the risk; all she needed to do was see where Lilly had gone and report the matter as having been told by Harry. She could deal with the fallout later. "Okay, give me a moment, you sit down." Harry sat in the seat as Alice opened her door to stand up.

"What are you doing?" He clearly didn't trust her yet.

"I'm just going to call in and let them know I'm not going into the office," she replied.

"Promise?"

"I promise," she replied, closing the door and dialling her sergeant.

After she had spoken to her sergeant, claiming she was ill, she hung up and got back into the car.

"So, if I go to Stratford rail station, you can direct me to the house from there?" she asked, hoping for a positive response. Harry nodded and then looked straight ahead waiting for her to leave.

Driving up the A3, Harry said nothing, so Alice didn't push him any further, not wanting to risk upsetting him. Occasionally she would try simple questions like, "How's school?" or, "Do you still like your computer games?" which elicited the same answers. "Fine… Yes… No." Certainly not giving anything away or indicating he wanted to talk.

Eventually they approached Stratford and the Queen Elizabeth Olympic Park.

"Where should I go?" she asked.

"I'm not sure. I can take you there from the station. It's not far to walk."

Alice decided to park in the multi-storey in the shopping centre and walk to the station from there.

Harry led the way from the station towards the house. But as he rounded the corner to the road, he saw that it was closed off with police tape and officers were stopping foot traffic. Harry turned to Alice.

"It's just down there on the right," he said, pointing down the row of Victorian houses. There were at least three ambulances outside. Alice turned to a man and woman in their 50s or 60s who were standing by the tape in front of them.

"What's going on?" she asked.

"There's been a shooting," the woman said.

"Drugs, I expect, in one of the houses."

Suddenly a stretcher was carried out and was put into one of the ambulances. It held a covered body. A second body followed and then a third.

"All dead by the look of it," said the man, not looking away from the scene in front of him.

"Far too much of it going on in this area. Used to be a good place to bring up the kids," said the woman.

"Yeah, unless you knew the Krays," said the man, laughing.

Harry tugged on Alice's arm.

"That's the house, that's where I went with Lilly." He sounded more shocked than afraid.

Shit, this is serious. Alice knew she should speak to the officers at the scene but at the same time, that could get her in trouble for lying about being ill, and for taking the risk of going there with a vulnerable witness in tow. Better to get back and report the concerns later. That way she could stick to the original plan, and say it was information she had been told by Harry.

"Come on," said Alice, turning to go back to the car.

Harry was asking Alice what she was going to do. All she could say was that she was working out what was best. She guessed Harry knew she had no idea.

Back in the car park, they were approaching the car when a voice spoke as if from nowhere.

"Leaving so soon, Harry?" Next to her, Harry stiffened. "You haven't introduced me to your friend."

Alice turned at the same time as Harry. The voice came from a large black guy. Harry froze in fear. Alice could tell how terrified he was.

"Police," she called out. "Who are you?" The man looked at her and then back to Harry.

"Police? Fucking police, Harry, I'm very disappointed. Which is your car?"

"What?" replied Alice.

"Your car, bitch, which is your fucking car?" He stared at her.

"I'm not telling you that, who are you?" The man drew himself up to his full height and stepped forwards, so he was inches from her.

Suddenly he grabbed her by the throat. "I said, where are your fucking keys, bitch?" he snarled. The man reached into his pocket with his free hand and pulled out a butterfly knife before expertly opening it and pushing it against Alice's abdomen. "Last time, bitch. Where are your fucking keys?"

Alice was terrified and her mind was racing. Protect Harry, that had to be the priority. Do as the man says, try and calm him down. She reached into her bag, pulling the keys out. The man snatched them before pressing the door button. Alice's car alarm sparked into life, flashing the lights and sounding that the doors were unlocked.

The man threw Alice towards her car like she was a rag doll.

"You drive, I'll sit with young Harry in the back. Any fucking around and I'll stick him and then you. Got it, bitch?" Alice nodded and got in. Harry climbed in the back and was shoved over by the man so he could sit behind her. "Where's your phone?" he said as he leaned forwards.

"What?" She had heard what he asked, she just responded out of habit.

"Fuck me, bitch, are you fucking deaf? Where is your fucking phone!" he shouted.

She reached into her bag on the front passenger seat. The man suddenly grabbed the bag from her and pulled out the phone himself and kept the bag by his side.

"Code?" he asked.

"Seven-four-six-three," she answered quickly so as not to anger him further. Although she couldn't see, she guessed the man had tapped in the number unlocking the phone. In her mirror she could see he was looking at it.

"Time to go for a drive while I work out who fucked us over." He indicated for Alice to start the car.

CHAPTER 22

"Room service," came the voice from outside the room. Anastasjia was already awake, in fact she had been awake most of the night. The clock by the side of the bed showed it was 6:30, though it felt like later, she had been awake for so long. Incredibly, Uldis was sleeping soundly. He hadn't even woken to the sound of the door being knocked.

She walked to the door before pausing. Last time she had opened a hotel room door Balodis had stormed in and attacked her. She looked out through the peephole to see a smartly dressed young man aged in his early twenties. His name was emblazoned on the Hotel Amigo badge. Still not wanting to take the risk, she called out, "Thank you, just leave it there," still looking through the peephole.

The young man leaned towards the door. "Okay, no problem," he replied, putting down a ladened tray before walking off down the corridor towards the lifts.

When she was happy he was far enough away, she grabbed her hotel dressing gown and opened the door. On the floor there was a tray with plates covered with metal and a cafetiere full of coffee, cups, saucers, napkins, and orange juice all laid out. She carefully lifted it into the room and saw that Uldis was finally awake, sleepily sitting up in bed.

"Morning, sleepyhead," she said. As she smiled, she felt the pain in her face from the previous day's assault.

"Morning," he replied. She noticed that he, too, winced as he responded. She was not the only one in pain.

She put the tray on the bed and sat next to him, lifting the metal covers off the plates to find two full English breakfasts. Uldis laughed. "Getting us ready to work in England." She was surprised by his casual humour; they were now going to be involved in something really serious.

"Are we going to talk about this?" Anastasjia asked. She remained deeply worried about the days ahead.

"Talk about what?" he asked, trying to sound as though he had no idea what she was talking about.

"This," she said in a raised voice. "This, today, England, smuggling people. And how about yesterday, you killed Balodis? Lots of things."

She looked at his face and suddenly saw how young he was, how naive, a country boy thrust into a new and violent world of corruption and crime. How could she not have noticed this before? She had been too busy thinking about how she was feeling and now they were going to have to travel to England with a group of people against their wishes, and all that money being laundered to pay for more of the crime he was being sucked into.

"I don't know what there is to talk about. We've been told what we have to do," he said.

"Oh, right, and you're okay with all of this?" she snapped.

"No, I'm not alright with it, but we're here and we're stuck with it for now."

Anastasjia shook her head. "Stuck for now? How does that work?" she said. "When exactly do we stop being involved in this? Once in it, we're in it. Can't you see that?"

She looked at his face. He wasn't angry, just concerned. He knew this could end up being his life. Not just now but for the time to come, possibly forever, she didn't know, and she couldn't guarantee his release from the company. In some ways it was easier for her. She had been rescued from a dreadful situation, one that meant almost anything was an improvement, so despite hating what they were being asked to do she was still grateful it wasn't as bad as what she'd had to do in her past.

"Look, Ana, I know it looks bad—" But before he could finish Anastasjia interrupted him.

"Yeah, you could say that. It does look bad, and I don't want you having any part of it." She stared at him; he looked calmer than she expected.

"I know," he said. "I don't want any part of it either but for the moment we have no choice. If we do as Daniels asks, maybe we can negotiate a way out for us. I don't know, this is all new to me."

"Shit, what the fuck have I got you into?" she said, shaking her head, and then moved to the edge of the bed, her hands over her face.

"Come on, Ana, please. I don't want us to part like this. We have to separate for a while so let's enjoy breakfast together and we'll try and work things out later." She smiled as he pulled her hands away from her face gently. He slowly pulled himself into a more comfortable sitting position.

They ate without speaking, both of them finding it surprisingly easy to finish everything on the plates. They both had a second coffee and Anastasjia gave Uldis an apologetic smile.

"Are we okay?" she asked tentatively. He smiled back.

"Yeah, I guess so." He shook his head slightly, partly trying to stop her from seeing it.

"I'm going to have to leave in a moment, it's a long drive to Dieppe," she said.

"I know, I'll help with your bag. I'm only a short drive away so I've a couple of hours yet."

There was a knock at the door. As Anastasjia was partly dressed, she went over and again looked through the peephole. Daniels. She opened the door.

"Sorry to disturb you," he began. "Not much time, Ana, if you are to make it to Dieppe. I just wanted to make sure you got away on time."

"Yes, of course," Anastasjia replied.

Daniels nodded. "Could I come in, just for a moment?" It was a request she knew not to refuse.

He stepped into the room and closed the door. Uldis reached for his dressing gown by his side of the bed.

"No, please," said Daniels. "No need to dress, I just wanted to give you the keys to the Aston, Ana." He held out a key for her. "The money is already in the car. Feel free to check if it is there, but I assure you, you won't find it." He laughed. "There is plenty of room for your suitcase."

He turned to Uldis. "How's the face this morning?"

"Okay," Uldis replied, but his wincing betrayed his words.

"Before you leave, I'll get the doctor to have another quick look at it for you." He reached into his pocket and pulled out another car key. "Keys to the Golf, it's in the car park." He smiled and tossed it towards Uldis who instinctively caught it.

"Thank you," he said.

"I won't see you in England, Ana, so I'll wish you a safe journey and we'll catch up soon. Possibly when you get back here or maybe in Riga, I'll let you know."

Anastasjia nodded. "When I get to England, where do I need to go?" she asked, suddenly realising she had barely been told anything.

"Like I said yesterday, nice and easy. Everything is programmed into the sat nav but just in case I'll text you the address. It's not far from the ferry." He reached into his jacket pocket and produced two envelopes and handed one to Ana and then one to Uldis. "Details of who to visit and the reason for your journeys." He smiled again. Then, in a voice that sounded as though he was just sending his children off on a holiday, he said, "Enjoy the journey and sorry for the long drive through. You should enjoy the hotels we've booked for you though." He smiled again. Anastasjia found herself smiling back as Daniels turned to the door. Just before he left, he suddenly stopped and turned back. "No mistakes, we are watching."

After the door closed, Uldis looked at Anastasjia, who spoke. "I'm guessing the drivers and maybe others will be working for the company, and they will be watching us in the same way we will be watching them."

"I guess so," he replied as he sipped his now cold coffee.

After they had finished eating and got dressed, Anastasjia looked at her watch, time to leave.

"I have to go." She looked at Uldis. Still he looked reassuringly calm. He got up and held her in his arms.

"We'll meet up soon and then once back here it won't be long before we're heading back to Riga." He was trying to sound reassuring but they both knew that with the company anything could happen, the plan for them could change at any moment.

Uldis helped her with her case down to the car park. She was surprised at the number of Aston Martins down there, along with Ferraris, Jaguars, Maseratis, and McLarens. This really was a hotel for the rich. She pressed the key and a beautiful Aston Martin Vantage AMR clicked into life, its lights flashing and the internal lights coming on. Before she left, he once again held onto her and then he kissed her gently on the forehead.

"See you in England," he said quietly.

"Yes, see you in England." She kissed him softly on his lips but even then, she felt him wince with pain. "Sorry," she said quickly.

"Don't be sorry, I'll see you soon."

She climbed into the car and pressed the start button. The car's 4-litre twin turbo V8 engine roared into life. She knew that sound from working at the car sales; the roar of the engine was somehow comforting. She lowered the driver's window and smiling, called out,

"There are worse ways to travel."

Uldis smiled back. "Yes, a Volkswagen Golf." He laughed.

Anastasjia felt the power of the car as she sped out onto the streets of Brussels. As she drove, she realised she had forgotten to start up the sat nav. She didn't know where she was going as she had been savouring the time she had left with Uldis. She activated the journey and was promptly told to turn around at the first opportunity. She smiled to herself again before seeing a junction she could spin the car around in.

*

The drive to Dieppe was wonderful, despite knowing why she was heading there. The thought of what those poor girls would likely be going through reminded her of her not-so-distant past.

She realised why the cars she helped to sell in Riga were so popular. The Aston was a delight. She would miss it when it was returned.

Arriving at the terminal, she joined the queue for the ferry. Getting on was easy enough and as Daniels had said, she had no issues with passport control and was treated exceptionally well. She suspected this was due to her car as much as anything. She wore large dark sunglasses to hide some of the bruising on her face.

She made her way to the restaurant, ordered some lunch and then took a seat at a small table by a window. The weather outside was clear, which meant the sailing should hopefully be calm. She was unsure of her sea legs, having never been on a ferry before.

She looked down at the sandwich wrapped in plastic and the bag of crisps and sighed, remembering the quality of the food at the 'Amigo', which had been exceptional. She thought about Uldis. He should already be on the ferry, sailing towards Hull after taking the short drive to Zeebrugge. She hoped he was okay. She looked outside again and as she did a man approached and sat in the chair opposite. *Please don't come on to me*, she thought, trying to ignore him. He had only brought a coffee with him so maybe he wouldn't be too long.

"Are you travelling alone?" he suddenly asked in what she guessed was a French-accented version of English.

Anastasjia looked over at him. He was a small, insignificant-looking man, dressed in a plain sweatshirt and jeans, carrying a bright red anorak. He wore black plastic rimmed glasses, and his short dark hair was parted on one side. It was difficult to judge his age, but she thought he was maybe mid to late thirties. She wondered how best to discourage him from continuing but decided against lying.

"Yes, I'm on business," she replied, immediately regretting it, wishing she hadn't given away the extra piece of information.

"Business? What kind of business?" he asked, sounding genuinely interested.

"I'm sorry," she replied. "I'm tired and am not feeling very talkative at the moment, please excuse me." She began to get up.

"Please, Ana, finish your sandwich." He said her name so casually, she almost missed it.

"Sorry, wait, how do you know my name?" She sat back down.

"Nothing to worry about, it's all part of my job. I'm helping to drive the youngsters for their exchange visits in England," he said. "I understand you will be helping once we're there?" He leaned forward and put both elbows on the table. "I'm just letting you know the journey and the exchange will go well and it's my job to help with that. Do you understand?" he asked. It was a threat; he was speaking calmly and quietly but radiated menace. She nodded. "Good, glad we understand each other." He smiled. "Finish your sandwich," he said, sounding upbeat.

As he finished talking Anastasjia felt the vibration of the ship's engines as the ferry moved away from the dock.

"Here we go," the man said, looking at her over the top of his coffee cup as he held it to his lips. She didn't answer, she had no desire to engage with anyone that she didn't have to.

CHAPTER 23

"Morning, girls," said the Dutch woman. One of the men stood behind her menacingly. Instantly Michalina felt sick at the thought of what she had done for them the previous day.

Some of the girls had been sleeping. Michalina was in a morning daze. The only light in the room was from the open door to the hallway, but as the woman spoke, the room light came on. It was clearly dark outside, and Michalina guessed it was very early.

"You have a ferry to catch, but before that you have a drive. So, I need you up and ready to leave in an hour." She smiled, sounding cheerful. She looked around the room then sniffed the air and shook her head. "Unfortunately, you all need a good shower. To be honest, you stink." The man standing behind her laughed.

The woman put her hand out towards him, and he handed her a roll of black bin liners.

"Okay, girls," she began. "I would like you to strip and put all of your clothes into these bin liners before we take you for your showers," she grinned and began to laugh, "and don't forget to wash behind your ears."

"What are we to wear?" said one of the girls, one who had been dragged from the room. The woman looked at her and then towards the man, before nodding. He stepped forward, quickly walking across the room and punched her full in the face, then again, and again. Blows rained into her cheeks and blood splattered from her now open wounds. Her nose and mouth were also bleeding.

"Enough," the woman said in a raised voice. The man let go and the girl fell to the floor, coughing and spitting blood. "Now, girls, I have asked nicely for you to put your clothes in the bags and be ready to shower." The calm had returned to her voice. "It would appear that young Mila here wishes to stay in Brussels for a while, at least until her injuries heal enough." She smiled. "If any of you wish to join her, we can arrange that." She paused before her face suddenly hardened. "So, get your fucking clothes off and put them in the bags."

All the girls undressed until they stood naked looking down and trying to cover their modesty as best they could. But Michalina had stopped worrying about this. Survival was the issue, and she did not want to end up like Mila who was still lying on the floor, coughing and spitting as she tried to breathe through the blood, her eyes closing as they became more and more swollen.

The woman looked at the man who grabbed the full bags and walked from the room. As he left another man appeared. Michalina guessed he had been standing just outside the whole time.

"Now girls, fall in line behind this gentleman and he will take you to the shower. Be quick or you can join Mila." The girls quickly fell into line.

After showering they were led back to the room, still naked. The girls were all shivering; the showers had at least been hot but now standing there naked she felt incredibly cold, also from fear of what was to happen next. Mila was no longer in the room. The sheet from the mattress she had been lying on had been removed but the mattress was covered in her blood. It still looked wet.

Michalina was relieved to see that on one of the other mattresses were piles of clothing – school clothing, socks, long skirts, shirts, pullovers.

She didn't have to wait long before the Dutch woman re-entered the room.

"Girls," she began, "as you know, I have been arranging employment for you in England so we will be leaving shortly for our journey." She smiled and continued in the soft, gentle voice. "You all look lovely and clean and certainly smell a lot better."

She nodded at the man, and he walked towards the piles of clothes. He pulled a bag from behind them, a 'Carrefour Market' supermarket shopping bag – and tipped it out. Combs, hairbrushes and deodorant fell onto the mattress.

"Help yourselves, make sure you all use the deodorant, we have a long journey." She paused. "Sorry, I mean, you have a long journey, not we." She smiled again. "Sadly, we must part ways but before you leave, I want you all looking smart in your school uniforms, smelling nice with your hair brushed."

None of the girls spoke; they had learned very quickly what would happen if they did and none of them wanted to join Mila, wherever she was now.

"Well come on then, quickly," she said, her voice raised now.

The girls began to look through the clothing for something that fitted. Some used the hairbrushes, all used the deodorant. The scene looked frantic as they tried to be as quick as possible. Some of it fitted well but on some of the girls the clothes were either too big or too small. Not so bad that they couldn't wear them but not great either. They still looked like a rag tag group but were at least all dressed the same.

"Excellent," the woman said, smiling once more. "The good news is you don't need to speak to anyone on the way to England. We have your passports, and you will be travelling with your teacher." She smiled. The girls looked at each other. Once again, her face hardened. "If anyone speaks or steps out of line, they will be brought back here to join Mila, is that clear?" The girls didn't move or speak. In a loud angry voice, the woman said again, "I said, is that clear?"

They all nodded or replied, "Yes."

"That's good. Things will be much easier for you all if you do as you are told."

Moments later another man appeared at the door. He was

noticeably smaller than the other men Michalina had seen and did not appear to be eastern European. He was wearing a plain sweatshirt and jeans with a red anorak.

"Are we ready to leave?" he said to the woman in a clear French accent.

"Yes, all ready," the woman replied. "Any problems, you have my number and if things get out of hand, they know what to expect. My colleagues will be following you."

"Excellent, let's look forward to a good journey," he replied in a cheery voice, his French accent now even more pronounced than before.

They were taken to the minibus, which was waiting outside the house. There were already girls inside, all wearing the same uniform. Some were clearly in their mid to late twenties and the uniforms didn't fit well. They looked ridiculous.

When they were all on board, there were fourteen girls in all, plus the French man and a large eastern European man was in the driving seat. Michalina was sure he was one of those in the kitchen she had 'sucked off'. Her body shook at the thought of it. Thankfully she had just had a brief smoke of 'H' before leaving, so was chilled. She could feel the effects beginning to wash over her. A couple of the other girls were clearly addicts as well and they looked as though they were having the same feeling. She wondered how the others could endure what was happening without it.

The minibus set off and Michalina closed her eyes and leaned back. As the 'H' continued to take its hold, she thought, *Nothing to worry about just yet*.

*

Michalina slowly opened her eyes. She had no idea what time it was, but it was light. The minibus was stationary in a queue of cars waiting to drive onto a ferry. She had no idea where she was but guessed it was in France.

She looked at the other girls. Some were still asleep, some looked terrified, others looked like they were resigned to their fate. The French guy was standing just outside the closed front passenger door looking ahead whilst the driver sat in his seat with the window open. He was smoking. Michalina could occasionally smell the sweet acrid smell of the tobacco wafting back towards her. She laughed to herself at the image. She looked back and could see the driver of the car behind. It was the man who had assaulted Mila. Clearly, he was standing in view so that they could all see him.

Finally, the car in front of the minibus moved forward and the Frenchman climbed back into the front passenger seat, allowing the driver to pull away. They stopped at the building where their passports were checked, and Michalina spotted the bag containing them in the Frenchman's hand. Michalina guessed it also contained some kind of fake consent forms.

After parking the minibus, the driver and the Frenchman got out.

Speaking in the best English he could manage, he said, "Ladies, we are shortly on our way to England. Unfortunately you cannot remain in the vehicle so you will need to come with me and my colleagues to the restaurant." He paused and looked at the girls. "You will all know what my associates are capable of, some of you more than others." He paused again. "Let me assure you, if any of you think you can get away from us or contact other passengers, you can't." He gestured towards the men. "They will have no fear of putting you in your place and in the worst case, letting you try to swim back to France. Are we clear?" He looked at them again, not expecting them to answer. "Okay, ladies, out you get. Go with these gentlemen to the restaurant. If you are good, they will buy you some refreshments." He smiled at them. Anyone watching would think he really was their teacher, and they were on a real school trip.

In the restaurant they were taken to a corner where there was a group of tables near each other.

"Sit," said one of the men.

It was the first time Michalina had heard any of them speak. The girls sat down, saying nothing. The three men stood together for a moment, talking in a language that Michalina didn't understand. Then two of them then walked over to the self-service counter and took a tray each. Michalina could see them grabbing various food items and drinks cartons. She glanced around the rest of the restaurant, wondering where the Frenchman had gone.

At that moment Michalina felt the engines of the ferry burst into life, causing the boat to vibrate. Slowly it pulled away, on its way to England.

CHAPTER 24

This was not looking good. Alice's mind was racing; how could she have been so stupid? Here she was, driving wherever this bastard wanted to take her and Harry. He had the knife, and he also had her phone. She may have been in control of the car but to do anything drastic would risk Harry, and she couldn't do that.

She also guessed his gang had been killed, presumably by another gang. And she also knew she had phoned work to report being sick, which meant they wouldn't be looking for her for at least seven days. Nyakim wasn't likely to be home until at least 7:00pm, maybe later, and when she did come home it would not be unusual to accept Alice's absence, as she was often out working or socialising with her team. Nyakim was unlikely to worry if she wasn't there.

The earliest would be tomorrow morning. That meant she was going to have to keep herself and Harry safe for at least another eighteen hours. And then there was the response from her team. She couldn't rely on the DI from the main office. The DI for the missing persons team would be better, at least he knew what he was doing and wasn't a sexist bigoted bully.

"M25 south." It was the first time the man had spoken for some time. In fact, he only spoke to give directions.

"Where are we going?" Alice asked.

"You'll know soon enough, just fucking drive and keep your mouth shut," he barked back at her.

Alice adjusted the rear-view mirror so she could see Harry. "You okay there?" she asked. He nodded without answering.

"I won't tell you again, bitch, shut the fuck up."

"You know the police will be looking for me?" she said, guessing he wouldn't try to hurt her whilst she was driving.

"Yeah, I guess so." He answered remarkably calmly, considering how he had shouted at her moments ago. "I've been thinking about that," he continued. "This car, too nice to be a police car. I'm thinking it's yours, right?" Alice didn't answer. "Yeah, thought so," he said, clearly responding to her silence. "That being the case, I'm thinking you picked young Harry up at home and brought him over to see me and the boys." She felt herself gripping the steering wheel tighter. "So, I've got to wonder, what's a police officer from Harry's hometown doing turning up in East London with young Harry in tow?" He smiled and leaned forward. He almost whispered in her ear. "I'm guessing you've not told anyone where you and young Harry were going."

She looked in the mirror and saw his wide grin.

"Thought so," he said triumphantly, leaning back in his seat. "Now shut the fuck up."

She turned onto the M25 where the signs were pointing toward Dover, M20, Channel Tunnel and M23. She had no idea where they were going but assumed it wasn't going to be the Channel Tunnel.

She was right. Not long after crossing the Queen Elizabeth Bridge she was directed to turn off and head south on the A21 towards the south coast.

Finally, their captor spoke again.

"Pull over in the next lay-by."

"Where?" replied Alice, not seeing a lay-by.

"I don't fucking know; the next one you see."

Alice drove on, finally seeing a bus stop. She pulled in, leaving the engine running.

Alice looked in the rear-view mirror as the man scrolled through the numbers on his phone and then called someone. He looked at her in the mirror and saw that she was watching him.

"No tricks or young Harry gets stuck, got it?"

She nodded in response.

Then he turned his attention back to the phone. Someone had clearly answered his call.

"Yeah, it's me." He paused. "Yeah, but my fam's dead so I need answers." Another pause. "Don't fuck with me. I know enough about you to bring you all down." A pause. "Just fucking tell me where you are." A longer pause. "Just text me the address and I'll be there." He pulled the phone from his ear and forcefully pressed the button to end the call, hanging up on whoever he was talking to.

Moments later a text message sound came, and he looked at his phone. "Drive on down here," he said, indicating she should continue. "I'll tell you where we're going, not far now."

Alice pulled away and waited for his instructions.

The man led them to a housing estate, and she pulled up next to a minibus that was parked in the mud outside a house. Much like the minibus, the house was unkempt. The paint was peeling from the door and metal window frames. Hanging in the windows were nicotine-stained net curtains that looked like they had never been cleaned.

"What now?" asked Alice.

He ignored her and looked at his phone, dialling once more. He put it to his ear, saying, "We're outside." He paused before saying in angry raised voice, "Yes, I said we, now get out here you fucking bitch." As before, he appeared to hang up the phone abruptly.

"Fuck, fuck, fuck," he kept repeating. He was clearly agitated and growing more and more angry. Alice could see Harry had moved as far from him as the back seat would allow and pressed himself against the door.

Alice looked over to the house and saw the front door open and two people step out. They walked down the path towards the car, passing the minibus on the front garden. She thought the man who brought them here was big, but this guy made him look positively average. He was wearing a leather jacket and looking at them threateningly. The woman was smartly dressed, maybe late forties or early fifties, her hair was immaculate, but she wore too much makeup. Alice noticed a slight limp.

"Out the car," the man behind her said as he opened his door. Alice climbed out and turned to see the man dragging Harry across the back seat.

The woman spoke first. "Who have we here and more importantly, why have you brought them here?" She spoke with an accent that Alice didn't recognise but she guessed was eastern European.

"Listen, all my guys are dead, and I want answers." He spoke loudly, too loudly.

Alice was aware that anyone in the nearby houses could hear.

"I think we had best go in and discuss the situation," the woman said calmly but in a forceful way. She turned and began to walk towards the house. The man in the leather jacket indicated they should follow. Their captor followed the woman. Harry looked first at Alice. She nodded at him, and he followed too. Then Alice and finally the large man entered last, closing the door behind him, and then they went to the kitchen.

"Please could I use the toilet?" asked Harry, politely.

"Yes, of course, child," she answered with a smile. The man in the leather jacket stood to one side and indicated it was under the stairs.

"Thank you," said Harry before leaving the room.

"Before we start, let me explain how this will work," the woman began, addressing the man who had brought them to the house. "I will ask you questions, and you will answer."

"Don't fucking tell me what I can do," he snapped back. "I want answers and I'm not doing what you want. Fucking bitch." The woman raised an eyebrow. She was clearly not afraid of him.

"Who is this young lady you've brought to me?" she asked calmly, completely ignoring the man's anger.

"She's a pig, something to do with you and this boy." He indicated towards Harry.

"Clearly, she is not a pig, she is a young lady. Are you telling me she is a police officer?"

Alice realised she was wearing her own clothes. There was no way the woman could know she was police by just looking at her. The man must have found her voice disarming because he, too, responded calmly. This was the first time he hadn't spoken in anger.

"Yes, a police officer."

The woman nodded. "And why are you here, young lady? And I don't mean because he made you. I mean what is your connection to this young boy and this rather rude gentleman?"

"Fuck you," shouted the man, to which the woman raised an index finger in the air, indicating he should stop speaking.

"Who are you?" asked Alice, looking directly at the woman, turning her question back on her.

"I'm sure you would like to know," she replied, "but, I want you to tell me what I ask." She smiled at Alice. "Now perhaps you could answer my question. What is your connection to this young boy and why are you with this gentleman?" Alice thought for a moment; she knew she had to say something. Keep it simple, don't give too much away.

"I work in Missing Persons; I'm just trying to find Harry's sister. She goes missing a lot." She found herself stumbling on her words more than she intended. *Why did I say 'she goes missing a lot'?* she thought to herself. She sounded like such an idiot.

"And have you had any luck finding her?" the woman asked.

"No," replied Alice. "I thought she might be visiting him." She nodded towards the now silent man.

The woman smiled again. "And do you have a phone?"

"I took it off of her," the man answered, sounding pleased with himself.

"I see, and did you take out the SIM card?" she asked. His face dropped. "I thought not," she said, remaining calm. "Perhaps you could go with my colleague here and find a suitable way to dispose of the phone and SIM card that won't bring the police here. Do you think you could do that without messing it up?" She was looking at him as if he was a naughty child.

"Who the fuck do you think you're talking to? Fucking bitch," he shouted, returning to his natural angry state.

"I see," said the woman. "I'm sorry, dear," she said to Alice. "I need to give your car keys to my friend here so he can take your phone for disposal." She smiled at Alice who knew better than to argue. She handed over the keys, removing her house and work locker key first. "Good, good."

She then looked towards the large man in the doorway. He reached into his jacket and pulled out a handgun and held it up against the other man's head.

"What the—" He began to speak. The woman put a finger to her lips indicating he should stop.

"I'd like you to hand this gentleman the lady's phone and go with him to suitably dispose of it. Maybe while you're out there, you can learn about how the police can track phones." The two men left and moments later Alice heard her car start and pull away.

"Now, young lady, when are you expected to be home or back in your office?" she said warmly.

"Look, they'll be searching for me now," Alice said, trying to appeal to her senses. "You need to let us go. I don't know anything about you, I'm just looking for Harry's sister. I don't care who you are." She knew she sounded desperate.

"Shhh," the woman said again, holding a finger to her lips. "I think we both know it's not that simple. Ah, Harry," the woman said as he returned. "What is your sister's name, Harry? Maybe I can help." She smiled again.

"Lilly," he said, looking down as if unsure of whether he should speak or not. He looked up at Alice for reassurance and when none came, he looked down again.

"Lilly, hmm, we do have a 'Lilly' staying with us here, maybe it's her." She continued to smile. "I'll see what I can do to help. Are you worried about her?" Harry nodded. "Very well, let's get you both something to eat and drink and we'll see what we can do."

Alice wondered if she should say anything else but realised there was no point. She just had to keep the two of them as safe as possible until the cavalry arrived. She knew the SIM card would be tracked to the address or pretty close, so that would be their best opportunity. She wondered whether she could convince the woman to let them go. She didn't look like she was one to be messed with. No, waiting was the best option.

Alice and Harry took a seat at the kitchen table whilst the woman made some calls. One was ordering them some food for collection. Alice assumed they didn't want it delivered as that would be too risky. The other calls were more interesting, though she could only hear one side of the conversation.

"Yes, we have to… Yes, as soon as possible… All of us…" She guessed they were talking about moving from the address, probably because she was there. She only hoped it wouldn't be too soon.

She was aware of occasional voices in the house, most of which she couldn't understand. The smell also gave their presence away. The acrid stench of stale sweat and smoke from cigarettes. When the food arrived, she was pleased to see it was pizza, although she struggled to eat. She was surprised how easily Harry did, though, he must have been starving. Every now and then the woman would leave the room and go upstairs. Sometimes she heard crying and sometimes pleading but it was quite muffled from where they were in the kitchen and difficult to hear.

Time passed until late afternoon. At one point she heard a vehicle revving as if under strain. Shortly after, she heard the sound of the vehicle's doors opening, eastern European accents and voices, male and female, nothing in English. There was then the sound of someone barking orders and various doors opening and closing.

Shortly after the people arrived, the woman came in and turned on the small television in the corner of the room. Alice was so busy thinking of her next move she hadn't even noticed it.

"News will be on in a moment," she said. "Let's see if we're on it." She laughed.

The news began, but only displayed the usual local stories of politics and general people struggling with their lives. *They've no idea*, thought Alice. Then she saw it, a mugshot of the man who had brought her and Harry to the house. But it wasn't a story of his disappearing or anyone trying to find him, it was a story of how he had 'committed suicide' by jumping off Beachy Head following his gang members being murdered earlier that day in a shootout. The story told how a car believed to have been used by the man had been completely destroyed in a fire near the spot where he had jumped.

The reporter said that police had announced there were no suspicious circumstances. *Shit*, thought Alice. *What's not suspicious about that?* Alice knew the car was hers, although from the images on TV, it was so badly destroyed the chances of identifying it as hers were remote.

"Oh dear," said the woman. "He did appear upset when he left here, don't you think?" Alice just looked at her without answering. "I expect your phone was in the car when it was destroyed," she continued. "Because that foolish man brought you here, we're going to have to move. It should be fairly soon, I'm just waiting for a call."

Alice couldn't help herself. Despite knowing that to remain quiet was her best option, her police training kicked in and she instinctively began to ask questions. "A call from whom? Where are we going?" she asked.

"I'll be perfectly honest with you, young lady, I don't know. What I do know is we don't know what to do with you..."

"Who's we?" she asked.

"None of your concern," she snapped back. "Everyone here has some use, except you." She paused. "Even Harry has one; there are people who will be prepared to pay good money for him, not here, but certainly on the continent." She smiled. Alice looked at Harry. He was staring at the woman with fear in his eyes. He said nothing. "You're quite pretty, I'm guessing late twenties or early thirties, older than we would normally use." The woman spoke as though she was an item, not a person.

"I don't know what you think you can make me do but forget it," Alice said, seething.

"Possibly," said the woman. "But remember, if you are no use to us, there are always people jumping off Beachy Head." She smiled again, this time a far more sinister smile than before.

Alice prayed that Nyakim would notice something was wrong sooner and contact her colleagues, and most importantly speak to the right ones.

CHAPTER 25

When Anastasjia went to stand up, without having finished her coffee, the Frenchman grabbed her wrist. "Going somewhere?" he asked menacingly. She snatched her hand away.

"Where do you think I'm going on a ferry out at sea?" she asked sarcastically. Before he could answer she continued… "I'm going out onto the upper deck. It might be cold, but I have no wish to converse with you or spend time in your company. The transfer you talk about will go smoothly as it is in my interest for that to happen. But don't think for one moment you can tell me what to do." He sat back in his chair, a dismissive look on his face.

She glanced over his shoulder at the rag tag huddle of girls she had noticed near the counter behind him. Drawn tired faces and badly fitting uniforms.

"I assume the girls over there are your responsibility?"

"They are, and they will arrive safely at their destination."

"Well, I know what I need to do, and I do it well, which is why I'm trusted with the company's cars. Company cars I suspect would pay your wages for several years, so before trying to pull some sort of seniority over me I suggest you examine where you are in the organisation and then lower yourself a few rungs on the ladder. Understand?" She smiled a knowing smile.

The Frenchman looked back at her, bemused. "Very well." He paused. "Please continue as you wish." Another pause before in a slightly more forceful tone, "I'll be watching… in case I need to speak to someone further up that ladder you speak about." Anastasjia didn't respond and instead turned away, moving towards the upper deck.

She was right in what she said to the Frenchman. It was freezing outside, and she was not really dressed warmly enough to stay there for too long. Finding a bench seat, she took out her phone and went through the contacts until she found Uldis.

She pressed the dial symbol and heard the phone trying to call.

"Sorry, we cannot connect your call, please try later…"

Damn it. He must be inside the hull or have his phone off. She really wanted to hear his voice and to see whether he was okay. It would have to wait until later.

Sitting back on the bench, she folded her arms, putting her hands under them to try to keep them warm. It worked for a bit, but she was still cold. She looked out at the English Channel, which was very uninviting, given how grey the water was. The small white horses dancing on the tops of the waves just went to show her it was not only cold in the air, but there was an icy breeze, making a bitter windchill.

She managed to last about 30 minutes before deciding she would have to go back inside. She didn't want to go back to the restaurant where the Frenchman was, or the girls who were clearly the ones being trafficked. *Poor things*, she thought, wondering what mishaps they had endured and would continue to endure in the future. She shook her head; it was best not to think about it.

She found the split-level bar and looked quickly around to check that the Frenchman wasn't in sight. He was nowhere to be seen. *Good*. She ordered a Coke, before wandering off to find a secluded seat where she could warm herself.

It wasn't long before she could see the English coast through the mist, in the distance, rising out of the grey sea. *Not too long now*. She tried calling Uldis again…

"Sorry, we cannot connect your call, please try later." She hung up. *He must still be on the boat*. Never mind, there would be opportunity once she got to her destination.

She put the phone back in her handbag. As she looked up the

Frenchman was standing in front of her. "What?" she said sharply.

"Now, now," he replied. "Try to at least be courteous."

She couldn't hide her disdain for the man and said, "I'll ask again, what do you want?"

The Frenchman raised one of his eyebrows, clearly not happy with being challenged by her. "Very well. I know we will part company soon. I have had a change of plan in that my destination has changed at short notice. I have also had a message from Mr. Daniels that he would like you to follow me to the new location, before you follow your sat nav to your destination to exchange the car."

"Why hasn't he called me?" she asked.

He looked at her smugly. "Maybe you're not as far up that ladder as you thought you were," he replied.

"I'm not doing anything you tell me to do," she said, trying her best not to sound intimidated in any way, and trying to sound as if she was superior to him.

"I'm going to call Mr. Daniels and see what he would like me to do." The smile disappeared from the Frenchman's face.

"Very well, as you wish but be quick, we will be moving from the ferry soon." He was right, the ferry was about to tie up.

Walking hurriedly onto the upper deck she flicked through her contacts until she reached Daniels' number. She quickly pressed the dial button, hoping he would answer quickly. If the plans changed, she needed to find out soon. They were already making announcements about passengers returning to their vehicles to be ready to depart. She certainly was not about to take the word of this smarmy Frenchman.

The phone rang twice before being picked up.

"Ana?" came the unmistakable voice.

"Yes, hi Mr. Daniels, sorry to trouble you—"

"No, trouble," he answered, interrupting her. "I expect you're calling about the change of plans."

"Yes, I—" Anastasjia tried to answer before he interrupted again.

"I'm sorry you had to be told by our colleague, I was able to get hold of him first."

Not as important as he thinks, thought Anastasjia.

"I would like you to follow him to our new premises and when there, the money will be removed from the car to pay our accounts. When that has been done, you can go to the pre-loaded destination."

"No problem," she replied. "Do you have any idea how long that will take?" She wanted to know for her own benefit; she was hoping to see Uldis soon and this might limit her time with him.

"Not too long," he replied. "I can't be more specific than that, I'm afraid."

"Okay," she replied, hoping it wouldn't take too long. "I have to go now," she said, realising they had just made the last call for passengers to go to their vehicles.

"Okay, Ana, safe journey," Daniels said cheerfully.

"Thank you," she replied before quickly hanging up and hurrying to the car bay and her waiting Aston Martin.

Back in the car, as she was about to close the door she saw the Frenchman looking at her. He was standing by the side of a Volkswagen minibus in which the girls from the restaurant sat, still wearing school uniforms. The Frenchman pointed at the back of the minibus and nodded towards her. She guessed he was trying to say 'follow behind'.

They would be leaving the ferry a short while before her, so she'd have to make sure she could catch them up when her car was released.

In the end, she left the ferry port before the minibus and had to wait for it. She guessed that they took slightly longer to get through as they were a bus apparently full of children. She knew that was not the case but with them dressed like that, she guessed that was the deception they used. She wondered if it ever failed, whether anyone looked more closely at the girls, but quickly discarded that thought. They wouldn't be using it if it didn't work. Sure enough, as she sat in the lay-by waiting the minibus passed her, slowing. She pulled out behind it and followed.

She occasionally saw one or two of the girls near the back seats looking out at her. She wondered what they were thinking and what they had been through. The girls she could see had vacant expressions; they were the expressions of the girls she used to work with before being rescued by the company, looking as though they had given up and were resigned to their fate.

Driving in the luxury of the Aston Martin along coastal roads, Anastasjia was astounded by the beauty of the English countryside. The car gripped the road, making the drive a pleasure. She hoped to be able to open it up again soon, when she would see how fast it could really go.

After about 30 minutes or so the minibus indicated left and turned down a partially made road. She followed after it but quickly stopped as she saw the state of the road. If she drove down this, she could wreck the underside of the car, not to mention the danger of stone chips. As she sat stationary, she saw the minibus stop and then the reversing lights come on as it reversed to where she sat.

The Frenchman got out of the front passenger seat and walked up to her. She did not want to get out and speak with him. She opened her window sufficiently to converse with him.

"Problem?" he asked.

"Yes, there's a problem," she said, exasperated. "Do you know how much this car is worth?" It was a rhetorical question, but after the Frenchman shrugged his shoulders, she told him. "About one hundred and eighty thousand euros."

He again shrugged his shoulders. "And?" he asked.

"And you want me to drive it down here? I'll wreck the car." Even at this point the roadway was worn, muddy and full of holes.

"You'll just have to take your time and drive carefully," he said calmly.

Patronising bastard, she thought to herself.

"The house is just up here, not far." He walked off back to the minibus and disappeared around the passenger side.

The minibus pulled away, splattering her bonnet with mud as it did so. She shook her head before slowly following at a distance. She felt every vibration and bump in the road as she slowly navigated her way behind the ever-distancing minibus. The car was filthy; she prayed it was not damaged, and if it was, she wasn't about to take the blame. Any damage would cost a fortune to fix. *You patronising French bastard*, she repeated over and over to herself as she gingerly made her way along the increasingly poor road surface.

Eventually she arrived at an open gate to a very run-down-looking farmhouse. The minibus was already parked in the yard in front of the building and the girls were being led out.

Anastasjia pulled up alongside and then got out to inspect the car. Fortunately, from her assessment the car only seemed to be dirty.

"Is it okay?" asked the Frenchman.

"Yes, no thanks to you and that idiot driver of yours," she snapped back.

He laughed and walked towards where the girls were standing at the door, clearly not sure what they should do next.

She watched as the Frenchman went to a large concrete flowerpot that held a very dead, miniature conifer plant and reached underneath, pulling out a key. He entered the building and was followed by the girls who were ushered into the lounge area. Anastasjia followed. She tried to hold back her horror when she saw the number of stained mattresses on the floor. Memories of lying in the cold and damp on rotting mattresses whilst waiting to be given to her next client made her shiver.

The girls all crowded together, looking at the Frenchman as he turned to the driver and indicated that he should do… something. Anastasjia couldn't decipher what he was telling him. The driver left the room and returned with a large cardboard box that he dropped onto the floor. He then opened the top of the box and began to empty the contents onto a nearby mattress.

"Okay, ladies," began the Frenchman. "I need you all to strip down to your underwear and grab a pair of bottoms and a tee shirt. Be careful not to crease the uniforms too much, we will be needing them for someone else soon."

The girls stood and stared, none of them wanting to be the first to move. The smile disappeared from the Frenchman's face. He glanced towards Anastasjia and then to the driver and back to the girls.

"NOW!" he shouted, making several of them jump, including Anastasjia who was still in that moment from years ago. She quickly snapped out of it. "Don't make me lose my temper," he continued as the girls broke ranks and started grabbing items of clothing, making no effort to check on sizes.

Anastasjia looked away.

"You show your vulnerable side," the Frenchman sneered.

The emotions brought on by her memories made her angry. "It's not vulnerable, it's human, something you wouldn't understand."

The Frenchman laughed and shrugged his shoulders. "Whatever." He threw the comment back at her.

"How much longer am I going to need to wait here?" She didn't have any desire to stay in his company any longer that she had to: and she knew Uldis would hopefully be on his way to her location soon. She still needed to deliver the car after the money had been removed and then pick up a replacement to take back to Riga and the showroom. The showroom seemed like a lifetime away but for the first time ever she found herself missing it.

The Frenchman smiled. "Wanting to leave so soon? Just when we're getting to know each other."

Still full of his own self-importance, thought Anastasjia.

"No, not at all, being with you is a pleasure," she said sarcastically. "But I do have work to do that doesn't involve being here with you." She scowled. He glanced towards her but didn't answer, then turned and walked out of the room leaving her with the girls and the driver.

"Wait!" she called after him with no idea where he was going.

"I'm bored with your conversation," he said as he walked, not looking at her. She followed him.

"I don't give a damn," she shouted after him. "I need to get going and I can't do that until the car has been cleared."

He stopped and looked back at her. "And I don't know where in the car the money is, and as you have made a big thing about how expensive it is, I don't want to start ripping it apart to get it." He nodded towards her, equally sarcastically, and turned to the door. "Understand?" he sneered as he stepped outside.

Patronising bastard, she thought.

Reaching into his pocket he pulled out a silver cigarette case, and quickly flicked it open and offered one to her.

"No, thank you." She couldn't believe he had a cigarette case. Did he think it was the 1960s? He took one for himself and returned the case to his pocket. Pulling out a Zippo, he proceeded to light the cigarette; he took a deep breath, drawing the smoke deep into his lungs, as though his life depended on it, before blowing out the smoke in a long slow breath.

"What are you going to do with the girls?" she asked, despite already having an idea.

"Don't be naïve," he replied.

"I'm not," she responded. "I know why they're here. I wanted to know how and when they get moved on."

"Unfortunately, I cannot answer." He looked at her, taking another deep draw on the cigarette before again blowing out the smoke. "I am not involved in distribution, just delivery." He spoke as if he was simply a delivery driver for UPS.

"You'll need to do something for them soon," she said, trying to impress her concern on him. "I can already see some of them sweating and becoming agitated. I'm guessing some of them are on something."

"You are correct," he replied, nodding slightly. "Some of them are, some of them have other reasons to be here, some even volunteered to be here, some of them volunteered to have a better life." He shrugged. "Maybe it is?" He smiled. With that, he dropped the remains of his cigarette on the ground and put it out with his foot, twisting it left and right until very little of the butt was left. He walked past Anastasjia to the van and opened the passenger door, pulling out a small holdall. "Time for a top-up," he said as he unzipped it. She followed him into the lounge where the girls were all still standing around awkwardly.

He pointed to four of the girls.

"You, come with me, I have your medicine." The selected girls stepped forward and followed him from the room. Not one of them was dressed properly. The clothes didn't fit, and they looked exhausted. Anastasjia suspected none of them had slept for at least 24 hours. The four girls looked dreadful. It was obvious they were going into withdrawal so would need something.

She followed them into the kitchen where the Frenchman put the bag down onto the worktop. Opening it, he pulled out four small wraps of what she guessed was either heroin or cocaine. When she saw the colour she could tell it was heroin.

"Who's first?" he said cheerfully as he began to prepare the first bag, tipping it out onto a dessert spoon before heating it up with his lighter.

One of the girls stepped forward, holding out her left arm, which revealed scratch marks and bruising from previous injections. The Frenchman handed the girl a rubber tourniquet that she quickly put over her hand and pulled above the elbow with practised ease. She pulled it as tight as she could, but no vein appeared. The Frenchman flicked her arm until the slightest trace appeared. Then he inserted the needle and slowly pushed the plunger until the liquid disappeared.

When the needle was withdrawn, the girl covered the entry point with her finger. She was clearly used to it. The same thing was repeated for the next two girls.

Finally, the last girl stepped forward nervously.

"What's your problem?" asked the Frenchman.

"I, I don't inject." She stuttered slightly.

"You do here," he replied, "if you want your fix?" He said it like a question.

The girl looked desperate and Anastasjia knew how she'd be feeling if she was in withdrawal. She felt sorry for the girl, knowing what she would have had to do for the men. It made her shudder again.

"Why can't she just smoke it?" she asked.

"If she wants drugs here, she gets injected," he said abruptly. He looked at the girl. "Well?" She looked at the Frenchman and then at the needle in his hand.

Slowly she held out her left arm as the previous girls had. The Frenchman put the syringe onto the kitchen worktop and then put the tourniquet on her upper arm, pulling it tight. The tightness on her virgin arm caused the vein to quickly stand out. With one hand he grabbed her wrist and with the other he picked up the syringe. "Keep still," he commanded. The girl steeled herself to remain as still as possible. "Just a scratch," he said as the needle entered her vein.

The Frenchman pushed in the plunger before reaching in his bag and pulling out a bag of cotton wool balls. He held it out for her to grab. He pulled the needle free and indicated that she stop the bleeding with the cotton wool ball.

Anastasjia said nothing. She wasn't happy but it was not her problem. Her problem was to get the car to its destination and pick up a replacement.

"Okay, ladies," said the Frenchman. "You might want to go back to the room and lie down for a bit," he said, sounding a lot like a doctor. The girls left the room.

"Coffee?" he asked casually.

"No," Anastasjia snapped back.

"It might be a while," he said.

Anastasjia shook her head and began to walk out of the kitchen, intending to wait outside.

"Please yourself," he called after her. "If you change your mind let me know. It will need to be black, though, we don't have any milk."

Anastasjia didn't look back but went outside to sit and wait in the car.

CHAPTER 26

The house had become a hive of activity. Alice had noticed a number of eastern European men and a couple of women in charge of groups of people they were herding from room to room. She guessed the ones being moved around were not all there willingly, and she also guessed that the smartly dressed woman who had been speaking to her earlier was ultimately in charge of everyone. Certainly, the men and women seemed to come to her for instruction. It was difficult to tell as most of the conversation wasn't in English.

Alice looked at Harry, who was sitting with her at the small kitchen table. She put a reassuring hand on his, and he looked up at her. He looked totally lost.

"Try not to worry. I know it's difficult, but you'll be okay, I'm sure," she whispered, trying to sound as reassuring as she could but at the same time, she doubted everything she was saying.

The woman re-entered the kitchen. "Not long now," she said cheerfully.

"What's not long?" Alice asked, trying not to sound alarmed.

"All in good time. Our other guests will be leaving first and then we will be leaving shortly after."

She was annoyingly upbeat. Alice could feel her emotions moving from concern to anger. "Leaving to go where?" she asked.

"Questions, questions, questions," the woman sang. "You'll just have to wait to see. I promise it won't be long." She smiled and left the room again.

"Wait," Alice called after her, suddenly speaking in such a raised voice that it made the woman stop in her tracks. She turned to look at them.

"Yes?" she asked sternly.

"You said Harry's sister Lilly might be here. Is she?"

The woman smiled. "I'll have to look and let you know." With that, she walked from the room.

Alice turned to Harry. "Hopefully we'll find Lilly and then we can look at getting out of here," she said, trying to sound positive to get him onside.

"How?" He sounded scared.

"I don't know yet, but I'll figure it out, just trust me, okay." She looked deep into his eyes. "Okay?" she asked again, squeezing his hand gently.

"Okay," said Harry quietly, nodding.

People continued to move around the house. It was noisy, with orders being shouted. Eventually the front door opened and the two groups of occupants were ushered outside. First out was a group of men. Alice could see them through the open kitchen door. A mismatched group aged between late teens and possibly mid to late 30s. Moving them along were some of the eastern European men she had seen earlier. She guessed there must have been about ten men in all. Once outside she heard raised voices and then the slamming of vehicle doors, the tractor-like sound of diesel engines starting up and the minibuses pulling away.

Then more voices and the sound of people coming down the stairs. Alice watched as a line of young girls emerged from the bottom of the stairs and left through the front door. Again, with them were a handful of eastern-European-looking men and women. They spoke with raised voices in a language Alice didn't understand, which was then repeated in English…

"Quickly, into the van, hurry." It was obvious they were being taken away.

"Lilly!" Harry suddenly shouted.

Alice caught a glimpse of a young, dishevelled girl in the group she thought she recognised, who was trying to look back, shouting, "Harry! Harry..." But she was forced out of the house, disappearing from view.

Alice went to follow but was almost instantly blocked by one of the eastern European men who said something to her she didn't understand.

"Sit down." The voice came from behind the man. It was the woman in charge.

"That's Lilly, that's Harry's sister Lilly, where are you taking her?" Alice said.

"You will sit down, or my friend here will make you sit down." The woman was not to be ordered about.

"Listen, lady, I don't know who you are or what you are doing but my job is to find her and so I'm going to go outside and see her, got it?" Alice was angry; adrenaline was pumping through her veins as she barked the words at the woman and went to push past the man.

With one hand, he grabbed her around the neck and lifted her up like a rag doll. Her toes were just about in contact with the floor, but she was choking. She grabbed his arm with both hands.

"Let go, please I can't breathe, let go," she managed to get out, despite the constriction of her throat. With almost no effort the man threw her back into the room, and she fell to the floor with a thud.

"Now, young lady, take a seat or my friend here will harm you, are we clear?" the woman said with a sinister calm tone that Alice found more menacing than if she had shouted at her.

Alice pulled herself up and sat back in the chair.

"Please can I see my sister?" asked Harry again politely, tears beginning to slowly roll down his cheeks.

"Of course, my dear. Not just now but soon, I promise," said the woman, trying to sound reassuring. "But first, before we go anywhere, we need to find out what your police friend here knows."

Alice was still rubbing her neck where she had been choked. "What does that mean?" she asked. "I don't know anything. I told you, I'm looking for Lilly." Alice was worried, not just for Harry and Lilly, but for the others who had just left the house. She remembered the man who had brought them here, and how quickly he had been killed, not to mention the deaths of Jordan and the gang members. Was all of that down to this woman? It was a puzzle; it was also a real concern. If they would do that, what would they do next?

The front door closed and Alice heard the sound of another vehicle starting up. She guessed it was the girls' turn to leave. That left Harry, herself, the woman and at least one man. Better odds, but still difficult. She remembered how he had thrown her effortlessly just a few minutes earlier.

Matters got worse when another man appeared.

"These gentlemen are going to take you to find out if you are of any use to us," the woman said, sounding increasingly sinister.

"What does that mean?" she snapped back.

The woman put a finger to her lips and then indicated to the two men. At her command they stepped forward. Alice leapt to her feet and backed into the room.

"You are going with these gentlemen. You can either go peacefully, or fight and go… less peacefully… Whatever you choose, the result will be the same. You're upsetting young Harry," said the woman.

Harry was crying, he was terrified. He had seen his sister be dragged away and now these men were going to drag her away, leaving him alone again.

"Me? You're the one upsetting him, you fucking bitch," Alice said, terrified but still unable to hold back her anger.

"Just take her," said the woman. The two men grabbed her.

"Fuck off, get the fuck off me!" She tried to kick out, but it was pointless. The two men lifted her off the floor. She turned and spat in one of their faces. With his free hand the man wiped the spittle on his cheek, rubbing it between his fingers. He smiled at her and licked the fluid from them. His calm reaction and smile filled her with dread. She had never felt as afraid as she was at that moment. The two men then dragged her from the room.

"I'm sorry you needed to see that, Harry," said the woman. "Let's you and I sit here and watch a bit of television for a while."

Alice was dragged easily up to one of the bedrooms upstairs. The smell of stale sweat filled the room. There was no furniture, but the floor was covered in mattresses, some of which were clearly stained. The walls had mould under the windows and in the corners. It also smelled damp. She was thrown to the floor.

"Strip," one of the men commanded.

"What?" She had heard him, she just hoped it was something else.

"Strip," he said again.

"Fuck you," she replied, trying to remain defiant. The other man had moved behind her. He effortlessly picked her up, a hand on each upper arm, holding her in place.

The man looked at her. Suddenly he slapped her around her face.

"Strip," he barked at her.

"Fuck off," she shouted back as the pain began to spread across her cheek.

He slapped her again in the same place.

"Strip," he barked again.

She shook her head, tears welling up in her eyes from the pain.

"Fuck you," she said.

He slapped her again. The pain was now excruciating.

"Strip," he said again.

Without saying anything, she shook her head, trying not to look up. The man grabbed her hair and pulled her head up. As soon as their eyes met, he slapped her again.

"Strip."

Tears flowed down her face. It was pain, fear and an acceptance that she had no choice. She slowly nodded. The man who had been hitting her stepped back and nodded towards the other who let go of her. She knew she had no chance of getting away. Her face was in unbelievable pain, and she could feel it begin to swell. Reaching up, she began to undo her top.

When she was standing in just her bra and knickers, she looked at the floor, trying to make a point that she had done what they asked, but the same man continued to bark the same command.

"Strip."

"Please," Alice found herself pleading.

"Strip." The man was looking at her. The other man was still behind her.

"I can't, please."

"Strip."

The man stepped towards her. She shook her head, she was sobbing, but knowing there was nothing else she could do she reached behind herself and released the catch on her bra then moved her shoulders forward, so it fell to the floor. The man was still watching as she put her hands to her hips and slowly lowered her knickers. She stood with one arm across her breasts and the other hand covering her pubic hair.

The man grinned as she felt the other grab her again and pull her to the floor. Alice didn't resist, she couldn't resist. She'd always told herself if she was in this position, she would fight to the death, but she couldn't. She could see the man had undone his trousers and his hand was now inside his underwear masturbating himself to an erection.

Within moments he was kneeling between her legs and then the sudden pain as he thrust himself deep into her. She looked to the side so as not to look at him and he thrust her several more times before he suddenly made a last effort. She guessed he had cum. He got off her and she lay on the floor unable to move.

The two men spoke, and they swapped places. Suddenly and effortlessly, she was flung over onto her front.

"Please, no!" Alice cried.

She knew it was hopeless as the other man proceeded to rape her from behind whilst the first man held her in place.

When he had finished the two men got up, leaving Alice lying on the floor. She found herself curling into a foetal position. Her face was still in pain, but it was nothing compared to this pain. She felt like the world she had previously occupied had ended only to be replaced by this new nightmare.

She hadn't noticed one of the men leave the room, but she did become aware when he re-entered, carrying a kitchen chair and a roll of heavy-duty cloth tape.

Putting the chair down, he indicated to the other man to pick Alice up. She had no strength left to resist. She was unceremoniously forced into a sitting position on the chair.

"Please," was all she could manage.

The men ignored her and continued to tape her arms behind her to the back of the chair. Each leg was then taped to a chair leg, trapping her naked and unable to move.

One of the men called out and the woman appeared at the door with Harry. Despite the tape, she was able to look up and see his shocked face. Any dignity she had hoped to maintain was gone. She was helpless. Harry was crying and looked away. Alice tried to reassure him, but no words came from her. She dropped her head and closed her eyes.

"We have good news," the woman began. "These gentlemen tell me we may have a use for you after all." Alice kept her head down and her eyes closed. At this moment she couldn't get past what had happened. "We do, however, need to know what the police know about our organisation," the woman continued. "So, Alice. It is Alice, isn't it?" she asked, clearly knowing the answer. "We've had a look at your I.D. we found in your pocket. Nice photo by the way." Alice didn't move or say anything. "Young Harry tells me you went with him into London to find his sister, is that correct?"

Without looking up Alice nodded.

"Good, good," the woman said. "What else do you know?"

Alice shook her head. "Nothing," she whispered.

"What was that?" the woman asked in a raised voice.

"Nothing," Alice repeated in a louder whisper.

"Knowing nothing is good but it's my job to make sure."

She turned to one of the men and held out her hand. He passed over a rolled-up bath towel and the woman put it on the floor in front of where Alice was seated. In the towel was a tool that looked a bit like a giant pair of secateurs.

Instantly the fear began to overtake the pain she already felt. How much more she could endure, she wasn't sure. Her mind was racing; she was exhausted.

"Please," was all Alice could manage.

"This is an industrial ratchet cable cutter; do you know what it's for?"

"Cutting cable," Alice whispered back.

"Yes, that's right, it will cut both copper and aluminium multi-core cable up to thirty-two millimetres thick." Alice said nothing. There was nothing she could say. Once more she tried to speak, and once more no sound came out.

The woman gestured towards the man, asking him to pick up the cable cutter.

"You've had quite a day, haven't you Alice?" Alice said nothing. "I know, I know," she said. "I'm sorry about my men doing that to you, but we needed to check if you were any good to me. If not, we would need to get rid of you and I really don't want to do that. What I need you to do is answer me. What do the police know about our organisation?"

"Nothing," replied Alice. "Please, nothing." It was true – she hadn't known anything about these people until that morning.

The woman pointed at her own breast and in response the man stepped forward and opened the cable cutter, pushing it against Alice's naked right breast, forcing the nipple through the aperture.

"Now, Alice, please don't make me do this. If I cut off your nipple you will be disfigured for life." The woman stepped forward and lifted Alice's head to look her in the eye.

"Please," replied Alice. "I don't know anything."

The woman indicated to the man to pull the device away. "No, not a good idea," she said. "Having just established you could be a valuable resource, we don't want to disfigure you. After all many of the men you service would like to fondle them." She paused. "I know." The woman held up her index finger and the man moved the cutters accordingly. "I'll ask again, what do the police know about our organisation?"

"No, really, please, please, we don't know anything." Tears streamed down her face again. She shook her head.

"Sorry, silly me, are you left or right handed? I never noticed." She smiled at Alice.

"Right," whispered Alice.

"Good, good, we've got the right one." She paused. "Oh, wait, you will need that finger for your clients." She indicated to the man to pull the device away, which he did. She held up Alice's head and smiled at her.

"Please stop, please. I don't know anything, please." She was shaking. The cold of the room on her naked body was beginning to have an effect. On top of the trauma of the rape, it was too much to bear.

"Of course, there is something we can do to help you remember, something that won't affect your ability to work for us." She stepped back, keeping in Alice's line of sight. She unzipped the side of her right ankle boot and peeled it from her foot. As Alice looked at the woman's bare foot, she gasped, and her eyes widened. The whole of her big toe was missing to at least a centimetre into her actual foot.

"You probably noticed my limp?" she asked. Alice continued to stare at the damaged foot. "Needless to say, it took a little while to heal but it hardly affects me now. In fact, you could say I've become a trusted member of the organisation. It took a bit of forgiveness first, as you can imagine." She smiled again and then nodded at the man with the cable cutter. Alice found herself curling her toes. "Please don't do that," the woman said, seeing what Alice was doing. "We don't want to remove more than we need to." The man forced it over her right big toe. The woman's smile dropped. "I'm going to ask you again, what do the police know about our organisation?"

"Please, I don't—"

Before Alice could finish speaking the woman had indicated to the man. Quickly and without a pause he closed the cutters.

Alice screamed, feeling the pain ricochet throughout her body, to the point she thought she would pass out. She began to rock frantically, the tape holding her in place pulling on her skin.

"There, there, Harry. It will be over soon." Alice heard the woman comforting him, but she was too wracked with pain to see anything clearly. She was crying, screaming out. "I know, I know, it's very painful." She stepped forwards and lifted Alice's head once more. "Now Alice, this is the time. What do the police know about our organisation?"

Alice shook her head violently. "I don't know, I don't know!" She screamed the words, her voice faltering in frustration and pain. The woman nodded.

"Okay, let's do the other foot."

"Please, no, I don't know, please!" Alice was screaming. The man put the cutting edges around her big toe on her left foot. "Please, I don't know anything, please," she continued to plead.

The woman raised Alice's head once more.

"What do the police know about our organisation?" Alice shook her head. She had no idea what to say. "Okay, Alice, I think I believe you. Let's get you bandaged up, and you can get dressed. Harry, you can come downstairs with me."

Harry stood up and followed the woman from the room. One of the two men set about helping Alice to dress and one of them wrapped her foot in the bath towel. She struggled to stand and when she was pulled up by the men the pain was unbearable. She looked down at her heavily bandaged foot. The blood was already seeping out of the wrapping.

*

The woman led Harry back into the kitchen and sat him down. "Would you like some water?" she asked.

Harry nodded. She took a glass from the cupboard and filled it from the tap before handing it to him.

"So, Harry, we need to decide what to do with you." The words filled him with terror. He had the vision of Alice's torment and pain fresh in his memory.

"Can't I go home, please? I won't tell, I didn't tell when they made me take the drugs." He rushed the words out, pleading in tone.

The woman nodded. "I understand. I need to think about what's best. I know you want to see your sister and if we decide to keep her, what would you do then? I expect you would still speak with the police."

"Please," replied Harry. "Please let me and my sister go, we won't tell anyone. If you want money my dad's really rich." He spoke quickly, hoping he could convince her to let him leave with Lilly.

"That's very interesting but it might be out of my hands. Your sister, Lilly, wasn't it?" The woman looked at Harry.

"Yes, Lilly, Lilly Voclain." At this, she stopped speaking. She looked shocked. "What did you say?"

Harry was unsure what he had said that was wrong. "Lilly?" he said again.

"Your last name, what is your last name?" She sounded almost frantic in her search for an answer.

Harry was confused. "Voclain," he said, still puzzled.

"Stay there," she commanded. She was looking concerned; something wasn't right, and Harry could see the worry on her face. She quickly left the room, taking her mobile as she walked out. Harry heard the front door go. Whoever she was speaking with, she didn't want anyone to hear.

Minutes later she returned. She looked even more shocked and upset than when she'd gone out. Whoever she'd spoken to, had clearly rattled her. *Maybe she knows Dad's lawyers could get her somehow, or he could hire private detectives to find her.* He wondered what it was that caused her reaction, it was obvious to Harry that his last name had spooked her. She put her phone on the side and leaned against the unit looking at him. She looked like she was searching for the right words but was struggling to find them.

"Okay, Harry, I'm going to try and get you home. I need to organise some things first."

With that, she left the room, and he heard her hurry back up the stairs. She had left the phone on the side. Maybe he could get it and make a call. Every time she went upstairs and came back down, he heard her, so he'd know if she was coming back. He dashed over to where the phone was and picked it up, but it was locked. His heart sank. But this was his only chance, so he stopped to think about it. She was probably 50 years old; how much about phones would she know? It would be something obvious, he tried the default 0000. Nothing. *Think, think, think.* 1234, still nothing. 1111…

Unlocked.

Harry froze. The phone was still set to the page of the last call, and it was a number Harry instantly recognised. It was his dad's home number in Weybridge.

Someone was coming down the stairs. He put the phone back and quickly sat down. The phone screen was still live. He looked at the screen and at the door. The woman approached and as Harry glanced back at the phone it went to black again. He breathed a sigh of relief.

"We are going to arrange a car to take you to meet Lilly and then the two of you will get a train to home, okay?" Harry nodded. "Alice will be coming with us, but sadly she will part from you after we meet with Lilly, her path will be different to yours."

He hoped Alice would be okay. He shivered at the thought of what he witnessed happen to her. He was also confused but elated to be going home. He wondered if it could really be happening. He then thought it might be a cruel joke. But why? And why had she phoned his dad? How did she know his dad? There were so many questions, he didn't understand. He then remembered Jordan and the men in London. Did his dad get them killed looking for him and Lilly?

He tried to tell himself it was impossible, but it was the only possible answer.

CHAPTER 27

As she sat there waiting, Anastasjia listened to the music that gently came from the speakers in the car. She had gone through the channels until she found one that played classical music. It was not normally her choice but somehow, she found it relaxing. She imagined what it would feel like for her and Uldis to be driving to Riga together. She knew that she wouldn't see him until she had exchanged vehicles. She guessed that she would drive the new car to Brussels again and from there it would be taken to Riga via a transporter, leaving her and Uldis to catch the train. Maybe she would get the chance to choose. She smiled at the thought.

Looking out of the windscreen she saw the Frenchman come trotting out of the front door, phone in hand. *What's the urgency?* she thought as he reached her. Not wanting to get out and speak to him, she pushed the button and let the window down.

"You have a job," said the Frenchman in a condescending fashion.

"Yes, I know," replied Anastasjia sarcastically. "It involves delivering this very expensive and now slightly dirty car."

"I'm not laughing," said the Frenchman. "Mr. Daniels needs you to take one of the girls to a new location."

Anastasjia frowned. "What location?" The Frenchman shook his head.

"I don't know, but it's urgent and you need to be ready to go. She will be arriving here in a few minutes. Once you have dropped her off you will return and the car will be emptied as the original plan, understand?" He was treating her as though she was stupid.

"Yes, I understand, but if the instructions are from Mr. Daniels why has he not spoken to me?"

The Frenchman stared at her.

"As we've already discussed, maybe you are not as important as you think you are." He grinned. Anastasjia was raging but didn't want to show it.

"Okay," she said. "When will the girl be here?" As Anastasjia finished speaking a minibus closely followed by a van came into view down the driveway. Both pulled up in the yard and the driver and front passengers all got out. She could see that the minibus appeared to be full of men. They all looked a little dishevelled. She guessed therefore that the van behind it must be the one containing the girl she was going to have to move. This was confirmed when one of the men opened the back of the van and the Frenchman went over to look inside.

"Lilly, Lilly Voclain?" the Frenchman called. No one answered. *Voclain?* Where had she heard that name? Anastasjia knew the name from somewhere. Suddenly it came to her. The garage in England they purchased Aston Martins from, she was sure that was the owner's name. She told herself it must be a coincidence.

*

Lilly had said nothing. She was not about to volunteer herself.

"Lilly, you must come forward, it will be better for you and better for everyone." The man was clearly trying to sound caring, but Lilly was not having any of it. "Very well, if I don't speak with Lilly, I shall take one of the younger girls and she will be beaten until Lilly identifies herself. How does that sound?" A look of even greater fear appeared on some of the younger girls' faces. Some of them were only 14 and 15 years old. She was petrified of what might happen to her but could not live with the younger girls being harmed on her behalf.

"I'm here," she said, stepping forward.

"Ah, Lilly. Come here, child," said the Frenchman, reaching into the van to help her out. Lilly's eyes adjusted to the sunlight. "I see you have a nasty bruise on your face. That looks very painful." Lilly nodded. "Yes, of course. You have no need to worry, it will soon be all over for you. But first, I need you to get into the boot of that car." He pointed at the Aston Martin.

"What?" asked Lilly.

"I know, it's going to be uncomfortable for a short while, and cramped, but I need you to get into the boot of the car." He smiled at her.

"But I can't—" Before she could finish, he raised his hand to stop her.

"I insist, you must. It won't be for long, I promise." It was odd. He sounded as though he cared, despite the instructions. That was the first time she thought someone was genuine out of these people.

The boot of the Aston Martin was opened to reveal a remarkable space for a sports car but still very small for a person to climb into. Also in the boot was a small suitcase. Lilly looked at the Frenchman.

"I, I can't get in there, there isn't enough room. I can't—"

The Frenchman pulled out the suitcase. At that, a woman Lilly hadn't noticed before now, opened the Aston Martin's driver's door and climbed out.

"What do you think you're doing with that?" she shouted.

"It will be here when you get back," the Frenchman shouted back.

Lilly looked at the woman. She was beautiful, although she could see bruising behind her sunglasses. Lilly wondered if she had gone through the same as her. It was odd she was driving the Aston Martin though, so maybe not.

"In you get," said the Frenchman. Lilly stood and looked, not moving. "Now, please. You must if you want this to be over." She thought hard. She had no desire to climb into the boot of the car, but she was being promised an end to her ordeal. She decided the outcome couldn't be any worse than she had already suffered.

Stepping forward, she put one foot in the boot and then tried to lie down. Her balance went and the Frenchman grabbed her, helping her into a foetal position. He was surprisingly gentle, giving her reassurance.

"Not long, I promise," he said before closing the boot.

Lilly could feel it pressing on her. It was cramped, and she couldn't move. She prayed he was telling the truth.

In the darkness, Lilly heard the Frenchman talking to the beautiful woman who had been in the driver's seat, or at least that's who she guessed he was speaking to.

"This is the location. Take this map. Do not use your sat nav, that will leave a record of this location and route, understand?" Lilly didn't hear a response. She was feeling cramped and uncomfortable. She could feel the hard floor of the boot against her hip bone. It was beginning to hurt. She hoped she had made the right decision. The engine suddenly fired into life; she guessed the woman must have agreed.

The car moved off, and Lilly could feel every bump and movement of the car. The last part of the van journey she had taken not long ago had been bumpy, but it was nothing to how bad it felt in the boot of this supercar. She knew all about the cars from her dad's showrooms; he was a bit of a 'dick', but he did get to drive nice cars. She had been the envy of her school friends when he used to pick her up after school. That was a while ago, when they got on.

It felt like the bumpy ride would go on forever, but then the car stopped. She could hear the sound of the thumping engine ticking over. Suddenly a roar and the car leapt forward, turning sharply to the right and accelerating away. Lilly knew they were now on a solid tarmac road and although cramped, she was glad. At least she wasn't being thrown around.

The journey seemed to go on, and on, and on. She could feel stiffness and pain in her knees and the hip pain was getting worse as she lay curled in position. Finally, she felt the car pulling over. The engine stopped and then nothing. She lay wondering what was going on. Then she suddenly had a thought. What if she was being taken to meet someone who was going to rape her? She began to panic. The trauma of the recent past started to wash over her, the space in the boot was getting smaller and the anxiety was rising fast. She began to shake and cry. *Please no, not again.*

"Let me out!" she shouted. She started to hit the inside of the boot. Maybe there would be someone who could hear her. *Bang, bang, bang.* She hit the inside of the boot as hard as she could. *Bang, bang, bang.* "Let me out! Help, help!" The boot latch clicked, and the door sprung open. The beautiful woman was there.

"Shhh!" she said. "It's okay." Another eastern European accent. She was one of them.

"Help!" she called out, hoping there'd be someone else nearby.

"It's okay, it's okay, you're going to be okay," the woman said soothingly, and gave Lilly a hand, helping her from the boot.

She stepped out and saw that the car was in a lay-by, secluded from the main road by trees.

"We have to wait here for someone and then you will be able to go. Are you okay?"

"Yes," replied Lilly, not knowing what else you were allowed to say to that question.

She wasn't okay at all. But what else was she to say? She didn't know who this woman was. A Mercedes 'A' class pulled into the lay-by behind the Aston Martin.

Anastasjia turned to Lilly and said, "Just wait here, while I make sure it's okay." That's when she heard the voice. The voice that had haunted her nightmares for so many years.

"Anastasjia, what a pleasure. You've come so far." Anastasjia froze, she hadn't heard that voice in forever. "I believe this young lady you are with is Lilly, is that correct?"

Lilly looked at the woman from the Mercedes car. Smartly dressed and attractive but, as usual, wearing too much makeup. She walked towards them. Anastasjia hadn't turned to look, she didn't want to see this reminder of her dark past, the reminder of the sex with countless men she was forced to endure, the beatings, the squalor, the deprivation. This woman was the one, the one who controlled it all.

She steeled herself to turn around and face her nemesis. The one person who filled her with absolute fear and dread.

"I thought you were dead," she said without thinking, a look of shock on her face. The woman smiled at Anastasjia, clearly enjoying the effect she was having on her.

"No, I'm very much alive, and you, look at you. You're doing very well, I understand." It was said as a comment rather than a question. Anastasjia still couldn't speak, but the woman continued. "Are you Lilly?" she asked.

Lilly didn't speak either.

"I have someone to see you," the woman said, indicating behind her. A large man got out of the driver's seat of the Mercedes and opened the rear door behind him.

Anastasjia watched as a slim spotty face emerged from the rear of the car.

"Harry!" Lilly called and ran towards him. He stepped aside from the door and Lilly threw her arms around him. He hugged her back, starting to cry, which set her off as well.

"Touching," said the woman before turning to Anastasjia. "It is time we left. I will see you at the house. After we have looked at the car you can continue to deliver it."

Anastasjia had still not spoken. She had watched the scene unfold in front of her, feeling the warmth at the reunion, and completely forgetting about the hatred that was rising in her for this woman. The man had already closed the Mercedes door and had got back in the driver's seat. The woman turned and walked back towards the car calling behind her.

"Hurry, Anastasjia, don't keep everyone waiting."

Lilly and Harry stopped hugging and turned to the woman.

"What do we do?" asked Lilly, unsure what was going on.

"Yes, of course," said the woman. She reached into her pocket and pulled out a roll of banknotes. She counted out ten of the twenty-pound notes and handed them to Lilly. "There is a town that way," she pointed. "Only a couple of kilometres away. It has a station, catch a train home." She smiled. "You should have enough left over for a sandwich and a drink each." She continued to the car and as she climbed in the passenger seat, Anastasjia could hear her laughing as she pulled away in the opposite direction to the farmhouse.

Lilly and Harry looked at Anastasjia as if they didn't quite believe they were allowed to go.

"You heard her," she said, and closed the boot before climbing back into the Aston Martin.

Harry and Lilly hugged again, both of them feeling the tears on each other.

"Come on," said Harry, and the two of them set off towards the nearby town.

CHAPTER 28

Alice was in unbelievable pain. The trauma she was suffering from the rape and the amputation of her toe was too much for her to bear. It was too much for anyone to bear. She knew her only hope was to try to stay awake. She could feel the blood draining from her and her body trying to shut down. *If I sleep, I'll probably never wake up*, she told herself.

She was glad to see Harry and Lilly set free, though she had no idea why. What she also couldn't understand was the decision to take her with them. They must have known it was a risk. It couldn't be good. From the back seat of the Mercedes car, she had seen the woman take Harry over to the Aston Martin where Lilly was standing with a very elegant-looking woman. She wondered who she was. She looked quite scared of the woman; that was no surprise, considering what she had done to Alice.

With the boot of the Aston Martin open she couldn't see a registration number but could tell it was a new-looking car, despite being quite dirty, and the fact it was beginning to get dark. She used the information to keep her mind busy. Hopefully if she kept thinking things through, she would stay awake.

Before leaving the car, Harry had looked at her with a mix of joy to see Lilly and sorrow for her. She had tried to smile back at him, reassuring him everything would be okay. The only good thing now was that with Harry gone, there was more room in the back of the car. The extra room wasn't easing the pain.

When she was back in the car, the woman turned to her and said, "Alice, I have some good news for you and some bad news." She smiled as Alice raised her head to look at her. What could possibly be 'bad news' after all that had happened to her up to now? The only thing she could think of was that they had decided to kill her. In some ways, that would be a welcome relief. "It would appear that your services are no longer required," she said, continuing to smile. "These gentlemen tell me you were an excellent fuck and that you showed great promise, however I have taken instructions, and you are to be set free from our organisation."

Alice couldn't quite believe what she was being told. There had to be a catch. She looked at the woman and, trying to muster an element of humour in defiance, said, "And the good news?"

The woman laughed, clearly appreciating her bravery in the face of everything.

"I'm afraid there is bad news." She paused. "Your survival will depend upon your good fortune and your ability not to bleed to death. I'm sure you are very happy for young Harry and his sister," she continued, "but what we cannot do is allow you to get home before we have had an opportunity to cover our tracks. Obviously, you know the house we have left, but you do not know where we are going."

Alice looked down and shook her head slowly from side to side. *What next?*

"You will not find us. Time will ensure that, so don't even try." Once again, she smiled at Alice. "You may have noticed it is getting dark?" Alice nodded. The woman nodded back. "We will shortly be taking you for a walk." She looked at Alice's face clearly, noting the pain and discomfort she was in. "Don't worry, you won't have to walk on that bad foot of yours, these gentlemen will carry you." She indicated to the driver and the man sat next to Alice. He was the one who had beaten her around the face and the first to rape her. She had no desire to be near him, let alone him touching her.

"Tell me, Alice, do you like dogs?" It was a question she wasn't expecting.

"What?" she managed to reply.

"Dogs," repeated the woman. "Do you like dogs?" Alice looked at her and shrugged. "I hope so. We will be taking you to a well-known dog-walking place. Not obvious but used enough." She smiled again. "Someone will eventually find you and take you to hospital to get that foot looked at. How does that sound?"

Alice struggled to keep her head up. "What's the catch?" she managed to ask.

"I see you're a bright girl," the woman replied. "Hopefully a successful career ahead of you. Yes, there is a catch. Obviously, we can't risk being seen, so we will take you there now. So provided you survive the night, there is a good chance you will be rescued in the morning."

Alice was trying to process the idea of being free whilst at the same time wondering if she could survive being out all night, bleeding and cold.

The car drove on. "There is just one more thing," the woman said, this time without looking round. "We need to blindfold you, just to make sure you are not clear about where you are when we leave you, just a little addition to your confusion. I'm sure you understand."

Alice didn't care, she was beyond caring. She had been raped and tortured, so even if she was to be abandoned overnight and might bleed to death, it didn't matter. She just wanted it over.

The man next to her pulled a black cloth from his pocket. He rolled it into a loose-looking blindfold and tied it around her head, making sure it was spread over her eyes. Alice didn't try to resist; she didn't want to jeopardise her freedom. She hated the blindfold, but if it meant she had a chance, so be it.

After a while Alice felt the car turn off the main road and eventually come to a stop on some bumpy ground. Alice couldn't see a thing. She could tell it was now completely dark, as there was not even a trace of light above or below the blindfold. The door opened next to her, and she felt one of the men pulling her from the vehicle.

She screamed. Not so much because of the physical touch, but because the pain in her foot was horrendous.

"Please, Alice, try and keep your voice down, you'll scare the wildlife," the woman said.

"Fuck you," replied Alice defiantly.

The next thing she felt was being picked up onto one of the men's shoulders. She was feeling weaker by the second, she knew the bleeding hadn't stopped and she was shivering from the shock, or the cold, or both. She was doubting her ability to survive every minute the nightmare continued.

The man walked on until he eventually stopped. Alice was lowered to the floor and propped against what felt like a tree.

The man removed the blindfold. The woman was nowhere to be seen. Alice guessed she didn't want to get mud on her shoes. *Bitch*, she thought.

The man walked away, leaving her where she was. Nothing was said as she heard him leave. She was alone. She did her best to adjust her eyes to the dark. She was in the trees, and it was dark. The density of the canopy seemed to make it feel much darker. In the distance she heard a car start and drive off. That must be the woman and the men. But she couldn't be sure. She stayed quiet, listening to see if they were coming back. She couldn't hear anyone; she was alone in the dark.

She tried to make herself as comfortable as possible. She was convinced that there was a better position than the one she was currently in, but as she tried to move, it became obvious she would be in pain whatever she did. She tried to settle into position and instead looked around at what she could see. The answer was nothing. Just undergrowth and trees. She couldn't make out what kind of place she was in at all. She just had the woman's word that it was a common place for dog walkers. What if it was some cruel sick joke, and she had been dumped in the middle of nowhere to starve or bleed to death? She knew the woman was capable of anything.

What she could do was hear, and it was obvious to Alice she was not alone here. Her mind was beginning to race. Was it mice? Rats? Snakes?

She had no idea, but it sounded like she was surrounded by whatever it was. She reminded herself of her earlier thoughts. In order to stay alive, she needed to stay awake. One thing was for sure – the sounds were going to help her stay awake.

CHAPTER 29

As Anastasjia reached the end of the driveway back to the farmhouse she saw another minibus had arrived, as well as another car – a Volkswagen Golf, which made her excited beyond belief. *Uldis*. She'd had another testing day. She was tired, shocked at seeing the woman who had been in charge of her previous life, she felt dirty and in need of a shower and she knew she still needed to deliver the car – her sat nav was telling her it was at least another hour with no traffic. Despite all this, Uldis was here, and none of that mattered anymore.

She pulled up and walked over to the house, pushing open the unlocked front door. The smell of sweat and stale tobacco was by now filling the air. She didn't know how many were in the house and the outbuildings, but it had to be at least thirty-five to forty. Men, women and in some cases, children, teenagers at the least.

In the kitchen chatting to the Frenchman and a couple of other men was Uldis. Her heart skipped a beat when she saw him. They all stopped talking and looked at her.

Uldis smiled, but it was the Frenchman who spoke. "No problems, I hope?" he asked.

"No, no problems. Who was the woman?" She knew full well who she was, but she wanted to know how much he knew about her.

The Frenchman laughed. "Ah Madam Kristine." He smiled. "She is very formidable." He nodded, pausing. "But very good at what she does. She will be here soon to clear your car before you carry on to deliver it."

Anastasjia's heart sank; she really didn't want to see her again. The good thing was that Uldis was there. She could sense he was being a little off with her, but she guessed it was because the other men were present.

"How are you, Uldis?" she asked. "Did the journey go okay?"

"All good," he replied in a clipped manner, clearly trying to avoid engaging in conversation.

"Would you like coffee?" asked the Frenchman.

Was coffee his answer to everything? But, what the hell, she was tired, it would help.

"Please," she replied. "Strong as possible."

She looked at Uldis again, but he remained quiet and avoided her stare. She hoped he was okay, and she would have a chance to be alone with him later.

As she sat down, she could hear movement around the house, people going from room to room but considering how many people were there, it was surprisingly quiet. There was very little conversation or voices she could hear. She guessed the 'residents' were under instructions not to talk.

The men continued to chat, a man's conversation of drinking and sex, generalising about the girls in the house and the ones they had previously come across. Uldis was joining in, which Anastasjia found hard to stomach. She hoped it was just bravado, but with her past she couldn't really complain. As little as a month ago she was doing the company's bidding with Jennings.

It was dark when the Mercedes carrying Madam Kristine and the other men arrived.

"Madam Kristine," said the Frenchman as she entered the house. Making a huge gesture towards her, he kissed her on both cheeks before stepping back.

"Claude," she replied, nodding at him and then joining the others in the kitchen. The Frenchman followed close behind.

Ignoring the others in the room, she immediately singled out Anastasjia.

"It's good to see you again," she said cheerfully.

Anastasjia couldn't believe she was so casual in her manner; she knew Madam Kristine remembered what she had been like when they first met. She knew what she had been made to do at her hands. Anastasjia was disgusted. She tried not to show it but did not answer the woman all the same.

"I see you are struggling to forgive our past," she said with what she presumed was fake concern. "We have both improved our situation, we are in a place where we can hopefully move on."

Anastasjia did not want to speak with the woman but did not wish to cause a scene either. She looked at the men who were all looking at her, including Uldis.

"Of course," replied Anastasjia, forcing a smile in return.

"Good," said the woman. "Now let's get that car of yours emptied so you can get on your way." She put her hand out to her. "Keys?"

She handed over the keys to the woman, who then passed it to one of the men she had arrived with. He and the other man headed out to the Aston Martin.

"Not long now and you can be on your way," said the woman cheerfully. "Once you have delivered the car, you will be provided with a replacement and then you can meet up with Uldis and continue to the continent at the port. I believe you would like to continue the journey with Uldis, or at least that is what Mr. Daniels tells me. Would that be correct?"

"Yes, if possible, what about the Golf?" she asked, looking at Uldis.

Uldis looked down, still trying to avoid eye contact. After what he had been through, she guessed things were finally catching up with him. She looked back at the woman.

"We will keep the vehicle here for the time being and Uldis can travel with you." She paused, taking in the room, and then continued. "You are both booked into hotels together on the way back to Riga, so you must do what you both can to enjoy the journey." She raised an eyebrow but said no more.

Anastasjia remained suspicious but couldn't help feeling excited at the prospect of the time alone with Uldis. Still, he said nothing.

The men who had gone to the car returned and handed the keys to the woman.

"All done?" she asked. They both nodded. She handed the key back to Anastasjia. "You're free to leave. We have booked you into the Oatlands Park Hotel in Weybridge, I think you'll find it rather pleasant," the woman said. "It's a shame you won't have time to enjoy their facilities, but you will need to drop the car at the garage in the morning and pick up the new one. The ferry leaves Newhaven at 5:00pm but you will need to be checked in before 3:30 so don't be late. Uldis will meet you near the entrance to the terminal. Got it, Anastasjia?" She hated it when she used her name; it felt like a violation.

"Okay," she replied. "I'd best get moving." She didn't want to leave Uldis, but she didn't want to be in the company of the woman any longer than she had to.

She walked out to the car and unlocked it as she approached. There were footsteps behind her that she hoped would be Uldis coming out to say goodbye, but as she turned, she was dismayed to see it was just the Frenchman,

"Wait a moment," he said, holding up both hands in front of him.

Before she could answer she saw the two men coming out the front of the farmhouse, carrying a young girl. Anastasjia looked at the girl and recognised her as the one he had injected with heroin earlier. She was in a bad way, sweating and going in and out of consciousness. Her head was swaying from side to side as though she was trying to stay awake but failing miserably.

"What's the matter with her?" asked Anastasjia, though she knew it was an overdose.

"This poor soul was not used to being injected," the Frenchman said with a grin. "And yet the dose we provided earlier didn't appear to be enough, so we had to give her a little top-up." He smiled at Anastasjia.

"What have you done, you fucking idiot? She's going to die." Anastasjia found herself shouting at the Frenchman.

"Alas, that may be the case." He paused. "She may survive if she were to get hospital treatment." Another pause. "You could drop her off on the way to Weybridge." He smiled.

"Are you fucking mad?" said Anastasjia. "I can't just turn up at a hospital with a drugged-up child, they'll ask questions. What do I say then?" The Frenchman looked remarkably calm.

"It will be fine," he said, gesturing to the men.

They took the girl to the passenger seat of the car, gently lowered her in and fastened her seat belt. Anastasjia shook her head. She would get caught; she didn't know what to do. She couldn't take the girl from the car, not with the Frenchman and his thugs standing there. Surely, they must know there would be CCTV outside the hospital. This was madness.

"I don't even know where to go," she said, trying to get the Frenchman to see reason.

"You sell these cars," he said. "Don't tell me you don't know how to use the sat nav." It was true, she did know, but she didn't want the risk. "Hurry now, Ana, we don't want her dying in the car."

Anastasjia ran to the driver's seat and jumped in, firing up the engine and then activating the sat nav to look for nearby hospitals with an A&E department.

"Eastbourne," she said out loud, looking at the girl, who was fading fast.

She put the Aston Martin into gear and set off, fastening her own seatbelt as she drove.

Trying not to damage the valuable car along the bumpy drive, she glanced at the girl over and over, trying to keep the car as smooth as possible whilst driving as fast as she could. Finally, she reached the main road and wheel spun onto the main carriageway. It was an opportunity to see how quickly the car would go, yet Anastasjia was not enjoying the speed.

"Come on, come on, stay with me." Anastasjia tried to get her attention. She knew it was pointless, but she had to try something. "Come on, don't die on me, stay with me, come on."

She was speeding past cars as if they were standing still, accelerating through the traffic at breakneck speed, hoping beyond hope there would be no police.

Finally, the sat nav indicated she should take the next exit. Following the signs, she saw the hospital approaching and screeched to a halt in the ambulance bay outside A&E. Two ambulance crew came running from the building as Anastasjia opened her door.

"Oy, move that, you can't park there," one of them shouted.

She ignored them and opened the passenger door. She leaned in, unclipped the seatbelt and did her best to lift her now dead weight out of the car. No sooner was she out of the car, Anastasjia dropped her on the tarmac. The two ambulance crew ran over to help. They assisted in getting the girl to her feet.

"What has she taken?" asked one of them.

"Heroin," she replied.

"When and how much?"

"I don't know," she replied, and then moved back to the car, leaving the ambulance crew holding the girl.

"Wait," called one of them.

"I can't, I have to go, sorry." She was already climbing into the driver's seat.

"Stop! Who is she?" the other ambulance crew called.

"Sorry," Anastasjia called back. "Sorry, I have to go."

She knew she couldn't help, even if she did know who the girl was. She closed her door and pulled away as quickly as she safely could.

She wasn't happy; she knew she had been seen. The ambulance crew would have recognised her accent as eastern European; they would have seen the car she was driving, and she suspected there was CCTV. What were the Frenchman and Madam Kristine thinking? Anastasjia knew the heat was on. She continued to Weybridge, following the sat nav, and finally arrived at the Oatlands Park Hotel.

She did not want to be hanging around in the morning with that car. She promised herself to get it to the showroom as soon as possible. She was tired and hoped to sleep. Somehow, she didn't think she would find that easy.

CHAPTER 30

Alice slowly came around. She had tried to stay awake but with the exhaustion and the loss of blood it was an impossible task. She was awake again now and promised herself she wouldn't fall asleep again.

It was still dark but even with the lack of light she could see the white towel around her foot was soaked in blood. Much of it was now congealed or dried and appeared black in colour. Some of the pain had subsided by now so she tried to move into a more upright position. She cried out as the pain once again shot through her foot. Tears streamed down her already stained cheeks.

She had no idea of the time; she could only go on the fact it was still dark. That could mean it was any time before 5:00am; that's when she thought it was likely to start getting lighter. She recalled the woman telling her it was a dog-walking path so hopefully there would be some early walkers first thing.

She could still hear the sounds of the forest. It was amazing how many sounds there were, although they were also quite frightening. What would she do if a fox or rat attacked her? She wasn't sure she could do anything in her state, let alone fight off an animal.

Here she was, lying in a wooded area on a dog-walking footpath, or at least she hoped. How the hell had she ended up here? All because she stopped to interview Harry on her way to work. No, it wasn't that at all, it was because she had been incredibly stupid, trying to show she was better than Missing Persons and should be on a Major Crime team. *Well, look how that turned out*, she thought. But the chances were, she would still be alive when she was found and that meant she could describe the people who were responsible, and hopefully, her colleagues would find them.

Enough of that. She was here, but why? She knew they had killed others, why not her? They did threaten her, so what changed? Why did they let her go? It didn't make sense. She knew they could be ruthless, better than anyone else. Look what they had done to her, not to mention murdering the man who had brought her and Harry from London.

She thought about that for a moment and then another thought came back to her; why did they let Harry and Lilly go? That was just as strange. The two of them could identify them as well. Why was that? The woman with the limp definitely got spooked at one point. None of it was making sense. Alice steeled herself to stay awake.

*

Lilly and Harry had reached the railway station.

"Normans Bay," Harry read aloud.

"Never heard of it," said Lilly. The station was deserted; there was no ticket office and no facilities, but there was a bench so the two of them sat down.

Harry turned to his sister. "Are you going to be okay?" Harry said as he looked at her bruised and battered face.

She smiled at him. "Yeah, sure. I'm sorry I got you into all this, are you okay?"

Harry nodded. "That police lady, I saw them cut her toe off." He looked at her.

"What? What police lady?"

"The one who came to look for us when we went missing, you've met her before."

Lilly was confused. "Why was she with you?" she asked, not really understanding what Harry was talking about.

"I told her where Jordan took us, and she drove us there, but they were all dead and the big man took us captive and drove us to the lady but he's dead now." Harry was desperate to tell his story and blurted out the words in one long flow.

"Scraggy, slow down, who is dead?" she asked.

"The men in London," he replied as though she should know who he was talking about.

"What men in London?" she asked, still confused.

"The ones at the house you took me to with Jordan." Lilly realised who he meant. She couldn't feel sorry for them, they had taken it in turn to rape her, giving her good reason to hate them.

"You said the big man was dead?" she asked.

"Yes, but that was after he made the police lady take us to the house where I saw you."

Lilly looked at him. This was clearly a lot to take in. "What happened to him?" she asked.

"They took him away in the police lady's car and threw him off the cliff in her car," he said.

"How do you know that?" she asked, shaking her head.

"I saw it on the news."

Lilly paused before responding. "If we only had a phone, I could call Jordan to pick us up," she said.

"He's dead as well," said Harry in response.

"What?" said Lilly in shock. "What do you mean dead?" she said to Harry, panic and confusion in her voice.

"They found him in the river, in his car. They didn't say it was him, but it was his car, and they said the driver was dead in the car."

Lilly shook her head.

She had already been through hell; she was not about to accept that Jordan was dead. It was obvious to her that Harry was mistaken. She loved Jordan, and he was going to help her so he must be wrong. He wouldn't be involved in this, surely?

"It's Dad," said Harry.

"What?" replied Lilly, not really hearing what he was saying. She was still trying to get her head around Jordan being dead.

"It's Dad," he repeated.

"What's Dad?" asked Lilly.

"All of it. The woman called him."

Lilly was even more confused than she had been a few moments ago. "What do you mean, the woman called him?"

Harry sighed. "The woman, the one with the limp, called Dad on the phone. Just after I saw you, the two men took the police lady upstairs and the woman called Dad." Harry couldn't understand why Lilly couldn't understand him.

"Let me get this straight," she replied. "When we left the house, the men in the house took the police officer upstairs and the woman phoned Dad?"

"Yes," replied Harry.

"How do you know? Did you hear her?" she asked, feeling quite angry that Harry would even think such a thing. She didn't have a lot of time for their dad, but he was their dad, and he wouldn't want them to come to harm.

"I didn't hear her speak, but she left her phone and the last number she called was Dad."

"You're mistaken," replied Lilly. It made no sense. If the woman had called their dad, he must have known them. She thought about being released; it had happened quickly and according to Harry it was just after the woman called their dad. He must be wrong.

"I'm not," snapped Harry, upset that Lilly wouldn't believe him. Lilly didn't answer. She sat back on the bench, looking straight ahead.

Minutes later the train to Eastbourne pulled in and they climbed aboard, not speaking, both annoyed. The train was deserted. They took a seat opposite each other and sat back. They were on their way.

Getting off the train at Walton-on-Thames station, Lilly and Harry knew it was only going to be a short walk home. They hadn't talked much but both were happy to be in each other's company. Harry had spent some time explaining to Lilly about seeing Jordan's car being pulled from the Thames and there being a body in the driver's seat. She was still hoping he could explain what had happened and why he had let her go with the men when he was supposed to be her boyfriend. Harry tried to say he wasn't, but she was having none of it.

Harry stopped speaking and Lilly guessed it was because he didn't want an argument. She was happy to let him change the subject; she didn't want an argument with him either. He looked tearful again. Spontaneously she put her arms around him and gave him a hug. He immediately hugged her back.

Arriving at the house, Harry asked her if she had a key.

"What do you think?" she snapped. She was right, it was a stupid question. He rang the bell. Nothing. He rang the bell again and with that, the hall light came on. The CCTV camera above the door moved and stopped when it was facing them. Suddenly the door opened, and Harry saw his mum. She stood with tears of joy on her face. He threw his arms around her and began to cry. Lilly waited a moment, not wanting to spoil Harry's reunion.

Her mum looked up from Harry, tears in her eyes. She put an arm up towards Lilly and invited her into the hug. Lilly burst into tears. She was a young child again, and moved forward to accept the arm of her mother. All three of them stood hugging for some time.

Finally, their mum let go and pulled them in, closing the door behind them.

*

It wasn't getting any lighter. Alice guessed it was earlier than she thought. A proverb from her childhood kept going round in her head: "A watched clock never moves." Her mother's voice was as clear as if she was sitting with her, and it brought a smile to her face.

The sounds of the forest were alarming. Every so often something unseen would run past her in the undergrowth, then there was the sound of foxes screeching, like a child in distress. Regardless of the noise, the temptation to close her eyes and sleep was overwhelming.

Think of something. Come on, Alice, think of something, stay awake.

She kept going through what had happened in her mind, over and over. Why had they let Lilly, Harry and her go? She closed her eyes. *Come on, Alice. Think. The boy in the car, Harry said he was Lilly's boyfriend, but he had driven Harry and Lilly to the gang house in London. And now he's dead, and so is the gang and its leader. Got to be connected.* The thoughts raced through her mind. *Kidnapping, slavery, wounding and murder.* She shook her head, trying to make sense of it all. *And yet they let us go.*

Lilly's boyfriend must be involved somehow. Maybe that's why they let Lilly and Harry go, but if that was the case, why her? But he's dead, so who killed him? Could it have been an accident? But Lilly's friend Julie is in hospital so who hurt her? Surely it can't be a coincidence?

She found herself more confused than when she started.

It was a serious, high-profile crime with ruthless people and yet here she was, alive and hopefully to be rescued soon, if she could just stay awake.

What else? There must be something. She went over the day in her head again. The details of her rape and torture she would never forget, but she tried to think of other things. Things she might have forgotten. The woman that Lilly had been standing with when they turned up with Harry. Who was she? She was beautiful, elegant and standing next to the open rear of a very expensive Aston Martin. It still made no sense to her, but she knew to try and remember as much as possible.

Suddenly a fox appeared in front of her carrying what appeared to be a dead mouse or some other kind of rodent. It was literally feet away and just standing and staring.

"Shoo, go, go," she called. But the fox never moved; it was obviously not afraid and could sense that Alice wasn't a threat. "Fuck off," she shouted at the top of her voice. The fox turned and trotted off into the undergrowth, its prize in its mouth.

*

"We need to call the police." Their mum went to pick up her mobile from the worktop.

"Not now, Mum, please. Can we get some sleep and speak in the morning?" She wasn't being obstructive, she just wanted to sleep.

"I just need to let them know you're safe, they're looking for you. Don't worry, I'll tell them they can't speak to you until tomorrow." Lilly was grateful, she had been to hell and back.

"The police lady!" Harry shouted out, sounding frantic. Lilly had forgotten about her with the euphoria of being home safe. She felt guilty for being so selfish.

"What police lady?" Their mum sounded puzzled but also alarmed by the tone of her response. "Who do you mean?" she asked, clearly not having any idea what was going on.

"The police lady had been tortured," said Harry.

"Tortured? Who was tortured?" Lilly thought her mum was sounding more and more concerned.

"The police lady that was looking for us, Harry saw her getting tortured, she might even be dead as well, I don't know."

"What? Dead? What do you mean, dead? Why didn't Harry say anything?" Diane was getting frantic.

"I don't know, he was afraid, I don't know."

"Sorry," said Harry.

"Oh my god."

Lilly watched as her mum activated the phone and dialled 999.

Harry, Lilly and Diane sat at the island in the kitchen, waiting for the police to arrive. Lilly wanted a bath, she wanted to sleep, but her mum had said the police asked her not to yet.

"Can I get you both anything else?" She had already given them both Horlicks and toast with jam, a favourite of their childhood. They had both drunk and eaten as if it was their first meal in months. Lilly watched as Harry shook his head.

"More toast would be nice please," responded Lilly. She watched as her mother smiled. It could be that she was pleased she was home, but she suspected it was because her mum was not used to her being so polite.

"What happened to you two?" Lilly knew the question was coming; she could feel tears forming in her eyes. "It's okay, it's okay, you don't need to say anything." Lilly was struggling to speak.

She was grateful her mum had seen her distress and backed off. She recognised how horrible she had been to her mother before all this had happened and here, she was being so nice to her. That was the hardest thing, part of her had hoped her mother was going to shout and be angry with her. It was what she deserved, but she also knew that wasn't her mum's way. Sure, she could lose her temper, but Lilly knew her mum would be caring, when she needed to be caring, and this was one of those times.

Their mum was standing by the toaster, waiting for it to pop.

"It's Dad," said Harry suddenly.

"You don't know that," Lilly responded, staring at Harry. "He doesn't know that," she said to her mum, as she was pulling the cooked toast out.

"What's Dad?"

"The woman who had us, she called Dad, she knows him."

"You don't know that," she repeated.

"I know what I saw." Harry was indignant, frustrated that she wouldn't believe him.

"What are you saying, Harry?" Their mum looked confused.

"I saw her phone and she'd just called him." Harry was obviously getting annoyed.

"I'm not saying you are wrong; I just don't understand what you're saying." She paused. "The woman who had you with her called your father?"

"Yes!" said Harry.

"I'm sure you've made a mistake," she said, trying to reassure him.

"Why does no one believe me?" Harry said, jumping from his stool and walking out of the kitchen to go to his room. Lilly kept quiet, watching her mother and brother.

"Please, Harry, don't be angry. Please, let's talk," their mum called after him. "What's he on about?" she said, turning to Lilly.

"He's convinced he saw Dad's number on the woman's phone."

"Who is this woman?" she asked. She seemed to be key to all of this.

"I don't know," replied Lilly, "but she was kind of in charge."

CHAPTER 31

Michalina had been given Naloxone and was on oxygen and fluids. The nurse was sitting by the side of her bed watching her constantly. She was moving in and out of consciousness, as she tried to stay awake.

She was going to have to remain in the hospital. This was fine by her, at least she was no longer in the house with the others. She had been unconscious when she arrived and had no idea how she got to the hospital. She remembered being in a car with a woman but little else. She didn't know whether she was going to have to go back to the house later; she hoped not, she just wanted to go home.

"How are you feeling?" the nurse asked, noticing she was awake.

"Okay," she managed to answer.

"That's an interesting accent. Where are you from?" She couldn't tell if the nurse was genuinely interested or just fishing for information.

"Poland. Well, the Netherlands actually."

"The Netherlands? I went to Amsterdam with my boyfriend a couple of years ago, it was lovely." She sounded bubbly.

"It's not all lovely," replied Michalina. She now had a good knowledge of the dark side of the city.

"I'm sure," the nurse continued. "I only visited the tourist bits." She smiled. "What's your name?" She was obviously trying to find out about her.

"Why?" Michalina asked, suspicious. She wasn't going to give away anything that might cause her a problem later.

"Well, I'm Josephine, Josie for short," she said. "I could call you

Patient, but I think a name would be better." She smiled at her again.

"I'm Michalina," she said eventually, feeling relatively safe.

"Not a very Dutch name," the nurse said.

Michalina told her, "It's Polish, my family is from Poland."

"Yes, of course, you said," she replied. "So, Michalina, we've given you Naloxone to help revive you and as you can see, we are helping you breathe with oxygen. What would really be helpful is to know if you only use heroin, or do you use other drugs? I've looked at your arms and although it looks like you've recently been injected, it doesn't look like you've done it for long?" It was obvious this nurse knew her stuff.

"No, not normally," she replied cautiously.

"Okay, we obviously can't give you heroin here but I'm sure we can help you with a substitute whilst you are with us. Maybe get you on a detox programme? Would you like that?" the nurse asked, clearly hoping she would agree.

"Please," replied Michalina.

"Good," she said. "I'm sure we can try and get you some help with your drug use and hopefully help you feel a lot better." She looked at Michalina reassuringly. "I'll be back in just a moment, Michalina." It was nice to hear her name being used by someone who was not going to exploit her.

"Thank you," said Michalina.

She was expecting one of the eastern European men to enter the room at any moment, or even worse, that French bastard who'd injected her. But so far, no one had come. After only a couple of minutes, the nurse returned with a young-looking man whom Michalina guessed was in his late twenties.

"Hi, Michalina, I'm one of the drug support workers at the hospital. I understand you came here having overdosed on heroin?" Michalina nodded. "Well, you'll be well enough to leave shortly. I wondered if you wanted any help with your habit?"

Michalina began to shake. She didn't want to leave, she would only get taken back to the other girls.

"Please, can't I stay longer?" She sounded desperate.

"It's not normal to stay," the man began. "What are you in the UK for?"

Michalina didn't know how to answer.

"I don't know," she began. "They haven't told me yet." She didn't want to say any more as she was still unsure if she was safe.

"Where are you staying?" the man continued.

She shrugged. "I don't know."

"Okay, Michalina, do you have any of your documents, a passport perhaps?" She shook her head. The Frenchman still had it. "Okay," the man replied with a look that suggested he knew why. "I think you may have been trafficked. Would that be correct?" he asked.

Michalina could not respond. Her eyes welled up and she began to cry. Tears streamed down her face.

"I know, I know," the man soothed. "Look, we can get you help but ideally you need to speak with the police."

"No!" she shouted.

"Okay, that's okay," the man said, not wanting to distress her anymore. "Let's get you rested and then we'll try and get you some support to safely get you home."

*

Just as she suspected, Anastasjia found it almost impossible to sleep. She was half expecting a knock on the door any moment. The hotel was only a short drive to the dealership, but she couldn't drop off until the morning. The CCTV at the hospital had probably been viewed by now and the car was in the hotel car park, leading them straight to her. She lay on her back thinking of what could happen. Hopefully the car couldn't be traced to the hotel, but they may figure out its connection to the showroom where she was heading in the morning.

She glanced at the clock, 3:30am. She would need to get some sleep. Even if the police were not waiting for her at the showroom, she would have to drive back down to the house at Newhaven in the morning and she did not want to fall asleep driving an expensive supercar.

She closed her eyes and tried to think of things that would help her sleep. She tried to slow her breathing whilst keeping her eyes shut. Tried to think of good things but everything came back to the previous day. It was no good, all she could think of was the drugged girl, and that young girl in the boot of the Aston Martin. *Who was she? And the boy? Why did they let them go?* She was not going to find it easy to get even a small amount of sleep.

She tried to think of Uldis. She knew he had been off with her when she last saw him but was sure it was for the benefit of the others at the house. Even if Madam Kristine knew about them, it was better the other men didn't. At least they would be together for the long journey back to Riga. *Then, who knows?* she thought to herself, smiling for the first time in a while.

CHAPTER 32

Nyakim was woken by the front door being knocked on loudly. *Who the hell is knocking this time in the morning?* she wondered.

'Bang, bang, bang.' Then a pause. 'Bang, bang, bang.'

"Alice!" the voice called from outside, loud enough to wake the neighbours.

'Bang, bang, bang.'

"Alice!"

Nyakim glanced over to Alice's side of the bed and saw it had not been disturbed. Alice had not been home by the time she went to bed, but it was odd that she still wasn't there yet. She tried to wake up.

'Bang, bang, bang.'

"Alice! DC Thomas!"

Grabbing a dressing gown, Nyakim turned on the hallway light and the banging stopped. She made her way to the door.

"Who's there?" she called through the closed door.

"Police." She was confused and still drowsy. Why would the police be here asking for Alice? She was working late.

"What do you want?" she asked. She was still reluctant to open the door until she was sure it was safe. She didn't know the time, but it was still dark, and it wasn't uncommon for Alice to be working into the night.

"We need to speak with DC Thomas," came the reply.

"She's not here, she's at work." She paused before the sudden realisation that something was wrong hit her.

The voice on the other side of the door spoke more quietly. "She never came into work yesterday; please could you open the door?"

Nyakim was shocked. What did they mean? She saw her just before she was going to leave.

Still concerned for her safety and not wanting to take any chances, she put the chain on the door and opened it enough that she could see the two uniformed officers. She was sure one was a sergeant, he had stripes on his arm anyway.

"I'm Sergeant Maurice Williams and this is PC Janine Walker, we've been asked to do a welfare check on DC Thomas."

"She never came home last night," said Nyakim. "You said she never came into work yesterday?" She looked at the sergeant's face and could see his concern.

"Yes, I'm afraid not, she called in sick."

Nyakim opened the door and let the officers in. "Come through to the kitchen." She led the officers to the room and offered them a seat. "Coffee or tea?"

"Please," said the sergeant.

"Yes please, same," the other officer said.

"Sorry, can we ask who you are?" the sergeant asked, holding out a notebook. Nyakim knew the question was coming but was unsure how she would answer.

"I'm a close friend of Alice's, she lets me stay over."

The sergeant smiled sympathetically. "Look, if you are Alice's partner, that's okay, no one needs to know."

Nyakim felt her eyes welling up; she had wanted to let someone know for so long. "Yes, she is my partner."

The sergeant smiled at her. "This must be a shock for you?"

"Yes. You've no idea how much."

She continued making the coffee, and one for herself at the same time, then sat with the officers and explained what had happened the previous day, how Alice had been going to visit a witness or something. She couldn't remember but she knew she was due to go and see someone and then go to work. The officers listened carefully.

"Where is she now?" Nyakim knew they didn't know, but the words just came out.

"We've no idea, sorry. I'll make sure you are updated with anything we hear."

"Thank you," she said. She was desperate to know Alice was okay but would have to wait and pray she came back safe. Nyakim thanked the officers and gave the sergeant her mobile number.

"I hope you don't mind me not saying we are partners, only I don't think either of us are ready for us to tell our families yet." She looked at the sergeant with watery eyes.

"No problem," he replied. "It's between you, me and PC Walker." He looked at the other officer who nodded in agreement.

*

Sergeant Williams and PC Walker returned to their car after finishing their coffee and making sure that Nyakim would be okay on her own. As they climbed into their seats, Sergeant Williams shook his head. "The shit is about to hit the fan," he said as he reached for his radio. "Control from PS Walker," he spoke into the radio.

"PS Walker go ahead," came the reply.

"DC Thomas hasn't been seen since leaving for work first thing yesterday morning, best call out the cavalry, and begin with the Detective Superintendent."

"Roger, wait at your location for further instructions," came the reply.

Sergeant Williams turned to PC Walker. "It's going to be a long night."

CHAPTER 33

Anastasjia lifted her case into the boot of the car, having decided to drive to the showroom early. If need be, she would wait for someone to arrive. The normal opening time was around 8:30am but she guessed there would be someone there early and maybe she could leave the car, pick up the new one and get on her way. It was only a short drive from the Oatlands Hotel to the Aston Martin garage in Hampton.

As she pulled onto the forecourt, she could tell that someone was there as the security bars had been removed to allow cars in and out. She parked the car and walked to the showroom doors – locked. *Damn it, there must be someone somewhere.* She went around the side of the building and came to the large shutter doors to the workshop. Still, they were down. She wondered what to do next. She was sure someone would be there shortly. Then she heard the door in the shutters being unbolted and turned to see a mechanic. She guessed he was a mechanic anyway as he was wearing British racing green overalls.

"Can I help you, love?" he asked. She looked at him and smiled.

"I'm delivering the Vantage AMR and am due to collect a replacement." She pointed towards where the Aston Martin was now parked.

Seeing the state of the car, he said, "Jesus Christ, lady, have you been through a ploughed field?" He put his hands on his hips and shook his head.

"Yes, I'm sorry," she replied, putting on her best innocent expression. "I took a wrong turn."

"Bloody hell, best we have a look at it," he said, already walking towards the car.

Anastasjia hoped it was only dirty; she really didn't want to have to start trying to justify the condition of the paintwork.

She needn't have worried, the car was fine.

"I'm afraid no one else is here at the moment," the mechanic said, clearly happy that the car was in good condition. Anastasjia suspected that if it was damaged, then it would have been his job to organise the repair, a job he could do without. "There should be some showroom staff here before 8:30 and Mr. Voclain is usually in before nine." Anastasjia smiled. "You can come into the workshop for a coffee, if you want, it's warmer inside."

"Please," she replied, and followed him.

*

William Voclain had been up since 6:00am. He had received a call from his ex, telling him that Lilly and Harry were home safely. That was pleasing, he just hoped that she was going to get a grip and parent them better. So far as he was concerned, if they went missing it was down to her. If it wasn't for the kids, he would have loved to cut her off and leave her to fend for herself. But what he was not going to do, was abandon his kids. He loved Harry and Lilly. He found Lilly hard work, but he could see a lot of himself in her from when he was a youngster – headstrong, opinionated. Harry, on the other hand, was a bit of a genius but over-sensitive. He was going to have to learn to man up. He did wonder why he had started to go missing too. It wasn't his nature. He decided he would call in after work and see him. He needed a firm hand. As he walked into the kitchen, Amalia and the children were already up and ready for the day.

"Much on?" he asked, knowing his wife would probably be dropping the kids off at a creche and having lunch with some friends afterwards. *Tough life*, he thought.

He walked over and kissed her on the cheek before heading out the door.

"No breakfast?" she asked, concerned.

"No, I'll grab a coffee on the way," he called back as he closed the door.

He climbed into his Aston Martin and moved forward to trigger the gates to the property, which opened, allowing him to pull out to the edge of the road. He was just about to leave when a woman stepped in front of the car, causing him to break suddenly.

Stupid woman, he thought to himself.

The woman looked at him but stayed where she was. What was the matter with her?

"Come on, lady, move!" he called out and gestured for her to move out of the way. The woman instead put her hands on the bonnet of the car and continued to stare at him. "Jesus fucking Christ." He hated being delayed. He opened the car door and leaned out so he could shout at the woman again. "Get out the way, I'm in a hurry." As he called out, he was grabbed from behind by a large man who in a single action pulled him from the car and punched him hard in the face. His nose exploded in a shower of blood, making him dizzy.

The woman walked to the driver's door and looked down at where he now lay.

"Hello, Mr. Voclain. I need you to go with this gentleman. Don't worry about your car, I'll be following you in it."

Voclain looked at the woman. "Who are you?"

"All in good time," she replied. "We need to get going." She indicated to the man who effortlessly lifted him to the nearby Mercedes car, where an equally large man was in the driving seat. He was forced into the back and the man sat beside him.

The car pulled off and was followed by the woman in his Aston Martin.

"Where are we going?" he asked. Neither man replied. "If you want money I can get you money. How much do you want?" Again, neither man said anything. Voclain reached into his pocket and pulled out a handkerchief and held it to his nose to stem the blood. "Is it the car? You can keep the car," he offered, trying anything.

Usually, his wealth worked in his favour, but in this case it did nothing. He eventually realised it was pointless speaking. He would have to wait to find out what they wanted.

The cars headed west and then south towards Chobham Common. It was early but there were dog walkers visible. The car turned into one of the car parks and pulled up. Voclain noticed there was a woman getting into a small SUV having just put her dog in the boot. She didn't look over at the Mercedes, but she did look at the Aston Martin that had followed them in. That was to be expected, everyone looked at the Aston Martin.

Voclain was pulled from the Mercedes and forced to stand in front of the woman.

"Who are you?" he asked, desperate to know.

*

Sure enough, just before 8:30am one of the showroom staff showed up. He was a middle-aged man, maybe in his mid-forties, greying slightly but sharply dressed in an expensive suit to impress the customers. Anastasjia introduced herself and explained that she was there to collect a car for export.

"Yes, of course, no problem. I'm fully aware. Let's go into the showroom and sort out the paperwork," he said pleasantly.

"Thank you," replied Anastasjia.

"Has the mechanic looked at the Vantage?"

"Yes, it got a bit dirty, but no damage."

"Excellent," said the salesman. "Would you like coffee whilst I do the paperwork?" he asked.

"No thank you, your mechanic was kind enough to give me coffee earlier. I'm in a hurry to catch a ferry so if we could just get the forms completed, I'll be on my way."

"Yes, of course," he replied as he flicked through sheets of paper.

Thirty minutes later Anastasjia fired up the replacement vehicle, an Aston Martin DBS Superleggera. She entered the Newhaven address into the sat nav and pulled off the forecourt. Not long now and she'd be catching up with Uldis for the drive to Riga.

*

"I would like you to climb back into your car," the woman said to Voclain.

"I'm not doing anything until you tell me what's going on."

The woman looked at one of the men who, taking her command, punched him in the face again, knocking him to the floor.

"Please, Mr. Voclain, get in your car. There is no need for us to make this more difficult than it needs to be." He looked at them and then sat in the car. "Good." She indicated to one of the men who produced two wide cable ties from his inside pocket. "Now, Mr. Voclain, I would like you to put your hands on the steering wheel, just as if you were going to drive."

"Why?" he asked.

"It's a temporary thing. We'll soon be on our way, and you will be left here with your car."

"I don't understand." Why bring him here to just let him have the car back?

"Hands on the wheel, Mr. Voclain." He did as he was told. The man put one cable tie around his left hand and the wheel and pulled it tightly in place. Voclain pulled his other hand away.

"What are you doing?" He was scared; his bravado was no longer driving his speech.

"The other hand, Mr. Voclain."

"Fuck you," he shouted. The woman shook her head and indicated to the man who again punched him. One of the men then grabbed Voclain's hand and held it on the steering wheel, whilst the other secured it.

"Who are you people?" he asked, unable to move.

"Who we are is not important. What I can tell you, is your children are safe. Amalia and the children are well and obviously well cared for. Harry and Lilly are now home and will also be cared for, as well as Diane."

"What have I done?" he asked. He didn't get it.

"Nothing, so far as I know, but someone has to take the blame."

"What?" Voclain was shaking his head.

"In order to make sure Harry and Lilly were safe, our operations were compromised and unfortunately all the evidence will show that you are the perpetrator."

"Main perpetrator, for what?" He was getting more and more concerned.

"Murder, slavery, prostitution and some other things." The woman was so matter-of-fact, Voclain struggled to understand. "There are files and paperwork in your office and at home that will show you as the person who has arranged everything. Obviously, we will have cleared any other areas evidence may be found. The main houses will soon be empty, and the people involved will have moved on. I myself am booked on a ferry this afternoon."

Voclain's head was spinning. "Just let me go, I won't say anything, I promise."

The woman smiled at him. "If only there was another way," she said and gestured to one of the men. He went to the back of the Mercedes and lifted a petrol can from the boot.

"Please, no." Voclain had lost his control and was now crying.

"Sorry," she said, "but someone needs to take the blame." She smiled as the man threw petrol over Voclain and then threw the canister in the car. "When your office is searched, they will find a suicide note, and when your body is discovered, it will be unrecognisable. The cable ties will have melted, looking like you did this yourself."

"No, please!" shouted Voclain as the man threw in a lit lighter, causing him and the interior of the car to burst into flame. The door was slammed shut, drowning out the screams.

Madam Kristine and the men got back into the Mercedes and pulled away, leaving the Aston Martin in an inferno.

CHAPTER 34

Alice blinked and closed her eyes again. The lights were too bright. She slowly tried opening her eyes once more, and half squinting. She managed to see there were people moving, shouting and calling out, mumbles of differing voices. She closed her eyes again.

"Hurry, I need those fluids." She could hear the voices, none of them making any sense.

"Hold still, try to relax."

"Just a scratch."

Alice tried opening her eyes again, this time trying to sit up at the same time, but she felt hands on her shoulders pushing her back down.

"Hold still, hold still, you'll be okay, hold still." The voice was calming and reassuring but it still made no sense. They must be speaking to someone else. Again, she tried to sit up, only this time she was held down more firmly. She felt something being laid over her body and tightened, restricting her movement.

"You're okay now, you're safe," the reassuring voice said. This time Alice realised it was aimed at her.

"Where am I? What's going on?" she asked. "I need to get help."

"It's okay, try not to worry about anything, let's get you fixed up first."

Alice still didn't know what was going on. She didn't even know where she was.

"You're on your way to hospital, shouldn't be long."

"What? What? But… I, I…" Alice couldn't speak; she was confused and still dazed by the bright lights above her. She realised she was in an ambulance. It rocked unsteadily as it overtook vehicles, speeding towards the hospital. Every turn and bump in the road seemed to cause her more pain. It was then that she remembered her foot, and this caused it to explode with pain all over again, as if it had just happened. She remembered the rape and torture, every painful soul-destroying moment of it embedded into every thought she had. She felt the tears beginning to well in her eyes as the images played over and over.

"Try and stay calm," came the voice.

'Stay calm'? If only they knew they wouldn't be saying 'stay calm', she thought.

Finally, the ambulance screeched to a halt and moments later the doors flew open. "Not long now, we've got you," the voice said, trying to be as reassuring as before but now it was sounding more stressed. Alice didn't care, she wanted it to all be over, the pain, the memories, the whole thing.

As the bed rolled into the building she heard the same voice as before.

"Female, mid-twenties to mid-thirties, severe trauma to the right foot including amputation of the right big toe causing severe blood loss."

"Quick as you can," other voices shouted.

"We need blood."

"Trauma room two."

More voices and lights, crashing through doors until coming to a halt. The hospital staff worked tirelessly over Alice, checking her and doing everything necessary to keep her alive. In the background she could hear the voice from the ambulance telling her what had happened. She had been found bleeding heavily in woodland, unconscious.

"Can you hear me? Can you hear me?" The voice sounded almost pleading.

Alice nodded as best she could.

"What's your name?"

"Huh?" she replied, unsure.

"What's your name?" The same voice.

"Alice." She said her name but was still struggling to understand what was happening.

"Okay, Alice, you're going to be okay, we need to get that foot treated. You've lost a lot of blood, but we need to get you fixed up and that means an operation. Do you understand?"

Alice nodded; she understood it would need fixing.

"Harry and Lilly?" she said, somehow expecting them to know what she was talking about.

"Who?"

"Harry and Lilly," she repeated.

"Are they relatives? Do you want us to get in touch with them? Have you got a contact number for them?"

Alice shook her head; she was feeling drowsy and wanted to close her eyes. She concentrated as hard as she could, desperate to stay awake a little longer.

The door opened and closed. Another voice.

"Are you Alice Thomas?"

"What?" How did they know her? "Yes," she managed to say.

"She's the missing officer from Surrey," the voice said. Alice tried to look around. She could feel she was falling into unconsciousness.

"Let's get her down to the theatre." The voice from earlier. Alice was wheeled from the room and down corridors towards surgery.

"Is Nyakim okay?" She just wanted to know she would be okay; this was going to be a big shock for her.

"Who's Nyakim, Alice? Do you want us to speak to her?" She could feel her trolley being raced down the corridors.

"My partner, tell her I'll be okay."

"We will," came the response.

Into another room and another voice.

"Not long now, we'll get you fixed up. You're going to feel drowsy." That was the last thing she remembered before the anaesthetic took effect and she slipped into a deep sleep.

*

Nyakim sat at the breakfast bar with the Detective Superintendent. Alice had previously spoken very highly of her and there was something about Helen Dorry you felt you could trust. She made her feel relaxed, despite her fear for what had happened to Alice.

Taking her time, Nyakim had gone over in great detail exactly what had happened the day before, recalling Alice getting up early and everything she had said. Nyakim searched for every morsel of detail she could find. Anything to find Alice.

Every so often Helen would leave the room to take a call, each time returning and reassuring her that they were doing everything they could to find her.

Helen's phone rang yet again. "Sorry," she said.

Nyakim smiled as she got up and left the room, and sat waiting nervously. Helen seemed to be away longer than on previous occasions, which only added to her concern. Finally, she returned. "Good news, she's been found."

Nyakim burst into tears. It had all been too much.

"Is she okay? Can I see her?" All she wanted at that moment was to tell her she loved her, and she didn't care who knew about it. If her family disagreed with her, then they could go to hell as far as she was concerned.

"She's okay." Helen looked relieved. "She's in hospital. I don't know everything, only that she should be okay. She's about to go into surgery for an injury to her foot—"

"Her foot?" Nyakim interrupted. "What's wrong with her foot?"

"I've not been told, only that it needs an urgent operation, but they're sure she'll be okay." Helen looked at Nyakim's face. "Look, I'm going to drive to the hospital now. It's about an hour away, near the coast. Do you want to come with me? I can't guarantee they'll let you see her straight away but at least you can be there."

"Yes please," she replied. "I'll grab a coat and my phone, I need to call work and tell them I won't be in."

"I'll wait," said Helen as she rushed off.

CHAPTER 35

As she pulled up in the queue for the ferry, Anastasjia looked to see if she could see Uldis. No sign of him or the minibuses, nor vans from the house. She sat back in the driver's seat and closed her eyes for a moment, listening to the music from the sound system. Taking a deep breath, she opened her eyes and once again looked around hoping to see him. Nothing, no sign. She shook her head. Why did she think things would change in the few seconds she had closed and opened her eyes? Dialling his number, she pressed call and waited for it to connect. After ringing for what seemed like an age, she hung up. He must still be driving or busy.

A full half hour passed and the vehicles in front began to edge forward onto the ferry. *Not long now*, she thought to herself, still slightly concerned she hadn't seen Uldis yet. She pulled into the space on the ferry and made her way up to the restaurant where she purchased a coffee. Just like on the journey over, she took a seat at one of the small tables, which reminded her of when she first met the Frenchman. She glanced around the room, hoping that he wasn't there. The room slowly filled and eventually she felt the vibration as the engines came to life and the ferry slowly moved away from the side of the dock.

Still with no sign of Uldis or the others, she wondered if they had missed the ferry or perhaps had been booked on a later one. She thought about it, but that couldn't be right. She was sure she was told there would be a 'delivery' for the continent and that she could meet up with Uldis. It was possible the plans had changed but she was sure she would have been told.

Finishing her coffee, she decided to get another and made her way over to the counter. She was going to need to stay awake for the next part of the journey, not that she was sure what the next part was. She knew it would involve going to Brussels first, but was she to go straight there? It would mean a four to five hour drive if the traffic was good. More likely she would be staying over somewhere. Madam Kristine had definitely mentioned having booked hotels for her. She contemplated calling Mr. Daniels or Uldis. Maybe try Uldis again first. She thought it would be the best option to start with.

She found his details on her phone again and pressed the call button.

"The number you have dialled has not been recognised." She looked at her phone, still hearing the message being repeated. "The number you have dialled has not been recognised."

What's going on? Why would this happen? Making excuses for the situation, she decided it must be because she was in the middle of the channel. She would try again in a bit.

She paid for her coffee and turned back to her table. *Shit*, she thought, taken aback by the sudden and unmistakable figure of Madam Kristine. She was clearly waiting for Anastasjia to join her. She put her coffee on the table and took a seat.

"Are you not going to offer me one, Anastasjia?" Madam Kristine asked, smirking. No matter how much time had passed since she worked for her, Anastasjia couldn't help but feel intimidated. So far as she was concerned Madam Kristine was 100% evil and she couldn't help but wish she was dead.

"Would you like a coffee?" she asked bluntly, not wanting to appear friendly in any way.

"Please, like yourself, espresso would be lovely." She smiled at her again.

"Here, you have this one, I'll get another."

"Thank you," she replied, taking the cup and sipping it. Once again, Anastasjia returned to the queue.

She had no choice but to act as though she wasn't concerned. She knew that despite being rescued from this woman by the company, she had still somehow managed to get herself back in with her. And somehow this woman had managed to get some sort of authority within the organisation. After paying for her coffee, she returned to her seat and sat down, noticing the coffee she had passed over had been finished.

"I expect you're wondering why we didn't meet you before driving onto the ferry?" she asked.

"It was what I was told," replied Anastasjia.

"Yes, of course," she replied. "Unfortunately, there is a slight change to the plans," she began.

Anastasjia stared at her, wondering what was going on now.

"We've arranged for you to spend the night in Dieppe, whilst Uldis and I carry out some company business in Amsterdam."

"Amsterdam? Where is Uldis now?" Anastasjia asked with anger in her voice. This was not what she was told, and it was all she had been looking forward to.

"Yes, yes, I understand how disappointed you must be." She nodded sympathetically. "It's a bit of a last-minute thing, really, but important business. It does mean that you won't see Uldis until you get back to Riga, I'm afraid. Still, the quicker we get the business sorted in Amsterdam the quicker you get to meet up."

Anastasjia shook her head. "Where is he now?" she asked again.

"Oh, he's on board, he just can't come to see you. He is watching over our cargo and making sure no one gets ideas above their station." She smiled. "I must say, I can see why Balodis trusted him, he's a very reliable young man indeed."

"Don't you dare hurt him," Anastasjia said, full of concern. She didn't trust Madam Kristine one bit.

"Hurt him? Certainly not. He is earmarked for a high position. All good, I assure you," she said. "Enough about business, Anastasjia, how was your journey? Did you get that poor young girl to hospital?"

Anastasjia didn't know how to respond. What was wrong with this woman? She must know that making her take the girl to hospital had put everyone at risk.

"Yes, she'll hopefully be fine," she snapped back.

"Good, that is good. Can I get you another coffee or something to eat, my treat?" she said, changing the subject as though they were best friends meeting for lunch.

"No, thank you, I'm fine."

"Okay, well I am going to get something. Please keep an eye on my seat until I get back, I'd hate to lose it." She smiled as she got up and headed over to the counter. Anastasjia shook her head; she was tired of everything.

*

As she came around in the recovery room, Alice felt like she was drunk. She struggled to open her eyes.

"Alice, Alice, I've been so worried. You're safe now, you're safe. I love you." Nyakim's voice was instantly recognisable. She smiled; she was so happy to hear her voice. She tried to speak but nothing came out. "It's okay, it's okay, try not to speak. There'll be plenty of time, just take your time, it's okay." Nyakim said, her voice reassuring.

Alice closed her eyes, still smiling as she felt Nyakim's fingers entwine with hers.

"We're going to need to find out what happened to you, but there's no rush, just get better first," another voice said. This was a voice she recognised but she couldn't place it immediately. Then it came to her – Detective Superintendent Dorry.

"Sorry, sorry," she managed, trying once again to open her eyes once more.

"Don't worry, no rush. I came to tell you Harry and Lilly are okay.

I was told you were asking after them." Alice managed to smile. "I don't want to go into what happened just yet, Alice, let's wait until you're fit and well and then you can tell us. We've already got some leads and have identified some of those responsible, so no rush. When you're well we'll record your account."

Helen told her what was going to happen, but she already knew the routine, she also knew about the cognitive interview techniques they would use, and that they would record it, so as to get the full story. She was not looking forward to it, having to relive the details, but she knew it would be essential to identify the woman driving the Aston Martin, the men, and most importantly the bitch that tortured her.

"I'm going to go and have a chat with the Major Crime team about interviewing Harry and Lilly. When you're better, give me a call and we'll arrange one for you too. Try not to worry."

Alice knew Helen, she liked and respected her, but how could she say that? 'Try not to worry,' how was she supposed to not worry? Everything felt like it had changed, all because she did something stupid. Alice scolded herself. Nyakim squeezed her hand.

"I'm sorry," said Alice, looking at her tear-stained face.

"What have you got to be sorry about?" asked Nyakim. "I'm just so happy you're going to be okay." She squeezed her hand again and smiled.

*

The ship's tannoy announced they would be docking in Dieppe shortly.

"We shall soon be going our separate ways, Anastasjia," Madam Kristine said.

Anastasjia did not want to engage in conversation. She had been sitting in silence with the woman she hated most in this world for four hours. She was not about to begin a conversation now. "When you leave the terminal there is a car park on the main route out of the town." She looked at Anastasjia as she spoke to make sure she was paying attention. "You will drive there and wait for the two minibuses."

"And do what?" she asked.

"This is where you will see Uldis." The woman smiled. There was something about her smile that made Anastasjia trust her even less than she did before.

The ferry docked and it was announced that passengers could return to their vehicles.

"Off you go, Anastasjia," she said, speaking in the same manner you would to a child. "See you in the car park."

Anastasjia didn't respond and left the restaurant to go to the car. She made a conscious effort not to look back as she went, although she sensed Madam Kristine's eyes burning into her back.

*

The drug support worker had been sitting with Michalina for quite some time and had finally got her to chat with him. He had told her his name was Sam, he had also told her he had looked at the CCTV from when she arrived at the hospital and had seen her left by a woman with an Aston Martin car.

Michalina had no recollection of anything; the last thing she recalled was a Frenchman injecting her arm.

"What was his name?" She didn't know. "Where was this?" Again, she had no idea. "Who was the woman driving the car?" Michalina shrugged.

She wanted to try to help but she had no idea. She had finally agreed to speak with police but didn't know what she could tell them. She knew enough to not speak about her drug dealers or Sebastian in particular as that would put her family at risk.

"I've given the police the CCTV, so hopefully they can do something with the car details."

She hoped this wouldn't take too long, she was desperate to get home.

CHAPTER 36

It was getting late when Amalia pulled onto the driveway of Diane's house. She had arranged a friend to call round and look after the kids whilst she told William's other family the bad news. She thought it best to do it in person. She knew that Diane hated her for 'stealing' her husband, but she also knew she wasn't the first and probably wasn't the last he had an affair with. This was going to be a difficult conversation.

As she climbed out of the car and walked up to the door, the security lights came on. Nervously she rang the doorbell. After a few moments she saw the unmistakable shape of Diane looking out of the frosted glass. She guessed she was looking through the spyhole to see who was there. Then the sound of locks and a chain being removed before the door opened.

"What do you want?" she asked coldly.

"Please, Diane," said Amalia. "It is important. I must speak with you and then maybe Harry and Lilly."

"What do you want to speak to them for?" Diane said, clearly not about to give ground easily.

"William is dead. Please, Diane, can I come in? I must speak with you." Amalia could see the look of shock on her face.

"Dead? What do you mean he's dead? I don't understand, what happened?" Diane still stood in the doorway with Amalia on the doorstep.

"Please, Diane, let me come in."

She stood to one side, allowing Amalia into the hallway. She was visibly beginning to shake; Amalia guessed it was the shock of the news hitting her.

"Come through to the kitchen." Diane led the way and offered her a coffee.

"No, thank you. Where are Harry and Lilly?" Diane looked at her. Considering the news, she seemed remarkably calm.

"They're both upstairs."

Amalia nodded. "Good, good. I'm so sorry to have to tell you this."

"What happened? Was it an accident? Heart attack?" Diane wanted answers and it was clear to her that she was not about to consider the feelings of the woman who had stolen her husband.

"Please, Diane, it was suicide."

She stared at Amalia, frowning, and shook her head. "What did you say?" The look on her face said she couldn't believe it. William was a bastard sometimes, but he would never commit suicide. He was successful and the business was doing better than ever.

"It was suicide. They found a note at his office." Amalia looked at Diane hoping she could understand.

"What? How?"

"He set fire to himself in his car. The police came around and told me. I asked to go and see him, but they wouldn't let me, they said he was too badly burnt. I thought I should come myself, to tell you and the children." Amalia looked at her with concern for both her and the children. Diane sunk down onto a kitchen chair, allowing it to take her weight. Amalia knew she may not like her, but the shock must be equally great for her, and she had teenage children to care for.

"I'm sorry," said Diane, forcing a weak smile in the most comforting way she could muster.

The two women sat at the kitchen island whilst Amalia recounted everything the police had told her. When she had said everything, she asked about Harry and Lilly.

"Do you want me to tell them?" It was a kind gesture, but Diane told her that this was her responsibility.

"No, that's fine. You get home to Sienna and Elena, and I'll tell them."

"Okay," she replied. "If I can help, or if they want to see me, they are always welcome."

"Thank you," she replied.

Amalia got up to leave and Diane showed her to the door. As she stepped out, Diane spoke. "Thank you for telling me in person, I know that couldn't have been easy."

"That's okay," said Amalia. "It's times like these that the children are the most important thing." With that, she gave a final smile, and walked to her car. As she climbed back into the car, she saw the door closing.

*

After closing the front door, Diane stood in the hallway. *This is going to be hard*, she thought.

As she returned to the kitchen, she glanced at the photo of herself with a younger Harry and Lilly. The three of them smiling for the picture and happy. They had been through much in the last couple of weeks. The police were due to see them in a couple of days so they could tell them what happened in detail. That would mean going over the horrors they had experienced, and now this. She sighed and made her way upstairs.

She knocked on Lilly's door and opened it, seeing the face of her daughter looking more vulnerable than she had for a long time.

"Hi, sweetheart. Could you come downstairs, please? I've something important to tell you and your brother." Lilly nodded, no disagreement or argument. That stubborn side seemed to have been forced from her. Somehow it made Diane feel as though part of her daughter was gone.

Harry's door was already open, and he was lying back on his bed with his hands behind his head. At first, she thought he was asleep but as she stepped towards the doorway, he turned to her.

"Is everything okay? Do you want me to come down as well?" he asked. He had obviously overheard. He was still so considerate and thoughtful.

"Please," she replied. Harry rolled into a sitting position on the side of his bed and Diane went back downstairs.

Harry and Lilly walked into the kitchen and sat at the breakfast bar looking at their mother expectantly.

"I've got some bad news for the two of you, I'm afraid." Her voice was beginning to tremble. "It's about your father."

"Has he been arrested?" Harry said, still certain his father was involved with what had happened to them.

"Shut up, Scraggy," Lilly said. She didn't want to believe him.

"Don't call me that." Harry was sick of being mocked and was not about to take it anymore.

"Please, you two, stop." Diane could feel the tears filling her eyes. Harry and Lilly could see it as well. They both stopped bickering and looked at her. "It's your father. I'm afraid the police have found him dead." Harry and Lilly looked at each other and then back to Diane.

"What do you mean, dead?" asked Lilly. Harry just stood open mouthed, staring at her, not knowing what to say.

"He apparently killed himself. I don't know the details, I'm so sorry."

"No," replied Lilly in a raised voice. "Why are you saying that? Why do you hate him?"

"I know, Lilly, I know it's hard to understand, I don't understand myself." Tears had begun to stream down Lilly's face. Harry just stood and stared.

*

Anastasjia had been waiting in the car park as instructed for at least

20 minutes when she saw the headlights of the two minibuses pull in. The first person she saw was Madam Kristine getting out of the first vehicle, quickly followed by Uldis who climbed out of the other. As she saw the two of them walking towards her, she noticed the Mercedes pulling up too. *Madam Kristine always travelled in that. Why wasn't she in there?* The two front doors of the Mercedes opened, and two very large men climbed out and stood behind her Aston Martin. Anastasjia climbed out of the car and looked at Uldis. He in turn looked away. What was going on?

"Anastasjia, another change of plan, I'm afraid," said Madam Kristine.

"What change now?" Anastasjia snapped back. She was getting sick of this.

"Hand over the keys to the Aston Martin to Uldis. He and I shall be travelling to Amsterdam. You will go with these gentlemen." She indicated towards the two men.

"You told me that you were going with Uldis on the ferry. Why are you taking the Aston Martin?" She was getting annoyed. "And why do I need to go with these two apes? Why can't I drive to the hotel myself?"

Madam Kristine took the keys from Anastasjia and handed them to Uldis, who still didn't look at her. *Bastard*, she thought. *He's been playing me.* She could feel herself getting upset, but was not about to let him see that.

"So where am I going?" she asked again.

Madam Kristine looked at her as the two men moved closer. "Unfortunately, your usefulness to the company has passed."

"What do you mean, passed?" she replied loudly, glancing round at the two men and then over to Uldis who was climbing into the Aston Martin. "What the fuck is going on?" She was now quite frightened.

"The thing is, Anastasjia, you have become a liability, not your fault but a liability nevertheless." Madam Kristine gave her a sinister smile.

"You saw Balodis kill Jennings and there is footage of you," she paused, "shall I say, enjoying his company before he died." She smiled again before continuing. "And then you were in the room that Balodis died in, and of course you were driving the car that the poor young girl with the serious addiction was dumped from, not to mention being seen by young Harry and Lilly before they were returned to their home. You are so clearly wrapped up in this whole saga."

"Who the fuck are Harry and Lilly?" asked Anastasjia.

"The young boy and girl you helped to reunite."

"You fucking bitch." Anastasjia was raging; she had been set up. "What about you? You're very obvious with your limp. What about Uldis? He killed Balodis, don't forget that."

There was a short pause before Madam Kristine responded. "Ah yes, of course you are quite correct, but I have earned the trust of Mr. Daniels over the years. I'm sure you thought I was dead or unfit to work, but here I am, doing very well and remaining elusive to the authorities." She smiled once more. "I will disappear for a while, helping the business from the shadows. Now young Uldis, what a find he is. I never liked Balodis, he was a thug, above his station, but Uldis, he is very measured and understands what is required. Of course, he also understands what will happen to his family if he doesn't do as we wish. The good thing for you is that he is doing fine, in fact better than fine, he will be promoted for services rendered."

"You fucking bitch." Anastasjia knew it was hopeless.

"Now, now, Anastasjia, let us part as friends. These gentlemen will make your journey as painless as possible." Madam Kristine gestured towards the two men who grabbed Anastasjia.

"No, please, wait, I can help. I've always done everything asked of me," she shouted. She tried to think of what she could say to change her mind. Madam Kristine said nothing, she was already walking towards the Aston Martin. "Please, I won't say anything, you can trust me."

Madam Kristine opened the passenger door and stepped in. As she did, she called back, "I'm sure we can trust you, Anastasjia, but this is about making someone look responsible for the things that have not worked out." She closed the door and the Aston Martin roared into life, then took off at speed towards the car park exit.

The two men dragged Anastasjia to the Mercedes and forced her into the back seat. Tears streamed down her face. It was hopeless.

CHAPTER 37

Michalina was nervous. She was grateful to the authorities in England for helping her and she had done what she could to help them identify where the other girls and men could be found, although as she told them, she had no idea where they had been staying. She couldn't tell them about Sebastian, he knew where her family lived, and she knew the threats against them were real.

She told them about the woman with the limp, who seemed to be in charge. The police had also been interested in the woman who took her to the hospital, but she couldn't recall her at all. She remembered her having an accent but that was about it. The police told her she had been driving a high-powered supercar but even this prompted no recollection.

That was at least two weeks ago. She had been clean for that time but knew the road ahead was rocky. She was an addict and probably would be for the rest of her life. Fortunately for her, her mother and father had no idea. She knew that Zuzanna had been told but after she'd done nothing to help her, she didn't really want to see her. But she was glad she hadn't told their parents. She had spoken to her mother on the phone and told her she had been trafficked, but had been working in the fields. It was always going to be necessary to lie to her parents to spare them the shame.

Her addiction counsellor in England had put her in touch with his counterpart in Amsterdam and after travelling home today, she would be seeing him tomorrow. First, she had to get through her first day away from his support. "One day at a time," that was what her counsellor had said and that was what she was going to do.

After stepping off the tram, she took the short walk to the family apartment. When she saw the front door, tears formed in her eyes, but unlike the last few weeks, they were tears of happiness. A new start, a chance to move on. She would even forgive Zuzanna.

She rang the doorbell and waited, excited but still nervous. She heard the door catch being pulled back and then she saw her mother's face. On seeing her, her mother cried out with joy and wrapped her arms around her, pulling her close and sobbing uncontrollably. Michalina cried and the two of them hugged as if it would be the last time. When she saw her father, he acknowledged her, but she could see he had deteriorated further. He looked older and weaker. It was clear he could no longer stand, even though he tried. A tear of recognition could be seen in the corner of his eye. She rushed over and kissed him on his forehead.

"Hello, Tata, I've missed you." She smiled at him, and he smiled back warmly.

"He has missed you, Michalina, but he is struggling a little more than when you last saw him," said her mother.

"Where are Szymon and Zuzanna?" she asked. She only just realised how much she had missed her siblings.

"Your brother is at college, he'll be home soon, he's excited to see you. He's talked of nothing else," her mother said, but she detected an element of anger in her voice. What was going on?

"And Zuzanna, is she at work?"

"We don't mention that name in this house," her mother snapped back at her.

"What do you mean? Zuzanna, what's wrong with her?"

Her mother's face suddenly changed, now displaying her full anger. "I told you we don't mention that name. You will not say it, do you understand?" Michalina was shocked by the venom in her mother's voice.

"But why—" She tried to ask but was stopped.

"I told you, no. We do not mention her name and you will respect our wishes. Do you understand?"

"But—" Michalina began.

"I said, do you understand?" her mother spat.

"Yes, Mama, I understand."

Michalina sat and drank tea with her mother and father. Her mother tried to ask about what happened to her, but she made it clear she didn't want to go into it.

"Poor child, poor child, you're safe now," her mother would say, trying to reassure her. Michalina would smile back and thank her but deep down, she knew things would never quite be the same. She could not stop wondering about Zuzanna. What had she done that was so bad? She would have to wait for Szymon. She knew he would tell her.

After a short while, she excused herself and asked if her mother minded her going for a lie down. She was tired after the long journey and the excitement of being home.

"Of course, of course." She hugged Michalina again and kissed her on each cheek, cupping her face in her hands, then finally let her go to her room.

In her room, nothing had changed. It was exactly as it was left except for Zuzanna's bed, which had been stripped and just had a bare mattress. She opened the shared wardrobe and, again, all of Zuzanna's clothes were gone. Had she just moved out? Michalina wondered if this was why they were annoyed, but surely not. She could understand how Zuzanna leaving her mother and her brother to care for her father would have annoyed them, but to cut her off in such a dramatic fashion? It made no sense.

She lay on the fresh bedding her mother had put on for her and closed her eyes. She couldn't sleep but it was nice to just lie back and relax.

A short time had passed when she heard the front door being

opened. She heard her mother telling Szymon that she was home. Michalina sat on the side of the bed and waited eagerly as he ran towards her door. As soon as she opened it for him, the two of them hugged.

"I swear you've grown," she said, laughing.

"I think you've got smaller," he replied.

"Tell me how you've been, how is college, are you doing well?" She asked lifelessly. She knew she was expected to ask, but couldn't hide that she was troubled.

"Whoa! Hold on, Michalina, one thing at a time. Is something wrong? Are you okay?"

She held his hands and led him to her bed where she sat and pulled him to sit next to her. Looking at him closely, she squeezed his hands. "Please, Szymon, tell me about Zuzanna."

Szymon suddenly looked nervous. "We don't talk about Zuzanna anymore, please don't ask me to explain."

Michalina let go of his hands and turned to face him. "Listen, Szymon, I need you to tell me where our sister is." He looked away.

"No, Mama doesn't want her name used in this house and I'm okay with that."

Michalina was shocked. "Because she is my sister." She paused. "And she's your sister too."

Szymon's expression changed to one of anger. "She's not my sister, she's a whore, a fucking whore." He threw the words at her.

"What do you mean? How dare you? She's our sister." Michalina was fuming. How could he speak that way about Zuzanna? She didn't know what she had done to upset everyone but to call her that…?

"She's not my sister, she's a fucking whore, and that's the end of it." He stood up and went to leave. Michalina stood up and grabbed his arm, turning him towards her.

"Don't walk away from me. Where is she? Why is everyone being like this?" she snapped at him.

"Don't talk to me that way," he snapped back. "I'm not a child and your sister is a fucking whore who sells herself for cheap sex." He looked enraged.

Michalina couldn't help herself; she slapped him hard around the face.

"You fucking spoiled, selfish little shit. How dare you speak of Zuzanna that way? Now I'll ask once more, where is she? And don't fuck me around, you little shit." Szymon could see how angry she was.

"She sells herself in a shop window in De Wallen." He looked down, embarrassed whilst holding his cheek, which had gone red from the slap she delivered.

Michalina felt her legs giving way. She sank down until she was sitting on the side of the bed that once belonged to Zuzanna, trying to process this. Suddenly Sebastian's words came back to haunt her: "Zuzanna is going to help you pay off the debt." She finally realised what Sebastian had meant by this. How could she have been so stupid, so inconsiderate, so distrusting of her beautiful and thoughtful sister, the beautiful soul that always sacrificed everything to help others? She felt tears coming to her eyes.

"Take me there," she said to Szymon. It was not a request.

"No way, I don't want to see her. I told you, she's a whore."

Michalina slapped him around the face again, harder this time.

"I'm not asking, I'm telling you." She was so angry with him. He was such a spoiled brat and refused to see anything from anyone else's point of view.

"Okay, okay, just don't hit me again," he said. "When?"

"Now," replied Michalina. "We go now." She grabbed her coat and left the room. Szymon followed. He hadn't even taken his coat off.

Walking out the door their mother called, "Where are you going?"

"Out, we won't be long." It was a lie. She didn't know how long they would be, she just knew they had to find Zuzanna.

*

"Last time I saw her she was down there." Szymon had taken her to De Wallen, to the passageway he visited on his eighteenth birthday.

"Where?" She wanted him to take her to the window. She wanted to see the exact spot her sister had sold herself to save her.

"I'm not going to see her again; she was on the right-hand side about halfway down." With that, he turned to leave. But Michalina was not finished with Szymon yet.

"And you're just going to leave me here, are you?" She was so angry with him. He had abandoned Zuzanna in her time of need and now her. She ignored him and walked down the pathway looking for her sister. It was getting dark, and all the windows were occupied but there was no sign of her. Maybe she wasn't working tonight or maybe she had moved on. She prayed she would find her.

She walked the length of the passageway but still no luck. As she walked back there was a familiar voice behind her.

"Hello, Michalina, long time no see. Looking for work opportunities?" Michalina froze. Turning slowly, she saw the smirking face of Sebastian staring back at her. "Or maybe a fix? I may be able to offer either." He continued to smirk. "Your sister was an excellent employee. Maybe you're ready to replace her, what do you think?"

"Where is she?" she asked.

"What, no greeting?" he responded without answering her question.

"Where is she, Sebastian?" she asked again.

"Alas, she no longer works for me. Shame, really, she was very good. I even tried her out myself. Hmm, yes, very satisfying." He laughed.

"Where is she, Sebastian? Please tell me." She found herself pleading, which was something she really didn't want to do.

"Yes, I understand your concern, but unfortunately, I don't know where she is. She has been sold on, and very profitable she was, too.

Obviously, she was earning me good money but sometimes you just have to cash in when the right offer comes." His smile widened. "Perhaps I could offer you this." He pulled out a small clear bag with a brown powder within. "Very high quality," he said.

She felt the urge to reach out and grab the bag, but her resolve was strong. She knew she had to find her sister and the words of her counsellor echoed through her head.

"Fuck off, Sebastian."

"Now, now…" he replied. Then his smile turned to a scowl. "Don't think I couldn't force you to work for me, because believe me, when I say it would be easy…" She could see he meant what he was saying. He continued with his threats. "I suggest you are the one who needs to fuck off. And if I hear you have been talking about me, then you, your brother, your mother and that crippled father of yours will pay for your mistakes, are we clear?" The look on his face was terrifying. She nodded submissively. "Run along now, Michalina, before I change my mind."

She didn't say anything else; she just turned and walked away. She had no idea how she would find her sister, but she promised herself she would never give up looking.

CHAPTER 38

Nyakim parked the car next to the police station.

"Are you going to be okay?"

Alice was eternally grateful to Nyakim for all her support. She had been home from hospital for a week now and Nyakim had taken time off from work to help her. Now the time had come to face work and her colleagues. She knew most would be okay with her, but some would be angered as much as she was. She'd left them short of staff, with no idea where she was, and that was down to her. She was still reeling from how stupid she had been.

"I'll be fine, thanks for running me here," she said. She leaned across and her lips were met by Nyakim's kissing her goodbye. She opened the car door and manoeuvred her crutches before hauling herself up onto her good foot. "See you later." With her arms now in the crutches she managed to raise one hand enough to wave.

"See you later, and take it easy. You're not actually back at work, remember, you're just calling in to say hello."

"I know, I know." She smiled and closed the car door and began to hobble over towards the building. She glanced back just in time to see Nyakim pull away, beeping the horn once and waving as she left.

Trying to keep her damaged foot off the ground she managed to get to the main doors. Thankfully there were no members of the public inside, so she didn't have to struggle to shuffle past too many people. As she passed through security, scanning her ID badge over the small pad, she heard a voice.

"Hi, Alice, what are you doing here?" It was Mary, the front desk operator. She liked Mary; she was one of the most helpful people in the station.

"Hi, Mary. I'm not working, I just wanted to get some company and see the office."

"Well, let me help you," said Mary, holding the door fully open until Alice was able to get in. Mary helped her to the lift and made sure the door didn't close before she was inside.

"Do you want me to come up with you?" she asked.

"No, I'm good, thanks."

"No problem," said Mary as the lift doors closed.

Up to the second floor and then walking to the missing persons office, she hoped that a friendly face would be in. As she peered through the open door, initially she thought the room was empty. But then a voice called out.

"Alice!" It was Dave, one of the older detectives, a really nice guy who everyone got on with.

He got up to greet her and put his arms around her in a hug. It was what she needed, reassurance that her colleagues were going to be okay with her. Dave led her into the room and sat her down on a chair by his desk. "Coffee?" he asked.

"Please," she replied. As he switched on the kettle, he turned back to her.

"We weren't expecting you back so soon. Aren't you still off sick?"

"Yeah," she replied. "I'm going to drive my partner nuts if I don't get out and see other people.

"I've got to ask," he began, looking a little nervous. "What the fuck were you thinking? You could have been killed."

"I know, I know, don't remind me. It just seemed like a good idea at the time," she said, still embarrassed. "What's everyone saying?" She knew she could rely on him to tell the truth.

"Well, I think everyone thinks you made a huge mistake but most of all, we're just glad you're okay. And at the end of the day, you did manage to get the two kids back, Harry and the girl... erm?"

"Lilly," Alice reminded him.

"Yeah, Lilly, you got Harry and Lilly back."

She knew that wasn't completely true, but if the team thought she had a hand in their coming home, that was fine with her. "You might want to steer clear of Jameson," he said quietly. For a moment Alice wondered whether there were others in the room, or it was bugged, neither of which were the case.

"What's his problem?" she asked. The hairs of the back of her neck stood up just at the mention of his name.

"He was ranting about you, calling you every name under the sun. I think Dorry has put a stop to it but he's not happy."

Alice shook her head. "Bastard," she said, loud enough for Dave to hear. "He's always had it in for me, ever since I refused to sit on his cock."

"You won't be the first and I doubt you'll be the last." She was grateful for Dave's support, but it didn't ease her concern over having to face Jameson.

The two of them chatted for over an hour before Dave finally announced he had a meeting to go to.

"Sorry, Alice. If I could stay longer I would."

"That's okay," she replied. "I'd best be going too." Dave came round his desk and gave her a friendly kiss on the cheek before bidding her goodbye and leaving the room.

She made her way to the lift and pressed the button. As she waited for it to reach her floor, she heard the voice she didn't want to hear.

"DC Thomas, my office now." It was Jameson. No acknowledgement that she was here just to visit. Just barking orders, as usual.

Shit, she thought.

For a moment she considered ignoring him and getting into the lift that had now arrived, but thought better of it. She turned to see his back as he walked back to his office. He couldn't even wait for her. *What a fucking bastard.* She struggled to turn around and then began to follow on her crutches.

"Come in and close the door," he barked at her when she caught up. She did as he said, not saying anything but still struggling with her crutches. "So, let's start with the lies, shall we?" he began.

Wow, she thought. He wasn't even going to offer her a seat.

"What—" She started to defend herself, but he interrupted.

"I'm talking now," he snapped. She remained standing on one leg. "You're lucky to still have a job in the department. In fact, if it wasn't for the Superintendent you'd be gone." His face was full of anger. "You lied about where you were, you lied about being sick, you left the county on a work job and told no one where you were going. What did you think you were doing?" He was ranting. She knew he had a right to be annoyed but this was ridiculous.

"Look, I know I made a mistake, boss, but—" Before she could finish, he interrupted again.

"I can only think you've got something on Dorry that's keeping you here."

"I'm sorry, but I've been through hell—" Again, she was interrupted.

"I don't care. You caused us all sorts of problems, not to mention the danger you put Harry Voclain in."

She shook her head.

"Don't shake your head," he shouted. "That should have been enough to get you disciplined, or even better out of the job completely. Yes, you were lucky they let you go, but it was you who put him in danger in the first place."

"He was being used for selling drugs, county lines, you must have heard of it, and his sister was being trafficked. I'd say that was more in danger than I put him," she found herself shouting back.

"Somehow you've managed to stay a detective, God knows how," he said, sneering at her.

"Because I'm good," she snapped back.

"You're not good, you're still in a job because political correctness won't let me get rid of you."

"Political correctness? What does that mean? What's that got to do with anything?" She had no idea what he was talking about, but she was getting angry. Jameson had treated her like dirt ever since she rejected him. "Look, I don't care about you," she said, feeling emboldened by her anger. "Like you said, you can't get rid of me, so I'm going to tell you something. I didn't sleep with you because you're old enough to be my dad. I don't find you attractive and you're married, you also disgust me. You need to get over it and get off my back."

Jameson's eyes narrowed. "Don't think I won't get you eventually," he began. "I've got rid of people far more clever than you and once Dorry retires, fucking her won't help you!"

Alice's mouth fell open.

"What did you say?"

Jameson smirked. "I know about you," he began.

Alice was startled. Was she hearing this correctly? "What's that supposed to mean?" she asked indignantly.

"I've heard about you," he started again. "If I'd known you were a fucking dyke, I'd have never tried to fuck you. Mind you, it explains why you wouldn't let me."

"How dare you?" she yelled back at him.

"Watch yourself, constable. If I can get rid of you sooner, I will. I don't want any fucking scissor sisters working for me." Alice was frozen to the spot. She didn't know what to say.

"What's wrong with same-sex relationships?" she finally managed to get out.

"Not had a good fuck before, have you?" he asked. "I can't imagine Dorry is very good." He was sneering at her now. "I read your statement; you were fucked. Two of them, wasn't it? Anal as well." He laughed. "Maybe I should give it a go, depends how much you liked it I suppose." His face was full of hatred.

She knew he was a sleaze but the bigotry and lack of compassion coming from him was shocking. At that moment it felt like he was pure evil. Tears welled in her eyes at the memories of what had happened.

"What's stopping me from reporting you?" she asked.

"And say what?" he asked. "Just remember, I'm the detective chief inspector and you're a lying constable who put herself and a young boy at risk after telling those lies. If anything comes from you about me, I'll just say you're lying again." He grinned. "Now get out of my office."

Alice was raging inside. She knew he had a point; nothing she could say would help people believe her. But she knew what would. As she made her way out of the office and back down in the lift, she reached into her jacket for her phone. She smiled as she looked at the screen, then stopped the record function.

She made her way to the end of the corridor and approached the Superintendent's secretary.

"Is Superintendent Dorry in, please?" she asked.

Before the secretary could answer, Helen Dorry appeared.

"Great to see you, Alice. Come in and have a seat." Alice followed her into her office. "What brings you in, Alice? Not that it isn't good to see you." She smiled.

"I just called in to say hello to my office," replied Alice. Helen smiled.

"It's great to see you back on your feet, but don't even think about returning to work yet. I want you to have all the counselling you need and time to recover."

"Thank you, ma'am," she replied, smiling back. She still had tears in her eyes.

"Tell me how you're getting on?" Helen had always been a great person to work for. She felt nervous but knew if she didn't do something, Jameson was never going to let go.

"Before I tell you about that, can I play you something?"

CHAPTER 39

Zuzanna felt herself slowly coming around. This was her second night sleeping in the apartment and the first time she had slept well in months. As she rolled onto her back the cat jumped on the bed and nuzzled up to her face. She was told it had belonged to the previous occupant but had been abandoned when she left. Zuzanna felt the warmth of her fur against her cheek. She slowly moved her to the side, allowing herself to sit up and lean against the cushioned headboard.

She glanced at the clock that only moments ago had woken her – 6:30am – time to get up and shower. Today was going to be a big day.

Zuzanna couldn't quite believe her luck, especially as she had been resigned to having lost everything – her family, her home, her friends, her dignity and her life. For the first time in months, she could see a future. Not the future she had dreamed of but one that was much better than she currently had and most importantly, away from that bastard Sebastian. She wondered how he was feeling. She smiled to herself, knowing he would have been fuming she had gotten away from his control. She could still see the look on his face as he was held against the wall by his throat, choking and struggling to speak. That was before agreeing that she could leave for a settled fee of a thousand euros, not much more than she would make him in a night.

She knew she was still going to have to sleep with men, but this time, she was assured it was not for money but as a way to encourage clients to make a purchase. She was actually helping her new company, rather than being the thing that was bought. She knew that still made her a sex worker – technically – but a wealthy client now and then was much better than drunk and sweaty men off the street, many covered in vomit and stinking of cannabis.

Today she was to meet her new boss, the manager of the luxury motor company where she was to be his personal assistant, organising deliveries of the cars so that they looked their best. She was even going to be in charge of a group of young men whose job it would be to clean the cars and move them on. She found the thought to be exciting. Finally, a new opportunity when all had seemed lost.

The only part of her former life she was going to miss, was Charlotte. She had supported her and kept her going when she was at her lowest. When her family had disowned her, she had contemplated suicide, but Charlotte turned her around and made her want to live. They had both suffered at the hands of Sebastian and the others that had used them as sex toys. But when they were away from De Wallen, they would hug and cry and comfort each other. They would even find things to laugh about. Yes, she was going to miss Charlotte and was grateful that the woman with the limp let her say goodbye before leaving Amsterdam.

That was three weeks ago. That morning had been like any other. She had arranged to meet up with Charlotte at hers so they could go for some lunch. Breakfast was a thing of the past. When you work in the shop fronts into the early hours, a lie in is one of the few luxuries you can allow yourself. She showered. *11:00am, just time to dry my hair before leaving*, she thought to herself. As she thought it, there was a knock at the door.

"Shit," she said out loud. If anyone was calling at this time it was going to be Sebastian or one of his cronies. Looking through the viewer, she was right. *Lucas, that little prick.*

"What?" she shouted through the closed door. Ever since he had brought Szymon to the De Wallen she found it impossible to look at him. He made her fume. She expected he was only doing as Sebastian had demanded but she would never forgive him.

"Erm, sorry Zuzanna, Sebastian wants to see you in his office at the portacabin."

Fuck, she thought. *What now?*

"Tell him I'll see him tonight," she called back.

"Please, Zuzanna, he insisted you come with me." He sounded scared. *Good*, she thought. She hoped that little shit was terrified. She stood back from the viewing hole and paused.

"Okay, wait there, I'll be out in a few minutes," she called back.

"Don't be long," he called back.

"Fuck you, Lucas, you little fuck. I'll be as long as it takes," she shouted back through the door before looking at Lucas through the eyehole. He looked so scared. Zuzanna smiled and walked away from the front door to the bedroom. She was going to dry her hair before she helped him. She guessed that would be long enough to scare Lucas but not annoy Sebastian too much.

After drying her hair, she used a hair band to put it into a ponytail. A quick look in the mirror at her slender frame, clothed in tight Levis and a tee shirt. No makeup, this was daytime and wearing makeup was the last thing she wanted to do. Reaching for the waterproof rain jacket on the back of the front door, she opened it and looked at Lucas.

"Come on then," she said to him as she put her coat on. Walking down the corridor ahead of him, Lucas followed on without saying anything.

"What's this about?" He shrugged, which made him look even younger than he was. Clearly, he was just following instructions.

The two of them made the short journey to the portacabin where she had first met Sebastian. It was also where she had been coerced into fucking Lucas. The memory made her shudder. If she had known what she knew now, she would have liked to tell Sebastian to fuck off there and then, despite knowing she had no choice.

Lucas stepped in front of Zuzanna and opened the door for her. If anyone else did this she would thank them, but she was not about to extend that courtesy to Lucas.

Sebastian was seated behind the desk looking surprisingly nervous. Seated opposite on the cheap chairs were two people she hadn't seen before. As she walked into the room the two of them stood up and turned to greet her. Sebastian stayed seated and said nothing. The woman was in her fifties maybe, quite attractive, the man was much younger, powerfully built and quite handsome but with a dreadful wound on his face that was clearly quite recent.

The woman glanced towards Sebastian, the look on her face suggesting she was not at all happy with him for not standing up, which was the polite thing to do. *I'm beginning to like her.* Zuzanna smiled.

The young man spoke in a language she couldn't understand. Then he spoke again in English.

"Zuzanna, my name is Uldis, do you speak Latvian?" She shook her head. "Polish?" he asked. She nodded. "Good," he replied.

The woman spoke to her in English. "So, Zuzanna, you can speak good English, Polish and Dutch, any other languages?" she asked.

"A little German," she replied. "Why?"

"We have a proposition for you," the woman began. "Do you think you could learn Latvian?"

"Hold on, we haven't agreed on a fee yet." The man held a hand up towards Sebastian, without turning to face him. Sebastian stopped.

"As I was saying, Zuzanna, before this rude man interrupted—"

"Wait a minute, you can't—" The man held his hand up again, stopping Sebastian from speaking once more.

"We have a job opportunity. You would be given a nice apartment to live in, a good wage, a good job helping to sell luxury cars to mostly Russian and eastern European gentlemen. How does that sound?" Zuzanna looked towards Sebastian who was clearly fuming.

The expression on his face made her fearful. She had felt his wrath before; the violence, the rape the degradation. She began to shake.

"You look afraid, child," said the woman. Zuzanna was not a child, but the way the woman said it was reassuring. She didn't know what to say. She looked at their faces, trying to understand what the catch was.

"I, I don't know," she said. She looked behind at Lucas who was looking at the floor, trying not to get involved.

"Are you concerned about Sebastian?" asked the woman. Zuzanna obviously looked as nervous as she felt. "Don't worry, Zuzanna," she paused. "The only thing is, we need to leave later today. We will pay Sebastian for your service so he will have no reason to feel aggrieved and we will be able to get your passport and anything you wish to take with you. Don't worry about anything. I promise you'll be okay and well looked after."

The woman turned to Uldis and nodded. Uldis reached into his jacket pocket and pulled out a roll of banknotes.

"This is a thousand euros. This will be compensation for Zuzanna leaving your employment," she said to Sebastian in a commanding manner.

"No fucking way, lady," he started. "She can make that for me in one night."

The woman looked to Uldis, who suddenly moved very fast, grabbing Sebastian around the neck with one hand, the money still in the other. In a swift movement, he dragged Sebastian from the chair and pulled him up the wall, so he was pinned. He pushed the money into Sebastian's mouth. Sebastian tried to resist but he was no match for Uldis, who was clearly hurting him. When Uldis let him go, he sunk to the floor, choking.

"So, a thousand euros is agreed," said the woman confidently. Despite removing the roll of money from his mouth Sebastian was still choking, and so said nothing. He didn't even look up, sitting defeated on the floor.

"Good," said the woman. "Well, unless you want to stay here and work for this piece of shit, Zuzanna, it's probably time for you to come with us. We'll go back to your place to get your things." She smiled again.

Zuzanna was still quite frightened, but she was intrigued by this woman and her offer. Anyway, what could be worse than working for Sebastian?

"Thank you," she said as she walked out of the portacabin.

"Our pleasure," replied the woman. It was at that point that Zuzanna noticed the woman walked with a limp. She couldn't help but glance down at her leg.

"Yes," said the woman, "I have an old injury that gives me a limp." She continued to smile at Zuzanna. "Nothing to worry about. Anyway, now Sebastian is sorted, please call me Kristine."

As they stepped outside, Zuzanna saw the Aston Martin.

"Yes, I see you like the car," the woman began. "This is one of the cars you would be helping to sell." Zuzanna still didn't speak, it all made no sense. "I shall be leaving you in the hands of Uldis who will be driving you to Riga where you will be living and working."

"In this?" said Zuzanna, not quite believing what she was hearing.

"Yes, in this." Zuzanna looked her in the face. There was nothing to suggest she was lying, though after everything she had been through, she was no longer that naive. Of course, she knew the woman could just be a good liar. "You are booked into a couple of nice hotels on the way so the two of you will get plenty of chances to get to know each other," she said cheerfully.

That's when the reality settled in. *Oh, she wants me to sleep with him,* she thought. *That makes sense. Though it's better just him than lots of others.* She smiled back at the woman.

"Good," she said. "You go back to your apartment; we'll be along in an hour or so to collect you. Make sure you have done all you need to do before we leave."

"Thank you," said Zuzanna, though she wasn't quite sure what she was thanking her for. She turned to walk away but suddenly stopped and turned back. "Sorry, wait, erm… do you know where to go?"

"We shall have a little chat with the young boy who collected you," said the woman. "I'm sure he will be happy to tell us."

"Oh, okay." Part of her hoped Uldis would hurt Lucas, not a lot but enough to make him pay. "Oh, one more thing, I don't have any family anymore, but I have a really good friend I'd like to say goodbye to, if possible, please," she asked. She owed it to Charlotte.

"Of course," said the woman. "Shall we say two hours?"

Saying goodbye to Charlotte had been difficult. The two of them hugged and cried. They had formed quite a bond in the relatively short space of time they had known each other. Although there was no certainty as to what was going to happen to Zuzanna, they both knew it couldn't be as bad as working for Sebastian.

They parted, promising to keep in touch, though they both guessed they would quickly lose contact with each other. A final hug and they separated.

"Good luck," said Charlotte as she left her apartment.

"And to you," replied Zuzanna. "If you get any chance to get away from Sebastian, do it. Run if you need to."

As she packed a very small bag, she could see how her life had nothing much of value left. Not just in a material sense but emotionally and socially. She had so little left to offer. Whatever this woman could give her, it had to be better than where she was at this moment. It certainly couldn't be worse.

As she walked out of the apartment building, she saw Uldis sitting in the car. As she approached, he climbed out, walked around to the passenger door and opened it for her. *Wow*, she thought. *It's a good start.*

"Ready?" he asked. Zuzanna nodded and the car roared into life before setting off.

The journey to Riga was 20 hours of driving and took four days. They stopped at three hotels on the way. Although not five stars, they were still quite nice and certainly better than Zuzanna had anticipated.

Uldis explained that on the rare occasions they asked her to entertain clients it would be her job to make the night as good as possible. They needed the men to be compliant the next day. Make sure they enjoyed the sex, he had said. Cater for their needs and she shouldn't worry about violence; if any of them were violent she could call for help. Most of her work was to be at the showrooms and entertaining was simply to give them coffee and conversation. But if she was required to sleep with them it would involve a night in a top hotel, all expenses paid. For Zuzanna this all sounded too good to be true. She also expected to have sex with Uldis and sure enough she did, at each of the hotels they stopped at. On the first night it had felt like a job, like any other client, but as the days went on, this view changed. She knew it was part of her work, but Uldis appeared to be quite caring. He never forced her.

When they arrived in Riga, Zuzanna was introduced to one of the showroom secretaries. She was tasked with showing Zuzanna the top clothing stores in Riga, and providing her with a wardrobe for leisure, business and entertaining. Everything was of the best quality.

Finally, she was taken to her apartment. It was fairly simply furnished but was okay and had everything she needed. It was better than the room she shared in Amsterdam with her sister. She thought for a moment about Michalina and once again, hoped she was okay. Although she had gotten herself into this situation, she also knew how easy it was to be exploited by Sebastian. She had only been in the apartment for an hour when there was a knock on the door. The woman was holding a cat and introduced herself as her neighbour. She explained the cat had belonged to the previous occupant and as she couldn't look after it, it was now hers. Before she could object the woman put the cat down and it ran past her into the lounge.

Here she was in Riga, three weeks after leaving Amsterdam, waiting outside the apartment to be collected for her first day at the showroom. The taxi pulled up and took her for the short drive. Getting out of the car she walked to the large glass doors into the building. She saw the secretary at a desk and went to speak to her. Before she could, the secretary pointed to an office with a large sign saying 'Manager.'

"You need to see Mr. Petrova, the manager." The phone rang and she quickly answered it.

Zuzanna knocked gently on the glass. The middle-aged man who sat behind the desk jumped up and beckoned for her to come in. "You must be Zuzanna. I'm Dimitrijs, the manager. I understand you will be part of the sales team answering to my new number two, Mr. Vidas." For a moment she looked confused. "Uldis, Uldis Vidas," he said.

"Oh, yes, Uldis, of course." It was only then she realised she didn't know his last name.

"Let's get you to work." He pointed at the desk on the other side of the room, and she took a seat. Reaching for the intercom, he pressed the button. It was quickly answered by the secretary. "Coffee?" he asked Zuzanna.

"Please."

Mr. Petrova smiled and pressed the intercom again. "Two coffees, please," he called through.

"Yes, Mr. Petrova," came the reply.

I could get used to this, thought Zuzanna, smiling to herself.

CHAPTER 40

For Mr. Daniels it was always a pleasure to see his employer's daughter. He knew she was being groomed to take over the business and had shown she more than had what was going to be required of her.

He pulled up at the large, gated property overlooked by CCTV cameras and without using the intercom the gates opened; he was expected. Taking the Aston Martin up the driveway he pulled up outside the grand property and climbed out of the driver's seat.

"Mr. Daniels, such a pleasure." He turned to look at the beautiful young woman standing at the door. In her arms she carried her young daughter, and her other daughter stood next to her. He held out his arms in a welcoming gesture.

"Amalia, it's been so long, you look fantastic. Your father I know is so proud." He smiled.

"Please come inside, we've much to talk about."

Amalia Voclain – née Romano – led Mr. Daniels into the house and through to the lounge, where she set young Elena on the floor in the area set aside as a child's play area.

"Sienna, please play with your sister and keep her entertained, Mr. Daniels and I have to talk." She sat down on the lounge suite and invited Daniels to join her.

"I'm sorry about Mr. Voclain—" he began. Amalia held up her hand to stop him.

"Please," she said. "We know he was an adulterous pig; I should have known that when he started our relationship whilst still married to Diane."

"Yes, but he is still the father of your children," Daniels pointed out.

"Yes, of course, but in the long run they will be better off without him, as will his other children."

Daniels paused before responding. "Yes, I wondered what you had in mind for them. They are not your responsibility, and neither is Diane, you really don't have to do anything for them."

Amalia suddenly looked very cross. "Mr. Daniels, family is everything. It is not Lilly or Harry's fault their father was a pig, it is not Diane's fault that the pig decided to have a relationship with me, and it is certainly not their fault the pig betrayed all of us by continuing to think he could fuck everything in sight, do you understand?"

Daniels looked taken aback. "I'm sorry, Amalia, I didn't mean to offend you or upset you. I understand your loyalty to the children, but Diane… she stopped being your responsibility when William died."

Amalia looked at him and smiled. "I have been able to rely on Harry to look after the children in an emergency. Diane always agrees to this, despite owing me nothing." She smiled again.

"That's very gracious of you. Again, your father would be proud."

"Thank you, Mr. Daniels, now we need to discuss business…" She paused. "As you know, the police have been here and have searched the house. Thanks to you, the material and devices they have seized will show that any connection to the businesses are only from him and not my family. For that, I am grateful."

"My pleasure," replied Mr. Daniels.

"It is where we proceed from here that we need to discuss."

"What do you have in mind?" he asked. He knew she was young, but she was good; her father had taught her well.

"I shall be returning to my family in Italy. I am, after all, the grieving widow who needs support from her family." Daniels nodded his understanding. "As the garage and showrooms are in my father's name and not William's, we won't be liable for his wrongdoings. The only thing legally owned by him is Diane's house and I will make sure they are not going after that."

Daniels nodded again. "What would you like to happen to the showrooms now?" he asked.

"I'm going to entrust that to you, Mr. Daniels. I'm expecting you to appoint someone appropriate to run the business."

He nodded once more. "I will look for a suitable person from inside the organisation as soon as possible."

"Thank you, Mr. Daniels. I knew I could rely on you." Another pause. "Now, tell me about our other operations?" she asked.

"Well, good news on all fronts – the girls are still being recruited and we have many workers across the board in various occupations, overseen by our team leaders."

"What of Madam Kristine?"

Daniels laughed. "She continues to do what she does, and she gets results. We couldn't have framed William without her help."

"Yes, she must be congratulated. Her first meeting with him was short but painful. I am concerned she may become a liability to the company."

Daniels pondered for a moment. "And when she is, she will be removed." He smiled.

"Good, hopefully not too soon." She smiled back.

*

Harry looked out of his window as Amalia's car pulled onto the driveway. His father had been dead for over two months, and he had seen little of his siblings. However, since his dad died, he felt somehow closer to them. He guessed it was because he now felt they were his responsibility.

He watched as Amalia climbed out of the driver's seat and reached into the back, where Sienna and Elena were. Seeing the girls, he raced downstairs to greet them.

"Hi, Harry, how are you?" Amalia called to him.

"Hi, Amalia, can I take Sienna and Elena into the garden to play, please?" he asked excitedly.

"Yes, of course, if it's okay with your mother?" she replied, looking at Diane, who was now in the doorway.

"Yes, of course," Diane said, pleased to see Harry so happy.

Harry picked up Elena and took Sienna by the hand, leading them into the back garden via the side of the house. Diane and Amalia went inside.

*

Amalia appeared with Harry's mother in the garden. She had told her the estate would continue to support her and the children, for which Diane said she was grateful.

"Harry," said Amalia, "your sisters and I are moving to be with my family in Italy at the end of the month." At this, Harry's heart sank. Although looking after them could be annoying, he loved being with them most of the time. "Your mother has agreed that you can visit as often as you wish, beginning with your next holiday. You can all come to my family home to stay." Amalia smiled. Harry looked at her, not believing her words. She had said this before, and he'd never once been over. Diane looked at his face and saw the sadness in his eyes.

"No, really Harry. You, me and Lilly are all going to Italy. Amalia has already paid for everything," said Diane.

Harry jumped up, excitedly. "Can I tell Lilly?" he asked.

"Yes, of course," replied Diane.

"I'll see you before we go, Harry," said Amalia, laughing at the joy he displayed.

"Thanks, Amalia," he said as he ran into the house and up the stairs.

Getting to the top of the landing, Lilly's door was open. He ran to the threshold and as he entered his sister turned in her chair and shouted at him. "Get out!"

Harry froze, looking at his sister's stern face. It slowly changed to a smile.

"What is it, Scraggy?"

"We're going to Italy for the holidays," he said excitedly. "And stop calling me Scraggy."

They both smiled; they both knew what they had been through.

CHAPTER 41

The detective was standing in the cold. It had only been about 30 minutes, but it felt like 30 hours. He was freezing. He was only wearing his suit and regretted leaving his coat in the office. Where was the inspector? She had been told about this at the same time as him and yet here he was, waiting for her.

Finally, her car pulled up and she climbed out. She was dressed in a thick padded coat.

"What have we got?" she asked the young detective.

"A body, been in the water for some time. Female, white, a bit of a state really."

A group of walkers had come across the puffy, bloated body of the young woman earlier that morning. From the looks of her, she had been bashed against the rocks by the incoming tides for the last few weeks. They couldn't see the beauty that led others to exploit her and degrade her before finally throwing her from the tops of the cliffs near Dieppe.

"I'll take you to her. I'm guessing if no one has reported her missing by now, no one will," he said as he led the inspector across the rocks to where her beaten body lay.

THE END

ABOUT THE AUTHOR

Les Holmes is a Royal Naval veteran and a former detective with the police. Whilst serving as a detective he became a specialist in public protection, starting in child abuse investigations, moving into helping vulnerable adults, victims of modern slavery, honour abuse and missing persons. He has worked on action teams during major crime investigations and after retirement he worked for 10 years as a crime trainer, teaching police officers and other agencies the skills he had learned. He is married to his wife of 30 years, has a dog, five grown children, and a lot of grandchildren!

Printed in Great Britain
by Amazon